PERMISSION TO SPEAK FREELY

SAMANTHA WALKER

HABENCOURT, LLC

Published by Habencourt LLC

https://samanthawalker-permission.com/

ISBN (Hardcover): #979-8-218-83317-6

ISBN (Paperback): #979-8-218-83318-3

ISBN (E-Book): #979-8-218-83319-0

First Edition: January 12, 2026

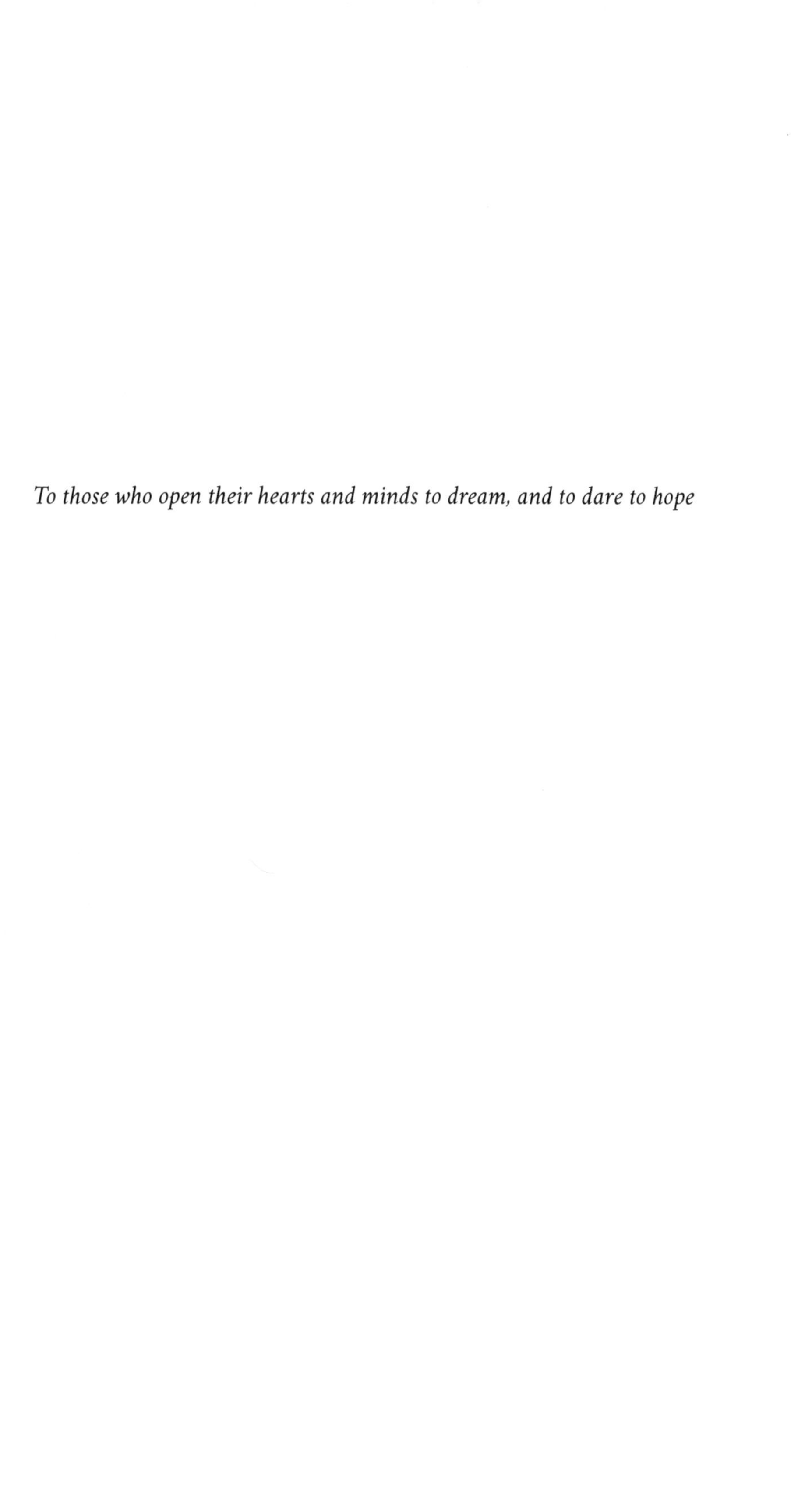

To those who open their hearts and minds to dream, and to dare to hope

PART I

1981-1990

1

IT BEGAN WITH A LETTER

OHIO, AUGUST 2001

Often described as hot-tempered, the weather in the Great Lakes region of the American Midwest was notoriously unpredictable. Unstable storm fronts often marched across the Great Plains, where they collided with other fronts roaring up the Ohio Valley before crashing into the water-laden air of the Great Lakes. The early weeks of August 2001 were no exception and a typical Midwestern summer storm raged over the Ohio Valley area wreaking havoc with airline schedules. Torrential rain pelted the terminal windows and winds howled, rattling the glass within their frames. Few local travelers, however, were worried. For the inhabitants of the region, the volatile weather was a running joke; if you don't like it, simply wait five minutes, it will change.

A crack of thunder jolted the terminal as the storm raged on and a bolt of lightning crackled through the sky, illuminating a growing backlog of passengers who stood idly by at the departure gates. Impatience gnawed away at what little good humor and tolerance the travelers had packed away with their tickets. The airport was quiet given the early hours and lack of departing flights, but there was still a constant drone of loudspeaker announcements and the bustle of people.

Amid the congregation of excited college students, senior retirees and business travelers that gathered in the muted lighting of the departure area, were two men in military camouflage fatigues and a woman. Sam, short for Samantha, had grown accustomed to these moments, but she dreaded them, nonetheless. Restless from the delayed departure, the boarding area had grown fidgety, but she and her Gerry were luxuriating in every unexpected additional minute they had together. The two men were Army and they were en route to rendezvous with their unit before heading overseas. This would be Gerry's last overseas deployment.

The ever-present Muzak in the background came forth with an upbeat medium tempo melody and Gerry suddenly twirled the woman around gracefully. Putting one arm behind his back, he held out his other hand in a silent question of *May I have this dance?* A set of golden flecked brown eyes, sparkling as if they were already dancing, enfolded Sam in their gaze as he took her hand and twirled her again before drawing her in close. At forty-four years old, auburn hair hinting at her Scotch-Irish heritage, her movements were light and practiced as agile sneakers deftly rocked to the rhythm.

As Sam twirled gracefully in his arms, swaying to the beat, Gerry's fatigues, clumsy and rugged, made him appear cloddish and off-balanced, while his cumbersome Army boots clunked heavily on the hard tile floor. They were a picture of stark contrast, yet Sam and Gerry moved in harmony as one.

The group of college students sniggered at the couple, poking each other, nudging and pointing as their snide comments of *How lame* could be heard filtering over the waiting area. The senior travelers, however—perhaps remembering their own times in the sun—merely looked on with dreamy, subtle smiles, and the business travelers were simply happy for a diversion. As the final stanza of the song faded into silence, Gerry dipped Sam with a flourish and ended the song with a kiss.

"I'm so glad I taught you to dance," Sam said with a giggle as Gerry lifted her to her feet, her smile matching the joy in his eyes.

Lt. Colonel Gerald Martinez, the man she had shared the last twenty years of her life with, was now middle-aged at forty-nine years old, with grey beginning to peek through his deep brown hair at the temples. He was, in Sam's eyes, depending on which way the wind was blowing, either insufferably cute with a boyish smile or just bloody handsome sporting a cocky grin. Today, the wind had that needle squarely in the insufferably cute department. It's hard to be handsome in those camo fatigues, Sam laughed quietly to herself—its discordant clash reminded her of a new exotic disease whose chaotic skin rash pattern resembled something the cat scarfed up.

Sergeant Stanley Ibbotson, Gerry's best friend of more than twenty years, his "wing man" who had seen him through it all, stood to the side waiting his turn. When he spied his chance, he darted in and gave Sam a mischievous poke from behind, causing her to jump and laugh. Over the last two decades, Stan had become Sam's dearest friend, and for her, it was just as difficult to bid him goodbye as it was to bid Gerry goodbye.

While Sam's heart unquestionably belonged to Gerry, she recognized that the topic of Stan was an entirely different matter altogether. At forty-five years old, through the grace of God and genetics, Stan was a gift to women; he knew it and he reveled in it. For some inexplicable reason, he had won the genetic lottery in the looks department. Magazine cover model material whose facial features were both refined and chiseled, the man had the most astonishing drop-dead smile that left a trail in its wake of female hearts going pitter-pat. With the build of a linebacker, this southern boy from Georgia, with the most charming of accents, was the complete package. A mesmerized waitress had once aptly described him as an *ebony Greek god*. Ladies' man, playboy, rake, Don Juan, Casanova, Romeo, womanizer—they all applied to Stan Ibbotson.

With an effervescent grin, Stan leaned in to give Sam a peck on a cheek that had already begun to crinkle in a huge smile. The corny tradition she knew was coming was a time-honored departure routine between the two, and both only vaguely remembered how the ritual had started decades earlier. The routine's soothing familiarity always put a smile on the sad act of saying goodbye. Privately, both Sam and Stan thought of it as a good-luck charm, and neither of them dared to tempt the gods of fate, so the tradition continued.

A sly Cheshire smirk replaced his broad grin as Stan joked, "Yo girl, I feel for ya 'cause you're gonna miss my dashin' good looks," as he struck the pose of a fashion model at a photo shoot.

Sam playfully shook her head back at him as she countered his joke, "Oh please, I am looking forward to the peace and quiet. I always feel like I'm in a Chippendale Calendar review around you!"

Stan's face lit up as he puffed out his chest in mock delight, and following the script, he dramatically adopted an exaggerated theatrical stance as he bodaciously exclaimed, "Oh. Can I be Mr. April? I've always thought of myself as more of a spring guy!"

His reward for his performance was a look of pained exasperation from Sam. "No? Well, I guess I'll hafta settle for bein' Mr. January then!" Playing her role, Sam melodramatically groaned, rolled her eyes, and teasingly socked him in the shoulder, thus ending the ritual. Oblivious to the commotion their goofy charade had caused, the trio stood in a huddle as the two men hugged Sam tightly, laughing and drinking in their last moments together.

There was one final departure routine left to be played out, and excitement hung in the air as Sam expectantly raised her eyebrows at Gerry, eager to see what he had chosen for them. Theatrically poised on the tips of his fingers, a simple brown paper-wrapped book magically seemed to appear out of thin air as Gerry presented it to Sam. Their "deployment book." They each had a copy, and reading it together, the book would serve as a conduit, a connecting link that would sustain the couple throughout the long months of deployment.

A charming moment of private intrigue and mystery, a beaming Gerry watched contently as Sam happily tore the book from its wrapper, the anticipation killing her as she read the title on the spine. *Guns, Germs and Steel: The Fates of Human Societies* by Jared Diamond.

"Ah, is there something you are trying to tell me?" Sam asked

Gerry quizzically as she read the book's jacket, noting the departure from their usual, more lighthearted topics.

"Well," Gerry whispered conspiratorially as he leaned in close, "You know germs, I know guns. Thought it would give us something to argue about!" His crooked smile told Sam just how much he was looking forward to debating her over the coming weeks and months.

Smiling, Sam lightheartedly scoffed as she kissed him on his cheek and warned him, "Be prepared to lose!"

Patting his cheek with each word for emphasis, Sam cackled. "The phone line is going to sizzle as I cook your goose!" They both loved a good argument and more importantly, neither liked to lose. Despite the grins on their faces, they each were already orchestrating their approach, mapping out a cutthroat strategy that would ultimately lead him or her to victory. With the scent of competition in the air, Gerry's final deployment was already shaping up to be fun and hopefully shorter.

In the breaking dawn of the morning, Samantha saw through the glass of the terminal windows that the early morning storm was lifting, its clouds moving off far to the east, and she knew the flights would resume soon. Using the actions to hide her nervousness, Sam straightened Gerry's fatigue jacket in a futile attempt at smoothing out the wrinkles, silently laughing to herself that, even after all these years, her nerves still got the best of her. It was a short stint this time, only four months left to get through, and then he would be home.

"Call me before you head out, if you can," she quietly told Gerry while privately chiding herself that she was being a silly old goose. The loudspeaker crackled with an announcement that their flight was now ready for boarding, disrupting their final moment.

When Gerry leaned in for one final hug and kiss, a flash of pink caught his eye. A simple heart-shaped pendant, less than an inch wide, kept company by a trio of engraved mini dog tags, hung on a gold chain around Sam's neck. He reached down for the pendant and his fingers rubbed over the stone, feeling its smoothness and the edges of metal, and a nostalgic smile moved across his face as he remembered the how and why he had given it to her. As Sam watched the memory wash over the man's face, she knew what he was thinking, and the same smile also crept across hers. It was a quiet moment where the silence said it all.

The unapologetic barking of the loudspeaker announcing another call for boarding broke the moment. Taking a deep breath, Sam reached up to pat Gerry's chest with both hands. Drawing herself up in her best imitation of a dour CO, she sternly ordered, "Stay safe, sir," but her decidedly non-Army rendition of the command only caused Gerry to teasingly grin down at her.

"Oh absolutely, ma'am," he said, while offering a loose two-fingered salute.

Solemnly, she turned and gave Stan one final bear hug, leaning forward to whisper in his ear, "Promise me you will keep him safe." Stan merely looked at her while quietly nodding and with that, the two men picked up their duffels and headed for the boarding gate.

Sam watched as two of the most important men in her life proceeded down the jetway for boarding. Several women turned and brazenly watched them as they passed, and Stan, enjoying their attention, strutted and brashly called out, "G'morning, ladies. Splendid day, innit?" That smile had them swooning.

Watching the gate attendants openly stare at the retreating men, their attention focused squarely on Stan's back, Sam derisively chuckled to herself, *Oh ladies, if you only knew.* She was all too aware that Stan's idea of a solid relationship was inversely proportional to his sense of fun. The man's aversion to personal entanglements added a new dimension to the definition of commitment-phobic.

A mixture of dread and sadness engulfed Sam as she watched the plane back out of its gate and taxi toward the runway, and she braced herself for the onslaught of feelings that always seemed to find her with every deployment.

Her companion for the ensuing months would only be a constant void that stalked her everywhere. Watching the plane roar down the runway and lift its nose into the wind, she bit her lip as she said a silent prayer for them, and held her book tightly.

·   ·   ·

SEVERAL HOURS LATER

Gerry's and Stan's flight was surprisingly quick, even for a nonstop. To their delight, the subsequent cab ride was both mercifully short and quiet, and the men easily caught up with their unit as it gathered on the tarmac for boarding.

The fat, wide-bodied transport that was to be their ride on the second leg of their trip to Germany stood with its ramps down and doors open. Surprised that cargo was still being loaded, Gerry shot a glance at his watch and saw that he had time to make good on his promise to Sam for that last phone call. Jabbing Stan in the arm, Gerry sprinted for a phone.

There was no answer to the electronic ringing on the line and a burst of quiet cursing erupted from Gerry as he realized he had forgotten the new term's schedule, and he slammed the receiver back in its cradle.

"Damn it," Gerry sputtered, knowing he had missed his window of time. Sam was undoubtedly already on campus and teaching. Stan, leaning up against the wall next to the phone, snickered at Gerry's use of questionable language and recoiled in mock horror as he kidded,

"Language, language, *mon colonel,*" his fake French accent superimposed on his southern drawl giving him a cartoonish air.

Gerry just flippantly waved Stan off with a *Yeah, Yeah,* but then turned to grab the receiver again. On second thought, he wondered, perhaps she was with her parents. Her father was losing his battle with cancer, and she often stopped by on the way into work. As Gerry dialed her parents' number, Stan idly watched a teammate in the distance say goodbye to his family, his toddling daughter hanging onto his pant leg as he hugged his wife. Stan was only half paying attention to Gerry when he spoke as Sam's mom answered the phone.

"Good morning, Betty. Yeah, it's me, Gerry. No, we're still in the States. Look, is Samantha there?" Stan could see a change in Gerry's expression as he watched his friend's face darken a bit, and then frown as the woman talked. When Gerry turned to shield his face for privacy, apprehension began to set in as Stan wondered what was being said.

Gerry momentarily looked a bit startled, even shaken, but had said little during the phone call. Slowly replacing the handset as he hung up, his disappointment hung in the air. He and Sam's mom were on shaky ground at the moment, but even so, Gerry had been caught off guard by the hostile tone and rancor in the woman's voice. There was a silent internal flush of concern as he struggled to understand her position, but Gerry's usual stoic expression quickly returned as he turned to Stan.

"She's not there—probably teaching," he briskly said while picking up his duffel and heading out for boarding. Stan had started to call out "what happened" but the rigid carriage of his friend's back told him it was best to let it go.

Picking their way through the center section already jam-packed with cargo, the unit filled the plane, choosing seats, stowing gear, exchanging jokes and barbs. Gerry scanned the interior as he entered the cabin, looking for a quiet, more secluded place. The solidly middle-aged officer preferred to be out of the lively trash-talking crossfire of the younger men. Especially today—this was his last overseas assignment. Last posting away from Sam and home.

Over the last twenty years, whenever he was deployed, he would write her a note—instructions and thoughts for "just in case I don't come home." *Twenty years…is it possible?* he thought to himself as he reviewed the last decades of service, and he wondered how Sam would view them. *Will she remember the same things?*

It had begun innocently enough with their first deployment together. He had forgotten to tell her not to use the back burner on the stove—he hadn't had a chance to fix it yet. A few other quick pleasantries and that was it, short and sweet. With each new rotation, a new collection of thoughts was written and each one was longer than the last. Gerry found he increasingly had more to say.

While intelligent with acute street smarts, self-expression was not Gerry's strong suit. Weapons, ordnance, strategy—those were topics he could discuss with enthusiasm and ease. But whenever talking of personal concerns, the things that truly matter, the man would simply choke up, his words dying in his throat. Gerry found that in the letters he could say things he could not say otherwise, for they allowed him to organize his words to convey his thoughts. He would put the letter in the mail bag upon landing, where, in time, Sam would receive it.

Sam looked forward to them, waiting impatiently for their arrival, but she never read them—they were not to be opened until Gerry came home. Sam would instead put them under the Army coaster on his desk, where they would remain like a silent sentry on watch, waiting for his return.

On that first night upon homecoming, the couple would go cuddle in their chair at sunset, and Gerry would read his letter to his Samantha. As she lay against his chest listening to the words, the vibration of his voice as he spoke seemed to impart a layer of understanding that went far beyond the words themselves.

It was through these letters that Sam would learn of Gerry's joys, fears, and his worries. And of his questions about the future. She, in turn, would write her own letter, a rebuttal of sorts, back to him. She would mirror his words and talk about her joys, fears, and worries. And she would answer his questions. When finished writing, Sam, as Gerry had done days earlier, would read her letter to him while still in their chair after sunset, thus completing the link.

All couples develop their own unique style of communication. This was theirs.

Finding a corner, a section with only four seats and away from the noise and activity, Gerry settled in for the long haul; its seclusion would allow him to think. As a teenager, he had been sent to Vietnam, an experience he strove to forget. He hated the jungle. He hated the Army. He hated everything about the whole thing.

While in 'Nam, he had longed for the streets that beckoned to him, and at the first opportunity after his tour was up, he returned home to Boston. The streets had not waited for him, and Gerry was stunned to find everything seemed to have rotated while he was away. He did not fit there anymore.

For a couple of years, he had tried to reassert himself, to reinvent himself even, but the pieces of the puzzle that had defined Gerry's childhood simply refused to fall into place. To his shock, he had found himself missing the structure and camaraderie of the Army. The Army had taught him new skills and new ways to use old ones, and out of that, a new awareness had emerged, one a self-reliant Gerry was unaccustomed to. Even more, to his astonishment, he discovered he missed being that new person he had become while in the Army. Twenty-two-year-old Gerald Martinez had re-enlisted.

And that was twenty-seven years ago. It had been exciting back then—full of adventure and the promise of making a difference. There had been so many assignments, so many overseas rotations, and so many letters.

As Gerry stowed his duffel, he looked over the unit. The younger fellas were still settling in, jousting as they traded seats, pulling out books, headphones, tapes, and CDs. He also noticed with satisfaction that many of them had begun to write their own letters home, causing him to smile as he wondered where they themselves would be in twenty-seven years.

After so many years, Gerry was beginning to tire of it all, for there seemed to be few changes. The adversaries were different, albeit many new ones were merely old ones disguised in sheep's clothing. There were new updated weapons with even more deadly firepower and lethality. There were even new locations, although some were becoming an annual tourist destination for him. But the outcome was always the same and looking over the last two decades, he struggled to see any real progress. He had grown weary of trying to stop a tidal wave with a teaspoon.

Arranging legal pads with some pens and pulling out his coffee thermos, Gerry was lost in thought when Stan arrived and took his customary seat next to his friend. Chattering away about how insane the loading process was, but not getting much of a response, Stan glanced over and noticed his seatmate was more subdued than usual.

"Ya good, dude?" Stan asked with a touch of concern, still remembering Gerry's reaction to his call with Sam's mom. Deep in thought, Gerry merely nodded. With the phone call still on his mind, Stan lightly tossed out, "Since when do ya call Sam's mom by her name.

What happened to callin' her Mom?" The pursed lips and a worn-out sigh answered the question better than Gerry's words.

"Eh, Betty isn't too thrilled with me these days," and without looking up, Gerry busied himself with rearranging his pens laying on the legal pad, content to let the matter lie.

The appearance of the second unit they had been waiting for signaled that their delay in takeoff was over. It also signaled a new audience for Stan. Boyish enthusiasm overtook him as Stan, always the life of the party, jumped up to find new seating where he could be the center of attention. Gerry could only shake his head in amusement as he watched the incorrigible Stan go off in search of fun, but he was grateful for the solitude. At the rate the second unit was loading, it would be a bit before takeoff, and pouring himself some coffee in his thermos lid, he settled back into his seat as he sipped.

Gerry's mind whirled with confusion and questions. What Sam's mom had said to him on the phone was jarring, and he had no idea what the family's matriarch had been talking about. Gerald Martinez was at a crossroads with Sam, the woman who had been his epicenter for two decades. He knew it and could sense it in the air, but he also knew what he had watched her go through over the years. What he didn't know, however, was what to do about it.

A deep breath cleared his mind, and Gerry was quickly lost in thought as he wrestled with a foe he couldn't quite see.

2

A STORY FOR ANOTHER TIME

Right from the very beginning, when they had first met, Gerry could sense Sam was different, and part of that difference was that she had been born with a hearing loss. In Gerry's eyes, as an outsider looking in, her parents had been harsh. They had insisted Sam, as a child, not only learn how to *deal* with the real world but to *live* in it.

Her parents chose not to put Sam in a school for the deaf, but rather had enrolled her in public schools, and expected her to learn to navigate on her own. Fostering self-reliance and resiliency, Sam's parents believed in the adage of the tree growing stronger in the wind and had tolerated neither coddling nor excuses.

Gerry understood Sam's parents' point of view and perhaps it had been the right choice. Society could be incredibly cruel—the children no more than the adults, they were just more blatant and honest about it—and Sam had brawled her way through life. He even begrudgingly acknowledged that if he had been in her parents' shoes, he would have done the same thing. But now he saw the aftermath of that decision with all its consequences, and Sam's battle scars ran deep. It seemed there had been no right answer.

In elementary school, a teacher of hers once used her for show-

and-tell. Parading Sam in front of the class, the teacher explained what being handicapped meant, that she was not as good as them, and was to be pitied and tolerated. That humiliation and the persistent abasement that followed, characterized Sam's childhood.

While some people develop a thick skin, Sam developed a suit of armor, and it had served her well for all these years—until now. Now, that protective coat of armor was between her and Gerry. She would push him away, and he would shove back, in a never-ending duel. Gerry had watched the personality of the woman he loved fade to black, and he was desperate to find a way to remind her of who and what she was. He was watching her shut down, the fight in her evaporating to a wisp.

CARGO TRANSPORT OVER THE ATLANTIC, HOURS LATER

The soldier had gotten up to stretch his legs and as he twisted his way around cargo strapped in for the flight, he spied Gerry sitting with a pen poised in midair.

"You writing to Ma'am, sir?" the soldier called out loudly over the plane's engines, catching the ear of another soldier seated nearby, who yelled out, "Again? You still writing those?" as he joked with Gerry, knowing full well their colonel wrote one every time.

Kidding about how thick the envelopes going home had gotten over the years, several soldiers gathered around, leaning on seat backs and crates, and began to josh their commander that Ma'am would still be reading it when he got home.

"Shoot, you going to need a winch just to hoist it into the mail bag!" chortled Private Elliot, who had begun to write his own note back home to his wife. Gerry glanced over at Elliot as the soldier slid into the seat next to him, perturbed that his privacy had been invaded.

Private Elliot had been waiting for an opening, hoping to have an opportunity to talk to Gerry. He had heard about the letters and they intrigued him. The long deployments had begun to take a toll on Elliot's own marriage, and friction had begun to creep in on his otherwise content family life.

Elliot was hoping there might be something in it for him and his wife as he asked with interest, "May I ask, sir…what do you and Ma'am do with your letters? I mean, do you keep them?"

A philosophical Gerry held a distant smile before answering softly, "No…we don't keep them."

Elliot was surprised, for he had been sure that Ma'am had kept the colonel's letters in a flowery shoebox, perhaps with a satin ribbon to tie it shut. Something about Gerry's hint of a smile made him ask, "Well, what do you do with them? You don't just throw them out, do you?"

Elliot's astonished voice held a tinge of horror for he had come to understand just how important the notes back home had become, but his question was met with silence, as Gerry's thoughts seemed elsewhere.

Gerry's copy of the "deployment book" stuck out of his duffel's side pocket, and when he hadn't elaborated any further regarding the letters, Elliot asked, "What are you two reading this time, sir? Another thrilling spy novel?"

The idea of them both reading the same book at the same time fascinated Elliot as much as the letters, but he also found it a bit sappy. "Do you ever get tired of all your routines, sir? I mean, you got your letter, your book, and your phone calls," the private asked inquisitively.

Gerry fixed Elliot with a long pregnant pause before asking, "How long have you been married?"

The slight smile on Gerry's face was mixed with a touch of nostalgia as Elliot answered, "It's been a couple of years now, why?"

Gerry leaned over to take the book from Elliot. As he leafed through the chapter markers he had tabbed to keep him and Sam reading at the same pace, he commented, "Because…you'll find it's the small things that matter, not the big ones. Those routines of ours are what hold everything together," before handing the book back. Watching Elliot turn the book over in his hands, Gerry explained the tabs. "We read the same pages at the same time. For a moment, regardless of where either one of us are, we are on the same page, both literally and metaphorically."

A faraway look crossed Elliot's face, and as he replaced the book in the duffel's side pocket, he realized he wanted to try something like this with his wife, so he asked, "How did you guys get started? With the letters and the book and all, I mean?" He was hoping for an idea.

But Elliot's seatmate had gotten up and was now standing in the aisle with a question of his own. "I've always wanted to ask, sir, why do you call her Ma'am? Like it's her name?"

Impatient to get back to the writing of his own letter, Gerry let out a good-natured chuckle as he told the soldiers, "Oh, fellas, there are way too many questions here. This is all a story for another time. A long one." Seeing their disappointed faces, he added, "I'll tell you what, catch me on the return and I'll tell you all about it," giving them a wink while smiling as the soldiers returned to their seats.

A story for another time. The phrase stuck in his head. *A story for another time.*

As any military strategist will tell you, initial battle plans rarely go the way you intend, and you must tweak or even revise them completely as events unfold. Gerry's plans, formed almost two decades ago, were no longer working, and it was time for a different strategy with new tactics. There could be no more traipsing across the world or even trips across the country. He needed to be home.

This letter was his last one. His last "military order," or his own personal "Five Paragraph Order," as Sam had grown to jokingly call them since Gerry's tendency to write with bullet points lent a similar air to his notes. With so much at stake, Gerry couldn't afford for it to be the usual lighthearted chatter with an amusing doodle in the margin. At 30,000 feet, in an uncomfortably cramped and noisy airplane cabin, Gerry racked his brain as he sought a way to make the light of his life fight for the person she was. There had to be a way for her to find her footing again, but the answer remained stubbornly elusive, flitting tantalizingly just out of his reach.

Retrieving a large tin full of cookies from his duffel, Private Taylor began to make the rounds up and down the aisle and he spied the older officer staring at the ceiling, oblivious to his surroundings. Gerry was startled by the movement in front of him as the young man offered him a tin with cookies.

"Would you like one, sir?" The soldier's mom had baked them for the guys on the flight over and Gerry eyed the cookies with delicious anticipation.

"Are those cinnamon pecan?" he hopefully asked. Nodding and bursting with pride, Taylor boasted that his mom had even put chocolate chips in them.

When Gerry took only one, the young soldier kidded him while urging, "You can take two, sir. I won't tell Ma'am." Amused looks crossed between the two men as Taylor joked while patting his own waist, "I know you're watching the spare tire, sir."

The barbed joke only led Gerry to chide back at the youngster, "Go ahead and laugh all you want, son. Your time will come!"

Catching a slight stutter step, a hesitation on the part of the young man as he turned to leave, Gerry quizzically asked, "Something on your mind, Taylor?"

Bumbling a bit, the young soldier wondered if Gerry would tell him something. "Sergeant Ibbotson said I should ask how you and Ma'am met. How did you meet her, sir?" While sipping his coffee, a guarded Gerry, with a hint of suspicion in his voice, asked the young private why he would want to know that as he shot an exasperated glance up at Stan, standing in the aisle with a malicious grin on his face. Stan knew he had jabbed his friend in the ribs, for the story was one for the ages.

Embarrassment crept over Private Taylor as he shyly described to his commander his disastrous dinner date with a young lady a couple of nights previous. "I didn't mean to do it, sir, I really didn't! It was an accident. I…um…knocked over the fondue and her sleeve…sort of… caught on fire."

Astonished, Gerry's cookie hovered midair as amazement echoed in his voice, "You set your date on fire?" He sympathetically gasped, "Oh my! I can see how that would put a damper on things."

"Oh sir, I've never seen anything like it," Taylor forlornly admitted while recounting the improbable events that led to the couple spending the night in the emergency room of a local hospital. "Those fancy cocktail dresses are really flammable—you shoulda seen it, sir! She went up like a Roman candle."

The story had seemed amusing at the beginning, but now a shocked Gerry could only sputter, "Is she alright? How badly was she…?"

"Oh, no, sir, we put it out," Taylor quickly interrupted. "She's gonna be okay."

Gerry rubbed his forehead as he skeptically looked at Taylor. "I'm afraid to ask, but who's we? And how did you put it out?"

"They were like a precision drill team, sir!" Taylor brightly said, clearly impressed. "One waiter grabbed a tablecloth and smothered the flames while a bunch of other waiters grabbed fire extinguishers and hosed her down, sir. From head to toe!"

Taylor gushed with relief as he explained, "The ER was amazed at how minor the injuries were. The docs said she'll be as good as new in no time." But then he sheepishly added, "once her eyebrows grow back." Watching the growing smirk on Gerry's face, Taylor defensively blubbered, "I tried to apologize, sir…but she won't talk to me."

"Really? I can't imagine why!" Gerry quipped as he struggled not to laugh in commiseration. He knew the boy's pain well. He had been there and done that.

Grateful for the diversion, Gerry tapped the seat next to him and invited the lad to sit down. As he finished his tale of that initial date with Ma'am, Taylor was amazed.

"No way, sir. How did you ever get a second date with her?" he asked, awestruck, while adding he suddenly didn't feel so stupid. Taylor's eyes instantly widened as he realized the implied insult. "Oh geez, sir, that came out all wrong." Shaking his head, Gerry only laughed while he admitted, "That came out exactly right. How did I get a second date?" he mulled while rubbing his forehead in wonder.

With a bemused look, Gerry gazed over at Private Taylor and offered some advice.

"I have asked myself that every day, and even after all these years, I still don't have an answer. Yes, Ma'am was thoroughly unimpressed with me that day, but she was equally impressed that I could laugh it off. You have already made an ass of yourself with your young lady. What have you got to lose?"

"So, in other words, no guts, no glory, eh, sir?" Taylor shot back, not entirely convinced his date wouldn't slam the door in his face.

Taylor, nonetheless, thanked him for the advice, and as the young man got up to leave, Gerry called out while saluting with a cookie in hand, "Oh and Taylor, kudos to your mom. These are great!"

A roar of laughter rolled through the cabin and Gerry looked up to catch a vaudevillian Stan telling jokes with a full audience, and he could not help but laugh as well, for his best friend was a comedian at heart. The talk with Taylor had given him another thought, one that meshed with the earlier one he had tucked away.

Sam had once told him that the path to the future was woven into the past. At the time, she was making her case for Gerry to take her to his hometown of Boston, to show her where and how he had grown up. She could not understand him, she had argued, until she understood his past. The thought's glimmer danced about in his head,...*the path to the future...a story for later...how they met...*The tendrils of an idea began to creep through his mind as he eyed their last "deployment book" tucked into the side pocket of his duffel.

The idea began to solidify into a concrete strategy: The path forward was through Samantha's past. Knowing now what to write and how to rekindle the fire, Gerry was smiling to himself as Stan collapsed into the seat next to him and asked, "Got ya rhythm yet?" knowing Gerry had been struggling to find his words. Glancing over at Stan with a crooked grin, Gerry picked up a pen with flourish and clicking its top, he ardently announced, "I'm going to apply her logic here and bring the fight to her," his enthusiasm reflected in the satisfied *I've got a plan* look on his face.

Without waiting for Stan to poke at him some more, Gerry proclaimed, "I'm going to tell Samantha a story, and I'm going to tell her everything. How we met, why we watch sunsets, how and why the letters got started, all of our adventures…all of it." He looked over at Stan, delighted with himself.

I'm going to remind her of it all, he repeated to himself while he rearranged the pad and pens with purpose, no longer paying any attention to Stan.

Growing up an orphan, the Army had become Gerry's surrogate family, but he was fascinated by Sam's ancestry from Scotland and the intrigue of having a lineage to trace. He had learned key phrases and names in Scottish Gaelic and thus, in his distinctive block letter printing, Gerry began his last "Five Paragraph Order" to Sam…

"Somhairlin, mo ghràdh," meaning Samantha, my love.

[GERALD, 2001: Quoted Text from Letter

"Somhairlin mo ghràdh,

Oh god Hon, how many of these have I written? With each deployment these get not only harder but I'm finding myself not wanting to be in the position of having to write one at all anymore. I'm sitting here and as I look around, many of us are writing our letters trying to maintain our tough veneer while wiping tears. I'm relieved this is my last letter to you.

"Yep Hon, got [the] promotion—be stateside by January. Only got a few years left before mandatory [retirement] then I'm all yours. Will be a nice nest egg for retirement, eh? I'm tired of the fight Hon, I'm tired of what I have put you through. I have been so selfish, so self-centered. I added up all my deploy time versus stateside time—I've been gone more than I've been there for you. I show up on your doorstep and yes, I said your doorstep, not ours. There hasn't been much of an 'ours' has there? I breeze in, stay a bit, and once again leave you to pick up the pieces on your own. To soldier on as they say. I'm so sorry it had taken me so long to see things. I just left you and all I want to do is get back to you to just hold you while sitting in that chair, laws of physics say not possible but somehow we make it work —my favorite place. My only place where I find my peace.

"I have so much I want you to know. Things that I don't say

enough, have taken for granted that you somehow can read between the lines and just know. I want to leave nothing unsaid. This is my last one and I want to make it a good one. I'm going to tell you a story. Our story. My memories. Forgive my rambling, Hon—I have a lot to say."]

[**SAMANTHA, 2024: Quoted Text from Letter**

"All these things you remembered and wrote about; did you ever stop to think that I was able to do all that because you were there beside me? It was you, hon. Somehow you gave me an inner strength, a direction that I didn't even know a person could possess. My letter to you will not be as eloquent or as profound but it will be as heartfelt.

"And yes, I remember every amazing moment. Let me tell you what I remember. Are you listening, Gerry? Are you paying attention to what I'm saying here? You should be, my love, for you might be surprised at what made you so special to me.

"Do you have any idea of just how immensely proud of you I am? Of us? Of our story?"]

3

DON'T SHOOT ANYTHING THAT MOVES

The pen's raspy scratching against the pad rippled through his fingertips as Gerry wrote, his thoughts engulfing his mind and overflowing onto the paper. Its jet engines roaring, the cargo plane not only propelled him forward to Germany, it also transported him back in time to the beginning.

ARIZONA, 1981

With a significant hearing loss from early childhood, the realities of life presented Sam Walker with challenges, and she knew the words "usual" and "routine" would not describe her life. She required flexibility. She needed physical environments she could control, for her hearing loss imposed restrictions and barriers in her daily life. Likewise, her personality also demanded this same flexibility since she bored easily. Beset with an insatiable curiosity that as a toddler led her to disassemble numerous household appliances to see how they worked, the ordinary was for Sam dull, tedious, and tiresome. Variety was the spice of life she craved, and she was always on a quest for knowledge, never wanting to be tied down.

This innate drive for freedom drove her parents nuts, for they viewed her failure to settle on one single vocation as a lack of ambition and direction. Sam instead freelanced independent jobs, often instinctively taking positions based on what she could learn from them, rather than what they could do for her career. As a student, she was enrolled in both a Forensics Ph.D. program and in medical school, where she focused on the field of pathology, but this was her summer hiatus. And with summer break came field season.

Throughout the years of the late 1970s leading into the 1980s, both drug cartel and *coyote* traffic along the southern border had increased, with predictable and regrettable consequences. The finding of human bodies in the desert was becoming commonplace at a staggering pace. Participating in a pilot program to beef up surveillance in underserved sectors, twenty-four-year-old Sam Walker had been working the border for several seasons now, and had gotten used to the desert heat and its parchness. First introduced to fieldwork and the desert years prior as an undergrad in forensics, the desert had grown on her and she on it.

Forensics was the science of death and Sam Walker, a forensic osteologist, had seen much of it. Her job was to assist in criminal investigations identifying human skeletal remains. Even though she was early in her career, she had already seen what seemed to be hundreds of ways humans kill each other, and every time she thought she had seen the last of it, someone came up with a new innovative method. Burned, shot, gutted, knifed, torched, strangled, flayed, caustic lime, mutilated, fed to hogs, etc. The list seemed infinite, and she would not live long enough to forget all that she had seen.

In The Desert Outside of Tucson

The leather of the saddle emitted a creaking groan when Sam swung off the back of her mount, a seven-year-old gelded Paint named Roughshod, gloomily wondering if she would be adding yet a new method to her list. As she pulled her saddlebags off Roughshod's rear, Sam's teammate for the day, Sheriff Deputy Profitt, dismounted alongside her. Leaving their mounts ground tied, both somberly began to make their way over to an area of interest. Two more officers, another deputy, and a border agent, who had come up from the border town of Nogales, Arizona, were standing guard over a patch of ground. Even from the distance, Sam could see evidence of a burial, and a hasty one at that.

Sam dropped the saddlebags into the dirt at her feet as she sighed, and standing with her hands on her hips, she stared at the shred of polyester navy blue material that peeked out from under the sand, faded from the relentless sun. She could see tips of finger bones poking up through the yellow desert floor, as if they were waving her over.

As she knelt down, the border agent began to summarize who he thought the victim was, but Sam held her hand up to shush him. Without even looking up at him, she bluntly told him, "I'm sorry, but please don't tell me what you think. It only distorts my assessment and analysis. This needs to be my interpretation of the facts—not of your opinion."

As Sam leaned over and shifted to a better position, the toe of a boot filled her field of view, causing her to straighten up and once again. lecture the man as she pointedly gestured at him. "Do you mind? Please don't stand on top of the grave. Move back."

She reached back to grab the tool roll attached to her saddlebags. The tools of the field were nothing fancy, and she scanned over an array of trowels, small hand shovels, dental picks, probes, tweezers, locking forceps and assorted small artists' paintbrushes, and larger ones homeowners use to paint walls. She chose a one-inch soft-bristled paintbrush and began to clear out the sand from around the skeletal elements she could see. After a few moments, one impatient officer leaned over Sam and asked, "Well, what is it?"

Sam could only shake her head at them in exasperation. It never failed to amaze her how patient law enforcement officers could be while waiting to apprehend a felon, but yet be so annoyed at having to wait for scientific answers.

"Guys, it is going to take more than fifteen seconds to determine what is going on here. As soon as I pull it together, I'll let you know."

The officers huffed as they retreated, muttering under their breath at her.

Chuckling at the officers' irritation with her, Sam worked to clear enough desert sand to reveal the pelvic girdle. Of all the bones in the adult human body, the bones of the hips were the most informative and accurate source of determining gender. The bones of the body that made up what was called the hips—the ilium, the ischium and the pubis—form certain angles. In males, those angles are usually narrow, but in females, due to the genetic blueprint for childbirth, those angles are wider.

The angles of the hipbones laying in the sand in front of Sam told her the victim was a woman. After photographing and documenting position and environmental conditions, she finally began to remove the bones. One by one, each element was carefully removed and placed in an anatomical position on a black body bag that Deputy Profitt had placed next to the grave. As she removed the thoracic area with the rib bones, she caught a smattering of very small, delicate tube-like bones underneath.

A harsh "Aw crap," escaped from Sam as the realization hit home. There had been a fetus.

Some days I really hate this job, Sam grouched to herself, catching the deputy's eye as she straightened up and roughly grabbed the camera to document the scene.

The skull yielded another vital clue as she removed the cranium from the ground and placed it on the body bag above the mandible. Together, they allowed Sam to make a quick preliminary field assessment—the victim was a Caucasian woman. Further examination of the pubic symphysis, an area of the hip that demonstrates consistent age changes, suggested she was young, in her early twenties. The cause of her death, and the manner in which it was inflicted upon her, would have to wait until further examination back in the lab. The border agent, who had been so sure the body was that of a missing cartel lieutenant, didn't work too hard at covering his disappointment as he helped load the remains in the jeep.

Roughshod had been patiently standing by, one rear foot raised in relaxation as he "rested his eyes," while Sam tied off her saddlebags behind the saddle's cantle. Playfully, she tousled Roughshod's forelock and ears, causing him to turn his head in hopes of a treat. Amazingly, Sam had a sugar cube in her pocket for him.

Deputy Profitt was quieter than usual on the ride back to the station.

When he had finally eased his mount back from a canter to allow it to cool down, Sam leaned over and casually asked, "You okay? You seem out of sorts." Profitt's 1,000-yard stare was focused on the spot between his mount's ears, but he had heard her.

After a bit, he quietly asked Sam, "Doesn't it bother you?" His tone was somber and Sam sensed he wasn't talking about the weather.

Sam edged Roughshod up closer so they were side by side as she asked, "Does what bother me?"

There was a downcast expression on Profitt's face when he looked over at her before answering. "The fetus? It doesn't bother you to see that? You act as if it is nothing."

Sam was surprised at his discomfort—those in law enforcement see much worse every day. They rode in silence for a while as he worked up to offering a painful explanation, "My wife and I have been trying for a child for years. To see one that never had a chance just pisses me off."

When Profitt scoffed apologetically at Sam for his outburst, she sympathetically assured him, "No need, I hear ya. I'd be pissed too—and I am, but we are trained to contain our emotions, to maintain a professional distance." Leaning over the space between the horses, Sam put a hand on Profitt's arm as she told him, "I'm just as ticked off as you, but I keep it under wraps."

After the horses had cooled down, Sam and Profitt nudged their mounts into a slow loping canter that carried them toward the station in the distance. Perched on the junction of the desert and Tucson, the building was more of an outpost than a main station—a staging area for search and rescue teams and law enforcement.

Manned with a small staff for regional patrol, it boasted the bare minimum. Linoleum tile floor, a Formica counter and several desks for shift officers were the front room accoutrements, while retention cells bracketed each side of the entryway into a small medical clinic.

Outside, a horse trailer stood beside a small corral with a hitching post. At the sight of the corral in the distance, Roughshod picked up his pace—he was as tired of the day's ride as was Sam.

Sam was at the front counter scribbling her signature on various forms as she signed out, when the deputy in charge of field surveillance slid up and leaned on the counter next to her.

Eyeing Sam for a second, he hopefully, but cautiously asked, "Would you be willing to take on a larger sector? I lost a team member today, and I'm looking for someone to be my eyes in a sector sweep outside of Nogales."

Sam's head was already shaking no as she sputtered in a skeptical tone, "Nogales? Deputy, I'm not an officer. And Nogales...well..." Sam's voice dropped off in hesitation. That was not an area she wanted to be in.

At Sam's hesitation, the deputy added, "Walker, you were at that meeting as well as I," referring to a multi-unit task force meeting assembled a month prior to address the cartel border issue. "You know how important it is to get a handle on activity out that way." He quickly added she would be paired up with a deputy, but then his next comment brought her up short. "I will make the arrangements for you to be assigned a weapon."

An academic, Sam did not routinely carry a firearm in the field, and her shocked expression caused the deputy to ask in clarification, "Do you have a problem with being assigned a weapon? I've seen you at the range. I know you can handle a rifle. Can you handle a hand-gun?" At his hopeful look, Sam heaved a sigh and nodded her accep-tance. "Great!" the deputy exclaimed as he gratefully handed her a file of paperwork and told her, "Go to the main armory in town and they will set you up. "

The armory and weapons lockers stood at the back of the police station, with a subterranean entrance ramp leading into a main entry point illuminated in harsh fluorescent lighting. As Sam stood being assigned a weapon, she naïvely asked when and where the training would be. The man behind the mesh grill cage window cocked his pencil in the direction of ads on the bulletin board for gun ranges and blandly told her, "Can't afford to train you, honey. You're on your own. Pick one and give it your best shot," snickering at his own pun.

Standing there, pursing her lips, and blowing out some air, she eyed an ad for a range not too far from her apartment. "Just how hard can this be?" she whispered to herself while noting their hours, and planned on fitting in some time the following morning before she was due in court.

As Sam drove down a desolate dirt side road at the outskirts of town, she spied a sign hanging on an old leaning fence post. The rough, weathered board announcing the gun range in large hand-painted red letters, was Sam's first clue that the ad on the bulletin board had been a marvel of marketing. The building was nothing like the picture, and she felt the chill of an ominous dread as she stood out in front staring at its façade. The rundown, decrepit building's greyed and weathered wooden exterior had been repaired so many times, Sam could make out not only clapboard siding, but shiplap and plywood as well. The only breaks in the solid wood walls were two dinky little windows and a wood door, with its screen door hanging loose.

An odd assortment of men rode up on motorcycles, and they loudly cawed back and forth with each other as they yanked the door open, allowing the sounds of rounds being expended to suddenly spill out over the parking area. They wore blue jeans and open shirts with the sleeves torn off, leaving frayed edges that seemed to accentuate Sam's growing frayed nerves as well.

Sam had always trained at well-constructed shooting ranges with stringent protocols—for both safety and behavior. Standing in the parking lot looking at the wooden building that screamed, *I'm a fly-by-night operation with no rules*, Sam thought to herself in shock, *You have got to be kidding me.* She wondered if she should just leave.

But then the door opened again to the sight of the range officer, who functioned not only as the gun range's gatekeeper, but its sheriff and even bouncer when necessary. Sam watched the welcomed sight as the range officer threw a couple of men out the door, tossing their cowboy hats in the dirt alongside them while he pointedly told them to not come back until they grew up.

Oh, okay, there is someone in charge after all. Won't be too bad, Sam told herself in relief, as she shouldered her gun tote and headed for the door.

The same sturdy-looking range officer, his face dark and leathery from years of desert sun, regarded Sam with suspicion when she opened the door and stood in the darkened entry area. It was a type of place where women were rarely his clients. "Wow," Sam muttered as she gazed around the room. Given the exterior, she wasn't expecting much, but the stark rough atmosphere still caught her off guard.

"You in the right place, lady?" the range officer asked, his voice drowned out by the incessant sharp gunshots that emanated from beyond the wall behind the counter. Sam didn't answer him at first as her eyes struggled to make out dark shapes on the wall behind the man. *Are those mattresses on the wall?* Sam marveled as she stared in disbelief.

"You looking for a lane?" the man asked as he gave Sam the one over while shoving a clipboard down the counter at her to sign in.

Mentally reassuring herself, *You're already here girl, get it over with,* Sam wrestled with an urge to bolt for the door, as she watched the man study her temporary permit paperwork issued just days earlier. She was assigned to the next available stall, in the middle of the row of twenty stalls or shooting lanes.

The Colt 1911 Sam had been assigned didn't feel right in her hand —and it bothered her. In her world, it was important to display confidence. Her hearing loss often led to her being overlooked, compounding the dismissal she experienced by being in a profession where, at that time, men chafed at the presence of a woman. Showing timidity was tantamount to shooting oneself in the foot—it relegated a woman to serving coffee.

Not wanting anyone around her, Sam asked to be moved to the last lane at the end. Until she and the gun got acquainted, and she gained that confidence—she preferred to be by herself.

Asking to see her weapon, the man gave her instructions of target distance, and when he finished with a few other range rules, Sam surreptitiously leaned over the counter. She just had to ask.

"What's the deal with the mattresses?" She stared in amazement at the bullet holes and then further asked in wonder, "Do they really add to the soundproofing?"

Looking up at them on the wall, the man caustically sneered. "Oh, they have nothing to do with soundproofing, luv. I caught my wife with my best friend on those mattresses. I keep 'em to take out my frustrations every time I have to deal with the nagging harpy." He punctuated his last word with an intense snuffing out of a cigarette in an ashtray. Flicking his lighter on a new cigarette, he added one last instruction as Sam went through the doors into the firing lane gallery. "Oh, and sweetheart…don't shoot anything that moves."

The firing range gallery was a long forbidding walkway, a cavernous space that dared you to stay.

Shadows flitted over the dimly lit walkway, and Sam could make out posters and signs on the wall reminding occupants of safety and regulations, a humorous attempt at following code for it was clear no one paid attention to them. A jarring contrast to the dimly lit walkway, the row of the shooting stalls that lined it on the left, and the men within, were starkly illuminated by their bays of hanging fluorescent ceiling fixtures that threw out harsh light.

While modern day propellant did not produce the smoke of yesteryear, the two small windows that served as the ventilation system were hardly adequate to abate the acrid smell of powder with its veil of sulfur. The smell and haze were overwhelming, and between the stench of gunpowder and of male sweat, Sam's eyes began to water.

Fixating on the last lane, Sam slowly made her way down the walkway, looking into each stall as she passed. She was acutely aware she was the only woman present, and the men openly stopped and stared as she went by. Sam made it a point to hold their gaze as she passed, even nodding at the group of motorcycle riders as they stood reloading.

The negative impression that the mattresses on the wall had made was allayed when Sam noted with relief that the stalls were constructed with concrete, rubber and steel. *At least they have a bullet stop,* she sniped to herself. There were even steel baffles, covered in acoustic material of sorts to redirect errant bullets down range. There appeared, however, to be little other attempts at soundproofing, and the noise was deafening. She noted safety precautions seemed to have been an afterthought, for few men wore ear muffs, and the only eye protection were sunglasses that some insisted on wearing indoors.

What a mangy lot, Sam thought, but she decided she would stick it out and look for a different range later as she settled into the last lane at the end.

4

YOU COULDN'T HIT THE BROAD SIDE OF A BARN

Intensely private, twenty-nine-year-old Army Lieutenant Gerry Martinez kept his thoughts close to the vest. His years of being on the street as a kid had taught him the value of this survival skill, one mastered early and kept razor-sharp: Never let your adversary read your fears or intent. Opponents had learned there were two games they were wise never to play with him—chess and poker. They would lose their sanity in the former, and their shorts in the latter. Gerry's ability to gauge opponents, seize strategic opportunities, and counter their attacks earned him respect, the coveted street cred. His size earned him fear.

Despite the unreadable poker face, Private Stan Ibbotson had a knack that bordered on genius when it came to decoding his friend's micro expressions. The twitch at the corner of Gerry's eyes and the set of his brow said the obvious—he was not happy. As September of 1981 unfolded, both men found themselves in southern Arizona along the Mexican border. Gerry had not been too enthusiastic at receiving the assignment to participate in the joint training exercise. He considered the task just a goodwill gesture mired in politics, and a waste of both time and resources.

He was not fond of the desert—too hot, too dry, and too yellow for a boy from coastal New England. Gerry's forte was hand-to-hand, and while he was imminently proficient in firearms, he found firearm training rote. He was also painfully aware of his shortcomings, which had proven to be problematic in the past—a lack of social skills and a volatile temper with a short fuse. For that, he was grateful that Stan had been assigned to the task force as well. They were so different, but they complemented each other fully.

The friendship between the two men had begun early, for Stan had shown himself right at the beginning. Two weeks back into the service after re-enlistment had found Gerry, then a private, sitting on a bunk bed as he wondered how best to entertain himself for the evening.

"Yo, bro, howdy, my lord ya a big 'un," floated out over the room with a heavy southern drawl as an even younger private sauntered into the room. "What's to do around here at night?" Stan had queried, throwing his gear on the lower bunk as the two men eyed each other. It was the beginning of a beautiful friendship, one worthy of Rick's famous line to Louis in the classic movie, *Casablanca*.

It was the beginning of a unique relationship that caused many Army COs' heads to shake in frustration. It was also the beginning of an incredible bond, one that many would spend years trying to decipher, before they appreciated just how special it was.

Stan, a charismatic charmer with a genial personality, good looks, and confidence to match, was a fun-loving attention seeker who routinely danced the fine line between being just a pain in the rear or being downright insubordinate. Stan chafed under the direction of most commanders, subjected to disciplinary hearings more times than not, but when teamed with Gerry, he became a valuable asset. What Stan lacked was discipline in the details and that, Gerry supplied in spades. They made a good team.

Shooting Range, Tucson, That Same Morning

Hating the desert, a grumpy Gerry could not help but be pleased as he got out of his truck, at the shooting range on the edge of Tucson.

His quick assessment of the rough, worn out building caused him to quietly chuckle to himself, thinking, *My kind of place. Old school, nothing fancy, just the basics.*

After several days out in the scorching heat of the desert, he embraced the relief of shade. He noted with an odd sense of satisfaction that the pitiful efforts at soundproofing did nothing to squelch the sounds as they reverberated throughout the building. Gerry welcomed the harsh metallic clicks that accompanied the staccato bursts of gunfire, some rapid fire while others more spaced out.

A gun range could be an intimidating place, but Gerry was never more at home than here; these sounds and smells were his old friends. Hand-to-hand was more challenging and satisfying to him, but it was the solitude of range work he gravitated to, even craved. Whenever the complexities of life overwhelmed him, it would be at a gun range he would find his center balance again. The feel of the metal on his fingers, the sound of the slide clicking into place, the calling forth of the patience and mental discipline necessary to effectively engage his target—all led to a Zen-like state that fed his sense of control.

With a shift in military focus and priorities toward preparedness and training, teams were frequently sent to different regions of the country consulting with officers of various agencies and organizations. Each region had its own unique style and quirks, with long-held bad habits. In the west, officers often wore gun holsters too low on the leg, lending a swagger to their stance as if they were squaring off for a show down on main street. The men in Gerry's current group were no different—that swagger was so ingrained in their psyches, they were not even aware that they did it. It had been the breaking of those bad habits that had led Gerry and Stan to suggest indoor range work that morning.

The commotion to Sam's left was loud enough to cause her to lift the earmuffs from her ears, and she leaned back out into the walkway to look down toward the entrance. A group of men had arrived, most in typical desert garb. *Oh, hello…hmm, who might you guys be,* Sam mused to herself as she paused for a second to study them, but then two more men in military fatigues joined the group.

Sam sighed wearily at the sight of the two soldiers. Her dealings with the Army on past forensic cases had not always been cordial, and as she watched the man from the front counter wave a clipboard at the taller of the two soldiers, leading him back through the door, Sam made a mental note to stay out of their way. Acutely aware that she only had so much time that morning, she quickly dismissed the group, and got back to her business.

Gerry and Stan assembled the nine men in their training group for a drill emphasizing repetition to build up muscle memory and speed. After a brief bout of grip and stance corrections, the two Army men left the group to practice on their own. Overall, it had been a productive morning and a good way to end the week.

As the training exercise ended, Gerry's ears picked up the cadence of a novice shooter, and when he looked up to see who it was, he spotted a young woman in the last shooting lane far down at the end of the line.

Gerry stepped sideways to maintain his view when several men took positions in a stall in front of her, blocking his line of sight. It had been a glint of copper auburn hair that had first caught his eye. He watched, intrigued as a tall, lean woman's confidence took a beating.

Despite the obstructed view, Gerry could see her face screw up in frustration as she grabbed a book, flipping through its pages in disgust, and he caught a glimpse of what he considered a beauty. There was no city girl sophistication in the tilt of her head, carriage of her shoulders, or her stance. She was a country girl, through and through, and even from that distance, an air of no nonsense and practicality hung over the stall.

Gerry stood mesmerized, watching her fight with herself as she tried to figure out what she was doing wrong.

[**GERALD, 2001: Quoted Text From Letter**

"I know you've heard all this before but I'm going to say it anyway. I love you. I always have, from that first day. God, you were so beautiful. Had gone to the range that day. You were there trying to figure out that gun. If there was ever anyone who needed instruction, it was you."]

BENT OVER PACKING up their gear and ammo, Stan was asking Gerry for the ammo can while waving his hand behind his back, but received nothing but dead air.

"Yo, Earth to Gerry," Stan spouted as he straightened up to find Gerry totally absorbed with his attention fixed. Following his gaze down the line, Stan discovered the source of Gerry's focus and he good-naturedly teased his friend, "Well, well, whadda we have here?" Nudging Gerry in the ribs, a euphoric Stan could barely contain himself as he gleefully announced, "This we gotta check out!"

Stan was always on the lookout for the opportunity to get Gerry into the game, and this looked promising. "C'mon," Stan goaded. "What can it hurt? You're an ordnance guy, that be a gun, and she's… oh hell, I dunno know what she's doin'. From the looks of it, she don't either."

Grinning as he grabbed Gerry's arm and propelled him down the line toward the woman, Stan excitedly jabbered at his friend, "Just go up and do your thing, man. If ya don't I will. I'm not spendin' Friday night stuck in a motel room with ya!"

Meanwhile, in that shooting lane at the end of the line, Sam's morning was not going well. Muttering a quiet "damn it," she berated herself as she disgustedly looked at the spread on the shooting target. A few of her shots had missed the target entirely, and the rest were all over the place. Panicking a bit, she fervently looked to make sure there was no one in the lane next to her. The last thing she needed was a headline in the local paper—"Girl's wild shooting kills local at gun range."

For Pete's sake, you're a country girl—suck it up here. You know how to shoot a rifle. This is nothing but a little itty-bitty rifle, she griped inwardly while grabbing the book on shooting. She had hastily picked it up at the library the night before, and the pictures were worthless. *How is anyone supposed to figure this out? And where do I put my bloody finger again?* She had been at this all morning without much success.

Stan was on a mission. Distracted, the woman that held Gerry's interest was totally absorbed in her task as she studied the book in her hand. Stan had hoped the sounds of the commotion he was making would break her concentration and she would look up, but her earmuffs muted his efforts against the background noise of gunfire. Clearly, it was up to him to do something.

The more Stan pushed Gerry down the walkway toward the far shooting lane, the more he balked and dug in, locking his knees in protest. Stan's football days proved useful as he had to practically shoulder his friend down the last twenty feet. Dragging him by the arm, Stan hauled a reluctant Gerry forward, and with a final push, he propelled him up behind the woman. And Gerry just blandly stood there.

Scoffing with irritation, an old country saying ran through Stan's head, *You can lead a horse to water, but you can't make it drink.* Stan desperately wanted to strangle him, and through gritted teeth, he motioned for Gerry to do something. Anything.

Impatient, a peeved Stan threw a pointed jab into Gerry's side while quietly mouthing, *Will you get up there? My God, you're such a wuss.* Gerry was afflicted by a case of terminal shyness and, tongue-tied, he awkwardly began to stammer nervously as panic seized him. He came across as a complete dolt. As he raked his fingers through his short, dark brown hair, his voice wavered and cracked a bit, before he shakily croaked out the only thing he could think of, "Um...ah... permission to speak freely, ma'am?"

The Army was not Sam's cup of tea. She had worked with it before, having confronted it many times in the field, and often butted heads over jurisdiction and procedures. And that was just the paper-work. Being a young female in a male-dominated field, men often felt compelled to instruct her on how to do her job. The Army was no different. Sam viewed the Army as dictatorial and chauvinistic, and having to deal with it was just a nasty fact-of-life in her job. And then there was the "ma'am." The Army had the most abrasive way of saying "ma'am," that had every woman on a crew fighting the impulse to reach out and perform an excerebration—the Egyptian mummification technique of removing the brain through the nostrils using a hook.

Sam was already dismayed over how badly her morning had gone, and had laid her gun down on the ledge to pick up the book again, when an interruption sent Sam's annoyance climbing into the red zone. The source of the interruption was the two guys in Army olive-green fatigues she had seen earlier, and the unwelcomed sight instantly put her on point.

"Oh lovely," she muttered to herself under her breath as she removed her earmuffs. Another rude elbow jab in his back from Stan prodded the bashful Gerry to keep at it.

"Ah, begging your pardon, ma'am, but um...that's not how you approach the target...ah...you're using the wrong stance, ma'am..." Standing rooted to one spot and with the book still in her hand, Sam just stared incomprehensibly at a tall, well-built man in olive green, as he made absolutely no sense. Although she couldn't help but notice how cute Gerry was, he was eclipsed by the fact that his companion standing behind him, Stan, was stunning.

While she watched Stan grimace and shake his head pathetically at Gerry, Sam worked to stifle the thought, *What a waste, a man that gorgeous in Army green*, as she fought not to stare at him. Meanwhile, Gerry's painful struggle continued.

"You, ah...you should blade. And you, um...you're teacupping the grip ma'am, and you're overthinking too much...ah, um...using way too much finger, causing your shots to pull and ah, well, you..." Given Sam's animosity toward the Army, she had bypassed working her way up to irritation, and slid straight into argumentative—instantly. *Whatever these two want*, she thought to herself, *it can't be good*. Belligerently, she eyed the duo as she stood with a hand on a cocked hip.

Gerry's attempt at conversation was a disaster and Sam stared at him in barely contained disdain. Disgust took over Stan and with exasperation, he melodramatically rolled his eyes while brusquely pushing his friend aside as he huffed, "Oh for cryin' out loud."

. . .

[Gerald, 2001: Quoted Text From Letter

"I thought I was being so clever but alas you were not impressed. Downright skeptical of me I might say. It was Stan who saved the day —'what he's trying to say ma'am is that you couldn't hit the broad side of a barn if it laid down and surrendered.'"]

"Why bless your heart, darlin,' aren't ya the sweet-talkin' charmer?" echoed off the walls as Sam sarcastically mimicked Stan's deep Southern drawl. Midwestern by birth, Sam's mother's family hailed from the south, the Tennessee hills more precisely, the hills of the Cumberland Gap, a land of moonshine and double names. Sammi Jo to her mom's family, sliding into a southern accent was second nature to Sam, and in a shooting range outside of Tucson, Arizona, Tennessee twang faced-off against Georgia drawl.

Unimpressed, Sam caustically sniped at herself for being surprised at Stan's lack of manners. *Well, what did you expect, girl? He may be gorgeous, but he's still Army.*

Impatient to get her morning back on track, she dismissively turned her attention back down the lane, leaving Gerry to throw a downcast glance toward Stan. Looking for an inroad, Stan leaned over to look at the book Sam had picked up on shooting, and while leafing through the pictures, he was prompted to comment,

"Ma'am, this book's all wrong for ya. It's for officers who've already been trained." *Oh, this one can talk,* Sam mockingly thought as she took a deep breath and turned back around to face the men again, now squarely focused on Stan. Putting the book aside and hoping to deescalate the tension, Stan casually asked, "How 'bout you let us show ya the basics? And trust me, ma'am, it'd be best 'cause your shooting's all cock-eyed," he added as he unleashed a devastating grin.

Sam rubbed her forehead for a second. *This is not going to end well,* she thought, for they had already called her "ma'am" six times in less than ninety seconds. But she needed help and she knew it. Telling herself it couldn't hurt to hear what they had to say, Sam checked her watch again for the umpteenth time, and then flashed what she hoped was a grateful smile as she told them,

"Okay fellas, I've got an hour or so before court." Inwardly, she cringed. *I'm so going to regret this.* The idea of spending a torturous hour with a guy who could barely string two monosyllabic words together was totally unappealing, *but oh, that other one* Sam thought as she reloaded her gun. That grin had worked its magic.

[GERALD, 2001: Quoted Text From Letter
"You still weren't impressed but at least you weren't calling security. Spent the next hours teaching you proper gun management..."]

STAN TOOK the lead as he exuberantly showed Sam what she was doing wrong, which, according to him, was pretty much everything. While Stan positioned Sam's stance, Gerry focused on her grip, and gradually there was progress. Slow, but steady. Best of all, she had become more consistent. Sam's grouping was still not the greatest, but at least all her shots were now landing solidly on the target. Even Gerry, who had been instinctively ducking each time she stepped up and toed the line to shoot, had stopped flinching. Conversation had been centered around shooting, but soon was comfortable enough for loose joking to creep in, and Stan, sensing an opportunity, began his bid for dinner.

"Doin' good, ma'am," Stan chuckled as he reset a new target. An impish grin crossed his face and he turned to issue Sam a challenge. "We're down to the last shot, so how 'bout we up the ante? If ya hit 'center mass,' eight or better, we'll buy ya dinner at the diner of your choice." Sam's internal klaxon, already glowing a solid yellow warning throughout the morning, was on the verge of blaring red alert again.

"And if I don't?" Sam questioned Stan, eyeing him warily with suspicion.

Without missing a beat, the flirting Stan smoothly returned volley,

"Well then, I guess you'll hafta buy us dinner at the diner of our choice!"

Stan's cheerful exclamation did little to squelch Sam's apprehension as she dubiously scoffed right back at Stan, "And the upside to this bet for me is…?" Her skepticism was accentuated by her arched eyebrows.

Flashing that cheeky smile of his right back at her as if she had just won the lottery, Stan exuberantly gushed, "Why, a delightful evening with us, ma'am! Whaddaya say?"

Stan stood clearly delighted with his logic, and then waited expectantly for Sam to accept the invitation that he was convinced she couldn't refuse. Gerry, meanwhile, simply inwardly groaned. Despite Sam's improvements over the last hour, there was no chance of her hitting eight or better on the target.

For Sam, while Gerry and Stan had been nothing but agreeable and polite, she suddenly found all their olive green suffocating, and in a flash, she simply wanted to be done with it all. Looking for the quickest way to extricate herself from the situation, Sam, without warning and in a single motion, unexpectedly pivoted, acquired the target, and fired without hesitation.

Not even bothering to check her shot, Sam glibly shrugged at the men, and began to apologize, "Sorry fellas, no dinner for you tonight…" but she did not finish the sentence as she took in the astonished looks on the men's faces. Following their gaze, she stared at the target in disbelief—she had hit it dead center. Gerry couldn't believe it either and a broad grin crossed his face—*they would be going to dinner!* There was a god after all.

Stunned, Sam began to explain to the men she couldn't make dinner that night, telling them that she was due in…but her sentence abruptly ended and hung in midair. There was a sharp gasp as her words faded away and her eyes widened, and Sam snatched a quick glance at her watch while cursing under her breath, *Crap! Court, I'm late for court.*

Sam frantically loaded her backpack and bolted off the range.

. . .

[**G**ERALD, **2001: Quoted Text From Letter**

"Thought all was good. You suddenly just said, "thank you, gotta go." You were gone before we could even get our act together."]

45

GERRY AND STAN were caught completely off guard. Racing to try to catch up with her, they could only watch in dismay and disbelief as her dusty blue pickup truck peeled out of the parking lot and onto the street. They could do nothing but stand there and look at each other. *What the hell just happened?*

5

YOU SNOOZE, YOU LOSE

Gerald, 2001: Quoted Text From Letter

"I went to that gun range for days, weeks even looking for you. Thought all was lost until there you were. Still bad but had to give you credit—you were trying to implement some of the techniques we had shown you. God, I tapped you on the shoulder convinced you would show me the door. You flashed that smile and seemed actually pleased to see me. Stan always said he knew I was a goner—had the look of a guy who had been struck by lightning."]

DAYS LATER

Gerry had left his phone number with the man at the gun range counter, asking him to call if Sam returned. Despite her pledge to find a new gun range to practice at, Sam hadn't had time to scout out a new range, so she went back. And when she pulled the door open to the firing alley after signing in, the man behind the counter remembered to call Gerry.

The range was quiet that day. Tucked into a shooting lane, Sam was intently focused on maintaining proper position. While trying to use the smooth follow-through motion that Gerry and Stan had worked hard to show her, she felt a tap on her shoulder, followed by an earmuff being lifted so she could hear.

"You're still pulling your shots." It was Gerry. While he was still wearing Army green, Sam was no longer on point when she looked up to see a shy smile.

"That's because the target is too far to the right," Sam quipped, flashing Gerry a grin that surprised not only him, but her as well.

That grin calmed Gerry's jitters, and he soon found his rhythm as instinct took over. Smoothly, he began to make grip and stance corrections while reminding Sam how to stay balanced during recoil. With each consecutive round, small readjustments were made, and confidence grew. Hers in her ability to shoot, and his in her.

Sam's world was ruled by the clock. Juggling three different vocations—forensics, academia, and medical research—meant organization was paramount not only for her success, but her sanity as well. As she checked her watch once more, she realized her time was up. She had a report to write.

"I'm so sorry, Gerry, but I really do have to leave," Sam said with a huge sigh. While patting him on his arm, she thanked him. "I can't even begin to tell you how much I appreciate your advice...and patience!" She then laughingly added, "I must have been an absolute horror of a student!" Gerry's expression fell as he realized she was saying goodbye, and as he reached over to check her weapon, he looked for words. Sam marveled at how expertly he handled her gun, removing the magazine and securing the pieces with ease in her gun tote.

"Ah, um...maybe we could try this again tomorrow?" Gerry hopefully asked as he handed the gun tote to Sam.

She cringed when she saw the hope fade from his face as she told him, "Believe it or not, I really do have a day job, and I have to get back at it. I have a report to write, among other obligations. I'm so far behind as it is..." Her words faded off mid-sentence as she apologetically shook her head.

Gerry couldn't think of anything more to say, but his frown of disappointment was unmistakable as Sam packed up her gear to leave.

Gerry's a nice fella, she told herself, and heaven knew he was as cute as a button, but there was something about him. Sam's years in forensics and with law enforcement had left her with a heightened radar and an overabundance of caution. She had long since lost count of the number of notification calls she had made, and the number of families she had watched receive the news of finding their loved ones dead.

He's too measured, too closed. He's too…calculating. Yeah, that's the word, Sam mused to herself as she nodded goodbye.

Both puzzled and deflated, Gerry gloomily watched Sam cross the dirt street to a local *cantina* with an outdoor patio. *I will never understand girls,* he complained to himself under his breath. *Us dudes are simple—we make sense.* Beyond perplexed, he could not decipher why Sam was so evasive; just when he thought all was going so smoothly, she zigged instead of zagged. Sam had Gerry buffaloed, but there was something unusual about her that held his attention. While he leaned up against the side of the building, tossing blades of dried grass into the wind, he watched her and contemplated his options.

She had taken a table out on the patio, and had removed papers from her backpack, using the salt and pepper shakers and table candles as weights against the desert breeze. *How do I break through that wall? What would Stan do?* Gerry wondered as he stood stewing, and within moments, as if on cue, Stan appeared, wanting to know the latest.

"We've already gotta reason to ask her to dinner," Stan wildly announced when Gerry filled him in on the latest. "She lost the bet, remember?" Stan was always a fan of keeping it simple.

Deep in thought while leaning over her table, a preoccupied Sam had focused her attention on double-checking her data while crafting the opening abstract for her report. Suddenly, her table was thrown into shade. *Unbelievable…these two again. Don't you boys have a home to go to?* she quietly wondered to herself, inwardly rolling her eyes. Stan confidently laid it all out.

"We're here to collect—ya owe us dinner, remember? Did you think we'd let ya back outta our bet?" He cajoled Sam expectantly. "C'mon, let us buy ya a *cerveza*. Ya owe us that much," he added while trying to butter her up with a melting grin. Sam sat pensively, sizing the duo up for a few moments before she finally, putting aside her reservations about the two, gathered up her papers and gestured for them to sit down.

[**GERALD, 2001: Quoted Text From Letter**

"We followed you to that *cantina* hoping to buy you a drink, remember? You were so leery of us, not sure just what we were up to but the stars lined up that day and you let us sit down. Thanks for giving me a chance."]

ONCE SAM GOT over the fact that they wore Army green, she was surprised to discover that Gerry and Stan were unexpectedly delightful companions, and the hours flew by.

"Well, doll, how do ya want to start?" Stan had begun, with a grin that took years for Sam to become impervious to. It was of course Stan doing the talking and Sam marveled at how effortlessly he flew through conversation. She began to giggle as he described the men in the group he and Gerry were training. "Oh, ya shoulda seen it. The dude just flipped his loaded rifle, loaded mind ya!" Stan blurted out while gesturing wildly, "at the ass of the guy in front of him. Talk 'bout givin' someone a bullet enema!" Stan screeched in disbelief at the man's carelessness.

As he jumped up to imitate the swagger of the men, Sam looked over at Gerry, who hadn't said much of anything...yet, and she caught him staring at her. She was startled when he didn't look away. He was so shy she was expecting him to, and she found herself staring back into deep brown eyes that held so much depth. The moment was interrupted by Stan plopping back into his chair as he finished his dramatic reenactment, exclaiming that he didn't know how well the desert tactical training scheduled for the coming week was going to go over. Sam and Gerry shared a private smile as Sam turned back to Stan and casually joked, "Maybe you should give them a reading assignment, like homework? Perhaps Sun Tzu's *Art of War* and its lessons of 'know thy enemy'?"

Gerry and Stan both stared at Sam for a second before Stan blustered out, "You've read Sun Tzu?" His voice said it all, and even Gerry leaned back in his chair in disbelief.

Irritation crept in Sam's voice as she shot back at them, "What? You don't think a woman can understand the concepts? Geesh,...talk about chauvinistic fellas. It doesn't require testosterone to understand it." Sam's eyes narrowed a bit at the two, and there was a brief moment of edginess that gave way to the lighthearted levity that floated over the table.

The last of Gerry's chicken tenders sat perched on the rim of his plate and Sam's fingers clandestinely inched across the table before she nimbly mooched it. Gerry's expression at her brazen theft caused her to merely chirp mischievously at him, "Hey, it was just sitting there—you snooze, you lose," and a crooked grin began to spread across his face.

The chicken tender theft had broken the ice, and much to her chagrin, Sam realized that there was way more to this Gerry fella than she had first surmised. Of the two men, it was he who piqued her interest. The discussion of Sun Tzu had slid into an argument of various WWII naval battle tactics, and by their third round of beers, all three were arguing the finer points of the naval battles of Guadalcanal and Leyte Gulf.

Gerry was beyond impressed when Sam began to compare the effectiveness and consequences of U.S. Admiral Halsey's, the commander of the South Pacific Area during WWII, command decisions between the two battle campaigns. Sam was equally amazed. Gerry, who couldn't complete a sentence socially, was exceptionally articulate and intelligent on military topics. She learned more about the differences between the Mark 13, Mark 14, and Mark 15 torpedoes than she ever needed to know.

Stan found himself refereeing a spirited debate between Gerry and Sam over the impact that the battle of Samar, a component of the overall Battle of Leyte Gulf, had on the final outcome of the Leyte battle. As Sam sat ardently making her case against Halsey's logic of taking his force north away from Leyte, she jabbed her tortilla chip in Gerry's face.

"...Halsey left the collective asses of Taffy 3 to swing in the breeze. I'm sorry, I know hindsight is 20/20, but Halsey let his ego cloud his judgement..." The tortilla chip hovered just inches from Gerry's face. Impulsively, he reached over and snatched it out of Sam's fingers and popped it into his mouth.

Over the crunching, Sam heard him playfully mumble, "Hey, it was just sitting there—you snooze, you lose!"

Astonished at Gerry's out-of-character audacity, Sam turned to order another chip and dip plate when she caught the sun's angle in the distance. She had lost track of time, and was genuinely startled to realize the sun had begun its descent. This time, it is Sam who was disappointed as she regrettably told the fellas she had a busy schedule the next day, and she needed to leave.

A disheartened Gerry's face was soaked in frustration as he sat watching Sam pack up her belongings, and Stan kicked his friend under the table. Gesturing with his head as he tried to be somewhat discreet, Stan hissed at Gerry to ask her out for a date. After another agonizing bout of hemming and hawing, the introverted Gerry finally managed to squawk something out, only to be shot down as Sam shook her head no. She was sorry, she said, but she had a commitment for the following day.

Threading her way through the tables, Sam stopped at the edge of the street and looked back over her shoulder.

[GERALD, 2001: Quoted Text From Letter

"I was so crestfallen when you turned me down for a date the next day. Oh, woman, you have a mean streak in you. You played me. Waited until you almost got to the street, looked back over your shoulder, gave me that sly smile I've grown to love so much, that mischievous twinkle in the eye—you were scheduled for body patrol along the border. Said cartels were in the area and were dangerous.

Given how bad you were with the gun, [you] wouldn't mind an escort. Did we know of anyone who might have the time? Damn near fell over myself saying I would."]

Stan sat on the edge of the bed as he tried to stifle his giggles at his best friend having the jitters and butterflies. Gerry was always so reserved and so in control. But as funny as it was to see him so unnerved, it also pleased Stan to see him this happy.

Stan sensed his expertise was required, desperately, and warming up to the task at hand, he grabbed another beer while he launched his lecture to Gerry as to what to say to women. Insulted at Stan's loosely veiled critique of his lack of social skills, Gerry erupted as he retaliated in protest, "Oh, c'mon, I'm not that bad."

Having just taken a swig of beer, Stan dissolved into a fit of hiccups at Gerry's remark, and his convulsive roar of laughter left him barely able to speak. When he could breathe again and with tears running down his face, he managed to croak out, "She's better with a gun than you're at talkin'. And she's bad. Do ya honestly wanna leave this to chance? Now let the master speak." In his glory, Stan continued with his dating tips and pointers, complete with energetic body animation and vocal incantations. As his friend droned on, Gerry resigned himself to his fate as he sighed and settled down on the bed for the long haul.

It's going to be a long night, he grumbled inwardly, reaching for another beer.

[Gerald, 2001: Quoted Text From Letter

"Spent all that night working out [the] best uniform configuration and what to say. Stan's going, 'Dude you're wearing a uniform—not many options.' Also told me it was best for me not to talk much. Best you thought I was an idiot [than] to open my mouth and remove all doubt."]

6

WHAT COULD POSSIBLY GO WRONG?

*F*OLLOWING *MORNING*

He and Stan had meticulously planned the day all out. A nice outdoor hike and then into town for dinner at the restaurant the two had scoped out the night before. As he navigated the dark streets toward their rendezvous point, Gerry mentally rehearsed all of the topics Stan had given him, topics that were guaranteed to be conversation starters. What could possibly go wrong?

It was half past six a.m. and the sun was barely rising. They had arranged to meet at the diner at the edge of town at sunrise, and the excited Gerry did not want to be late. Knowing what a stickler Sam was for being on time, Stan had made it abundantly clear; if he was late, she would leave without him. The day was forecasted to be in the nineties and sunny—a typical desert day. After all the previous night's deliberation, Gerry had opted for wearing the light tropic weight service khaki pants with a belt rather than the usual fatigues. Stan, always the optimist, had argued that he would be better dressed for the anticipated dinner date later if all went well.

A hopeful Gerry had also packed an extra T-shirt and a nicer cotton shirt in his rucksack for the occasion as well. The rest of his ensemble included a simple T-shirt, his green utility jacket, patrol cap, and boots. Stan had talked him into acquiring a local wardrobe staple —the bandana. He was now officially part of the western desert scene.

Pulling into the parking lot, Gerry looked around for Sam's dusty light blue truck, but it was nowhere to be seen. The only vehicle off to the side was an old jeep. Thrilled to have beaten her there, Gerry hit the steering wheel with an exuberant *Yes!*

Elated, he smiled to himself as he parked along the same dune as the jeep and rehearsed once again what he was going to say when Sam arrived. As he exited his truck, he was staggered to hear a woman's snippy voice rise up out of the dark and rattle off three curt, short-worded sentences.

"'Bout time you got here. Been waiting an hour. Coffee's cold." *No way* roared through Gerry's head as he jerked around and realized Sam was sitting on the dune next to the jeep with a flashlight and clipboard on the ground. She had clearly been sitting there a bit.

Astonished, Gerry could only sputter, "I thought we were meeting at sunrise," and was taken aback by Sam's blunt snap of, "No."

Ticked off and exasperated, Sam heaved herself off the ground and, while pushing her way past the stunned man, gruffly pointed out, "We were beginning our search at sunrise; we're an hour from the border. Let's get a move on, time's a-wasting."

Gerry desperately scrambled to recover from his blunder, and as he threw his gear in the back of the jeep, he wondered why he just couldn't seem to catch a break. Gathering up all her papers and gear into her backpack, Sam looked up just in time to catch his pitiful expression.

Halfheartedly acknowledging that perhaps she hadn't been as clear as she should have been regarding the timing, Sam sympathetically leaned in and whispered to Gerry, "Don't worry about it, gave me time to begin the paperwork." Thinking he might appreciate having something to focus on, she then asked Gerry if he wouldn't mind driving while she finished putting the last of the paperwork in order. Sam's crooked smile as she climbed into the jeep's passenger seat signaled that she had already forgiven him for the slipup.

The sixty-nine-mile drive down from Tucson to Nogales was uneventful, and it allowed Gerry to take in the beauty of the desert. A typical desert morning, crisp and in the seventies it was early enough in the fall that flowers were still blooming; reds of paintbrush and bottle-brush, the yellow bell shrubs dotted the landscape along with all the various cacti; the stately saguaro, stout Arizona barrel cactus and the more comical pear were all mixed in with mesquite and palo verde trees.

With Sam absorbed in her task, Gerry mulled over the morning's bungling misstep. He had noted Sam's attire for the day—similarly outfitted with khaki cargos, T-shirt, a cotton overshirt with a utility vest, hiking boots, and a boonie hat. She even sported a bandana. Pleased with himself that he had chosen his outfit well, Gerry happily thought the worst was behind him, and allowed himself to daydream of great expectations for the day.

The miles ticked by as they closed in on the border and Sam began to take note of the mile markers. Leaning over, she gave Gerry a nudge and pointed out over the landscape to his left, telling him, "When you get the chance, cross over the interstate and head for that rock formation." They were at their designated search grid coordinates.

As she spread the map out on the jeep's hood, she traced the day's itinerary and route, explaining to Gerry the key rock formations to use to keep his bearings.

Leaving Gerry to study the map, Sam began pulling together her various field kits—a camera kit along with the forensic and medical kits—and when satisfied all was in order, she then assembled her survival gear. Knives, essential medical gear, ropes, and emergency items were all laid out on the ground and double-checked. Gerry chuckled to himself as he watched her carefully lay the Colt 1911 down as well. He was fascinated by some of the equipment, especially the forensic kit, but it was her attention to detail that he considered stellar.

Everything had a place, every box was checked off and as he watched, he thought to himself, *She'd make good Army material.*

In a final act, Sam retrieved a couple pairs of snake chaps from under her jeep seat.

"Best put these on," she instructed as she handed Gerry a pair along with his binoculars and canteen. Catching the hesitant look on his face as she leaned over to buckle hers on, she explained that they would be walking a good portion of the day.

Through experience, she had seen firsthand the consequences of getting lost in the desert, and thus removed two compasses from her backpack. One she duct taped to the jeep's roll bar, the other she taped to the driver's side mirror. She also checked to make sure she had a small one attached to her vest. They were finally good to go.

The day took on a predictable pattern: drive until you spot a suspicious lump, then get out and investigate. Repeat and repeat again. All was suspect—dead animals, trash piles, even peculiarly shaped cacti caught their attention.

[GERALD, **2001: Quoted Text From Letter**

"I fell in love with you that day, did you know that? Oh, it was the snake. If it hadn't been for the snake, the cactus wouldn't have happened. We had been on patrol all morning, seemed like it was the most natural thing to be with you in the desert looking for dead bodies. Not your typical first date."]

THROUGHOUT THE MORNING, all had been quiet. So uneventful that it was even boring. All of Stan's guaranteed conversation starters proved to be nonstarters, as Gerry's attempts bombed. Mindful that they were already behind schedule, Sam kept her eyes glued to the binoculars and rarely even glanced his way, let alone met his futile forays into conversation with anything but a noncommittal, disinterested grunt.

A rock outcropping next to an arroyo provided some welcomed shade as they pulled in under a rock ledge, and scrambling up to its vantage point to scan the horizon, the pair saw nothing suspicious.

The desert seemed uncharacteristically quiet. A line of shrubs and cacti along the bank adjacent to the outcrop provided even more shade, and offered a pleasant, inviting place to stretch out and relax. Desert willows, mesquite, even a small palo verde tree all decorated the area—it was the usual desert wash.

Both Sam and Gerry were tired, hot, and dusty, and they looked forward to taking a break from the day's heat and glare. Preoccupied with trying to come up with something witty to say, Gerry absent-mindedly sat down on the largest log of a long toppled tree, next to a large grouping of cacti, oblivious to what was hidden in the shadow of the log.

[GERALD, 2001: Quoted Text From Letter

"Sat down on that log for a break. Here I was trying to be some badass and I was so focused on impressing you that I never checked my surroundings. You just put a hand on my shoulder and told me not to move. I looked down and there was this huge diamondback in coil strike position—ready to take a bite out of my ass. In one motion you grabbed the stick, trapped the head, grabbed the tail, twirled it around a couple of times and chucked it into the brush. Dusted yourself off, sat down and took out a couple of energy bars, handed me one with a, 'You hungry?'"]

STUNNED EMBARRASSMENT FLOODED Gerry and he could feel the heat rise on his face, and he knew he was beet red as he watched Sam dust her hands off on her pants after letting the snake go. When she came up next to him, he averted his eyes so she wouldn't see how mortified he was.

Sam was digging through her field bag, and with an air of success, she mumbled, "There ya are," as she triumphantly pulled out a couple of granola bars. Nudging Gerry with her knee, she expected him to instinctively move over, but he sat as still as a rock while staring at the ground.

Sam leaned over and tapped him on the shoulder. "Hey, scoot over, you're hogging the log here."

It had happened in a flash and was over before it even registered. Gerry had gotten up at Sam's prodding to make more room for her, and had casually stepped backward up onto the log. There had been only the faintest of crackling sounds as the rotting log gave away and in a flash, it was over. He had fallen backward into the cacti grove. Sam had just begun to sit down, asking Gerry if he was hungry, but shot back up when she sensed Gerry beginning to fall. With granola bars in her hand, she watched a slow motion horror film. The seat of Gerry's pants impacted first, then his back, followed by his arms.

Dropping the granola bars where she stood, a gurgled, "Oh my God," escaped Sam as she rushed over to help him up, but her exclaimed question of "Gerry, are you all right?" was met with silence as Gerry's mind took it all in.

His silence didn't last long. Caught up on the spines as he struggled to get up, Gerry erupted in a flood of cursing that left even Sam impressed. Helping him to his feet, Sam caught herself repeating "Oh my God," over and over as Gerry's profanity reached a crescendo. Sam heard Gerry take another breath to launch into a second tirade, when he abruptly fell silent mid-word with a stunned look on his face. Instead of a second round of cursing, Gerry, standing in wide-eyed shock, and with spines sticking out of his rear end, began to apologize profusely to Sam.

"I'm so sorry, oh geez. I'm swearing," Gerry blubbered, more embarrassed by his language than by the cactus, as he kept repeating, "Oh God, I'm sorry. I shouldn't be swearing at you." For a moment, the comical apology brought levity to the seriousness of the situation, and there was a slight hint of a smile on Sam's face as she interrupted him.

"Gerry… Gerry! Stop apologizing. I know you aren't swearing at me. I've heard worse. Shoot—I've probably said worse. No worries here. Now turn around." Sam spun him around and was stunned to see pieces of cactus arms stuck to his arms and back. She was astounded at the level of the damage, with broken off spines and glochids everywhere—virtually every inch of bare skin on his arms was covered.

[GERALD, 2001: Quoted Text From Letter

"Little did I know [the snake] was only the beginning of my humiliation that day. You had me so rattled I sat on that cactus. The look on your face was total disbelief. In a span of minutes I went from being the white knight saving you from the cartels to you having to save me —twice."]

ON HIS BACK, spines had penetrated his T-shirt, and she could see tiny spots of blood beginning to seep through. But it was the tush that caught her attention. While the snake chaps had saved the thighs, his backside had no such protection, and the lightweight pants Gerry had on offered little resistance to the spines penetrating them. Gerry's rear end had taken the brunt of the fall—the full weight of all 220-plus pounds of him onto the cacti.

Her singsong of *Oh my God* resumed its cadence again, and Gerry took a hard swallow before he asked Sam, "What? How bad is it?" For once, it was Sam who was silent as she stood staring with her hand to her mouth. She had managed to stop saying *Oh my God* out loud but it continued to scream in her head.

The incident momentarily rattled Sam as she reached for her med kit, frantically reviewing her options. They were so far out in the desert that, realistically, there was no way to get him to a clinic; the spines had to be removed in the field. After laying out her instruments, she went about extracting the spines from his arms and back, and their easy removal caused Sam to glibly reassure herself, *Oh this is going to be a piece of cake,* as she carefully cut the T-shirt off piecemeal. Gerry squirmed with irritation at her caution, wanting to just yank the shirt off, but Sam stopped him as she explained they shouldn't disturb the remaining glochids on his bare arms and that it was best to use a glue patch.

As Sam began to prepare the glue-impregnated gauze mix, she tried to take on an upbeat mood. She cheerfully explained how the glue trapped the glochids, allowing for easy removal after it dried. Applying the glue/gauze mix to his arms, Sam attempted to lighten Gerry's embarrassment with a joke that women paid good money to get a hot wax job like this. Gerry was unresponsive as her joke fell flat. Every muscle in his body seemed to be in full contraction as he stood, staring unflinchingly straight out into space with his jaw set tight.

Nothing had twitched during the entire process of applying the slurry mix, and his unease was so suffocating that Sam found herself taking short breaths as to not gasp for air. When Sam finally looked up at Gerry's face, she could tell he was beyond distraught, and she made a hasty retreat to deal with the spines in his posterior.

The smaller, lighter spines had not penetrated far and Sam was pleased when they were as easily extracted as those on the arms. There was a momentary thought on her end that this whole thing would be nothing but an awkward joke. The larger sturdier variety of spines were deeply embedded in some well-toned gluteal muscle and even worse, they resisted all efforts to come out when she pulled.

At first, Sam just thought she needed to apply a different pulling angle and more force. Gerry had been totally stoic during the procedure up to that point, not one whimper or gasp. Not even a twitch had escaped him during the extraction of the spines on his back and arms.

But now, as Sam strained to remove the embedded spines on his rear with a hard steady tug, he flinched while emitting a squawking cough that left him panting in pain. She backed off to reevaluate the situation, using her forceps to manipulate the fabric of his pants to see where the hang up was. Clearly a Plan B was required. But Plan B was going to be very humiliating because, embarrassingly, Plan B required Sam to run her hand down the inside of Gerry's underwear. Sam sat there for a moment deliberating as to whether she should let the unsuspecting Gerry know what she was going to do or just go for it; she opted to tell him.

"Okay, here's what we're gonna have to do," Sam began to explain, wincing as she apologized. "Your pants are hung up on the spines and if I try to force things, I'm just gonna make matters worse. Several spines seem to have broken off below your skin...and I'll probably have to dig them out. What I need to do is cut the spine shafts between your skin and clothing, and I'm going to be using wire cutters." Sam didn't know how to say the next part. Taking a deep breath, she tried to keep her words and tone professional as she bluntly told Gerry, "I'm gonna have to put my hand down the back of your underwear."

When she paused to look at Gerry, she wasn't sure if he could even hear her anymore for he just stood there mute. She pulled out the wire cutters and, sliding her hands down between his buttocks and underwear, began snipping spine shafts as she encountered them. When the last spine was cut, the pants could be eased down to survey the injuries on the buttocks—it was carnage.

[GERALD, 2001: Quoted Text From Letter

"You were so damn composed, oh so professional when you told me to drop my pants. There I was, standing with my drawers around my ankles, you pulling cactus spines out of my bare behind. I kept waiting for the sarcasm that had to be swirling around in your head. I just knew you were dying to say something, [but] you never did."]

THERE WERE INDEED thoughts swirling around in Sam's head. She was beyond incredulous. *How can anybody be such a klutz?* Her initial shock and concern had given way to anger at having lost an entire day and she now fumed, *First he's late and now this?*

Kneeling behind him while removing the remaining shaft sections of the cut spines, the absurdity of the situation hit home. *Wow, what this must look like to anyone watching.* A flash of an image crossed Sam's mind—some retired ladies out on a birdwatching hike up on a neighboring bluff, binoculars in hand. *Hey Mildred—get a load of this!* A smile danced at the edges of her mouth.

Gerry was silent, his mind totally jumbled as he tried to comprehend, but he had heard every word Sam had said to him. *This can't be happening. Well, you sure impressed her! You're standing here butt naked, arms wrapped up like a mummy and her pulling spines out of your ass.* His internal diatribe was interrupted by a strangled chortle and a glance behind him confirmed its source. Sam was on her knees, her head in her lap, arms wrapped around her stomach. In one hand she held forceps and in the other, tweezers. Her boonie hat bobbed as her shoulders heaved with laughter. Her composure had cracked.

Gerry closed his eyes and tilted his head heavenward. *This day simply cannot get any worse.*

[GERALD, 2001: Quoted Text From Letter

"We didn't find [any] remains that day, which I was glad for. Gave me a chance to ask you to dinner. I used the excuse I had to make up for being such an 'ass.' Totally expected you to kick me out of the truck. Instead, we went for a beer and tacos and watched the sunset—the first of 20 years' worth."]

7

CAN I ASK YOU A QUESTION?

The ride back to Tucson had been an odd assortment of easy joking and stiff conversation as the awkwardness of the "cactus" still hung over the pair. Sam had been mulling over the day the entire drive back, in awe as to how it had gone. But try as she might, she couldn't bring herself to be upset with Gerry. If anything, she was impressed with how he handled what had to have been the most humiliating moment.

I would have just completely lost it, Sam joked to herself as they arrived at the sheriff's office parking lot to drop off the jeep and retrieve Sam's truck where she had parked it in the predawn hours. After swapping vehicles, they then headed back to the café where Gerry had left his truck earlier that morning. Eyeing the rucksack he had packed with the nicer cotton shirt, Gerry inwardly worked to suppress his disappointment. That hopeful dinner now seemed completely out of reach.

"Ah, um…I, ah…" he had begun when Sam cast a glance his way as she pulled into the slot next to his truck, but he dejectedly shut up as he got out. There was no way, after his fiasco, that Sam was ever going to go to dinner with him.

Sam had begun to shift into reverse to leave, when Gerry impulsively stuck his head through the passenger side window and began to falter again. Sam lightheartedly chided herself for being such a sucker for adorable, and her smile grew ever larger when she realized she was beginning to find Gerry's stammering endearing.

Gerry had been staring at the dashboard, not wanting to meet Sam's gaze for fear of seeing a look that screamed, *Will you just shut up and go away*, but instead, he heard a quiet "Gerry?" followed by her touch on his arm. He looked up to a smile that was friendly but also mischievous. Realizing she was more amused than angry with him, Gerry suddenly found his voice.

"I'm really sorry about today and I know I totally messed everything up. You okay with me buying you dinner? I need to make up for being such an ass." *Ah, girl, just be kind and put him out of his misery*, Sam thought to herself as Gerry stood looking cuter than he had a right to.

Sam shouted to herself, *You don't have time for this*, but was astounded at what came out of her mouth instead. She heard herself blurt, "Are you hungry? You up for a bite? Come on, hop in." With a toss of her head, Sam grinned as she enthusiastically chirped, "I know just the place."

An astonished Gerry jumped in before Sam could say another word, and as she made a U-turn to pull out onto the highway and head into the Catalina foothills, he could not believe his luck. He had been so convinced she would have nothing more to do with him.

An amazing panoramic view greeted the dusty light blue pickup truck as it pulled into a scenic bluff overlook. The Tucson valley with its surrounding mountains was majestically laid out below them, and to the side was an incredible turn-out area for picnics. But as they pulled in, a skeptical Gerry tried to keep the disappointment out of his voice as he quizzed, "This is dinner?"

He had been envisioning a candlelight meal with perhaps a mariachi band delighting them with soft background music. But as he looked around, he saw a small taco stand set up over to the side, bustling with activity despite its relative remoteness.

"Best tacos in Arizona!" Sam declared passionately. "Homemade taco sauce they jar themselves and their handmade tortilla chips are to die for!" she exclaimed while barely containing her enthusiasm as she ran for the food truck.

The stand was deceptively unassuming. As they studied the wooden handwritten menu hung on a nail to the left of the window, Sam turned to Gerry with a serious, ominous tone.

"Okay, important, earth-shattering questions. No margin for error here!" With a grin, she pointed to the sign and asked, "Soft shells okay? They have hard for the tourists." When Gerry indicated soft was good, her tone grew even more stern. "Good, now the critical question here, it's make-or-break time." A devilish smile broke over her face, and with her head cocked to the side as if in challenge, Sam dared him, "Mild or hot sauce?"

Gerry only smirked, "You're on, lady," and said to the server at the window, "Hot. *Picante*." And he threw Sam a sly grin as he turned back to the server and added, *"La salsa para tacos más picante que tengas,"* translated to the hottest taco sauce you have. *Whoa,* Sam thought, totally impressed that a Boston boy knew Spanish and could handle a salsa that undoubtedly had habaneros in it.

"You may regret that," she admiringly warned Gerry as she turned to the server to add a six-pack of beers to the order.

When the server stepped back into the trailer, his voice became muffled as he asked a question, and Sam didn't answer as expected. Gerry had been watching her all day and knew Sam could read Spanish well, but yet, he suddenly realized, she didn't follow Spanish verbally all that well.

Gerry sidestepped Sam to go up to the window, telling her, "I got this," as he pulled out his wallet, but Sam caught the confused look on Gerry's face as he wondered why she had ignored the server. A discouraged sigh bubbled up in Sam for she knew the look well, the offhanded side glance of someone trying to figure out what her problem was—but she had misheard. Her hearing loss was always a turning point in a first date and she hated explaining it, for most didn't know how to deal with it, and it often ruined the evening by changing its tenor. She knew Gerry would ask about it before the night was over...and she was already dreading the moment.

Laden with all the food trays, bags, and a six pack of *cerveza*, Sam led Gerry to her favorite outcrop. Geological activity millions of years ago had created the perfect picnic area with large rocks whose surfaces had been sanded smooth and flat by the winds throughout the millennia. Level with an unobstructed view of the valley floor below, Mother Nature had even provided the most amazing boulders with back support for easy chairs. As the pair laid out their spread, an eagle soared above, floating on the updrafts looking for its dinner.

They still had an hour or so before sunset but the air already had an edge as the temperature dipped. Sighing contentedly, Sam laid the tarp from the truck on the rocks and set up the camp stove. Looking over at Gerry taking in the view, Sam serenely told him, "Best sunset view around. I watch it whenever I can."

Taking a deep breath, Sam picked up her beer and straightforwardly asked, "Okay, Army Lieutenant Gerry Martinez, who are you? I kinda like to know a bit more about my dates before I see as much of them as I have of you. We kinda have this 'ass backward,'" she said, smirking a somewhat devilish look.

Gerry cringed a bit as he shot back, "Oh God, you are never going to let me forget this, are you?" At first, Gerry was hurt, thinking Sam had sniped at him, but her grin said otherwise.

"Oh, not a chance! I'm having *waaaayyyy* too much fun with it!" Sam giggled and Gerry's expression only made her laugh harder. "I'm sorry, but you gotta admit, that was…well, let's just say I've never had a date quite like that before…" Not able to finish, Sam was losing her composure again and Gerry sat there, shaking his head in chagrin at her as she began to rock in hysterics.

Her fit subsiding, Sam was wiping away some tears when she noticed how gingerly Gerry was sitting, and lightly teased, "How's the tush?" For a split second, horror raced through Gerry's mind when he thought she was going to ask him to drop his pants again. He refocused back on her voice just as she was telling him, "Ya know, you really do need to go to a clinic and have those punctures checked for infection and what not, especially the two on the right cheek. I had to dig to get them out and yo—" Seized by panic, Gerry abruptly interrupted, cutting Sam off mid-sentence hoping to redirect her attention to anything else but his rear end.

Stan's advice had been simple. Whenever the conversation dies, just ask a question and Gerry desperately fumbled for one, so he just asked the obvious,

"Can I ask you a question?" Startled at the abrupt change in topic, Sam busied herself, offering Gerry another taco while looking at him expectantly, waiting for his question.

Just ask a question, Stan had said, like it was so easy, but right then, Gerry couldn't think of anything. The cries of eagles soaring redirected his gaze upward and he caught the setting sun. "Ah...why are we watching the sunset? I mean, is there a reason you do it?" he asked, knowing it was a lame question but it was all that came to mind.

"You have never watched a sunset?" Sam asked in shock. "Oh, are you in for a treat! The colors alone are worth it."

Gerry's expression revealed the level of disbelief of a true doubter. In a skeptical voice, he countered, "No, seriously, it can't be 'cause it's pretty." Sam reflected for a second, and when she looked up, there was a philosophical air to her expression that took Gerry by surprise.

"I watch sunsets to remind me that I'm part of a much bigger picture, part of an interlocked system of planets and stars and energy, something older than time," she revealed while looking at Gerry. She waited for him to start laughing at her.

Instead, he pondered what she had said for a second or two and then asked, "What did you think of Carl Sagan's *Cosmos*? You know, the documentary—did you watch it?" Secretly shocked at the question, Sam only smiled before answering. "I saw the documentary, but have not read the book—just haven't had time."

"Yeah, me neither," Gerry admitted, as they both sat looking at each other, pleased they had found something in common. In between bites of the taco, Gerry mumbled, "Can I ask another question?"

Sam teasingly fired back, "Only if I get one, too. What do you want to know?"

"What book are you reading right now? Let me guess, some drippy romance novel set on a deserted island!" Gerry asked, smiling playfully.

He was genuinely surprised when Sam laughed saying, "I've never read a romance novel. I rarely read fiction if at all." Sam threw an embarrassed look at Gerry because she knew she was different. "Yeah, I know, I'm not normal!" she said, hoping to deflect to a different topic, but Gerry was curious.

"What do you read?" he asked as he shifted his weight off the sore right buttock cheek where the two deep spines had been dug out. It was beginning to throb incessantly. Sam leaned over and grabbed her backpack, pulling out a textbook on microbiology and its impact on human biological and cultural evolution. The title stopped Gerry cold as Sam held it up for him to read.

"Ah, well, that's different," he muttered and after a moment's pause, he asked, "Any chance I can get a do-over?"

Gerry's perplexed look over the unusual subject had Sam grinning as she quipped, "Nope, choose your questions more wisely next time!" She wasn't expecting the huge smile that broke out over Gerry's face and surprised, Sam teased, "What are you grinning at, you big sap?"

"There's going to be a next time?" Gerry cracked expectantly, hope reflecting on his face that maybe the day hadn't been a total loss after all.

When Sam had revealed the textbook that was her summer reading, a momentary *Ewww* had flitted across his face and Gerry knew she had caught it, so he asked her why she was reading that particular book. For the next half hour, Gerry, who thought he knew his military history, sat dumbfounded as Sam weaved in and out of the history of humanity, describing how it had been directed by the smallest of things, and more armies had been laid waste due to microbes than by bullets.

"Can I ask another question? I'll owe you two later," Gerry quizzed as he watched Sam attack her taco with gusto. Grabbing a napkin and dabbing her face, Sam merely nodded *Uh huh* as she swallowed her bite. "Why don't you read fiction?"

"Oh, I have, but I generally read for information, not entertainment. As a rule, I'm reading to learn something."

In the waning daylight, delicate shadows had emerged over the valley and now crept up over the cliff face where Sam and Gerry sat. Shards of pale orange and pink colored Gerry's face, highlighting an indifferent expression as he studied her. It was now Sam's turn to shift uncomfortably as she lightly exclaimed, "I know, I'm weird!"

Well, that went over well, Sam snippily thought to herself as Gerry apathetically studied her.

Sam had misinterpreted the silence of Gerry's scrutiny. The comfort of the day had eased his extreme shyness. No longer stammering, his run-on sentences that had been so prevalent that morning in the desert were barely noticeable now. But she began to notice other things, behaviors she had caught hints of the day before in the *cantina*. Every now and then, if she switched topics on him too quickly, he would fumble and mentally flail a bit before finding his way.

Gerry also didn't catch facial cues well at all. The type of funky looks she and her friends would lob at each other while kidding around either flew right by him or he took it badly, not realizing it was a jest. And then, he often retreated into a silent stare that pierced right through her.

There was a joke that flew around the labs on whether bacteria wondered about us as much as we wondered about them as we studied them under the microscope. Under Gerry's stony analysis, Sam felt like a petri dish of *E. coli*.

Is he even breathing? Sam wondered to herself as she returned his stare, haughtily thinking, *Well, two can play this game*. Suddenly, the hand holding the beer bottle flickered and Gerry raised it to take a sip before breaking his silence and resuming his cross-examination. His deadened tone left Sam wondering if it was a question or a statement.

"So, you don't read mysteries?"

As Sam tried to think of something else to talk about, she distractedly said, "Yeah, I have, but why would I read about something I do every day? I'd rather read about something I don't know." And as she looked out over the valley, Mother Nature provided the diversion she needed.

"Oh, oh, look! Harris hawks!" Sam excitedly squawked as she eagerly climbed over Gerry's lap to grab a pair of binoculars. Gerry sat, holding up his beer high in the air as Sam scrambled back across his lap while enthusiastically exclaiming, "The dark birds with bright white butts. There's four, no, five of them! Cool!" Absolute delight danced on her face as she handed Gerry the binoculars. "I love watching them—they hunt in packs you know," she cheerfully explained watching the spectacle.

Rejuvenated by the unexpected sight, Sam turned back to Gerry.

"All right, back to Twenty Questions. It's my turn and I get two." Sam was all business when she fixed Gerry with a penetrating stare as she interrogated him.

"Since you are so unimpressed with my summer reading, what book are you reading currently?" In incredulous mock horror, Sam screwed up her face when Gerry admitted he was reading a treatise on the Battle of Amiens 1918, a critical battle during WWI. "And you give me crap for my book?" she questioned in disbelief before continuing, "Okay, what's so special about this Battle of Amiens?" Gerry's face creased in delight and he eagerly jumped into describing the book.

"In early August of 1918, Allied troops smashed through enemy trenches just outside Amiens, France." The earlier coziness between them that had so abruptly disappeared, returned just as suddenly, and caught Sam by surprise. Totally at ease, Gerry had undergone the same transformation she had witnessed back in the *cantina*, from being unable to interact to being totally confident and relaxed, and its reemergence had her wondering.

While Sam leaned back against the rock face to listen to Gerry's narration, she was as intrigued by that transformation and what drove it as she was with the Battle of Amiens. "Known as the Hundred Days Offensive, it was the first in a string of offensive victories that led to the end of the First World War and November 1918 armistice..."

And suddenly Sam shot upright and cut Gerry off as she blurted out, "Wait a minute, 1918?? Yeah, the Spanish Flu! Just what I was talking about." She grabbed the textbook she had thrown aside and shook it at Gerry.

"The Spanish Flu decimated the world during WWI, changed battles. Probably had a huge impact on your Battle of Amiens!" Sam's face lit up at the connection when she eagerly got up to sit next to Gerry, and as she handed him another beer, she bluntly ordered, "Tell me what you know about this battle."

As Gerry continued describing the battle to Sam, she casually picked up the extra taco sauce jar, but struggled with a lid that simply refused to be opened. Giving up, she leaned over to grab her backpack for pliers when Gerry absentmindedly reached over, gave the lid a twist, and then lazily handed it back to her. Sam smiled when he didn't miss a beat.

[**SAMANTHA, 2024: Quoted Text From Letter**

"I fell in love with you that day too—repeatedly—and in the days that followed. And not because of the cactus. You have a cute tush, babe, but it's not that cute. Besides, I am a professional after all and not swayed by anatomical attributes! And to say you were socially awkward back then would be kind; you weren't much of a talker but when you did, you made it count. While sitting there watching the sunset, I fell in love with how easy it was to be with you and how easy it was to laugh.

As we talked, I fell in love with this inner strength that seemed to emanate from you. I didn't understand its source back then, but I did recognize its significance. You could easily have been brash and loud while trying to impress me with your exploits, but your intelligence betrayed you for you displayed a curiosity about almost everything. I fell in love with you that day in the desert, after the cactus. Remember that taco sauce jar? You were telling me about a book you were reading, and I could not get that sucker open. You, without even pausing or even slowing down, reached over and cracked that lid like it was nothing and handed it back to me. Was just the most natural thing and

I remember looking up at you—MY HERO! No, you weren't saving me from the cartels, but at the moment, it was just as important."]

Daylight was in its last throes as the sun's edge was disappearing beneath the horizon and Sam and Gerry were the last remaining spectators at the lookout. As the taco truck pulled in its shingle and dropped its awning, closing up for the night, Sam got up to dig out the camping lanterns and busied herself setting them up around their picnic site.

"Is there anything you don't have in that truck?" Gerry joked when she pulled out a kettle to boil water.

As she screwed in the stove's propane cylinder, she lazily asked, "Coffee, tea, or hot chocolate?" holding up containers.

As Gerry pointed to the hot chocolate, he shyly asked Sam, "Why don't you speak Spanish? You read it better than me." Gerry was intrigued. He had noticed she hadn't followed the server from the taco stand when he had given the cost of the meal.

Sam had been waiting for the question and sighed heavily as she thought, *Well, let's just get this over with.* To the sounds of water beginning to boil, Sam explained her hearing loss, and how she was not able to follow Spanish well. It was a rapidly spoken language with many nuances, and she often misheard those important differences. Nodding silently in recognition, Gerry began to understand the miscues he had detected in the *cantina* the day before.

She was expecting Gerry's silence for it was generally at this point that most of Sam's dates were looking for a door. Sam filled the moment by asking Gerry about something she had noticed he did. "You always call me Samantha. You know, you can call me Sam, most people do."

With a slight head bob, Gerry just lightly acknowledged, "I know, but you hear me better when I call you Samantha, must be the extra syllables. Besides, I like how it rolls off the tongue," and as he smiled at her, Gerry hoped he hadn't embarrassed her.

As she handed him his mug of hot chocolate, Sam almost pinched herself to make sure she wasn't imagining things. Not only had Gerry not been put off by her hearing loss, he had made an adjustment to accommodate it. Sam was in shock.

There was still a hint of that surprise in her voice as she asked, "Speaking of Spanish, how do you know it? You're from Boston!" She teased Gerry with the nasalized Boston dialect.

"People speak Spanish in Boston, you know," Gerry retorted as he chuckled at Sam's mimicking of the Boston accent. "I learned it on the streets. It was why I was sent here. Well, one of the reasons." The comment opened the door for Sam to ask what had been on her mind.

"Why are you guys here? Why did they send you and Stan here to Arizona?"

Settling in against the rock cliff, Sam watched the light from the lanterns flicker off his face as Gerry simply answered, "I know how to fight."

It was the way he said it—not boastful, just matter of fact. It was a statement with a tinge of remorse. She wondered why he knew how to fight, but her gut said not to ask. He described what he and Stan were doing, and where they were scheduled—Texas, now Arizona, then California, Colorado… They were in each place for a few weeks, and with a sinking feeling, Sam realized he was a flash in the pan. They would not be staying for long.

The sun had disappeared behind the distant mountains, all of the day's heat vanishing into the dark along with the light, when Sam realized just how late it was. The hours had flown by and neither had noticed. With a report to write, due on Monday, she filled the awkward silence with a subdued apology when Gerry asked if she would like to get together the next day. The trip down from the foothills into Tucson was quiet, the easy joking and chitchat from the evening replaced with a stiff reserve as Sam, surprised at how comfortable she had been with Gerry, was mentally reminding herself not to get too attached. He would be gone in a couple of weeks.

Arriving at the café where Gerry had parked his truck, the two looked at each other and both blurted out at the same time that they had enjoyed the evening, causing them to break out in nervous laughter. Sighing, Gerry dolefully said goodbye.

"Well, I'll be seeing ya," he said as he got out and collected his gear.

Sam, just to break the silence, lamely echoed his words, "Well, I'll be seeing you, too," and pulled out to turn around in the lot. He gave a weak wave while standing next to his truck.

As she swung back around alongside Gerry, Sam stopped the truck long enough to lean out the driver's window with a mischievous smirk on her face, and authoritatively instructed Gerry, "You really need to have the tush checked out, especially that right cheek!"

[GERALD, 2001: Quoted Text From Letter

"I had breakfast with you the following morning, then lunch, then dinner, then breakfast again. You began to wonder if I had a day job, but I didn't want to leave. I had never met anyone I could talk to so easily. We could talk for hours about everything and nothing at the same time."]

8

THEY GENERALLY NEVER ARE

FOLLOWING MORNING
Sam couldn't sleep. The events of the day had her tossing and turning, which only riled her up more, so she threw in the towel and got up to work on her report. It had been just a bit after three a.m. when she clicked off the lamp and finally turned in for the night. Sam's hearing loss prevented her from hearing the soft knocking on her apartment door, and Gerry stood, looking around and deciding what to do next when he spied a phone booth illuminated by the light of the streetlamp. Tucking the carryout bags under his arm, he fished out his wallet and, finding Sam's number, he headed for the pay phone.

Gerry put on his most cheerful tone when the groggy voice mumbled an unhappy *Hello.*

"Hi, Samantha, thought you'd like some breakfast!" He was met with silence before Sam pulled herself together enough to dozily grumble, "Huh...who's this?" as her mind still struggled to separate the abrupt shift to reality from the dream she had been awakened from.

"It's me...Gerry...um, Gerry Martinez. I brought breakfast." Still trying to shake the cobwebs out, Sam's faintly garbled *Who?* was followed by another stretch of silence. Rubbing the sleep out of her eyes, it finally clicked for Sam when Gerry asked hopefully, "Can I come in?"

"Ah…Yeah," Sam grunted and plopped the receiver back into its cradle, sitting up on the edge of the bed as she struggled to snap awake. Staggering to the door, Sam pulled the window curtain back and looked out to the sight of Gerry standing in the night lights, rocking back and forth on the balls of his feet. Bleary-eyed, she had to will her fingers to undo the door lock as she cracked the door open and wearily asked, "Gerry, what time is it? Is everything okay?"

Gerry had been startled for a second at the sight of Sam at the door. She looked different, and it was a few seconds before he answered, "Oh…ah…it's a few minutes after five a.m. Thought you might be hungry," holding up a carryout bag from a corner store.

She did look different. Although tall for a woman, five-feet-six, she seemed smaller as she stood in the doorway in an oversized T-shirt, her hair a complete mess. For a brief moment, Gerry had witnessed something few others had: Sam without her body armor on. But in the time it took for her eyes to adjust and focus properly on him, she had it back on and securely fastened when she let him into the apartment.

"Could you give me a few? I'd like to get dressed," Sam said, although it became more of a directive when she added, "Kitchen's that-away. Feel free to make some coffee."

The apartment was spartan, clearly a temporary rental, with nothing on the walls except a topographical map of the area and a large blackboard with data and info entered. Photographs were taped at various spots along the edge of the blackboard frame. There was a timeline drawn along the bottom with hatch marks along its path indicating events or where evidence had been found. Along the right side, competing hypotheses, of which one had warranted multiple question marks, and Gerry wondered if it was her favorite theory, or simply the one with the least data.

He was still studying the blackboard when Sam came out of the bedroom, now in creased chinos and a crisp white cotton shirt with a brooch at the neck. She had a tan tweed blazer thrown over her arm. Gone were the sturdy hiking boots, and in their place, she wore more fashionable lace up oxfords, and her hair had been combed neatly in place. The pair of dark rimmed glasses she was sporting gave her a studious appearance and she looked more like a college professor than the tough field rat he had spent the day before with. Sam had not worn makeup at the gun range, or yesterday, and the transition had him gaping at her as she hunted around the living room looking for her briefcase.

"Have any ideas for me?" Sam glibly asked as she passed behind Gerry, headed for the kitchen to get the coffee started. Still trying to take in the transformation, Gerry couldn't help but stare as she disappeared around the corner.

His attention returned to the blackboard and behind him, he could hear the faucet running water into a kettle followed by the *whoosh* of the gas burner igniting. Sam suddenly appeared at his side, joining him as he studied the board.

After a few seconds, Gerry pointed to a photo that was set apart from everything else, with multiple checkmarks on its border, and asked, "What's the deal with that one there?" Sam walked around Gerry to the other side of the blackboard where there was a map on the wall.

Gerry could almost see the thrill of the hunt on Sam's face as she announced, "That one? That is my pet project—a mystery of sorts. Look closely at that photo. See the odd piece of metal at the base of the tree in the distance?" Gerry stepped close to the blackboard and studied the grainy image. There was a light smudge against a tree in the background. "Well..." Sam said as she leaned forward and tapped the map, "that was found here a year ago, in 1980. Now this one..." Sam leaned in front of Gerry to reveal another photo tucked in behind the first, and then went back to the map to point out another spot as she continued, "was found here in 1978. Do you see the piece of metal?"

Knowing Sam wouldn't have it up on the board if the metal piece wasn't there, Gerry scrutinized the photo and finally saw it, another faint smudge laid in the same odd angle as the first. Lifting the second photo, Gerry saw there were several more taped to the board behind it, and Sam just tapped the wall map as she rattled off dates going backwards in time.

"1977, 1975, this one—1972 and finally, this one over here," she said, tapping an outlier location some distance from the others, "was found in 1969."

The implication of what Sam was hinting at hit home, and Gerry's eyes widened as he turned to ask, "These are all connected?" His jaw slackened in amazement. "All these others? Are they part of this, too?"

"Naw," Sam said as she came back around Gerry to stand in front of the blackboard again. "This site here is an archaeology dig I'm helping a colleague in Colorado with. Some of the skeletons had pathologies, and I'm running down what diseases would have caused them." Moving to indicate another area of the board, Sam further told him, "This over here is a mass grave in Texas. I was part of the initial dig and I'm just following the analysis."

And then pointing to the center mass of charts, photos, and notes, Sam described her current forensic case, a couple of bodies found in a desert gully outside of Tucson.

Waving his hand along the bottom, Gerry asked, "You working out the timeline? It looks like you don't agree with it."

"Actually, I do," Sam remarked as she turned to look at Gerry, "but the detective on the case doesn't. I keep looking for what is bugging him but…I'm just not seeing it. At the moment, the coroner has tagged the case as an accidental death, a drowning, but the detective seems to think it was a homicide."

"How can you drown in the desert?" Gerry asked with incredulity, but the shrill whistle of the teakettle beckoned Sam and as she headed to the kitchen, she threw out over her shoulder, "They were caught in a canyon by a flash flood." Gerry reluctantly tore himself from the board to follow.

Grabbing several plates and mugs, Sam hastily began clearing off a week's worth of files and paperwork, glancing over with a sheepish,

"Sorry, I didn't know I was having company." Gerry, who had a tidy place for everything, was astounded at the disarray on the table.

"How do you find anything?" he asked in wonder as he started to shove papers into a pile for her. Reaching over, Sam put a hand on his and stopped him, "Touch that…you die! I know where everything is, so let me do it."

Looking over at Gerry, Sam reluctantly admitted with a shy smile, "This is nice. Early…but nice. Thank you for thinking of it." Munching into the bagel from the gas station, Sam stopped and peered at it closely with skepticism, trying to figure out if the black spots were poppy seeds or baked in weevils. Gerry was also suspicious of the bagels, turning them over to inspect, tapping their hardness on the table, and the two looked at each other with screwed up noses, chuckling a bit, as Sam suggested, "Ah, how about we grab a bite to eat in town. I have to turn my report into an office in Tempe, about one hundred miles from here. It would take about an hour and a half or so, but we should be arriving in time for breakfast diners to open. Are you interested in tagging along?"

Of course, he was.

On the ride over to Tempe, Sam sat wondering, for she just couldn't wrap her head around Gerry. He was a conundrum, gyrating from an awkward geek to very articulate and then back. What more, he seemed to need to start over every time he met her. Not quite at square one, but there was this need to reassure himself of just where he stood with her. It was on the trip over to Tempe, that Sam discovered that if she didn't force things, but just waited him out, Gerry would eventually get there. It wasn't until Sam was pulling into the laboratory parking lot that Gerry finally reached the same level of comfort and ease that they had enjoyed the night before.

Sam was gathering up her blazer and briefcase while telling Gerry, "It is going to take me a while to sign this over and check in with the lab." Pointing out a dead-end street to their left, she explained, "There is a bookstore down that street that I can meet you at when I'm done. They have a nice café and such, and they cater to the early morning crowd. They are open way before anyone else, with good coffee!" she told him as they separated in the parking lot.

The bookstore was old—not as old as Tempe—but it had been there awhile, and Gerry was transported back in time as he stepped over the threshold. The building wasn't a modern strip store, it was a standalone wooden structure with a magnificent ornately carved oak front door with a heavy brass door handle, and it groaned rather than creaked when it swung open.

Its spacious interior, belying its previous function, defied traditional store layouts. It had been an old stable, a way station back in the days of wagon trains and stagecoaches, and the current owners had allowed the internal structure to remain as much as possible, walls being the old wooden stalls.

God, what a place, Gerry marveled to himself as he took in the smells and textures, running his hand along an old, weathered beam framing an arch. Planks had been reused as paneling on the walls with the imprint of a horseshoe hinting at a rich and colorful past.

An elderly woman sat at the main checkout counter, a marvel of craftsmanship in its own right, and she looked up at his entrance and smiled. Admiring its intricate carving and workmanship, Gerry knelt down next to the desk and wondered out loud, asking the desk itself, "Where did you come from?"

The old woman's face lit up as she ran her hands over its hand-hewn top, worn and polished from centuries of use, and described how the desk had been in her family for generations, moved from a northern California mining office where gold was weighed. The wonder on Gerry's face as he reveled in its history caused the woman to ask, "You a fan of history, hon?" as she smiled warmly at him for she already knew the answer before Gerry said, "Oh, yes, ma'am."

"Well then," the old woman said as she waved her hands, "the history section is over to your right. Yell if you can't find what you are looking for. The coffee pot is to your left by the window and the café will be open in about an hour." After wandering about the store, Gerry found himself heading back up to the old woman at the desk who put down her crocheting when she saw him. "Couldn't find anything, hon?"

"Oh no, ma'am, I, ah…" Gerry paused as he sought the appropriate wording. It was easier to find words if he didn't look at the person, so he stared at a crack between two wooden floor planks as he told the woman, "Still getting a taste for the old place." When he finally summoned the courage to glance up, he found the old woman watching him with a serene look on her face.

Glancing around the building, Gerry stumbled a bit as he put his thoughts into words, "I was wondering, um…if you could, ah…recommend something for me. I want to buy a book…for a woman."

"Well, you're in the right place," the old woman said, laughing. "What type of book do you have in mind? A romance novel, perhaps?"

Recalling Sam's view of romance novels from the previous night, Gerry snorted, "Oh definitely not!" The old woman had to stifle a giggle at Gerry's horrified look.

"Okay, well then, how about a mystery? There is a new one by Mary Higgins Clark, do you know her?" Gerry stood, slowly shaking his head.

"No, ma'am, I don't," he said, but then questioned, "She's good?"

"Yes, I think your lady will like her," the old woman yelled over her shoulder as she traveled across to the mystery aisle. Gerry could hear her muffled voice float out over the stacks, "Her latest, *The Cradle Will Fall,* was just published not too long ago," as she ran her fingers along the spine titles looking for the book in question. A soft *Ah* told Gerry she had found it. As Gerry read the summary on the back jacket, he nodded *Yeah,* while thinking, *This will do nicely.* And as she rang up the purchase, he had another idea.

"Do you have the book *Cosmos* by Carl Sagan?" he asked with a sly smile, pleased with himself at his idea. With the older woman's nod, Gerry smiled, "I'll take a couple of those, too."

"A couple…two?" The old woman looked at him, not sure she had heard him right. Beginning to grin, Gerry merely nodded before confirming, "Yes, ma'am. Two, please." The woman now looked at him with suspicion as Gerry stood there looking like the cat that ate the canary.

Sam scurried along the street headed for the bookstore. The meeting at the lab had taken well over an hour and a half, far longer than she had expected, and she figured that by now, Gerry would be ticked off to no end as she grabbed the brass door handle to the bookstore. Nodding a hello to the woman at the desk, Sam scanned the store for Gerry, but he was nowhere.

As she made her way up and down the aisles, she looked for him among the other browsers and finally wandered out to the café area, where there still was no Gerry. Now standing back in the main desk area, hands on her hips, Sam scowled to herself as she muttered with annoyance out loud, "How can I lose a guy who is six-feet-three, for crying out loud?"

The older woman overheard as she stepped up on a little footstool and asked as she looked down at Sam, "Are you looking for a tall man with dark hair? He's over in the corner behind the history section."

Sam shook her head a bit, explaining, "I just came from there and he's not there."

The old woman had an odd countenance about her as she asked, "Did you check the floor?"

Baffled, Sam just shook her head as the old woman told her, "Oh he's on the floor, back by the reading desk in the corner," pointing over to the back of the store. Sam's eyes had widened in a silent *What* as she went back down from where she had just come from, and peered around the last stack. There, wedged into the back corner, tucked in next to a reading desk, was a huddled man sitting on the floor, his knees drawn up to his chest.

Sam stood quietly, a picture of stunned and mesmerized, for Gerry held a book tight to his face, his eyes shiny as if lit from the back, as he eagerly absorbed every detail within the pages. He was oblivious to Sam until she touched his arm as she knelt down next to him.

The light touch of her fingers stroked his face. She asked, "Gerry," her voice just barely above a whisper, "what are you doing on the floor?"

Gerry's features were muted, almost a watercolor rather than a fine line drawing as he turned to her and murmured reflectively while sighing, "Oh, like old times, I guess," looking so much like a little boy who had just discovered a treasure map to the world.

"Old times? What do you mean by old times, Gerry?" Sam quietly asked as they sat on the floor together.

A hint of nostalgia was revealed in his smile as Gerry looked up at Sam as he told her, "I used to spend a lot of time as a kid reading in libraries." Helping Gerry up off the floor, Sam took his hand, and as she led him out through the main lobby, she caught the glance of the old woman at the desk with her crocheting.

"I see you found him," she said with a laugh and Sam laughed back, shaking her head.

"Yeah, he wasn't where I was expecting!"

As Sam and Gerry were going out the door, the old woman's needles stopped clicking for a second, and she could be heard saying, "They generally never are."

9

ARE YOU UP FOR AN ADVENTURE?

As they got back into the truck, Sam confessed that she needed to stop off at the nearby Native American reservation to drop off some medical supplies, something she hadn't planned on. Part of the reason she had been running so late was there had been an emergency request for supplies, and she had to wait for the items to be rounded up.

"Do you mind?" she asked, and for Gerry, it was like Sam was of two different worlds—the rough edged forensics versus a much more conciliatory and sympathetic medical. They had meant just to drop off several boxes of supplies at the clinic and be on their way, but instead they were sucked into helping with a vaccination program that was short-staffed and behind schedule.

It had been a long day, with crying babies and cranky adults, and climbing back into the truck, they looked at each other while Sam began to apologize profusely, "Whew, what a day. I know this wasn't what you had in mind. I am so sorry."

She stopped short when Gerry, with a smile, interrupted, "I'm not. The only thing I had in mind was spending the day with you. This was incredible. Thanks for letting me help."

Gerry was stupefied when he realized how easy the day had been for him. He was not only amazed at being a part of the clinic and how effortless it was to fit in, but also at how he seemed to be able to find words around Sam. For some reason, the words seemed to flow when she was there, and he didn't have to struggle to understand things. Around Sam, he wasn't always having to be on guard, analyzing every word or action, and it blew him away.

"Well then, at least let me buy you dinner," Sam insisted as she threw her briefcase behind the driver's seat and started to climb in. But Gerry was already one step ahead of her.

"Okay, and I know just the place, too."

Sam could only utter a surprised, "Really?" wondering what he had in mind as Gerry kicked her out of the driver's seat and took the wheel.

Her wonder broke into a grin when they finally arrived back in Tucson, and he turned on the road headed up into the Catalina foothills, the same road from the night before.

"Oh, you've got good taste!" Sam chortled as he pulled into the lookout and parked near the taco stand. Leaving Gerry to order the food, Sam hurriedly went about laying the tarp and blankets on the rocks before the sunset.

She had already pulled out the camping lanterns and camp stove, and had it all arranged when Gerry arrived with tacos and beer. As the sun began to set, Sam leaned over to ask him something only to be shushed.

"Quiet, I'm enjoying the moment here. Oh, look at all those colors!" he said with a smirk, knowing Sam knew he was just kidding. With a grin as wide as the Tucson Valley below them, Sam handed Gerry a beer and, clinking bottles, they both settled in to watch the sunset, neither saying a word.

As the last rays of the day disappeared, Sam got up to light the lanterns, and Gerry asked for them to be placed nearby and one behind him. Puzzled, Sam obliged, but wondered what he was up to.

"C'mere," Gerry waved with his hands, making a spot next to him on the rock for Sam to sit, and he pulled out the mystery novel, Mary Higgins Clark's *The Cradle Will Fall*, he had bought at the Tempe bookstore. Drawing Sam in closer, he wrapped his arms around her as he held the book between them in his lap, and then opened it to flip to the first chapter.

Looking down at Sam's bewildered expression, he told her, "We have all week to finish this," and then began reading out loud. Sam laid her head back on his chest and closed her eyes. As he reached the end of the page, he looked down and asked if she could hear him okay.

Sam softly nodded *Yeah,* not moving, but after a few seconds her voice whispered, "Gerry? I could get used to this." Reaching down to turn the page, Gerry thought to himself, *So could I,* and resumed reading.

ELEVEN DAYS LATER

The *cantina's* bustle was beginning to slow down, the lunch crowd having long cleared out. Waiters were clearing tables and setting up for the dinner rush, their chatter in Spanish punctuated by the clinking of silverware and dishes. Stan and Gerry sat at the *cantina's* outdoor patio and Gerry was melancholy. The *cantina* had been the site of his and Sam's first dinner, and what a couple of weeks it had been.

Stan had been on pins and needles that first day, the day of the cactus, wanting to know how things had gone. His laughter was as embarrassing as the cactus debacle itself, and lasted far longer as Gerry had listened in horror to Stan recounting that story to anyone who would listen. Gerry seriously doubted there was anyone left in Arizona who hadn't rolled in hysterics, and they were headed for California in a couple of days, which was a much larger state.

Over the past days, Stan had been an enthusiastic onlooker for the relationship, cheering and coaching with ideas, but even he knew all good things must come to an end. As Gerry described what book Sam was reading and why, Stan had screwed his face up in disbelief, telling Gerry, "Dunno if I should be in awe of her or scared outta my wits."

Gerry laughed as he took a swig of his beer and quipped, "I'm finding it best to straddle between the two, easier on my nerves." But

Gerry grew more somber when he looked up and quietly marveled to Stan, "It's been incredible."

Stan sighed, and closed his eyes for a second before reluctantly saying, "Ya know, Gerry, we gotta go. It was nice while it lasted, but ya gotta say goodbye. Ya know what they say, there's a lotta fish in the sea, dude. Don't get stuck on this one." Stan looked up and saw Sam weaving her way down the side street toward the *cantina*, and her expression was sour.

Sensing a "Dear John" conversation coming, Stan jumped up and abruptly announced, "Got somewhere else to be, bro," leaving Gerry to sputter at Stan's rapid departure.

"What? What gives?" Gerry asked as Stan began to leave. Stan leaned in closer to warn Gerry.

"Sam's comin' and she looks like a bullfrog who just swallowed a bad fly. I'm outta here."

As Stan passed Sam in the street, he twirled back around and called out to her while walking backward, giving her two thumbs up. "It's been real, girl. Best of luck to ya!"

Sam also spun around, and as she walked backward herself, she teasingly yelled back out to Stan, "Aw shucks, I'm going to enjoy the peace and quiet with you gone. I've felt like I've been in a Chippendale calendar review around you!"

Stan's pace as he walked down the side street suddenly perked up, and he began to strut conceitedly as he shot back, "Really? Hot damn! I've always wanted to be a Mr. April!" His face was creased in a huge smile as Sam threw him an *Oh please* look as she waved Stan goodbye.

As Sam sat down at the table with Gerry, she raised a finger at the waiter, catching his attention and Gerry couldn't miss the not-so-pleasant jaw set.

"*Oooh*, you don't look happy. How did court go?"

With a huff, she snorted, "It didn't. The yahoo was acquitted."

A *you have got to be kidding* look crossed Gerry's face as he asked, "What are you going to do now? What's next?"

Moving the salt and pepper shakers around the table in an endless circle, Sam simply admitted that there was nothing they could do. They had lost, the defendant had won.

"But the evidence…" Gerry's words trailed off when he realized the case really had been lost.

Sam looked glum as she reached over to steal Gerry's beer for a swig. "Anyways, enough of my day."

For a moment, Sam and Gerry didn't say anything, neither of them wanting to end what had been a lovely couple of weeks.

"Gerry, I've been meaning to say…" Sam suddenly understood how Gerry must have felt when he couldn't pull words together. Her words simply weren't there. Not the ones she wanted. Taking a deep breath, she tried again. "It's been a wonderful couple of weeks, and I'm really gonna miss you, more than I'm going to want to admit."

"Um, hey, ah…" Gerry leaned over the table to stop her as she was now playing with the candle in the center. He took her hands into his, but suddenly found the table candle as fascinating as Sam did when he didn't want to say anything. He stared at Sam's watch—it was different. It was an old military tactical watch from the Korean War that she had found in a secondhand shop, and it was too big for her wrist, but Sam didn't care. She had said it was the best watch she had ever had. It had taken everything she had thrown at it and it still ran, on time. Gerry sat watching the second hand tick around the watch face, and he was consumed by an odd feeling that it was talking to him.

He did a light shake of his head to clear his vision, staring at the watch again before looking up into Sam's confused face.

"Gerry, are you all right?" she questioned as she leaned over to peer at him with a touch of concern.

Gerry brought his gaze up to Sam's and defiantly declared, "This doesn't have to be goodbye," but Sam quickly withdrew her hands from his.

She reminded him, "Gerry, you guys are headed out all over. Arizona is not on your schedule again and, to be honest, even if it were, it isn't on mine."

"Whaddaya mean?" Gerry hadn't thought about Sam's field season ending, it hadn't entered his mind at all, but it weighed heavily on Sam's.

"Field season is ending and my time in Arizona is ending. It's time for me to go back to school, and to reality. I'm in med school—grad school, remember? I've got classes that will be starting in a few weeks, not to mention I've got to prepare for the classes that I'm teaching next term. And I've got…" Her last sentence was shut down by Gerry's crestfallen look.

She was right, Gerry knew it, but as he sat there, his hands on the table near hers, he saw her watch again. And then he saw his. He was mesmerized by their second hands as they swept around their dials, ticking in precise unison, and as the hands each closed in on the numeral 12, Gerry realized they were moving in tandem, clicking 12 at the exact same moment. They were in perfect synchrony.

Gerry suddenly grabbed Sam's hands again and lightly shook them as he implored, "Let's make a deal. We'd both still have our careers, we would both each stay true to ourselves and our goals. Neither of us will ask the other to give anything up. Let's just see where this takes us. If it doesn't work, well then, we've tried." Taken aback, Sam wondered how a guy who couldn't interact with strangers or be in group settings, always knew just what to say.

"Gerry, how are we going to do this?" It was a rhetorical question for Sam—she really wasn't expecting Gerry to have an answer, but he did, a somewhat eloquent one, she noticed. Sam also had noticed his stammer had disappeared, and his sentences were now smooth with words not forced.

"We can meet on the weekends, when I'm on leave. We'll make it work. We can meet halfway in between wherever we are. I'll come to you, you can come to me. I'll save my leave time. You have time between terms. And you have your summer field season." Gerry's expression pleaded for Sam to reconsider as he added, "I dunno, but we gotta try. Do you honestly want to quit without trying?"

Sam sat with a blank look as she considered his words and Gerry took that as an encouraging sign—it wasn't an outright goodbye. He chuckled as he quipped, "If nothing else, it won't be boring!" with a silly grin that Sam was really beginning to fall for. She started to giggle as well, and they were both still laughing when the waiter came to take their order. When the waiter returned with Sam's drink, Gerry pulled out something wrapped in a brown paper bag and placed it in front of Sam.

"Oh geez, Gerry!" Sam exclaimed, embarrassed that she hadn't gotten him a going-away present, but then to Sam's surprise, he pulled out a second identical package, and then placed it on the table in front of him. Smiling at Sam's baffled look, he nodded for her to unwrap the package. And as she did, he began to unwrap his. They were both holding copies of Carl Sagan's *Cosmos*.

"So wherever we both are, we each know the other is reading the same book at the same time," Gerry softly explained, and as he leaned in to give her a kiss, he asked, "Whaddaya say? You up for an adventure?"

It took Sam and Gerry months to read that first book together, but it linked them over the distance and ultimately over time as well. It was never the big dramatic events or acts that led them through their times apart, but rather it was the little things that built the bridge and maintained the connection.

The act of each reading the same passages as the other was a type of rubber band, stretching to allow them to go where they needed to go, but always keeping them tethered to each other, and in the end, pulling them back together.

Sam even read a few fiction novels.

[GERALD, 2001: Quoted Text From Letter

"I know you remember all this. I just want you to know that I remember it all too. I haven't forgotten one thing about that day or the days that followed. Now 20 years later you still rock my world and cause my heart to skip a beat. You are simply the most astounding creature and I still can't imagine why you chose me."]

10

WHADDAYA THINK?

ENNESSEE, 1982, 8 MONTHS LATER
The enthusiasm and delight that dominated the new relationship in its fledging stages, guiding and sustaining it throughout the turbulent learning of each other's ways—was on the wane. Dating for about eight months now, Sam and Gerry struggled to make things work, but the long distance proved daunting as they floundered in their search for footing, and the excitement faded into frustration. The romantic promises they had made to each other that afternoon at the *cantina* had been impulsive and unrealistic.

Still early in their relationship, they had yet to learn how to sand smooth the wheel upon which their schedules rolled. They had woefully underestimated not only those schedules, but also their independent natures as well, which threw wrenches into every plan, at every turn.

And then there were the quirks. Quirks that at first were cute and endearing, but as time scratched that veneer off, they began to wear badly, especially Gerry's knack for withholding and concealment. Sam was quickly finding that Gerry Martinez was a man with countless mysterious boundaries.

When Sam was given the opportunity to teach at a local college in

Tennessee, she leapt at it. Sam and Gerry were still a state apart, but they were now within striking distance of each other and they often took a convenient train to each other's world.

It was the first weekend of May 1982, and Gerry's birthday was around the corner, and like many men, that event was a nonevent. Sam, however, was determined to do something special to honor the day, but every time she'd ask him his age or what his favorite meal was, Gerry would be mysteriously cryptic and flippantly dodge the question. It would be Stan who provided the answer.

Laden with all the birthday fixings for dinner, an exuberant Stan barged into Sam's Knoxville apartment without even knocking on the door. As in Arizona, the apartment was just a temporary rental for the teaching year. A small set of rooms over a garage, it sufficed by having four walls and a roof. Sam had been grateful it came with hot running water, for there were few other amenities aside from a dorm-sized refrigerator and small two-burner electric stove. A long rolling tool chest, the kind mechanics used in garages, was provided as both the kitchen counter and cabinets.

The bedroom was dual-purpose as the sleeping quarters and Sam's office, with the Murphy bed becoming an office desk when folded into the wall. Its drawing power had been its proximity to the campus and to the rail station. That and a rooftop balcony with a stunning view of the sunsets.

Stan's rude entry caused Sam to jump, botching the frosting for Gerry's birthday cake. Muttering under her breath, she shot an unflattering look at Stan as he dumped the contents of the grocery bags on her counter. Unaccustomed to men having such a strong bond where they each filled a void in the other, the relationship between Gerry and Stan mystified her.

Sam had witnessed similar relationships between partners in law enforcement and elsewhere, where bonds were formed under intense pressure, but she had never been the one sandwiched in the middle, that person who was the "three's a crowd" person. She was still trying to determine just how she felt about this Stan character.

But despite her misgivings and simmering resentment about the guy, it was through Stan, ever-present, that Sam gleaned most of her information about Gerry during those early days of their relationship. It was from Stan that she scored his favorite meal, a basil pesto lasagna with enough cheese, fat, and calories to choke a horse. And it was from Stan that Sam unearthed Gerry's greatest hidden skeleton, the one he was petrified for her to know.

The birthday boy had been given an extensive list of errands to keep him occupied and out of the way for several hours. Stan's hum was barely discernible above the background noise of cooking food and clatter of utensils as he busied himself with grating the asiago, mozzarella, and parmesan for the main dish.

Comically decked out in a woman's cooking apron, a towel thrown over his shoulder and a beer tucked tightly next to the stove, Stan's lively humming became a crescendo accompanied by occasional animated spoon bopping on a stockpot and a jitterbug as he pulled the meal together.

Assembling the last of the ingredients of the lasagna, Stan's hum erupted into a full-bodied chorus that resounded throughout the apartment as he strutted his stuff, a wooden spoon as a microphone; the man could sing and what a voice.

A besotted Sam stood in the archway between the kitchen and the living room, enthralled as he performed a concert for an appreciative audience of one. Stan, Sam was discovering, was a man of many talents.

Putting the finishing touches on Gerry's birthday cake, a double fudge chocolate confection with chocolate buttercream frosting—her Boston boy had a ferocious sweet tooth—Sam casually asked Stan how many candles, not realizing the enormity of the question. Stan, a man rarely at a loss for words, only danced around his answer.

How hard can it be? Sam beefed to herself as she watched Stan, caught off guard, squirm as he fended off her question with one of his own, "Gerry hasn't told ya?"

Her initial puzzlement had turned to irritation and Sam erupted in exasperation, "I know Gerry has his secrets, but his birthdate can hardly be one of them," she snapped while slamming the candles on the table far harder than she had intended to.

In the eight months she had known Stan, that smile of his had never left his face, but he wasn't smiling now and Sam's earlier puzzlement, the one that had slid into irritation, had now evolved into a full-blown worry.

Tension was mounting throughout the kitchen when without warning, Stan just blurted it out, "He dunno how old he is." A straight-forward statement that caused Sam, more bewildered than anything, to just stop and stare at the man blankly.

"How can Gerry not know?" Stan had always assumed that somehow his best friend had mentioned his past, but now he found himself uncomfortably shifting his weight between his feet, as he mulled his options in hopes of sidestepping the topic.

Seconds passed before a quiet resigned voice was heard over the boiling water on the stove, "Gimme a few, lemme finish the lasagna prep and I'll join ya in a bit."

Stan, infused with natural charisma, was the master at handling people, and his outgoing, affable nature always put everyone at ease with a sense of wonderment. Now, eerily subdued, his sudden personality reversal sent a chill of dread through Sam as she went about decorating the living room for Gerry's surprise. To her disappointment, the evening had taken a turn with the festive mood having evaporated into the growing fog of uneasiness that now hung over the apartment.

His solemn expression spoke for him before he even said a word when Stan came in and sat down, not next to Sam as his custom, but rather sat to face her from across the coffee table. A shiver of alarm raced up her spine as Sam watched him struggle to find words, his characteristic gift for gab having failed him. After several false starts, he began by asking a question.

"Have you ever noticed Gerry's scars, the ones on his back, chest, and stomach?"

With a chill, Sam realized Stan's speech, normally full of loose-flying Southern contractions, was more formal. Even his Georgia drawl had softened.

"Um, well…yes, of course, I've seen them," a bewildered Sam answered as she wondered why Stan would even bring them up. She had seen them on that first date, when she removed his T-shirt after the cactus incident—they were hard to miss. They had given her such a start that day and she had stifled a gasp as she went about removing the cactus spines.

Long since healed, the scars were still prominent. Some were cruel with wide jagged margins and others were razor-thin lines so delicate that they seemed to have been drawn with a fine etching pen. Several had healed in such a way they were kind of charming, cute even, if you overlooked the fact they had been made by a knife.

The ones on his back drew an intriguing map, a constellation of sorts that was Gerry's own unique star formation, only the stars were bullet holes and cigarette burns, and hinted at a childhood full of violence and pain.

Stan's striking face was expressionless as he leaned forward with his elbows on his knees. He warned Sam that he had little to offer her in the way of answers—Gerry didn't share much with him either.

He started at the beginning. Gerry had been born on the streets, not in a hospital, and his mother was probably a runaway—very young and a prostitute. He remembered many men in and out of the room he called home, and he would be put in a closet whenever they came. Stan inhaled deeply as he paused, looking for a way to say what he knew was Gerry's most painful secret. Decades later, the secret was so raw for Gerry that it still festered. His shoes kicking at a piece of lint in the carpet, Stan told Sam, "Gerry doesn't remember ever having a name, the girl just referred to him as 'the Kid.'" The revelation caused Sam to stutter, while in total disbelief.

"Gerry isn't his real name?"

"As real as any other you'd want to give him, I guess," was Stan's soft reply as he shrugged dismissively. Fighting to wrap her head around what she was hearing, and desperate to find anything she knew about the man to be real, Sam couldn't stop herself and blurted out, "And May 7th? That's his birthday, right?"

"No," was Stan's curt answer as he shook his head. When he realized she still didn't get it, he spoke frankly and with irritation while enunciating each word slowly and deliberately. "Gerry has no idea when, where, or how he was born. May 7th is simply the date that social services formally put him into a program. They needed a date to put into the box on a form." Stan's voice was sterner than Sam had ever heard him speak. "The doctors guessed at how old he was."

More confused than ever, Sam's mind whirled with the contradictions of what she thought she knew versus what Stan was now telling her, "But he was adopted, right?"

Pursing his lips, Stan answered quietly after a hesitant moment, "In a manner of speaking, yeah, he was. He was placed into some type of foster program connected to the military." Sam couldn't stop herself from interrupting because she had so many questions.

"Where did the name Martinez come from?" Stan shot a look of disdain at her from across the couch, somewhat surprised at Sam's naïveté.

"From the family that fostered him in the program. You didn't actually think he was Hispanic, did you?" She had never heard of such a thing, and as he described what little of the program he knew, the stunned look on Sam's face led Stan to shrug and say, "It was the sixties," as if that explained everything.

Was everything she knew about the man a facade? was only one of the jumble of questions that raced through Sam's mind.

Impassively, Stan leaned closer toward Sam and simply admitted, "Gerry didn't lie to you and wasn't trying to deceive you. It's just that he truly doesn't know." While a disoriented Sam assured Stan that she was sympathetic to Gerry's reluctance to reveal his past, she did not understand *his* and pointedly asked him, "Why are *you* so scared of me knowing of Gerry's past?"

Getting up to check on the dinner's progress, Stan faced her question head on, "I'm 'fraid 'cause if y'know, ya might leave him...and that'll destroy him."

The disclosure threw Sam for a loop, and she was still reeling when the sound of Gerry's rattle of the doorknob all but ended the conversation, but not Sam's shock. Snatching the candles off the kitchen table, she hastily threw them in a drawer—there would only be one token candle tonight.

The exposure of Gerry's past set off a chorus of alarm bells, but as they echoed in her head, it was all starting to make sense: the social awkwardness, his guarded behavior, a lack of trust coupled with his boiling anger issues. Gerry's trigger temper was explosive when released, but also compartmentalized, for he never raged in private or with people he knew.

When his anger erupted, it was always in public social situations where he felt overwhelmed. He was a seismologist's dream, a constant Kilauea eruption rumbling at the surface, that occasionally blew with the force of Krakatoa whenever his sense of control was threatened. Within the confines of the Army, however, that rage was contained and he excelled.

Stan's confession regarding Gerry had another effect on Sam. There was now a glimmer of comprehension regarding the unusual symbiosis that existed between the two men. A seed of understanding surrounding their complex relationship had been planted and had begun to grow as Sam realized that during Gerry's early years in the Army, it was Stan who kept Krakatoa from exploding his career. It was Stan who had guided and helped a misplaced and socially inept street boy navigate the confusing array of contradictions that made up society.

Gerry, the man, took on a whole new dimension for Sam as she took a step backwards to process all that she had learned, and she decided that she needed to see this place, and the real Gerry, which included this "Kid." She needed to see just where Gerry was from, just how different his life had been from hers and just how different it was from the present.

The path to their future was woven into his past she had told him, arguing she couldn't see how they were going to survive, if she didn't understand this undercurrent within him. Pushing, she wanted Gerry to take her back to Boston. Not the Boston she now enjoyed with him at the waterfront with its beautiful parks and cafes, but the dank and grimy Boston where he had roamed the streets.

It took months to make a dent into his steadfast refusal, but ultimately, he yielded.

[SAMANTHA, 2024: Quoted Text From Letter

"I fell in love with you on a cool, crisp beautiful autumn day in Boston, with the leaves all crimson, orange and yellow. An ominous chill was in the air that caused you to put your arm around me to keep me warm. Do you remember taking me to your old neighborhood, Roxbury, where you grew up? Remember that day? I will never forget it hon, for my world spun on its axis that day. We walked those streets, and you pointed out where you used to hang, where certain events had happened. I was horrified by what I was seeing and hearing."]

BOSTON, 1982

The day was a beautiful New England autumn day, almost a year to the day from when the couple first met, and Sam and Gerry were en route to Roxbury, the neighborhood of Gerry's past. Gerry had been adamant against taking the subway, the "T," insisting instead, that they take a cab. And Sam could tell he was apprehensive. He had already warned her that it wasn't like where she had grown up, but Sam had misunderstood the depth of his concern.

Privately, Gerry was panicking because he believed once she saw he was just a "nothing" who had lived beneath even the bottommost rung of the social ladder, she would shut the door on him. He was convinced that once she knew the who and the what of those years, who he had been and what he had done, she would leave him—just like his mother had.

Do they know where they're going? the cab driver thought as he eyed them suspiciously in the rearview mirror, and he cautiously commented, "Are you sure this is where you want to be? This is not the type of neighborhood to go sightseeing in, especially a well-dressed white couple."

"Not a problem," Gerry had answered; he had grown up here, an admission that startled the cab driver who now looked at the young man in his backseat in a totally different light.

"This is your hood?" the driver asked, astonished, turning around to take the fare payment. Gerry didn't look like a thug anymore. At least not at that moment.

Sam threw a quick glance up at Gerry and almost did a double take. She wasn't sure when or how the change had begun, at which second the process had taken hold of him. The changes had been virtually instantaneous. Gerry's face, normally so stoic and impassive that even she had trouble knowing what he was thinking at times, was now unrecognizable.

It took on a distinct darker tone that was flat and dull, almost two-dimensional, as the cab drove down the street. His features grew leaner, the lines around his eyes and mouth crueler and gone were the soft brown eyes with golden flecks that mesmerized her so. The eyes now were deep and without life, and angry.

Old memories invaded and took Gerry over, and Sam watched, almost captivated, as even his body seemed to undergo a transformation. As a scientist, the process was compelling, and if it hadn't been her Gerry, it would have been fascinating to watch. But he was her Gerry, and the metamorphosis was both startling and upsetting. His body took on new characteristics that seemed to seep out. The carriage of his shoulders, the angle of his head, and the gait of his stride—they all changed. Gerry, the Army Lieutenant transformed into Gerry, the street thug, in the interval it took for him to exit the cab.

The tone of his voice altered from soft to a harsh rasp, and the cadence of his words became distorted, no longer spoken, but rather spat sharply with a mean quality that scraped skin raw. Cocky arrogance exuded from every pore as if he were daring those on the streets to challenge him. His confidence, in both his past knowledge and his present abilities, drew him up even taller than his six-foot-three frame. Arriving at the wellspring of his anger, Gerry the street thug had returned home.

The streets, despite the glorious sunny day, were ugly—there was no other way to describe them. The gusty winds of fall blew trash around on the bitter tense streets that were littered with belligerent youths loitering in doorways, viewing them with baleful stares as they began to walk the sidewalk. Gerry abruptly swung Sam around to his left side as he put his arm around her. She shivered, partly from the cold chill but also in part to the shock of Gerry's demeanor. He instinctively tucked her in tight, and the closeness allowed her to realize that he was carrying. She could feel the knife sheath and the pistol as she ran her hand around his waist. He had moved her to his left so his gun hand would be free.

Compelled to return the stares of the boys on the corners and in doorways, Sam turned to face them, but Gerry sharply jerked her and dug his hand into her shoulder with such force that she winced in pain.

"No," he hissed under his breath, sounding more like a cobra than the man she knew. "Do not acknowledge—you own the streets. Walk as if you own the streets," he said as she felt him reach down to flip the safety on the handgun.

Much had changed in the eight or so years Gerry had been gone, but a lot hadn't either. He made a beeline, clearly looking for something specific, and he found it: an old redbrick, dilapidated, vacant building. They stood across the street from the building, Gerry's face stony, as he coolly took in every detail—missing doors, broken windows, chipped brick with gang tags.

He had not uttered a word since his warning for her to own the streets and Sam, unable to remain silent any longer, asked him as she studied the building with curiosity, "Gerry, where are we?" But Gerry did not respond. Not to Sam's question or to her presence, and she sensed a seismic shift occurring in him as his present collided with his past.

As a child, whenever emotional turmoil threatened him, he had walled himself off in a cocoon of safety. Standing on that street, Sam watched in amazement as Gerry the street thug was now replaced by that child, building a protective wall around himself. Gerry had been holding Sam's hand when she felt his fingers grow cold, and she knew what the building was.

She tried again to get him to say something. "Hon, did you grow up here? Was this your home?" she asked, hoping, as she looked over at the depressing building, that it wasn't. Sam hung her head at the silence but then she felt Gerry's fingers twitch in her hand. "Sweetheart," Sam murmured while touching his face, "you need to talk to me. Why are we here?"

For the first time since they arrived, the gray expressionless face was broken by a faint smile. While Gerry still didn't look at Sam, there was a shift in his energy. His raw anger mellowed and his fingers curled around Sam's as he took a deep breath, and then stepped off the curb to lead her across the street to the building.

Without hesitation, he leaned in and stepped through the broken window on the first floor. He knew precisely where he was going and there was no need for a flashlight. You could tell someone lived there; there was detritus of human waste and discarded items strewn about with small makeshift living areas in corners.

Leading Sam by the hand, Gerry made his way up to the second floor, stepping over the holes in the floor covered with wood planks, and around several sleeping bodies. In their drug-induced stupor, the sleeping bodies didn't even bother to move, and Gerry paid them no heed, giving them nary a glance as he was careful not to trod on them.

Gerry focused on a back room near a fire escape landing. A room with no hanging door, windows broken with a plastic film hanging over them, yellow with age, and a rotted mattress on the floor. Three youths, no more than ten or eleven years old, jumped upright off the mattress as the couple entered the room. Each child held a weapon—a sharpened stick, iron bar, and a jack knife—and their eyes burned orange with the fire of hatred and defiance.

Motioning for Sam to stand aside by the doorway, Gerry approached them and began to gently talk to them.

"This used to be my crib, I used to hang here," as he waved his hand around the room. "I was called Kid back then." The boys' glare shifted warily between Gerry and Sam, and then back to Gerry.

Distrust hung over the room as one of the boys, tossed his gaze back at Sam and sniped, "The bitch? What's with her?"

A faint smile hovered on his face as Gerry stood unperturbed by their hatred. "The *lady* is with me… and she is my guest." Leaning down closer to the boys, Gerry pulled out some folded dollar bills and held a couple to each child as he asked, "We just want to stay and look around for a little bit. I promise, we won't touch anything and we will be gone when you come back."

Sam watched in amazement, not daring to move as the "Kid" from a not-so-distant past stood before the "Kids" of the future, both understanding where one had been, and the others were going. Each saw the other's reality with total clarity. With the agility of alley cats, the boys pounced on the money in Gerry's hand and bolted from the room, their footsteps echoing down the stairs as they frantically raced to get out of the building before he changed his mind and wanted the money back.

Footsteps also echoed loudly as the little boy who used to live there, now in the body of a grown man, slowly walked around the room. Going over to a narrow closet, barely a foot wide, Gerry opened the door. Kneeling down next to the doorknob, he rubbed his fingers over the wood, almost caressing it, while submerged in the past. It was then that Sam saw them, the fingernail scratches on the wood near the latch; someone had been kept inside.

She saw Gerry's expression but couldn't describe it with words and she knew not to say anything as a myriad of emotions darted across his face. Heartache washed over her as she watched shame, anger, defiance, even regret, all cloud the face of that long-ago lost child. But what she saw most was fear, not of the streets, but of how he was certain she must now think of him.

Standing back up and looking out past the window plastic, Gerry stood, watching a slow drip from a pipe while lost in thought, as if transfixed by an old memory. Finally, in a voice that was both apologetic and sarcastic, he spoke. "I'd offer you some coffee, but I seem to be fresh out."

He was no longer cocky as he turned to her and announced, his voice softened to a hollow version of the man she knew, "Well, this is my home," gesturing to the four walls around them. "Whaddaya think?"

[SAMANTHA, 2024: Quoted Text From Letter

"I had lived such a charmed life. I always had food on the table, a roof over my head and parents that took care of me. I always knew where I came from and knew what having a family meant. I listened to you describe your childhood so nonchalantly and so matter-of-fact. How you had to fight the others in your gang for food thrown on the floor at the end of the day. How you had to fight for a safe place to sleep. How you had to steal warm clothing to survive Boston's winters. Your existence was all about fighting. It was at that moment, babe, that I understood the enormity and the scope of what you had accomplished. The sheer magnitude of what you had overcome amazes me to this day."]

11

TUTORING IN THE FINE ARTS

*D*read seized Gerry as he watched Sam take in the surroundings. Her eyes, narrowing at the sight of the warped closet door, slowly scanned the room, stopping for moments here and there, as she began to grasp it all. She struggled to ignore the stench of the rotting mattress. The window plastic suddenly fluttered in a breeze with a sharp crackling snap, and Sam jumped. While it was fall, the room was stifling and she was finding it hard to breathe.

Sam was in shock as tremors of comprehension roared through her. She had thought after Stan had described Gerry's upbringing, his origins…that she understood. She had painted herself a mental picture and had persuaded herself she was prepared. *I know what to expect,* she had convinced herself.

My God, Sam gasped to herself, her attention focused on the water dripping from the pipe. It was making an odd sound—the drops were rhythmically splashing onto a multihued mat of algae and bacterial slime with a sucking squish—it turned her stomach.

But it was the gouges on the closet door frame that stole her breath. Sam ran her fingers over them, trying to feel the little fingernails that made them. She struggled to erase an image of her Gerry, as a little boy, scared and desperate, trying to get out. *How could you lock someone in here?* shrieked in her head as she stood in front of the narrow gap in the wall that served as a linen closet. It wasn't even a foot deep, and she just stood appalled, shaking her head. Sam was suddenly aware that the fingers were real—Gerry was standing next to her, holding her hand.

Sam swallowed hard and for a second, Gerry thought she was angry, or worse, repulsed. Not sure of what to say to him or how to act, Sam turned and hugged him as tight as she could and looking up in his eyes, she could tell—he was terrified. Gerry gave her a weak smile. He knew he had to talk, to tell Sam things, but he just couldn't.

"Let's go for a walk," Sam suggested as she reached out to take his hand.

When they were back out in the open air on the sidewalk, Sam gently prodded Gerry. "I have an idea. Would it be easier if you told me a story? A story... about someone you once knew, about a little boy who used to live here?" Will that be okay?"

There was a faint nod of his head, an inkling of a smile. "Yeah" Gerry murmured, "I think I can do that."

"Now," Sam softly asked as Gerry took her arm and they began to stroll, "what does this little boy want me to know?"

Boston, 1957, 24 years earlier

The young boy, perhaps four or five years old, was hungry. The girl who had been caring for him suddenly wasn't there anymore, and had been gone for several nights now. He would hide in the closet when he would hear other people, but the girl was never with them. He was on his own.

The summer of 1957 in Boston was average, no hotter or drier than others, but the room was stifling with no breeze. He had seen the girl get water from a dripping pipe off the fire escape and a desperate thirst drove him to try, finding a tin can to put under the dripping pipe for a drink. But he was still ravenously hungry.

The girl had taken him to the street a few times, and although he remembered the way, he wasn't big enough to climb through the broken window on the first floor. Piling up debris and boxes next to a hole in the wall, he climbed up and fell out onto the sidewalk below. All day he scrounged for food off the sidewalk, but it wasn't enough, and despite the day's heat, he grew cold in the dark. Too small to get back into the building that was his home, he huddled in the recesses of a door's overhang and waited for salvation.

A hand shook the boy's shoulder, and he woke up to see a blond-haired boy looking at him. Thin and in ratty clothes, with his face streaked with dirt, the blond boy poked the child and asked, "What's your name, kid?" but got no response. The blond boy knelt down and looked the child in the eyes and made a decision. The child was led by the hand across the blocks of Roxbury to another building, where in the basement, there was a horde of children like him. Of varying ages, they were all boys on their own. The street boys gathered around the newcomer, debating whether he was worth their trouble, but finally someone handed over some food.

The gang renamed the child Gerry and began to teach him the art of survival on the streets. They began to teach him how to steal, how to pick locks, how to be a look-out as crews stripped cars, how to determine what food out of trash bins was edible, how to spot and avoid the gun and drug runners—all the essentials.

At the end of the day, one of the older boys would throw food on the floor for the younger ones, not big enough to steal from stores or scavenge dumpsters and parks. Chaos reigned when the younger boys would all scramble to stuff as much in their mouths and pockets as they could.

The newcomer was the smallest of the group, and he stood no chance as they pummeled him. Gerry's tutoring in the fine arts of hand-to-hand combat had begun.

Boston, 1982

As they strolled, Sam strained to comprehend while trying to imagine what it must have been like, and she stupidly asked what he did about going to school. The sunlight had worked its way over the sidewalk, pouring out from between buildings, and Gerry's face was now illuminated in a soft eerie shadow that highlighted his shame.

"Didn't go," he said, biting his upper lip. "Didn't go to school as a kid." Trying to reconcile the intelligent, well-read man before her, one who had been to college, with this fact, she stumbled as she began to articulate her next question.

"How did—" but Gerry quickly anticipated her thought and interrupted, "I sort of taught myself to read."

Boston, 1959, 22 years earlier

Gerry had survived well enough to stay in the gang, and after a couple of years, he had gotten tall enough to get back into the building that had been his home, and he took over that back room again. Learning to improvise with available materials, he devised booby traps and intricate alert systems to forewarn him when trouble was coming. Gerry's tutoring in the fine arts of strategy and defense had begun.

He had studied the labels of food cans he stole and quickly learned which words spelled out what and from there, he would pick up a smattering of other independent words for other necessities. He had learned the basics but not everything.

One day, Gerry shoplifted from a small general store and had gotten caught by the shopkeeper. The older man stood before the grimy youth, ribs sticking out and in shabby clothes with a can of cat food in his hand. A swollen split lip, black eye, and bruises, along with skinned knuckles, were all trophies of his latest fight. Without saying a word, the shopkeeper held his hand out for the can, and Gerry begrudgingly gave it to him. Then the hand came out again, and the youngster emptied his pockets of everything else he had stolen.

The store owner leaned over and asked the child, "You planning on eating the cat food?" The look on the boy's face told the man all he needed to know—Gerry had thought it was a can of tuna.

Motioning for the boy to follow him, the man led the child through the store to the back soda fountain where his wife manned the counter. Patting for him to climb up onto a stool, the couple gave Gerry the first true meal he had ever had in his life—a whole plateful. At first, he would take a bite and then put a bite in his pocket, take another bite and put another bite in his pocket, but the wife leaned over and stopped him.

"No," she gently said, "you eat here." The ramifications of that act of kindness paved the foundation of what was to be Gerry's future and reverberated throughout his life.

The couple insisted that the boy learn to read. *Can't have him eating cat food*, they argued, and they struck a deal with him. If Gerry went to the library for the weekly reading class, then they would give him a plate of food daily. It was an easy choice, a bargain in the eyes of a street child, and he figured he would just scam them into thinking he went along.

The wife took Gerry to the most magnificent building the seven-year-old had ever seen, the local public library over on Vine. That first day, the scrawny little boy stood at the base of a bookcase, looking down the row and the sight of all the books captivated him as he was overwhelmed by the array of textures, smells, and colors. And then a librarian gave him a book to hold.

His innate intelligence unleashed, Gerry was a voracious reader and ravenously consumed everything he could get his hands on. At first, mysteries took him places and stimulated his imagination, then he studied maps and learned the sciences. Even a book on medicine in the field caught his eye, but history predominated his energy, especially military history. He devoured everything in sight.

Every Friday after the reading class, he would go to the store soda fountain and read to the woman behind the counter, and she would give him a plate of the daily special, followed by a milk shake. For a short time, a small sense of stability had crept into the youngster's life, but his windfall was not to last. Several years later, the shopkeeper was killed during a robbery and once again, Gerry was a street kid loose in the wind, and back to scavenging and stealing.

One day soon after, he had dug a box of half-eaten doughnuts out of a trash bin and was tucked in a doorway sharing the delight with a dog he had befriended. The two "street mutts," who had forged a bond as they looked after each other and provided a measure of solace, were enjoying the sweet treat when a group of older teenage boys demanded it be given over. In an act of defiance, the young Gerry refused and one of the teenagers pulled a gun from the back of his pants, shot the dog in the head, and then pointed the gun at him. Gerry's tutoring in the fine arts of anger and hatred had begun. And so did his tutoring in weapons.

The calories and protein from those extra meals had brought forth a growth spurt in that scrawny little boy that quickly propelled him to a size large enough to take on the bigger boys of the gang. He now could hit back, and hit he did. He soon had the lion's share of food and clothing, thus ushering in the final component of his indoctrination of the street's lessons. Gerry's tutoring in the fine arts of offensive fighting had begun.

Even after he learned to read, the young boy, and later the teenager, would still go to the library, find a corner where he didn't have to watch his back, and where he would be safe and warm. Through the yellowed pages of dog-eared books, he would dream of a different life, one that was on the other side of the tracks.

12

FERAL STREET CHILD

Boston, *1982*

The streets were buzzing with the news of their presence and every once in a while, someone would nod to Gerry in recognition as he and Sam passed. They knew who he was and the tension was gone, but there was no reunion, no one was happy to see him.

Gerry stopped and stared across a desolate street, its chain fence folded back along the sidewalk where thieves had broken in. Sam watched, knowing something had happened there and she waited to see if he would voluntarily say something, but he didn't.

So she encouraged him, "Do you want to tell me about it? and then reminded him. "It's just a story…it can't hurt you."

Boston, 1967, 14 years earlier,

The car had shown up around a week earlier. Like clockwork, it arrived daily at the same place at the same time and the two men inside, well dressed, but out of place in their military dress shirts and slacks, strode confidently into the building, unconcerned by the neighborhood or its reputation. They were oblivious to their surroundings or just didn't care. Either way, the crew that worked that block and the surrounding ones had gauged it for what it was—an easy mark.

The teenager watched the men climb the stairs to the building and snorted derisively at the stupidity of it all, it was a booty call—the building was a bordello, a whorehouse. Gerry knew he had about thirty minutes before the men returned, but he would need only a fraction of that to get what he wanted.

Snapping his fingers, Gerry set the younger boys into motion with a sharp toss of his hand. Ten years had passed since he had been taken in by a street gang and he had used those years to study and learn, and he applied his lessons of the streets well. In 1967, no longer a defenseless child, Gerry now ran the crew and while he was only fifteen years old, he was physically big, already close to six feet and solid.

Training daily to perfect and hone his fighting prowess into a remarkable set of skills, he had forged himself a formidable reputation that even adults heeded. His crew was the largest, most efficient and the most proficient in the area, instilling a sense of pride amongst the boys that cemented them together, for they lived well and fought well.

Popping the door locks on the car, a nicely polished black sedan, Gerry noted the government plates and he sneered with satisfaction, *Won't save 'em*. He expected a nice payout. He trained his crew with the same intensity he pushed himself, drilling the young boys almost daily and each knew his role precisely. There was no hesitation, no confusion and no questions. The boys descended on the vehicle like a swarm of army ants.

With practiced precision, the boys slid four cinder blocks under the frame while Gerry jammed a knife in each of the tires. He wasn't after the tires, he wanted the rims. In a matter of what seemed only seconds, each of the boys sprinted off carrying away his prize. Head and tail lights were stripped, side mirrors were torn off, and the license plate was removed—all with a flick of a screwdriver.

As ringleader, Gerry handled the front seats, pulled the radio and anything else of value. The men had stupidly hidden a satchel under the driver's seat, and one had left his jacket strewn over the front seat-back. All were quickly snatched up and as the teenager backed out of the front seat, he popped the glove compartment open, and there lying on top of folded maps, was a handgun; it slid into Gerry's back pocket.

It was at this moment in time, on a clammy, muggy, and grey day, that for a young street kid in Boston named Gerry, celestial karma, divine destiny, and human contempt all slammed together to send his life careening down a very different road. A spur-of-the-moment thought had set everything in motion. He had taken a closer look at the jacket and noticed it was Marine.

Nice, Gerry smirked as he fingered the insignias and service ribbons, already anticipating what he could pawn them for. In a rash split-second act of smug arrogance, the teenage outcast took the name plate off the jacket and left it prominently displayed on the dashboard, the name was Harris.

The car's condition didn't register with Major Derrick Harris at first...and then he saw the blocks. Front doors were ajar and as he stared at the interior with its dangling wires from the radio, he exploded. "Son of a bitch...aw shit," he raged, but then realized his jacket was gone. "Those stupid..." he sputtered and then frantically reached down for the satchel—it was gone as well. A horrid thought raced through his mind and he scrambled across the car seat to pop the glove compartment—the gun was gone. "Shit! Damn those..." he thundered as he slammed his fist against the car seat.

He had been enraged over the car, but now entered the realm of a full-blown-seething rant over the missing gun. Out of the corner of his eye, he caught the name plate sitting on the dashboard, just above where the radio had been—his name staring at him—mocking him.

He flew into an apoplectic fit. Harris crawled back out and threw a tantrum, stomping his feet and kicking the sides of the car.

It wasn't the lack of transportation; that was just a minor inconvenience. It wasn't even the satchel, since that was more tiresome than anything for it was just routine paperwork. While the missing service pistol was a problem and he needed it back, he had disregarded protocols—it wasn't even the gun.

What had sent Harris over the edge was his name plate on the dashboard. He screamed at what remained of the car…and at the streets.

"I will get you for this," Harris bellowed at the buildings. "I will run you down. You shitheads don't know who you are dealing with."

Major Harris's first line of attack was limited, as his impropriety with the gun meant keeping the situation under wraps. A couple of low-profile MPs were assigned to track and locate the crew, and they performed their job well. The younger children had been found easily enough, but the one Harris really wanted, the *capo*, was tougher to run down. The MPs were at a distinct disadvantage with the older street urchin, who with a decade of street smarts in his back pocket, was cagey as he toyed with them as a predator often does with prey.

Their standoff waged on for days as the streets watched in amusement at the game being played out before them. Gerry knew every alley to run down and every crawl space to hide in; he simply couldn't be caught. Day after day, he would taunt the MPs as they tried to corral him.

Harris shifted to a different plan of attack and as denizens in positions of power often do, cages were rattled, careers threatened, and palms were greased. The local law enforcement gang unit bartered with the rival gang and made them an offer; give up this Gerry kid, and they would pave the way for the new gang to take over his turf. It was a deal made in heaven, and betrayed as law enforcement swept the area in a dragnet, the young crew boss was ultimately cornered. A jubilant and puffed-up Major Harris made a point of going down to the jail house and smugly gloated at the boy imprisoned behind the bars.

"What's the matter, punk? Cat got your tongue? Not so high-and-mighty now, are ya?" Harris gleefully cackled as he strutted away with the cell guard, who ran his night stick along the metal doors as to rattle the bars. The next few days hauled Gerry every which way from one evaluation or medical exam to another, always in handcuffs after sucker punching a couple of security guards in an attempt to escape.

[SAMANTHA, 2024: Quoted Text From Letter

"You always laughed at me for being so protective of you. You called me Mama Bear, a title I wore with pride and took to heart, and I still watch over you even now. I fought for and defended you not because you were weak and needed coddling. I fought for you because you deserved it, and also because I knew hon—you had been thrown to the wolves.

"Years ago, I had dropped a file you had given me to put in the safe and papers spewed out all over the floor. As I was picking them up, my eyes fell on one in particular. It was the report from the local Social Services and their recommendation for you after your last arrest."]

GERRY HAD BEEN TUTORED WELL by the streets, its lessons of survival and fighting absorbed and applied with precision. An exemplary student, he had learned the stark lessons the streets' social discord had taught him—and they taught him reclusion, insecurity and distrust. He was of two identities, mirror images. One was eminently capable, and Gerry would exude a cool assurance while handling the streets and the gangs that ruled them, but the other was confounded by people with its society. He didn't trust society. When confronted by it, he often retreated into a realm of silence as a defense mechanism and now, in society's clutches, he wore that silence like a cape.

The more he was poked and prodded, the more sullen he became. Never speaking a word during the whole affair, he would just glare through slitted eyes, waiting and plotting. Social workers, doctors, psychologists all threw up their hands in disgust and moved on—they had other cases to deal with.

· · ·

[SAMANTHA, 2024: Quoted Text From Letter

"They had included your so-called birth certificate and labeled you as a Feral Street Child. They classified you, based on your history, as beyond redemption and felt rehabilitation would not be successful. They recommended you be sent to an adult prison for incarceration. You were fifteen years old with no name to speak of, who didn't know his birth date, didn't have a family, or had ever been to school or a doctor. You had never even been to a ballgame. I read it all. I read the psychological evaluation—I still remember the words, the adjectives that seemed so bleak on paper—Antisocial, violent, amoral, incorrigible, irremediable, irreparable. I read the medical report that listed the broken bones, the cigarette burns, the knife gashes, and the bullet wounds. And I read the social report—oh that was the most damning of them all. A social worker had written a note on the bottom of the last page and suggested an alternative option to prison which was some military foster program. Acknowledging that you would be probably sent to Vietnam, her last line stated it so clearly. [You were in all likelihood destined to die on the streets and perhaps you could find your place if you went to Vietnam.] I never told you I had seen that report as I assumed, or rather hoped, you would tell me when you were ready. Did you think I wouldn't understand and that I would think less of you? Did you think I would no longer love you?"]

WEEKS LATER

The courtroom was nothing fancy—it was night court and the proceedings were as simple as the room itself. Several months had passed since that fateful day where the streets had betrayed him, and Gerry now sat in a hard chair behind a hard table facing a hardened judge. The social worker attached to his case hadn't bothered to show up, and his public defender didn't even know who Gerry was, for he had the wrong case file in front of him on the table.

The judge, his years on the bench etched in the fatigue on his face, sighed at the familiar sight before him. Gerry was no stranger to the juvenile court system, but now, he was no longer a child. He would be treated as an adult. A rebellious Gerry slouched in defiance while the judge outlined the options that would define his future.

"You have a choice," the judge sternly explained as he leaned over the bench to look down at the repeat offender before him.

"Do you understand the program that social services is promoting as I have explained it to you?" The silence in the courtroom was broken only by feet shuffling and papers rustling. The hardened delinquent said nothing.

Gerry's act of ignoring him only tested the judge's patience even further and his voice became more authoritative as he stated, "Son, if you do not answer me, I will have no choice but to send you to adult jail. Now, are you going to accept the program or is it jail?"

Gerry chose the program.

[**SAMANTHA, 2024: Quoted Text From Letter**

"[I have] only one picture of you [...], babe. The one taken in Boston at the park with the disposable camera we bought at the last moment. You hate that picture, but I love it, you know why? Because you are not in uniform, hon. It is of the Gerry I know, the one that belongs to me and not the Army. Yeah, I could [display] your service photo—you know the one where you look like you are undergoing a proctology exam. No way, that is not my Gerry. I'm impressed with the Army Gerry but that is not who I love or who I cherish. That Gerry is the man in the picture.

"The Army did not make you what you became, it was merely the vehicle by which you traveled your journey. Nor was it me. Yes, I supported, maybe even goaded you at times, but they were your decisions and drive, and those accomplishments were yours and yours alone. You dragged yourself out of that hellhole. That was not luck, that was resolve and that was choice. You may not have known your past, your beginnings, babe, but you could see your future and you chose to change. It was a test of character that few pass.

"I marvel at you sweetheart for rising from the ashes and I am so proud of you Gerry for showing such grit and determination. You have an inner core of strength that I don't think I've ever seen in anyone else, and I have never been so proud to have been with anyone as I was with you that day in Boston. I am honored to have been on that journey with you. Do you have any idea just how strong you are?"]

13

IT IS YOUR CHOICE

The trip to Boston's back streets had a tremendous impact on Sam. She had always been impressed with that inner strength of Gerry's right from the beginning, but now, knowing the source of that strength and what it took to acquire it, she stood in awe. The little quiet clues, inconsistencies in Gerry's behavior that had nagged her, now stood as giant billboards with flashing neon arrows that were hard to miss.

Having gotten a glimpse of Gerry's early childhood social experiences, she now could see the hidden insecurities he had kept so carefully disguised, and Sam set out on a quest.

NORTH CAROLINA, *1982, 2 MONTHS LATER*

The Officers' Ball happened once a year and was one of the larger social events in the area. Officially, it was a meet and greet for all officers, where they could mingle without the distraction of work, but rank, however, was ever-present—front and center. Unofficially, it was at events like this where officers of all ranks sized up their competition for future positions, laying the groundwork and cultivating those all-important collaborations to be drawn upon later in their career.

The counterpart of the Christmas Party of the business world, the Ball was a grand winner-takes-all, take no prisoners and show no mercy affair, that presented dangerous waters for officers to navigate.

While he had owned the streets with impunity and had understood their subtle nuances completely, the capriciousness of human society confounded an otherwise competent and accomplished Gerry. His anxiety, driven by a fear of being judged, criticized, even demonized by his past, at times overwhelmed him and now, caused him to break out in a cold sweat at the mere mention of having to attend that year's Ball, the Ball of 1982.

In preparation for that event, Sam had spent weeks teaching Gerry how to socialize with peers and superiors, and how to be comfortable with the art of small talk. She also spent those weeks teaching Gerry the art of trust. Extending the trust he had in his military brethren to the community at large. Trust that she would not judge him for his past. And to have enough trust in himself to take a leap of faith when necessary. And she tried to teach him how to waltz.

Her toes had been crushed, like grapes being pressed into fine wine.

"How?" came her painful groan while leaning against the cabinet massaging a foot, "can you orchestrate complex offensives, implement deft evasive maneuvers, are nimble enough to negotiate the most challenging of training courses, and…yet…are unable to perform the simplest of dance moves?"

She had not asked in that sweet endearing tone that Gerry found so cute, nor was she making an inquiry. It was a rhetorical question that dripped with incredulous disbelief. Sam wasn't interested in his answer at the moment, and Gerry knew it. His latest misstep had caught her little toe in a grinder as he shifted and pivoted his weight, and at a loss for words, he shrugged an apology. "I'm really sorry, Hon. Um…let's just go have lunch." He was hoping to put an end to the lesson.

"No, let's not," Sam grumbled as she gingerly put her shoe back on and grabbing Gerry by his shoulder, she twisted him back out into the clear space they had made in the kitchen. "We're going to give it another go," she said, her face a portrait of dogged determination. Her quiet utterance of "Next time, I'm wearing steel-toed boots" only caused Gerry to hang his head.

There appeared to be no end to his misery he sighed, there would be a next time. Taking a deep breath, Sam reset the record player again, placing the needle crackling as it found its groove and turned to resume the lesson. "Okay, Lieutenant Gerry Martinez," she grimly muttered as she held out her right hand for Gerry to take.

Quietly beseeching the gods, Sam bravely asked, "May I have this dance, sir?"

Gerry's frown only accentuated his dismay as he dejectedly quipped, "If you insist."

Placing his right hand on her waist, Sam took Gerry's left and slowly began a soft *1, 2, 3, 1, 2, 3*, as the music began playing, its speed dial turned to low.

"Gerry, look at me, not your feet. Look up." She was following, he was leading, and as she dipped her knee into the box step, she called out, "Left foot forward and I will step back—your right foot goes to the side."

Gerry's overextended step to the right jerked Sam off balance, causing her to draw him up to a halt, exasperation on both of their faces. "Gerry, you don't jump into the next step. This is a gentle glide here. You're not vaulting the low wall. Just slide your foot to the right and the rest of you will follow, okay? Let's try this again."

Counting the beats in the music, Sam caught the cadence and with a *1, 2, 3*, she started the step again, "I'm going to go back, you are going to come forward with your left and then *s..l..i..d..e* your right foot sideways, no further than your shoulder—Gerry! You're mangling my fingers!" came her anguished cry over the record player.

Sam and Gerry were waltzing. To Sam's amazement, in an elegant ballroom reminiscent of the turn of the century with gorgeous carved wooden trim and stunning candelabras, they were waltzing. Gerry had been astonished when Sam had come out of the bedroom in the ball gown, kind of embarrassed by all the glamour. It was a jade-teal velvet gown with an off-the-shoulder neckline and straight skirt, slitted to the knee. It fit her style and personality to a T. Sam hadn't been sure they were going to get there but finally, Gerry's feet and head began talking to each other and coordination set in.

"Didn't think we'd make it, did you?" Gerry playfully whispered in her ear as he led her out on the floor and drew her in close.

Sam's smile was full of pride but she still joked, "Oh thank god you have dress shoes on and not boots!" as she looked down at his feet. Still, Sam wasn't taking any chances and elegant couples decked out in silk and sequined ball gowns and handsome dress uniforms could hear a soft, *1, 2, 3, 1, 2, 3,* as the couple would dip and sway.

Lt. Colonel Alan Lawson stood over to one side, a patriarchal lion surveying his pride and his domain, and he watched with great interest as thirty-year-old Lt. Gerry Martinez waltzed to the music with his date; the couple was clearly enjoying the evening and each other. Lawson was the type of commanding officer who liked to know the complete man who served under him, and that included knowing their families.

Overall, Lawson was pleased with his staff at how well they were maturing and growing into their roles, all except the new transfer Gerry Martinez. The young lieutenant was a conundrum, with raw talent off the scales but all seemingly for naught since his inner workings lacked balance and control. An odd duck who seemed more at ease with enlisted than commissioned, Lawson's new acquisition was proving not to be an easy man to contend with.

The colonel was most curious about the woman who seemed so comfortable on his arm as they floated about the parquet floor. He had made a special point of inquiring about her as he had told Gerry to be sure to introduce the woman to him and his wife Colleen that evening.

[GERALD, 2001: Quoted Text From Letter
"If something happens to me, know you are and always will be the

most precious thing to me. I would have thought of you that morning —I do every morning and I would have smiled, for you fill my heart with joy. If something happens to me, thank you for spending the last 20 years with me. Thank you for being so patient, for being so understanding when I would be so pigheaded and dare I say demanding. You have given me such confidence and support in who I am and what I can achieve and I am everything because of you. While everyone else saw just a street kid from Boston you saw something more and I can't even begin to tell you how special you make me feel.

"Tough as nails you are—you see right through me. And you never put up with my bravado or my crap. I was so used to using my size, street attitude to intimidate, bully my way through life. Not you. Early on I heard an officer's wife ask you if you were scared of me—I had lost my temper and was being somewhat of an ass—I know, hard to believe. You looked at her and said 'why would I be scared? If I can drop a 2000 pound horse I surely can handle a 200 pound jackass, especially since the horse appears to have been smarter.' My ego took quite the bruising in those early years—you simply didn't back down. You didn't walk away either.

"'I don't do big, bad and stupid well. Big I'm used to, bad doesn't scare me and stupid I have no use for.' Remember telling me that at the Officers' Ball? You turned on your heel and walked away, leaving me standing like an idiot in front of my superiors. I have never forgotten that moment. I was so embarrassed but I deserved that and more. I was being such an insufferable cad."]

As the song ended, Lawson watched the couple intently as they joined others at the bar, and he couldn't help but notice how at ease the normally testy Gerry was in her presence. Catching Gerry's eye, Lawson wiggled a finger at him, motioning that it was time for him and his date to come over for a proper introduction.

Sam had caught the wiggle, too. Patting Gerry's arm as she looked up at him, she smiled as she reminded him, "Game time, hon. Now, remember everything we've rehearsed. You've got this." She flashed a huge smile of encouragement while she took his arm. They had been over it so many times. What to say, how, the practiced witty comebacks and how to field unexpected questions.

Steering him around moving couples, Sam quietly whispered when she saw Gerry's frozen face, "Gerry, smile and relax. This isn't a performance review." She felt the resistance in his arms for a fraction of a second before she felt his knees lock up, and an *Oh no* raced through her. Gerry's face was white, ashen with a sheen from sweat. Sam waved weakly over at Lawson and his wife, using the movement to hide the deliberate opening of the clasp on her purse to dump its contents on the floor. Exploiting the diversion, Sam loudly exclaimed, "Oh my heavens," as she made a commotion, pulling Gerry down with her as she bent down to retrieve her makeup and keys.

"Gerry!" Sam hissed sharply. "Look at me, pick three things in the room." It was a coping mechanism commonly used to regain focus during a panic attack. "Now, focus on three sounds. Okay? Now, move your arms and hands. Pick up my lipstick and give it to me. Smile and look at me. We're good. You're good." She hauled him back to his feet and smoothed out his uniform jacket.

As Sam rolled up with Gerry in tow, she skipped over Lawson and went straight for his wife, Colleen, first.

"Oh lordy, leave it to me to cause a ruckus," Sam exclaimed as she caught Colleen's amused eye, and then sheepishly giggled, "I do apologize for that commotion!" Sam smiled broadly as she introduced herself, "Why Colonel Lawson, sir, it is a delight to finally meet you!" while giving him and his wife both reserved hugs.

Looking for a way to shift the focus away from Gerry, she cheerfully quipped, "Why bless you, hon," as she snagged a couple of drinks from a caterer's tray as he went by. While handing the drinks to Lawson and his wife, she looked around, pretending to have lost the caterer. Touching Gerry's hand, Sam redirected his attention toward the caterer who was now making his way through the throng of partygoers and sweetly asked, "Honey, would you go grab the caterer before he makes a getaway and get us a couple of drinks as well?" She hoped the task would give Gerry the time he needed to refocus.

The brief redirection was all Gerry needed and his confidence and composure both had returned along with the drinks, when he walked up and caught Sam mid-sentence telling Colleen Lawson, "...and that won't fly."

Colleen watched Sam greet her husband with her unique style of a greeting she called the "Army hug," and, intrigued, she had Sam demonstrating the various grips and when to use them. Much to Lawson's dismay, Sam and Colleen were using him as a prop and the two women were laughing delightfully as Colleen enthusiastically shook her husband's hand in practice. There was a look of gratitude on Lawson's face when Gerry had returned to save him.

Sam steered Gerry through the series of friendly topics that they had so carefully rehearsed, and by the time the server returned with the canapés, the colonel began to think he had perhaps misgauged the young officer. As the young couple took their leave for the dance floor, an enchanted Colleen Lawson leaned over to whisper to her husband that she didn't understand what he was making such a big fuss about; Lieutenant Gerry Martinez was charming.

The trip to Boston's underbelly had exposed Gerry's insecurities, his fears of being judged and of being found wanting, and it added itself to the pressure of his new position under Lawson, with its new responsibilities. He depended so much on Sam to help him do socially what a five-year-old could easily master, and for Gerry, it was embarrassing...and overwhelming. And at that moment, it all came to a head.

The orchestra music moved from a slow waltz tune to a faster Viennese waltz pace and many couples were soon swaying to its quicker rhythm. The music seemed to grow fainter in Gerry's ears and he had looked down at Sam, but was perplexed to realize he wasn't hearing what she was saying clearly. All of Gerry's fears and doubts, the emotional stress from the past year, had welled up to the surface.

The catalyst hadn't been any one specific event, but rather the building pressure under the Gerry Krakatoa volcano simply had reached its breaking point, and it had finally erupted. One moment,

Sam and Gerry were dancing, waltzing so elegantly and then suddenly, in full display of the entire ballroom, Gerry turned on his date like a viper, unleashing a stream of malicious acid-laced profanity directed solely at her. The hurled vulgar obscenities, unutterable under any circumstance, stunned Sam speechless, and she watched uncomprehendingly as Gerry was consumed by raw hatred.

Sam had seen on his face the pain that accompanied the hatred, but in an instant, his anger became hers and she exploded. Colleen Lawson gasped in horror, her conversation with several wives stopping midsentence.

Oh my word, Sweet Jesus, she quietly said to herself as she watched in shock as Gerry's face transformed into a demon. She glanced over at Colonel Lawson, who had been chatting with colleagues, but her husband's face registered the same shock as hers.

Bloody hell, I hate it when I'm right, Lawson spewed to himself while watching the scene unfold and quickly putting his drink down, he bolted out across the room to end it.

Sam was aware that everyone was watching, and she didn't care. Instead of dropping her voice to the expected demure whisper, Sam, in her fury, and with a voice strong enough to carry up over the music, erupted to shoot the last volley.

"I don't do big, bad, and stupid well. Big, I'm used to, bad doesn't scare me, and stupid I have no use for," she spat at Gerry while spinning on her heel to leave him standing alone, fury darkening his face and fists clenched at his side. Dancing couples scrambled to part like the Red Sea as Sam plowed through the astonished partygoers.

Gerry didn't even know he had erupted—he couldn't hear the words. He only felt the fear and rage. He watched in shock as Sam left him standing alone on the floor, and the horror of what he had done and said swept through him, followed by a tsunami of humiliation. They had been only words, but he had used them adroitly as weapons. Gerry had no sense of the "why." He couldn't attack the fear and insecurities that still haunted him so he had attacked Sam.

There had been so much at stake for him that night, latent fears and insecurities bubbling to the surface, and anger had used them to do its bidding. In their moment of victory, that trifecta of fear, insecurity, and rage reminded Gerry that they were his true masters.

As Gerry stood in the center of gawking partygoers, sweat dampening his face and clothes, a thought came crashing down on him; he had been a fool to think he could escape that trifecta by merely putting on a uniform.

The ballroom had stopped, couples frozen in position while the music kept playing. Watching Sam stomp off, Lawson altered his intercept course and caught up to her just as she retrieved her coat from the hat check.

"Yes," Sam snapped when Lawson asked if she was all right. He watched as Sam, red-faced from the embarrassment, apologized to him as she shook her head in dismay and disbelief. "I'm so sorry, sir. I...ah, I don't know what to say."

Her mind couldn't quite grasp what had happened, and Sam just reiterated how sorry she was. Sam's eyes scanned the vestibule and she was still shaking her head when she asked Lawson, "Sir...I need to leave. Where can I catch a cab?" Lawson reached over in hopes of placating Sam, but when he touched her bare arm, he could feel the cold sweat from the fight. Putting his arm around her shoulder, he steered her over to the side.

"I'll take care of this. You wait here," he told her, and with a sharp toss of a hand at a soldier, he arranged to have someone drive her home. The Army had caused her enough grief for one night. As he watched Sam leave with the driver, Lawson's focus shifted, and his previous concern for the woman was now blatant scorn toward the young lieutenant.

Gerry had retreated into an alcove alongside the ballroom, trying to command his anger into submission and regain his control. Anger was Gerry's friend, one that had reliably stayed with him throughout everything. Anger had kept him alive on the streets. Anger had gotten him food and a place to sleep. Anger was his constant companion, and anger was what he was expecting from Lawson as the colonel strode a purposeful path toward him across the polished dance floor.

Lt. Colonel Lawson was a good-looking man with shiny black hair that crowned a lean face gifted with lively eyes and a genial smile, but disgust had clouded and contorted those lean features into grim determination as he approached. Momentarily defiant, Gerry's raw rage boiled up again at first, but dissipated when Lawson's face only showed disappointment in the long pregnant pause before he began to speak.

Lawson pulled him aside away from the crowd of the room, and away from the onlookers whispering behind their hands and turned backs. The band had resumed playing but uneasy stares from attendees were still tossed their way.

For about ten minutes, Lawson did all the talking and Gerry's color changed from the blood-red of rage to the crimson-red of embarrassment. For those ten minutes, Gerry did all the listening and as Lawson turned to rejoin his wife and the festivities, he ended his fatherly advice with a quiet, "It is your choice."

[**GERALD, 2001: Quoted Text From Letter**

"What I've never told you is that a colonel came up to me afterwards and rather bluntly told me that being a military spouse is a horrifically tough job that tears at the fabric of their being. That it takes a very special type of person to handle the stress and responsibility and to do it alone. That women like you were scarce and were to be cherished, not dismissed. That if I didn't have the brains to see that then I didn't deserve you and to step aside for there were at least ten other men in the room who would gladly take my place. Said I couldn't change being big but fixing bad was doable and not being stupid I could work on. Said it was my choice."]

SHE WAS SITTING on the couch, her legs curled up beneath her, when Gerry returned to his apartment. She barely gave him a glance as he cautiously entered the living room. Sam had been sitting there trying to understand. The fight was like most other fights, a small thing that poked at simmering resentment. The final trigger had been an offhanded comment Sam had made about enjoying the evening without Stan being in their face riding shotgun. In 1982, the couple was still in the early moments of their relationship, and the constant navigation around a seemingly omnipresent Stan was suffocating to Sam.

What had staggered Sam the most was the venom. Their disagreement over Stan hadn't been that big of a deal, for privately, they had laughed over the very topic many times before. Yet the level of Gerry's fury was astounding. He had been so blinded by his rage, Sam doubted he even knew who she was as he attacked her with his words. They had been far sharper than any blade. He had eviscerated her.

She had changed into sweats, her face was freshly scrubbed clean of makeup, and Gerry couldn't miss how tired Sam looked sitting there staring off into nothing. Kneeling on the floor in front of her, he didn't know where to start. Gerry knew she wouldn't believe anything he said, he barely could believe it himself. He started to place a hand on Sam's knee, but carefully withdrew it—the vibrational energy in the room was so heavy. Instead, he shamefully admitted, his voice catching on the first words.

"I...I know you don't want to hear this right now, and I don't blame you. I want to say two things and then I will shut up. One, I am sorry. I'm an ass. And two, I do love you, more than I can possibly make you understand. I...I..." His words fell off as Gerry couldn't even begin to explain anything. Sam sat on the couch unresponsive, staring at the fireplace. There was no anger on her face, no flush of anything; it was as if he wasn't there, and Gerry inwardly pleaded, *My God, Samantha, say something.*

Taking the hint from the devastating silence, Gerry reached for his car keys and as he headed for the door, he told her he would stay at the base for the night, but would be back in the morning.

The sound of her sigh reached him before her voice. "Gerry, come back here, please. Sit down and hear me." Still staring at the unlit fireplace, Sam sat quietly withdrawn but after a moment, words were whispered. They were not so much as directed at Gerry, but seemingly just toward the walls of the apartment themselves. "I know down deep, you didn't mean what you said," Sam whispered in a voice that quivered with heartache. "I even know you don't know why you did what you did, why you popped off like that. But..." Sam's voice faded to silence as she heaved another heavy sigh, and when she finally lifted her head to meet his gaze, Gerry had to avert his. He couldn't face her, and what more, he didn't want to face what she was going to say.

Sam was so exhausted that she couldn't even cry tears. They just hovered at the outer creases of her eyes, gleaming in the reflective glow of the table lamp. Her words were carefully chosen, devoid of emotion, and spoken barely above a whisper.

"I don't care because this is not okay. It is not okay. Do you know how painful that was to hear you talk to me like that? To know you can think of me in such degrading terms? It is taking every fiber of my being not to walk out and never come back."

Tears formed in Gerry's eyes at his shame of her words, and Sam could tell from the awkward fluttering of his hands how upset he was, but Sam wasn't moved by them as she announced, "I'm going home tomorrow, and when or even whether I come back, is up to you."

A chill of panic seized his chest, racing down his body through his legs, causing him to catch his breath as his heart pounded a cadence in his ears. Sam's leaving was unexpected, but down deep, he knew he hadn't given her much of a choice.

Getting up from the couch, Sam bitterly told a disheartened Gerry staring at the floor, "I love you and I know what I saw tonight wasn't you, but I never want to see it again. There will be no second chance, Gerry. Either you get this anger of yours under control, or I'm walking away."

Turning to head into the kitchen, all Sam said was, "Let's see if we can have a civil evening, shall we?" All Gerry heard in her weary voice was disappointment, frustration, and sadness.

14

THE ONE YOU FEED

Three Days Later

Gerry had the rest of the weekend to reflect upon the debacle of the Ball and more importantly why he had exploded, and he was no closer to a solution. Taking refuge in the gym, Gerry vented his wrath by pummeling a punching bag into submission, his frustration and anger focused on the swinging canvas bag as he showed it no mercy.

Tucked into the side of a doorway, hidden from view, Lt. Colonel Lawson stood watching the young man, so determined to obliterate his foe but not comprehending who or what his foe was. Returning to his office, Lawson arranged for Gerry to report immediately when he came on duty.

A despondent Gerry cringed at the summons for he knew what it was about. His behavior at the Ball had been appalling and was the talk of the base as the gossip made the rounds. Disgusted looks and snide comments had already inundated him that morning, none of them remotely flattering.

Even Stan, who always understood him, had lashed out at him. And then there was Lawson himself. It would have stung less and been less humiliating if the man had raged and yelled at him, but his quiet talk-down had cut more deeply.

Lawson had also spent the weekend consumed by the events of the Ball. He prided himself on his empathy for the service men who served with him, but his instinct and experience told him that empathy wasn't what was needed here. Not if he was going to get to the bottom of this.

In a "Hail Mary" pass, Lawson called for Stan to report, much to the private's apprehension. Stan was well known for pushing the boundaries of a commanding officer's tolerance, often losing a stripe on his sleeve in the process, and when the summons was issued, Stan's teammates had quipped, "Well there goes another stripe!" Relief flooded Stan as he stood in Lawson's office. For once, he wasn't being reprimanded, but rather Lawson was looking for information, an inroad to understanding Gerry. A devilish grin broke out across his face as Stan thought for a moment.

"Have I gotta story for you, sir!" he said as his face lit up with a memory.

Lawson glanced up at the chagrined Gerry standing at attention before him and was pleased to see the contrite demeanor. *Good,* he thought as he pondered how to get through to the young man.

"Thought any more about our little chat the other evening?" Lawson genially inquired.

Begrudgingly, an ashamed Gerry had to admit, "Nothing but, sir."

Deciding to tread lightly at first, Lawson began amiably, "Your date—I enjoyed meeting Sam, you two make a nice couple," but then went on to reveal how he had the most interesting conversation with Ibbotson the other day. With a roguish smirk on his face as he remembered Stan's tale, Lawson slyly commented, "That was quite the introduction you two had," referring to how Gerry had sat on a cactus in the Arizona desert when the couple had first met. A panicked look swept over Gerry's face when Lawson laughed at Stan's vivid description of that day.

"Yep, he gave you two up, spilled the beans, the whole pot as it were." Shaking his head in disbelief, a huge grin creased Lawson's face as he lightly quipped, "Not sure how I would have fared."

But then Lawson astutely changed his tactics, his smile evaporating into a sharp frown. He now sat studying the uncomfortable Gerry's expression from across his desk and revealed he had told his wife. "I couldn't help myself," Lawson deadpanned coldly. "I just had to share that story with my wife, Colleen. I think she is still laughing."

Lawson's piercing dark eyes held Gerry in a steady grip, shredding any remaining resolve left on his part. Unsure of what to make of Lawson's sudden callous demeanor as he kept up his hostile tone, Gerry could feel not only the sting of embarrassment rise up under his collar, but also his old friend, anger.

The vitriolic digs had done their job as Lawson, pleased at how well his ploy had worked, watched in barely contained amazement, at just how shallow the anger resided under Gerry's skin, and moreover, just how easily it dominated him.

"How long have you and Sam been together? Plan on keeping her or is she just a short-term notch on your belt?" Lawson bluntly asked, watching as the muscles in Gerry's arms flexed from fists clenching behind his back as the flush of ire crept up his neck.

Lawson's earlier pleasant tone was now icy as he pointedly enunciated his words purposefully, "That was not a rhetorical question, Lieutenant. I am expecting an answer. Now, I believe my question is plain enough—do you want to keep Sam in your life?" Not sure how to answer, Gerry, his mind locked in his familiar battle of rage, couldn't seem to pull words together in a sentence, so he set his jaw and stood there silently.

Lawson left Gerry still rigid at attention as he got up to pour himself another cup of coffee and lazily meandered around his office, taking in the photos on shelves. Out of the blue, as if it were a spur of the moment thought, he abruptly turned toward Gerry and confessed, "I was a lot like you once. Anger boiling over and raging at the slightest thing—ready to punch out anybody's and everybody's lights."

At first, Gerry thought he had misheard. The unexpected admission momentarily blindsided him, causing him to stare in disbelief, for

Lawson was the calmest, most levelheaded officer he had ever met. The man never raised his voice or really even reprimanded, but instead believed in giving a soldier all the tools needed to do the job properly. Lawson also was known to give a soldier enough rope to hang himself for he believed in a man figuring out his strengths and weaknesses on his own.

Lawson had yet another surprise for Gerry as he walked back around his office to his desk.

"I'm part Native American, did you know that? My grandmother was Native American," Lawson quietly revealed, the skin around his eyes creasing with laugh wrinkles at Gerry's expression.

While fixing a steady gaze at the young man, Lawson's hostile stance softened as he explained, "My grandmother told me a story when I was young—a story that has guided me throughout my life and career. It is how I live my life and how I choose my direction, and it is a story I'm now going to tell you. The story I'm going to tell you is my grandmother's version of the Two Wolves."

Gesturing for Gerry to pull up a chair, Lawson settled back down in his desk chair, his face bathed by the warmth of the memory as he began.

"A grandfather is walking with his small grandson along a path, telling the little boy a story. 'There are two wolves that live deep inside me,' he says to the boy, 'and they are with me every day. These two wolves; one embodies evil and all that evil is. Not only the evil directed at other men in the form of superiority, arrogance, and envy. Traits like jealousy, greed, hate, lies, even false pride also inhabit this wolf. And then, finally, there is the evil that we use against ourselves such as guilt, regret, and self-pity. This wolf is the manifestation of all the negatives I carry with me each day, all the negatives of the human soul and existence.'

"'The other wolf embodies everything positive within me. All the good seen in humanity: joy, love, kindness, empathy, generosity. Traits like truth, compassion, faith, hope as well. And like his counterpart, this wolf resides in me every day, too. These two wolves are in every living soul and in every person. They are constantly at war, each trying to destroy the other. These two wolves, born of the same spirit, will fight to the death to rule supreme. To look at them, they appear identical, but they are opposites. They represent opposing paths, outcomes, and destinies. They fight every day, never stopping to rest until one wins. And only one can remain.' The little boy looks up at his grandfather and asks, 'Which wolf wins?' The old man smiles at the innocence of his grandson and answers, 'The one you feed.'"

Lawson leaned forward across his desk and stared at Gerry as he made his point. His resolute expression still burned with the same intensity, but was now tempered with an understanding that only came from intimate knowledge.

"These two wolves are inside of you right now, and they are at war. You are feeding the negative wolf, and if you are not careful, the positive will starve. You determine which wolf lives." Lawson had shown Gerry the rope that may hang him. Now, he hoped to show the young man how that rope could be used as a lifeline.

Reaching over his desk for a business card, Lawson gently gazed at the card for a moment and a trace of a peaceful smile appeared, hinting at a distant memory as his fingers stroked it in reverence.

Holding the card out for Gerry to take, Lawson's eyes revealed hope when he suggested to Gerry, "The time you spend in the boxing ring, spend it here instead. You will be taught how to use an opponent's aggression against themselves. Moreover, you will learn to recognize it in yourself and tame it."

The card was for a local dōjō, an Aikido dōjō.

[**GERALD, 2001: Quoted Text From Letter**

"From that moment on I vowed I would never do anything to cause you to walk away. I resolved to be not only the man you wanted, but the man you respected and trusted. I know some days I fell short, but I hope overall I have made more checks in the win column than not."]

· · ·

THE DŌJŌ DIDN'T LOOK like much that first day. A stark, nondescript building easily missed in the throng of everything else. Its interior, as simple and basic as you could get, wasn't any more impressive, with faded white cinder block walls covered with charts. The men on padded mats upon a hard linoleum floor, going through their training hadn't been all that interesting either, just a bunch of guys in pajamas.

For Gerry, the idea of this Aikido that Lawson was promoting was down three for three as he looked around, annoyed at having wasted his time. Gerry was almost ready to leave when the *sensei*, a teacher or instructor of Japanese martial arts, who had been watching him, came over.

"You are Lieutenant Martinez?" he asked. When Gerry nodded yes, the *sensei* smiled softly, telling him, "Colonel Lawson hoped you would come by." Lightly touching Gerry's elbow, the *sensei* gently asked, "Please, allow me to teach."

Initially skeptical, Gerry immersed himself into the martial art of Aikido, and wearing its mantra of self-control as a cloak, he made huge leaps in his composure. Central to it all was the ideology of him not trying to abolish fear, but to recognize it and control it, rather than allowing fear to control him.

Each time Gerry stepped onto the mats, he would enter another world that captured his entire being, now focused in mind and body. Initially, his military training had him barging ahead, bull-in-china-shop style while almost tackling his opponent, but as Sam watched, his self-control grew, as did his respect for both his opponent and himself.

For Sam, it was breathtaking. Gerry's unswerving devotion to Aikido was absolute, and in just a few months, his improvement was stunning. When Sam had first heard about Lawson suggesting martial arts, she worried that all Aikido would do, would be to just give Gerry yet another way to fight. But, as Sam would lean up against that wall, watching the students in their *gi*, the white uniform for Aikido students, with its white belt, she would wonder. *Did I always know, or did I merely suspect? Is my surprise not only due to how well Gerry is doing, but that I didn't realize at all?*

All that time, from the moment she and Gerry had met in Arizona to now, there had been another person inside of Gerry, the real Gerry no longer consumed by distrust or dominated by anger. Over the weeks and months, Sam could see the change in that angry wolf. As its dominance receded and its hold on Gerry slackened, the angry wolf began to tuck its tail in submission and slink backwards into the dark.

Japanese Aikido is one of the most widely practiced Budo in the world and is a discipline where one is taught to harmonize rather than clash with an opponent. Not just a means to kill an opponent, Aikido is heavily influenced by meditation practices that emphasize internal self-development as well as external physical fighting skills. The student is taught to handle weapons with compassion and understanding. Its founder, Morihei Ueshiba, is widely quoted from his book *The Art of Peace*, "To injure an opponent is to injure yourself. To control aggression without inflicting injury is the Art of Peace."

Gerry carried that quote in his wallet for decades. Aikido was only the first of the martial arts that Gerry mastered, and it ushered in his lifelong devotion to them. Karate, Judo, Jiu-Jitsu, and Krav Maga were all studied; different colored belts, one black, one brown, and others just in the early stages.

Lt. Colonel Alan Lawson had given Gerry the tools necessary to vanquish the wolf and he had used them all. Through the study of martial arts, he had begun to learn, understand, and ultimately master his angry wolf, the one born on the streets.

[**SAMANTHA, 2024: Quoted Text from Letter**

"In the beginning you didn't want to marry or have kids, then [later on] it was me. We made quite the pair, didn't we? I understand why, babe, for you had your demons too. You had that explosive temper that ruled you in those early days and left you paralyzed with fear. Gerry, that temper didn't define you. It was a tool you adopted in order to survive and once the reason for the temper was erased, so was the temper itself. It simply wasn't who you were, and I loved you for it. I was proud of you for recognizing it and conquering it. You hoped you had been the man I trusted, the man I wanted and the man I needed. Oh sweetheart—everyday.")

SEVERAL MONTHS AFTER THE BALL

It was a stalemate between doctor and patient as Gerry just sat, watching. He was not glaring, there was no animosity, for the doctor was more of a curiosity than anything. Seeing a psychiatrist had been Lawson's idea—an order, actually—so Gerry sat, his bearing just as rigid, sitting in the chair as if standing at attention.

When the timer on his watch went off, he nodded as he got up and left the office, politely closing the office door behind him. Aside from the usual greeting, Gerry had said nothing. The doctor sighed, uncrossed his legs and placed his clipboard on his desk. He had no more answers this week than last.

After the Ball, Lawson had requested an evaluation and the young medical officer had been tasked with deciphering Gerry's psyche, and the source of his anger. Frustratingly, information from his subject was not forthcoming, and the doctor had begun to explore other avenues. He had questioned attendees at the Officers' Ball and had spoken to Lawson himself.

The doctor had even summoned a reluctant Stan for a conversation in hopes of exploring Gerry's background. A murky picture had begun to emerge for the doctor of the persona that was Gerry Martinez, but there were still crucial elements missing.

Sam was aware of the man watching her as she sat grading papers with a cup of coffee, and she had seen him last week, too. The man hadn't even tried to hide his scrutiny behind a newspaper or any other prop, but rather was blatantly obvious as he overtly followed her every move.

The intense stare unnerving, it had become clear to Sam that it was no coincidence the man was getting a cup of coffee at the same time as she. The man casually glanced down to place his coffee cup onto its saucer, but started in surprise when the table he had been watching was now empty. Fervently, he scanned the mess hall, but Sam, the object of his curiosity, was nowhere to be seen.

A quiet *Crap* escaped from the doctor as he reached behind him for his jacket to leave. Her voice coming up from behind surprised him.

"Looking for me? Who are you?" Sam sharply grilled, as she took note of the insignia on the man's collar and his rank. A captain in medical. Introducing himself, the doctor explained his interest and that he had questions.

"If Lt. Martinez agrees, would you be willing to talk to me? I'd like to hear your side of things and how you see him," he said hopefully. Sam warily sat down across from him as she studied him.

"I have worked for a year to earn that man's trust, and I will not betray that," Sam coolly informed the doctor. "If you want information, you're going to have to earn your keep and figure it out for yourself." Sam stared back at the doctor, looking to see which way he would dart, but he was steadfast and didn't blink. "But let me give you a heads-up, Doctor. Do I call you captain or doctor?" Sam asked as she paused for a second.

The doctor gave a small smile as he answered, "Whichever you are most comfortable with," waiting for what he hoped was a clue from Sam.

"If you are going into battle against Lt. Gerry Martinez," Sam evenly told him, "then you have already lost. I guarantee you, he has analyzed you, he has evaluated you, and he has dissected you. He already knows your every weakness. It's what he does." The doctor leaned across his chair, his elbow on its arm rest and chuckled confidently at Sam's adamant position.

"That's just fine, ma'am, it's what I do, too." His grin emphasized just how much he was going to enjoy the battle.

Sam watched the doctor leave, and tilting her head in amazement, she scoffed an amused, "May the best man win." She would do anything to be a fly on the wall for this one.

Gerry had surprised the doctor by agreeing to let Sam talk with him. The doctor probed, trying to ascertain Gerry's true feelings regarding the meeting, but there was only the faintest glimmer of amusement on his patient's face.

"She will not betray me. She won't tell you anything," Gerry had said, challenging him, almost daring the doctor to prove him wrong.

"Interesting choice of words, Lieutenant," the doctor had responded as he recalled Sam using the same word, *betray*, just a few days earlier. "Who betrayed you? Who don't you trust?" His questions received no answers.

"How much do you want me to say to him?" Sam had asked Gerry later that evening, surprised he had agreed to the meeting. "What do I tell him?"

"The truth," Gerry told her, smiling. There was a look of uncertainty on Sam's face that prompted Gerry to give her a hug while saying, "You are my Mama Bear. You will say nothing to hurt me, I know that, so tell the man what he needs to know to do his job."

A beautiful sunny day greeted Sam and the doctor as they strolled through the park, each clutching a specialty coffee that had begun to be all the rage. As they walked, he questioned Sam about herself and her relationship with Gerry, learning of their dueling lifestyles and how they coped, but what he really wanted to know was how Sam saw Gerry.

"Well, for starters," Sam began as they strolled along the park's path, "Gerry is one of the most capable men in his unit. He's calm, decisive, and there's no ambiguity. And patient. My God, is he patient. And if he's in uniform, on base, or in the field, look out! His confidence in the Army is absolute."

Sam stopped for a moment, searching for how to say it next and finally, she admitted, "I don't get it. I don't understand how he can be so unshakable, so together in one setting, and then be so clueless in another."

Yes, the doctor thought, as his ears perked up, *this is the Martinez I need to hear about, not the Army Lieutenant whose brass buttons are always in order.* Putting on his best professional game face, the doctor's expression encouraged Sam to continue as he listened for clues.

"The Army is so easy for him, but civilian social settings—they boggle him. The bravado that carried him on the streets doesn't apply here, and he knows it, so he memorizes what to say and do in given situations. It's like he has a playbook and he flips through the pages, looking for the appropriate play for that situation. And when there is no preplanned play diagram for him to refer to...he doesn't know what to do, so he clams up and says nothing."

Sam abruptly stopped talking. Having exhausted all that she was comfortable saying, she was suddenly worried she had said too much already. In the quiet moment, Sam couldn't tell if the look on the doctor's face was the professional doctor facade he wore, or if it was genuine, until he spoke.

"You admire him." It wasn't a question as much as a statement, a professional assessment.

"Yes, I guess I do," Sam admitted in between sips of her coffee. "He's an impressive guy. I'd be a puddle of mush on the floor if I had gone through a fraction of what he has. He may not always say the right thing, or respond with the smoothest of words, but he's got himself together more than most."

"Yes," the doctor nodded with professional smoothness. "I am beginning to see that." Watching a couple walking their dogs ahead of them on the path, the doctor turned to Sam. "Now, tell me about this trip you took with Lieutenant Martinez to Boston..."

As the morning wore on, the doctor's boxes on his diagnostic checklist were checked off or eliminated, and a diagnosis emerged: an extreme case of shyness exacerbated by his upbringing on the streets. Gerry's anger was an overlay—it wasn't innate, but rather learned, and was deeply rooted in subconscious distrust.

But there were some glaring inconsistencies as well, with behaviors that were not associated with shyness. The largest? What Sam perceived as Gerry's inability to comprehend social cues and body language. He didn't always understand idioms, humor, metaphors, or anything that was not clearly defined and often made inappropriate responses during conversations. He used his Army uniform as a crutch, a coping mechanism where he extended the structure of the military onto civilian life. The path meandered through the park, and when they reached the end, the doctor had one last question for Sam.

"These social cues you say he misses and doesn't understand, I want to ask you something and I need you to not answer me today, but to think about it for a bit."

"Doctor," Sam interrupted, taken aback somewhat at the insinuation that what she was seeing wasn't real. "I'm not making this up. Gerry truly doesn't respond appropriately at times." The doctor chuckled a bit as they approached Sam's car.

"Oh, of course they are real. But perhaps the cause is not what you think. My question to you is, does he truly not understand or does he not trust?" The doctor went on to clarify. "When these miscues happen, did he truly not see them, or did he not trust his interpretation of what he was seeing? Those early years on the streets were his formative years psychologically. We humans draw on our experiences to interpret social cues. It's instinctive and we take it for granted, and Lieutenant Martinez's childhood experiences are different from most."

Sam sat in her car, chiding herself over her glib dismissal of Gerry's "it's just shyness." She had blown it off as just a little quirk—at times, she felt it was even cute. She hadn't known what she was expecting when she had met with the doctor, but now, as she pondered what he had said, an appreciation of the challenges Gerry grappled with daily sank in. While she knew it wasn't what he had meant, she laughed as she remembered what he had said that day in Arizona when they had first met—*at least it won't be boring. Well, honey,* Sam chuckled to herself as she shifted the car into gear. *We sure do make quite the pair, don't we?* Pulling out of the parking lot, Sam had intended to go home but she instead turned toward the medical library. She had some research to do.

15

NICK THOSE NUTS AT 1,000 EASY, SIR

That first full year of their relationship had been rocked by unexpected discoveries and full of emotional tension for Sam and Gerry. The couple had anticipated strains over their schedules and careers, but their stressful trip to Gerry's Boston childhood streets, and his subsequent disgrace at the Ball, had added a psychological layer that at times dulled their enthusiasm and sapped their strength.

By the early spring of 1983, however, the pendulum had swung, and there was change in the air. Turmoil gave way to understanding and to a string of successes and accomplishments, both personal and professional.

For Gerry, his quest was to prove himself, not only to the Army, but to Sam and his own self. Aikido's philosophy of control and confidence took hold, and he was rewarded with a promotion from lieutenant to captain. There had been no one to ask when he made first lieutenant, and Gerry was acutely aware that there would be family present for the other servicemen who were also being promoted. He was desperate for Sam to attend the ceremony, and he did ask, but knew she would not be able to make it.

Sam was in Missouri, with not only a full load of teaching, forensic, and research obligations, but as a student as well. It was a time in her life where Sam measured her successes not in promotions or accolades, but in stability and progress toward a goal. Forensic cases came and went, ebbing and flowing with farm planting seasons or the fall hunting season, when human remains were usually found.

The mixture of interacting with her students, to that of being a student herself in medical school, fulfilled her days. The data collection phase of her Ph.D. research was finally coming to a close, and she was ready to begin writing the dissertation. For Sam, the peace of a predictable routine brought great satisfaction as she watched uncoordinated pieces from the chaotic jumble that was her life, simply beginning to fall into place. For Sam, a ray of peace erupted with the click of each piece of that puzzle.

NORTH CAROLINA, 1983

Gerry rigidly stepped forward as his name was read and he craned his neck a bit so the pins could be easily attached. As he saluted and stepped back into formation, he casually flicked his eyes toward a sound off to his right, and was stunned. Sam had worked her way to an empty chair along the back, but had a clear view to the stage. The blush of pride Gerry felt when he caught the admiration on Sam's face was not so much due to the fact that he had made a rank, but rather that there was someone who cared enough to be proud of him.

As Gerry stepped off the elevated platform, Sam wormed her way through the crowd toward him. They met in the middle of the room, ignoring the excited ceremony attendees milling about them, congratulating proud members of their families.

"You're here." His astonishment was evident on his face and in his voice.

"Of course I'm here, silly. Wouldn't have missed this for anything," Sam lightly joked as she ran her fingers over the newly pinned rank insignias and adjusted his collar to the crisp crease she knew Gerry liked.

"But your schedule…how did you…" his voice again trailed off in wonder.

"Eh," Sam waved her hand in the air dismissively as she answered, "Med school will still be there and my students—I swapped classes with someone. I get to teach population genetics to the first-year grad students next week." Her face screwed up in an unspoken *Ugh*. "But you, sir, are worth it!" she told Gerry, pausing slightly as she stole a quick look around to see if any of his superiors were looking before she gave him a big kiss.

Standing back to look Gerry in the face, Sam solemnly asked, "Did you ever imagine, in your wildest dreams, Gerry, while sitting in that library back in Boston, that you would be here, where you are now, doing what you are doing?"

"No," Gerry warmly chuckled, as he momentarily thought back to those days and drawing Sam back in, he wrapped his arms around her in a hug. "Not even close," he soberly admitted, and out from under his hug, Gerry heard Sam's muffled voice.

"You should call him, you know, just to say thanks. Pernecki has to be so proud of you, too."

Yeah I should, Gerry thought, hugging Sam tight, and as he perched his chin on her head, he reflected on the road he had just traveled. Amazement accompanied the pride that welled up in his chest, as he marveled how fate had taken him from where he had been then, to where he was now.

KENTUCKY, *1977,* GERRY'S MEMORY OF *6 YEARS EARLIER*

At the conclusion of his Vietnam tour, Gerry took a hiatus from the Army and returned to his Boston streets, but the streets no longer enticed him. At loose ends and dissatisfied with his direction, he had rejoined the service in 1974 and hadn't looked back since.

In his early Army days, he had no aspirations of being an officer, for at that time, he hadn't had a formal education. He had gotten his GED as a teenager before Vietnam, and that was good enough for the Army. Gerry had considered himself enlisted material. Predictably

Gerry had moved up through the enlisted ranks and was now three years later, in 1977, a corporal.

It would have come as no surprise to anyone who had encountered Gerry on those Boston streets that he would excel at training and weapons, any and all, for survival in the concrete jungle cultivated an exceptional array of hand-to-hand skills. Once described by a trainer as being almost instinctive catlike reflexes, those skills were such that on the field, he stalked and pounced on his prey, cornering them before dispatch. Just as he had trained his youthful street crews, he both enjoyed and shone at training the newer members of the unit under him. It was those training skills that would show him a different path.

Stan had gotten him into a bar fight—an altercation that had been begun by Stan's indomitable personality, which usually had everyone enthralled. That evening, however, that personality had put him in the crosshairs of a displeased husband, and Gerry had stepped up to defend his friend.

The young lady had been pretty, very pretty, and Stan, being Stan, had chatted her up with expert flirtation. Her husband had objected.

A summons to a CO's office was expected after the bar fight, but the order to report to Pernecki's office was not, and Gerry fretted. A bar fight couldn't be the reason the colonel wanted to see him because colonels weren't interested in things so mundane, that's what subordinates were for.

Colonel Patrick Pernecki, a short, stout man with a ruddy complexion and slicked back light brown hair just beginning to grey in broad streaks, turned his attention to the matter at hand: a twenty-five-year-old Corporal Gerry Martinez and his sidekick, Private Stan Ibbotson.

Colonel Pernecki was an officer who prided himself on not only recognizing the talents of the soldiers under his command, but utilizing those talents, and what galled the man more than anything was the waste of unseen potential. With his innate leadership presence and training skills, the young Corporal Martinez had caught the attention of those above, and he was now squarely on Pernecki's radar.

The dust-up at the bar was of little concern to Pernecki, a second file on his desk, however, was. He wanted to float an idea past the young man.

Gerry had been standing before Pernecki's desk, rigidly at attention for so long, that he had begun to wonder if Pernecki had forgotten he was there. Expecting a lecture, Gerry mentally steeled himself by focusing on an obscure spot on the wall above the Colonel's head. When Pernecki finally spoke, he surprisingly announced that the meeting was an impromptu performance review.

Making a show of scanning Gerry's file, Pernecki began dramatically reciting paragraphs from a review from Gerry's previous CO, one Captain Blaylock.

Blaylock had praised the young corporal as being steady under pressure, calm, and decisive. But he also had mentioned Gerry's sniper skills, and Pernecki flipped through the pages of the file to find the proper phrase that had caught his attention.

"Ah, yes…Blaylock says here—you can nick the nuts off a bee at 500." His voice registered complete disbelief. With a flick of his head as he scoffed, Pernecki cynically muttered under his breath to no one in particular, "I didn't know bees had nuts."

The dry comment had no effect on Gerry, who had not moved an inch, and was still staring intently at the spot on the wall above the officer's head.

Blaylock did have a criticism, however. And it was Gerry's hair-trigger temper off the field. Pernecki leaned back in his chair, tossing the file aside and unsympathetically asked Gerry if he agreed with that review, fully expecting him to object to that last remark.

Gerry stoically commented, "No, sir, I do not."

Pernecki had been looking forward to hearing Gerry's excuse for putting an irate husband in a head lock. Much to his surprise, however, rather than defend himself for the bar fight, with his eyes never leaving the spot on the wall, Gerry instead quipped, "Nick those nuts at 1,000 easy, sir."

An amused Pernecki resumed his meeting as he told Gerry, "I'm aware of your Boston street background and that you view yourself as enlisted material." Sensing that Pernecki hadn't called him in for a talk-down, Gerry had begun to allow himself to relax a bit, but was still waiting for the shoe to drop. The shoe dropped when Pernecki remarked, "I would like you to consider going to Officer Candidate School."

Gerry's eyes flickered from the fixed spot on the wall to Pernecki as he stood in wide-eyed disbelief. Not considering himself officer material, he reminded the colonel that he had never gone to college and would stagnate behind a desk.

Pernecki went on to highlight the advantages and rewards of being an officer that he hoped Gerry could relate to and concluded with a postscript, "I will be proud and support you, regardless of your choice, but I truly believe the enlisted ranks are not your destiny—I believe this is." Handing Gerry the file regarding OCS, Pernecki fixed him with a steady gaze as he solemnly told the young man, "All I'm asking is that you think this over."

It took several years for the officer to emerge. Gerry sailed through the college courses and the subsequent OCS, for academics and concepts of leadership came naturally to him. What had not, however, were the social interactions with the other candidates, for the camaraderie of the barracks was gone. In stark contrast to the enlisted life, Gerry struggled to interpret the most obvious of social signals, and Stan spent hours on the phone as counselor.

The months dragged on interminably, but in the end, the Army had itself a newly minted lieutenant. Stan had once embarrassed Gerry by using the metamorphosis of a cocoon into a butterfly to describe the transformation, but the analogy fit. Despite all of Gerry's misgivings, the lieutenant bar suited him.

Without Gerry to anchor his ebullience and incessant drive for entertainment, Stan drove Colonel Pernecki and his staff to distraction, and the exasperated commander found himself in a quandary as he contemplated what to do with the boy. Pernecki had smoothed the way for Gerry by helping to arrange a posting with Blaylock, Gerry's former commander. He also arranged a special gift for Blaylock.

He sent Stan, as well, with a note in his file saying the performance of the two as a team was outstanding and they should be utilized as such. It was the beginning of a phenomenal partnership where, throughout the years, wherever the Army sent Gerry, so went Stan.

NORTH CAROLINA, *1983*

The memory of Pernecki's astonished look at his quip of nicking nuts at 1,000 caused Gerry to chuckle faintly, and Sam looked up from the embrace to catch his distant smile. At Sam's unasked question, Gerry gently sighed as the fond memory faded, and he admitted, "Was just thinking about Pernecki. Thanks for reminding me."

The ceremony was over, but they still stood in a bear hug as attendees filed out around them. After a moment, Sam's voice was even softer when she asked, "Do you know where they are going to send you this time?" Gerry's hug grew tighter when he revealed his transfer orders, as if the intense embrace would soften the news.

"I'm here temporarily in North Carolina until I go to Germany, but then I'm being sent to Georgia when I return stateside." Gerry felt Sam's deep sigh at the news, although she had been prepared for the transfer.

While unhappy he would be leaving North Carolina, Sam thought to herself, *At least he is still on the East Coast.*

With Georgia being within a day of Missouri, their organized moments of being together were still safe, although she made a mental note to check out train and plane schedules before his return from Germany.

16

TOOK ME WEEKS TO LIVE THAT KISS DOWN

*D*uring the Cold War, priorities shifted for the military and emphasis was now on being prepared and maintaining an ever-present state of readiness. Training for tactical skills, weapons skills, confidence, and conditioning now was a crucial driving force. In addition to revamping how the soldiers themselves were trained and prepared, the infrastructure and organization of the Army also underwent changes. There were times where it seemed everything was in a state of flux and everything was transitory or short-lived, the buildings, the personnel and the procedures.

A Few Months Later

Amidst this chaos, the recently promoted Captain Gerry Martinez sat in his makeshift, temporary office. It was spring of 1983 and the Army had put him in the barracks with the unit. His new office was an unimpressive old utility room with a small broom closet attached and he could even still smell the bleach and other cleaning supplies. It had been raining for days—weeks, it seemed—and the early spring weather had left everything damp and cold, with mud everywhere.

Well…Gerry forlornly sighed to himself, as he moped, *at least Sam's coming tonight for the weekend.* His mood lightened.

The Friday early evening hours seemed to have crawled to a standstill, and unable to concentrate, Gerry anxiously checked Sam's flight information yet again. A last-minute staff meeting had forced Sam to fly in on a later flight than usual, disrupting Gerry's tidy schedule, and now past dinnertime, he was impatient.

He had eagerly asked Sam to meet him at his office on the base that night, for another one of their quirky routines—their walkabouts, a stroll where they would tour the base, walking arm-in-arm. He would introduce Sam to people, point out buildings and describe activities. The routine cemented Sam's presence to the area, and he found that presence provided a compass whenever he lacked direction.

And at the moment, he was lacking direction. Scowling, Gerry reviewed his new unit's performance this past week. They were young, untested fresh faces whose efforts matched the sloppy weather, and Gerry wondered if he was expecting too much out of the youngsters. The late hour and the rainy weather, lamentably meant his walkabout would have to wait for another day. Gerry fidgeted as he silently told himself Sam should be here shortly, but then, he had said that to himself an hour ago.

A chorus of groans erupted from the rec room in front of his office and Gerry glanced out at a table of three men playing poker. Stan was holding his cards so close to his face that only his narrowed eyes were visible. To his left sat Brady Caldwell, and he had a tell—a slight tilt to his head when he got excited.

He must have a good hand, Stan deduced. The third gentleman at the table, Mark McIntyre, however, was convinced Brady was bluffing. Stan folded, Mark called.

"Aww shoot," groaned Mark as Brady cackled in his ear while scooping up the sticks of chewing gum that served as poker chips. Both Mark and Brady had entered the picture the year after Gerry and Stan first met.

Each of the four men brought his own skill set to the table, and they soon found themselves on the same team. The four men formed an unshakable friendship during those early days, a friendship that endured the march of time.

From Idaho, Brady was, despite his surname, the son of German immigrants and had entered the Army after failing to be drafted for the NFL. Built like a square with two pistons for legs and a body that filled doorways, his teammates nicknamed him Sherman, after a Sherman tank. His beefy sausage fingers could handle the most delicate of tools, and would float skillfully over intricate wiring and connections. He was great at working with explosives.

Mark was as tall as Brady was wide, and he reminded Sam of her family's Tennessee roots of ridge runners who used to run moonshine. Lanky and lean, Mark's caginess and suave demeanor reflected his hometown of Las Vegas, and he always had an angle and a hustle. A mop of strawberry blond hair with a slew of freckles over the nose and cheeks deceivingly oozed a sweet country boy charm, but those lively blue eyes and a crooked smile always seemed to hint that he was scoping you out to be his next victim.

Gerry's transition to an officer broke up that team of friends, but with the current rash of temporary personnel relocations, the four men inexplicably found themselves at the same base station at the same time. Mark and Brady, old friends but now in new roles, were once again reunited with Gerry and Stan.

While the soldiers often called each other by their nicknames, Sam collectively referred to the four men as her Four Musketeers.

[**GERALD, 2001: Quoted Text From Letter**

"Thank you for being my kindred spirit, my soul mate. For being the reason I get up in the morning, for reminding me why I fight and for whom. Thank you for showing me I didn't have to always be on guard, that I could trust, that I could believe. Thank you for showing me how to love, how to be loved. Remember how embarrassed I'd be saying I love you in public or god forbid kiss you in front of the unit?"]

. . .

SAM SAT SANDWICHED in between two soldiers in the back seat of the station wagon, listening to one of the soldier's parents carry on excitedly about seeing their son. The soldiers had boarded her flight during a layover and graciously had offered to give her a lift to the base since they were going by there anyways.

The last-minute change in plans had led to a frantic race to grab the flight, and it had been one of those times where trying to maintain a long-distance relationship was hard on the blood pressure.

And exhausting, Sam thought to herself when fatigue overcame her as she leaned back into the seat, clutching her overnight bag and briefcase as shields. Breathing deeply, Sam allowed the hum of the tires on the road to soothe her adrenaline stoked thoughts. She closed her eyes for a moment, forcing herself to relax, and allowed the happy voices to fade into the background.

The traveling soldiers from the airport had let Sam out as close to her destination as possible, and as she watched the taillights disappear around a curve, she scrutinized her surroundings with a huge sigh. At first glance, the base was not impressive; it was chaotic and gloomy with equipment everywhere.

No wonder Gerry sounded so tired and down in the dumps on the phone, Sam thought as she took in the disarray. The darkness of the night only added a dank shroud that, when combined with the constant mist, had cast a depressing pall over the area as she scanned the base trying to get her bearings.

Standing in the middle of the service road, Sam was startled when the harsh bray of a jeep's horn snapped her out of her reverie. After asking for directions, she followed the pointing finger to her destination of a nondescript cookie cutter building in a row of the same.

Cacophonous chatter enveloped Sam as she opened the door and made her way down the hallway to its source, a central room that served as a rec room and just about everything else. Sam was surprised at the number of men present. It was a Friday night and she was expecting most to be at the bars, but the relentless crappy weather seemed to have dumped everyone's spirits down the toilet.

Adding their numbers to the aggregate of unmarried soldiers were a slew of cheerless, melancholy family men. The construction of the on-base accommodations for those with families was still a work in progress, and in the meantime, many married soldiers also found themselves assigned to the barracks, as they unhappily waited without their families, biding their time.

At numerous tables sat groups of men playing poker, cribbage, and a board game called Risk, appropriately a war strategy game. One long table sat against a wall with a couple of soldiers clearly studying, with textbooks and stacks of papers askew.

Another held two men working on an old radio of sorts, its parts and tools spread out in disorder. An unexpected sight greeted the woman as she glanced over at a small table tucked into a corner—a soldier knitting a sweater, a beautiful cable-knit sweater of shimmering opal yarn. Its recipient was going to love it.

Stan caught the flash of civilian clothes. Jumping up from the table, he nearly upended his gum sticks as he raced over to engulf Sam in a fierce bear hug while vivaciously exclaiming, "Sam, *mon amour*. You have arrived!"

Their reunion, however, was cut short by another familiar voice off to Sam's left that was fast approaching. A gravelly deep male voice blurted out, "Geez woman, you've got the aging process backward! Supposed to look older, not younger!" On the move, Brady could move amazingly fast for such a brick of a man.

Snapping her head in the direction of his voice, Sam jokingly shot back, "You are so full of crap, Brady. Be sure to get yourself a powerful laxative!"

Staggering dramatically as if he had been stabbed in the heart, Brady theatrically croaked out, "Oh, I've been wounded." The goofy repartee that characterized their relationship had begun.

"My gosh, you boys are a sight for weary eyes!" Sam squawked as Mark, standing an easy six-feet-four, had effectively swept her off her feet with his enthusiastic embrace.

It had been close to a year since Brady and Mark had last met up with the woman they jokingly called their Musketett, and they were not to be denied as they, along with Stan, descended upon her, demanding bear hugs and kisses.

[GERALD, 2001: Quoted Text From Letter

"I had just been transferred, settling into my first command, remember? You had come down for the weekend. You strolled in like you had been there forever, like you owned the place. It had been a tough day of drills, hadn't gone well and the unit was on edge. I watched through the door of my office just in awe as you worked the room as they say. Half the guys knew you and you greeted them with hugs and that smile of yours. I watched as you introduced yourself to the rest, none of them sure of what to make of you. And then it happened."]

THE LIGHTHEARTED BANTER was easy and free flowing, and its effects were immediate. Stan, in the grips of his overwhelming need for distraction and sport, sashayed over to the jukebox that had been hidden in a utility closet—it wasn't quite regulation. As a Motown tune by the Supremes floated out over the room, Brady excitedly grabbed three flashlights from the utility closet, tossing one each to Stan and Mark.

Using them as microphone props, the trio broke out in a flamboyant karaoke song as they sang along with Diana Ross. They wildly gestured for Sam to jump in, and she without hesitation wormed her way in between Mark and Brady, joining her three friends in putting on a spectacle.

The backup singers were Sam, Brady, and Mark as they pretended to be the Supremes. Stan, of course, was Diana Ross. Blessed with a powerful and stunning voice that matched his good looks, he could have been an opera singer—he certainly had the chutzpah of an entertainer.

As the song ended and the four friends stood laughing and enjoying their reunion, Sam caught the amused faces of other soldiers in the room. Several she had met before, but she struggled with their names. She understood the importance of uniforms promoting unity, identity, and solidarity, but for her that caused a problem; the soldiers all looked alike. A bunch of olive-green guys with the same haircut, dressed exactly alike and with name tags that were not always easy to read.

As the years started to go by, their individuality began to blur. To counteract this, Sam adopted a technique she had observed her mother use. A minister, her mother was the classic social butterfly who routinely met thousands of people but was afflicted with a bad memory for names. In her defense, Sam's mom had cultivated a technique to avoid embarrassment; she simply called everyone honey or dear—it saved her mother a lot of grief. Sam found herself doing the same thing for exactly the same reason.

"Hey, hons, how're you fellas doing?" was heard when Sam hailed several soldiers as they got up to welcome her. Looking over at the others, she addressed each in turn, and greetings the likes of "Ah, good to see you again, sweetie," and "Oh, you're looking good, dear," were heard as she made her way around the tables, hugging each one, inquiring about their families. More than one proud papa whipped out an array of baby pictures, and soon croons of *Oooooh* and *Aww* filled the room.

Swinging around to the main table in the center, she was met with a sea of unfamiliar faces looking at her with suspiciously blank expressions. Missing nary a beat, the dialogue continued.

"Forgive me fellas, where're my manners? I'm Sam and I'm a package deal with Captain Martinez." Multiple sets of eyes followed the mysterious woman as she circled the area, lightly grilling each man about what his position was within the unit, and handing out restrained Army hugs.

Acquiring the Army hug had been part of Sam's initial learning curve in those beginning years with the Army. She had no problem hugging the stuffing out of young enlisted, young lieutenants, or even a captain or two; they were all fair game. On the other hand, stalwart sergeants and officers with oak leaves on up—the rank of major and above—required a different touch, one more reminiscent of a stiff-armed waltz, which allowed her to still be friendly without being too personal.

The admission of her relationship with their CO and her presence had startled the newer men as they sat taking in the commotion. Gerry had been riding their tails for the last couple of weeks and animosity had been building. The words blunt, grumpy, and demanding had all been among the softer descriptive terms thrown his way. As the newer men watched the genial whirlwind that swirled around the room, they found themselves laughing along with the older men although they were still apprehensive. There was no way this lady belonged to their CO.

Spying the open door, Sam looked over inquiringly at Stan. *Is that Gerry's office?* was her unspoken question as she cocked her head in the direction of the door. One of the new recruits, having caught the look and being taken in by the joking atmosphere, cheekily answered, "Why sure is, sugar." The sassy comment raised an eyebrow or two, and it would soon come back to torment the youngster.

While Sam was en route toward the open door, another song came on the jukebox, this time by Elvis Presley, and the trio of Stan, Mark and Brady was besieged by another bout of horseplay.

In a flash, all three men were comically on their knees, flashlights in hand, serenading Sam with dramatic and overly exaggerated moves. They never failed to amaze her—they were such rascals, those three. As she stood there, pretending to wipe away tears and holding her hands to her heart, she loved them all for it.

[**GERALD, 2001: Quoted Text From Letter**

"Stan put a song on the jukebox and the next thing I know he, Brady and Mark were clowning around, on their knees serenading you. In a span of five minutes, I watched you achieve what I hadn't been able to do in weeks. In the time it took for you to walk the length of the room, their expressions changed from weariness to smiles, laughter and cracking jokes."]

As Sam finally threaded her way through the tables en route to Gerry's office, a seasoned unit member cast a stern stare at the "fNG" (or more politely called recruit, boots, etc.) who had the audacity to call her Sugar. No one could say when it had begun, but somewhere along the line over the last couple of years, her courtesy title of address, ma'am, had evolved into her name.

Sam was simply called Ma'am, with a capital M. The older soldier marched across the room and stood before the newbie, his stern stare becoming a contemptuous glare.

Leaning forward, he put his hands on his hips while thrusting his face into the boy's as he growled, "Don't know how you were raised, moron, but around here you will address her as Ma'am. You do not address her as Sam. She is not a dearie. She is not a honey and she sure as *hell* is *not* a Sugar. To you, she's Ma'am. Are we clear?"

[**Gerald, 2001: Quoted Text from Letter**

"You walked into my office and kissed me. Not a peck on the cheek, oh no, that would have been too proper. You planted one on me. The unit had gathered outside the door—hooting and hollering, cat calling, applauding their approval. When you realized we had an audience—what did you do? You bowed to the unit. Bowed woman. Only you. You remember all that? It was as if 'heads up people, the queen is in the building.' I thought being a CO was about maintaining control and discipline. You showed me it was about maintaining respect and praise. By the time you left that weekend that unit adored you. Took me weeks to live that kiss down."]

17

FINDING THEIR RHYTHM

*S*am had stayed within arm's length in North Carolina that spring for as long as possible before leaving for Costa Rica, where she had managed to snag a three-week job analyzing burial remains. While visiting on weekends and several times staying for even an extended long weekend whenever her schedule had permitted, she worked to help Gerry find his rhythm.

The soldiers still ribbed Gerry about the kiss and for a bit, every time Sam would walk into that rec room toward Gerry's office, there would be a good-natured *Whoop, Whoop,* like a police siren going off from one of the guys. They had grown to enjoy ribbing Ma'am as much as they did Gerry.

When Sam had first arrived at the base months ago, she had been new to that sector of the base, and Gerry had been anxious to show her around the place to get her impressions. It was during those walkabouts, Sam having taken Gerry's cocked elbow, that their steep learning curves regarding how to schedule their time, and the finding of their common ground, flattened. During those walkabouts, their relationship began to solidify and take on a personality.

For Sam and Gerry, the anchor that common ground provided was more important than ever, for by any definition, their relationship was unconventional for its day and time. Sam's colleagues and friends were aghast at what they deemed a superficial relationship which gave off a cavalier, laissez-faire vibe, and heads shook in wonder at the legendary "two ships passing in the night" attitude. Sam and Gerry both knew their relationship was different, and enjoying the uniqueness that kept it fresh, the couple didn't mind the work it took to keep it so.

To their delight, as they dug into each other's worlds in their quest to unearth that common ground, the couple found it was composed of a solid matrix of "boths." Both had careers, both were organized, both were stubborn and tenacious, and both were driven. There was, however, one glaring difference, one that often made or broke a relationship. And it was this difference that had friends and colleagues running a betting pool as to how long the relationship would last.

Gerry was governed by rules and regulations. He understood, appreciated, and agreed with the need for flexibility in the military and combat—he even espoused it. It was his rules of life that were indelibly engraved in bronze. He lived and died by the book, and he always had a Plan A with backups B and C. For Gerry, life was best lived under the commandment of A + B = C. He was addicted to organization and consistency.

Sam was not. Professionally, she was deliberate, analytical, and organized with a fierce attention to detail, but her personal life, however, was decidedly more free-spirited. Her desk was a quagmire with a system that wasn't always obvious to those around her, and only she could navigate. Like Gerry, she had her Plans A, B, and C for negotiating life's pitfalls. But she also typically had Plans D thru F or even more floating in the background. Flying by the seat of her pants fit Sam's personality well, and she had no qualms about switching between plans at a moment's notice.

And then there was "Time." For those betting on the couple, when the issue of competing schedules was factored into the equation, it seemed all bets were off. It was during those walkabouts on that base, when Gerry and Sam reworked their concept of time, and it was reflected in a simple handwritten sign that hung on a wall in Gerry's apartment in North Carolina: *Her Time + My Time ≠ Our Time*. The phrase described their philosophy and it reigned with impunity. The concept of time governed the couple's world.

The couple had divided their time into two categories. There was Her Time and His Time in one group, and then there was "Our Time" in the second. Running side-by-side, Her and His Times were for the careers of Doctor Sam and Army Gerry, and respecting their sanctity, neither allowed much to intervene with their attention focused solely on the task at hand. Those career timelines marched forward in a linear fashion, with goals to be achieved and deadlines to be met, casting aside anything that stood in their way.

Their separate careers left little time for their relationship, so they created a new dimension of time that could be superimposed on those career timelines, much like the storm layer on an online weather radar map. They called their private dimension "Our Time," and gave it autonomy and the same importance and authority to rule, as their careers.

"Our Time" consisted of pockets of moments. They weren't spontaneous, but were rather created, carved out pauses within their careers. At the core of Sam's and Gerry's "Our Time" lay their competing schedules. As a rule, Sam's academic schedule was more flexible than Gerry's rigid Army roster. Depending on the term's teaching schedule and her forensic case or research load, she would take a Friday afternoon flight or train out and return on a red-eye Sunday night, or the wee hours on Monday morning.

Likewise, if Gerry's Army schedule was weekly, then they alternated weekends, with him coming to her. During those weekends, Army Gerry and Doctor Sam ceased to exist, only to reemerge come Monday morning. During "Our Time," careers were put on the back burner.

In contrast to the career timelines, "Our Time" was flexible. If Gerry's Army schedule was a week or two per month off, he would then join Sam at her home, or in the field for those weeks. If Sam was in between academic terms and research projects, then she would go stay with Gerry at his base station for those weeks. "Our Time" was adaptable, and during the weeks-long field seasons or months-long deployments, where coming together wasn't possible, it spun around letters and a phone where they would read a book together.

"Our Time" transcended being just a concept; it was a living entity that could be a demanding dictator. It required constant vigilance and subservience, for in order for it to exist and function, the packets of time had to be carved out and maintained. It was tempting to steal a few hours here or there when obligations swelled, but "Our Time," intolerant of career pressures, would refuse to yield, expecting its demands to be met.

Regardless of where they each were or what they were doing, "Our Time" hovered and bound the couple together. It didn't belong to Army Gerry or Doctor Sam. It belonged to Sam and Gerry, and they guarded it with the ferocity attributed to a parent protecting its young.

At first, the tug and pull of each one's lifestyle with them trying to maintain their professional careers as before, but yet make time for each other, made things seem misplaced and out of sync. But soon, the tug-of-war became a dance, where the orchestration of their schedules moved in tandem to a clicking metronome, and through it, they learned to live in the moment.

They learned how not to get hung up on where they were expected to be, who was in charge, or even who was right. They learned to just revel in and appreciate when the laws of physics regarding time and space, brought them together for a moment.

That dance was a slow relaxing waltz, where they effortlessly glided into each other's schedule as easily as they did into each other's arms on a lazy Saturday evening, or into that Army base in North Carolina.

North Carolina, 1983

Nowhere were the differences in their approach to life more apparent than in civilian social situations where Gerry's A + B approach didn't tally with a more freewheeling civilian society. Sam's abbreviated field season in Costa Rica had come to a close, and she chose to return to Gerry's home in North Carolina rather than to hers in Missouri. The three-week stretch that remained of her summer hiatus was a golden window of time where in the solitude of Gerry's off-base apartment, Sam spent the days studying for grad school, catching up and preparing for med school, and finishing her field reports from Costa Rica.

From her conversation with the psychiatrist months earlier, after the Officers' Ball altercation, Sam now knew what Gerry was dealing with. It had a name, Extreme Shyness, that sometimes could descend into social anxiety, and it was a gift from his time on the streets. Sam researched the condition and the available treatment protocols, and the ones that had caught her eye—the ones that when she read about them, she leaned back in her chair and smiled—were exposure therapy and role playing as coping mechanisms.

Within the confines of the Army, Gerry knew his role and place without question, but his larger role as captain placed him in more social settings than ever before, both among his peers and off-base. Soon to be deployed overseas to Germany, someplace he had never been, Gerry fretted a bit. Recognizing his heavy reliance on Sam to both coax him out of his shyness, and to guide him in social settings, he began to worry that over in Germany, he would muck it up.

Stan and Sam spent as much time as possible helping, introducing Gerry to a wide variety of situations he would encounter. Many were in real time, going to restaurants or ball games, attending gatherings, or even just strolling in a park watching children play. All the things he wasn't exposed to as a child. Many other times, however, there were staged charades, little skits or parodies where he could try out various responses, hear how they sounded and felt, until they rolled off his tongue with ease.

At times Sam would ramp up the comedy and would dress up as a German barmaid serving beer during Oktoberfest, a store clerk giving him the run around, or act out various commanders he would be serving under while in Germany. She thought she would start with an easy one, Lt. Colonel Lawson, a commander Gerry already was at ease with.

Sam stood in the bedroom, adjusting the jacket, and a look of disgust crossed her face as she viewed herself in the mirror. She was a caricature. Of her Musketeers, Stan's uniform was the closest to fit her, but even as she tugged at the shoulders and arms, it was a hopeless cause. She had used rope as suspenders to keep the pants up and was now struggling to keep the jacket on. It was Stan's dress jacket and she didn't want to wrinkle it too much, so she had carefully rolled up the sleeves and used large rubber bands to hold them in place.

Standing in front of the mirror, she placed the dress cap on her head, adjusting the angle just right. She had been studying Lawson's mannerisms for days, trying to catch his carriage of the shoulders, the way he flicked his cigarette when animated. With a final silent rehearsal of the man's gait, she nodded at her image in the mirror, *It's now or never sweetheart,* and flung open the door into the living room.

Lawson had a unique stride, and as she strutted across the living room like some runway fashion model with a hip disorder, Sam knew she had nailed it. Gerry started hiccupping, almost strangling himself in his attempt to maintain his composure as he roared in hysterics. Gerry would be expected to handle units in front of the commander at times or to give meeting updates, and Sam wanted no glitches.

After making a circuit around the small living room, pretending to be Lawson inspecting nonexistent units, Sam parked herself in front of Gerry, her arms crossed, Lawson-style, flicking a dusting cloth as if it were a cigarette.

Having met the man only once before, Sam was making it up as she went along, and in trying to keep it lighthearted, she opted for the satirical approach rather than factual. She found herself drawing upon every war movie she had ever seen, and John Wayne loomed large.

"Martinez! Up, front and center! Assemble the troops for review and I want to see the whites of their eyes!" Sam bellowed as quietly as she could, given they were in Gerry's apartment. Gerry was still struggling to regain his composure as the dress cap slid down Sam's face.

Maintaining her character, Sam barked, "Why are you laughing?

Stand at attention, boy," smacking him in the small of his back with the dusting cloth, and Gerry snapped rigid in attention.

"Yes, ma'am," he said, forgetting she was Lawson.

"Ma'am?! Where do you think you are? The bar? I will have you cleaning the latrines for that remark!" A thought drew Sam up straight as it went through her head and she dropped out of character for a moment as she whispered to Gerry, "Do they even call them latrines anymore?"

The charade continued as Gerry gave his "update" to the pillows lined up on the couch and Sam, as Lawson, would sigh ridiculously, ask the pillows and lamp for their opinions and suggestions, and cross her arms as if not impressed. So uninspired by Gerry's oration, she made him run through it several more times. It was all Gerry could do to finish his part.

"Did I say at ease? What do you have to say to me?" Sam playfully growled as she flicked the dust cloth she still had in her hands at him. Gerry pulled himself together from laughing and walked up to Sam, removing the cap from her head while putting his arms around her, and then bent down for a kiss.

Standing with her head against his neck, Sam murmured, "You know, I don't know how the Army does things, but I'm pretty sure it's not a good idea for you to kiss your CO." Gerry pushed her away to look her in the face, his eyes widened in horror.

"Oh geez, thanks a lot for that image!" he said before turning away to sit back down on the couch with a shudder.

"Oh, it could be worse!" Sam yelled out as she left for the kitchen, and Gerry only screwed his face in disbelief as he yelled back,

"How?"

"Well," Sam said as she stuck her head around the corner to look at him, "You could do what many of us who lecture do." At Gerry's expression of *Huh?* Sam explained. "You know, when apprehensive about lecturing in front of a huge crowd, it is often suggested to imagine everyone in their underwear. You could be standing in front of Lawson wondering if he was wearing boxers or briefs." She chuckled as she disappeared back into the kitchen.

Gerry sat motionless on the couch, his mouth still open in disbelief, when he heard Sam suddenly exclaimed, "Ooh, ooh," as she excitedly came running back into the living room with an impish smirk on her face, "Or maybe, Lawson wears one of those newfangled thongy underwear things!" She waved her hands behind her as she demonstrated on her rump, before disappearing back into the kitchen.

Gerry just closed his eyes, thinking *Oh my God…I will never be able to face that man again.*

But it was when Stan would join them that Gerry found himself stretching his limits. Not only was it two against one, with the tempo of Sam's and Stan's incoming salvos growing faster and more intense, Stan was also a master of manipulation, and in knowing Gerry so well, he knew which buttons to push and where they were hidden.

In keeping with their deployment destination of Germany, the old TV series of *Hogan's Heroes*, set in WWII in a German prison camp, was adopted as the running theme.

While the three friends had their own comedy hour of charades going weekly with Stan's performance of the character Sergeant Schultz sending the trio to the floor, the skits had the serious purpose of exposing Gerry to possible scenarios, even if they were fictitious. Using Gerry's knowledge of military history, and of WWII in particular, they hit upon familiar themes and topics and held debates on campaign strategy, all while in the characters of Hogan, Schultz, and Klink.

They invented scenarios where Hogan and General Patton conspired against Schultz and Klink, where Patton got Klink drunk at a bar while Schultz stood by repeating his well-known line of claiming to know nothing! They rewrote history where Hitler and Chamberlain found themselves on the beach of Omaha during D-day running for their lives, as Lawson roared after them in a tank, gun barrel blazing. They were endings no history book would ever recognize.

For all of Sam's role-playing and dress rehearsals, however, it was an unexpected incident that showed her just how far Gerry had progressed, and drove home just how well he was beginning to assimilate into social settings. Gerry worried about Sam. She was at times, in his view, surrounded by unsavory characters, both in the field and in forensics, and he wanted her to know how to defend herself, and be confident in handling herself in uncomfortable situations.

Along with basic defense moves, Gerry was steadfast in his belief that Sam should know how to box. Moreover, he wanted her to be able to hold her own in the boxing ring. At the end of one sparring session, he had misjudged her determination and had let his guard down—she clocked him a good one, without gloves.

The black eye that had resulted from that punch was impressive and a humiliated Gerry dreaded the ribbing and jokes that any self-respecting unit would undoubtedly throw at him. An unsympathetic Sam, however, basked in the glow of her lucky shot as she playfully mocked him.

"Aww, honey, just get it over with!" With a huge, crooked grin on her face, she held his face in her hand as she inspected the eye, taking in the rainbow of colors. "Oooh, I see a couple of colors I've never seen before!" she teased devilishly.

Peeved by Sam's lack of pity, Gerry was ornery as he watched her wipe down the kitchen counter with the sink sponge, and he sniped, "Get it over with? Get what over with?"

As Sam stopped in front of Gerry, she tapped him on the chest with the edge of the sponge as she spoke, "Just let them get it out of their systems! Stand in the middle of the room and let them take pot shots at ya."

Gerry had viewed Sam's advice with scorn and derision. *Let them take pot shots at me? Not a chance,* he blustered to himself as he headed across the rec room toward his office, but from the amused looks and snickers that followed him, he knew the word had gotten out. *Get it over with,* Sam had said.

Okay. I can do that, Gerry thought as he abruptly stopped and spun on his heel. Facing the room, he held his arms out.

"Okay, let me have it, fellas. Have your fun. Give it your best shot."

One of the men, blubbering with laughter, lampooned Gerry as he called out, "Looks like Ma'am already did!" This sent the room rolling in convulsions as Gerry stood there, acknowledging the mockery.

Two soldiers sat side by side in chairs, leaning against the back wall, balanced on the rear chair legs with their arms crossed over their bellies. One cheekily leaned over to his companion as he deliberated Ma'am's possible boxing style. "Hmm. What do you think? Ma'am a boxer-puncher or a slugger?" He was barely able to keep the smirk off his face.

The other soldier made a show of pondering a bit before he jeeringly quipped, "Looks like Ma'am might be more of an out-puncher to me!" He then called out to Gerry, "May we recommend some quality practice time with the bob-and-weave maneuver, sir," the "sir" barely audible in a cloud of giggles.

"Wow, she clobbered you a good one!" a private marveled as he walked up for a closer look. "Sir...how did she..." He did not finish his question as he stared in amazement.

Not wanting to admit that Sam had snuck one by him, Gerry shook his head as he offered an excuse in his defense. "Hey guys, she caught me unaware. I was bent over, off guard..." he said, but he was interrupted by a barb that came flying from across the room.

"Ah...so you're saying you were unfocused and unprepared while confronting a superior foe?" one of the men said, parroting a line Gerry often used during training.

"Okay guys, we're done here," Gerry said with a laugh as he turned to go to his office.

But just as his hand reached the handle, a soldier called out, "Ya know, sir, I've always respected Ma'am. Now...I'm downright scared of her!"

Grateful at how lighthearted the teasing had been, a huge grin broke out over Gerry's face as he looked back over his shoulder and said, "You should be! She packs a powerful wallop!"

18

WELCOME TO CHAOS!

*T*here were no shortages of topics to use in those skits, for weather, politics, history, famous people were all readily available and eagerly scooped up. The more skits and role playing Sam and Stan threw at Gerry, the more proficient he became at absorbing their impacts.

As the date for deployment drew near, Gerry was pleasantly shocked to realize he wasn't fretting as much about Germany anymore. The topic of conversation turned toward a leisurely last get together with the gang—Sam and her Four Musketeers.

Boston, Following Week

They settled on the weekend before they were scheduled to leave, where they managed to find a day where all five had a clear spot—Boston was on. Gerry loved Boston, not the streets he had left behind, but the history and charm of the wharfs, the Boston with its colonial architecture, cobblestone streets, and historic brass adornments. Whenever possible, the gang would meet there.

As Gerry packed last-minute overnight bags, Sam used the excuse to run to the drugstore for more toothpaste, but she had plenty. She was down a different aisle for a home pregnancy test.

Home pregnancy tests were new back then—a revolution on how women, and men for that matter, handled that dramatic shift in priorities. Sam hid the package from Gerry, not wanting him to know anything until she was sure. It was positive and a stop in a clinic later confirmed it. She was pregnant. There was nothing like a dose of cause and effect to draw you up short and she had spent the last week deliberating, taking in the news.

What did she want and how was she going to get it? She told Gerry the night before they left for the Boston get-together. Gerry considered a phrase of three syllables excessively wordy, and Sam hadn't thought it was possible for him to be any more silent, but he was. He was a deer caught in headlights.

It was Mark who put it together. There had been little clues along the way, but what gave it away was the neon sign with the big flashing arrow over her midsection. She had ordered an iced tea instead of a beer. Brady was a tad slower on the uptake, but when it sank in, a huge grin spread across his face like an avalanche, slow at first, just a rumble, but once unleashed, the rush could not be contained. Jumping out of his chair, Brady rushed over to Sam and knelt down on the floor next to her chair.

"You…you…you're pregnant?" He was astounded at the news.

Annoyed at Brady's look of disbelief, Sam snarkily quipped, "It's been known to happen in the history of humanity. You don't have to act so shocked." Mark and Brady looked at each other for a second, and then hollered out at about the same time in the crowded café.

"We're gonna have a baaabbbbyyyy!" but Mark stopped short, his eyes wide open as if he just thought of something, and he turned back to Sam asking, "It is a baby, right?" Only to yodel out again, "We're gonna have a baaabbbbyyyy!"

An astonished Sam could only nod an affirmative as she watched the two make a spectacle of themselves. Gerry, still the deer in headlights, sat there looking extremely uncomfortable as his buddies ran around the table in a frenzy. His effort to calm the storm was to no avail when Stan, who couldn't contain himself any longer, rose from his seat and burst out into a song that celebrated the wonder of having a child.

Multiple sets of mesmerized eyes followed Stan as he strolled through the seated tables, crooning out the lyrics. He stopped in front of one table and locked eyes with the three young women who sat adoringly swooning. Sam sat slouched back in her chair, shaking her head in wonderment at the scene as Stan continued his performance in unabashed glory.

Gerry looked horrified, and every time Stan looked their way, Gerry tried to motion for him to sit down, but Stan just pretended he didn't see him. As Stan belted out the final chorus, the crowd erupted in applause and shouts of encore, and excited congratulations for Sam could be heard over the commotion.

"Well…I think I need a refill," Sam briskly announced as she got up to head over to the coffee bar station. Several waitresses leaned over the bar, making eyes at Stan as he snaked his way back through the tables to where the group was sitting.

"I think my knees just buckled," one of the waitresses remarked dreamily as she sighed. Her companion, staring with infatuation, wistfully told her, "Be careful not to fall on top of me. I'm already on the floor." A middle-aged waitress, armed with a no-nonsense demeanor and a towel over her shoulder, sauntered up to the counter and fixed Sam with a questioning look that hovered between disgust and impressed.

"You know, most women normally settle for just one fella, but you? You have four?" Rolling her eyes at Sam, she scoffed, "Oh honey, they've got to have medication for this!"

"Oh my heavens, no, no, no!" Sam laughed as she busied herself with adding lemon to her iced tea. She dryly remarked to the waitresses that worldwide, usually it's the men who have multiple wives, not women having multiple husbands. Looking up at the women across the bar, Sam added baldly, "There's a reason for that, ladies— one's enough!" Looking over at the table, Sam motioned with the iced tea spoon, "The second tallest one with dark hair is mine, the other three are collateral baggage." The waitress with the dreamy sigh perked up at the comment.

"Oh, so the ebony Greek god is available?" Hope shone in her eyes at the thought.

Sam just scoffed while tossing her head, "Depends on your definition. That boy plays the field so you'll have to take a number to get on his schedule, and he's the biggest child I've ever seen. He just was released from Army purgatory and I have no doubt they're keeping the lights on for him. He'll be back." Her voice was full of exasperated frustration.

The older waitress leaned over the counter, eyeing Stan while she suspiciously asked, "What'd he do?"

Sam could only snort a derisive answer as she collected her tea and turned to head back to her table. "This time? Let's see…he broke into his CO's quarters, stole the man's shorts, and ran them up a flagpole for all to salute. It's a very old joke, with a very predictable outcome, and shock of all shocks, the CO was predictably…" Sam paused as she searched for a socially acceptable word to use. She settled on "unhappy."

The dreamy waitress held her chin in her hand while she leaned over the counter watching, as Sam collected the four men and headed out the door onto the street.

He can run my shorts up a flagpole any day, she thought with a sigh.

[Samantha, 2024: Quoted Text from Letter

"I fell in love with you on a beautiful, sunny early summer day in Boston, a last-minute get together before you all deployed. You, Stan, Brady, and Mark—my four Musketeers—we were all happy and carefree as we enjoyed the moment. You all were in your day duds that day and we left the café for the wharf, remember? We passed a small park along the thoroughfare where some moms with their young kids were enjoying the summer breeze—four little girls, all in pigtails and bright summer shifts, wearing sandals. A boombox was playing and just as we got up alongside of them, Bad Moon Rising began to play, and the little girls gleefully began to dance to the beat. Stan, Oh that man was unbelievable, and I know why he was so important to you, hon, why he was such a good friend.

"Stan squatted down and began to dance with one of the little girls and in a flash, each of you scooped up a little girl and began to dance too. I stood there just watching this scene, totally transfixed while mesmerized and captivated. You three all squatting, dancing this cute but funky little sidestep while Mark, being so tall, simply picked up his partner in his arms, her little legs swaying to his movements as he danced. Your hands dwarfed the hands of the little girls as you held them.

"Times were different back then and no one feared you guys would hurt them and people on the sidewalk, people in the park, the moms and me all watched you—four rather large men in military uniforms behaving with the joy of children. When the song ended, the onlookers groaned, the moms applauded, the little girls curtsied and you four bowed. I was so proud to be there with you and that moment is one of my most precious memories, one that will be forever cherished."]

IN THE FEW remaining days before Gerry's departure for Germany, Sam and Gerry wrestled with the prospect of being parents, and all that it encompassed, the good and the bad. Everything had been upended and they began to talk about what they each wanted. Sam was adamant, she would have the child regardless of whether they kept it, but she knew. While the conversation had floated around adoption, she knew that wasn't going to fly for her. Sam wanted it to be a joint decision, but Gerry's game plan was avoidance—that and feigned ignorance. Gerry had sidestepped any culpability by blithely announcing, "It's your decision," as if he hadn't been a party to it.

Sam caustically shot back, "News flash, this was not an immaculate conception—you were there. This is just as much your decision as it is mine. Don't you dare act as if it's mine to take care of."

To say Gerry was reeling was an understatement. He had no foundation from which to draw, no family experiences, and underneath it all, despite the phenomenal gains he had made in his social development over the last year, he was still very much a child of the streets.

Early on, neither of them had wished to marry because there were too many complications. She, at this time of her life, strove to make it in a man's world where women were still considered a novelty, and faced an uphill battle. Sam had learned quickly and early that no exceptions or leeway would be given for family issues. Having a husband was a liability, for it was viewed that her loyalties were divided, and her job performance would suffer. Having children was out of the question.

He, on the other hand, did not understand the concept whatsoever. Street life had a code, a creed with its rules, and Gerry found he was content with swapping out the street code for the Army code. While the Army instilled a shell of family life, the social concept of family eluded Gerry. His childhood on the streets was rough, with friendships and loyalty being earned and maintained vigorously.

If you dropped the ball, they would drop you, sometimes permanently—friend or not. He had buddies, even deep, long-lasting friendships in the Army and some, like the Musketeers of Stan, Mark, and Brady, he would even die for. But again, that devotion was earned. To Gerry, society didn't seem to have rules—everyone and every family was out for themselves. To have that level of devotion and honor automatically bestowed at birth, rather than earned, was almost incomprehensible to him.

Gerry needed time to process, and he didn't see how he was going to do that in Germany, so he went straight to Lt. Colonel Lawson.

"I'd like to be excused from deployment, sir," Gerry asked as he was standing in Lawson's office, hoping for a waiver.

Gerry's request came as a surprise to Lawson, for he had been keeping tabs on Gerry over the past months since the Ball, and was pleased at how well he was doing.

"What's this about?" Lawson asked, barely looking up from his paperwork. Gerry tiptoed around the subject, reluctant to give anything but the basics.

"Ah, Samantha, sir."

At the silence that followed Gerry's simple answer, Lawson looked up and worriedly asked, "Everything okay?" He caught Gerry's uncomfortable shift in his stance before the young man answered.

"No sir, she…ah…she has a medical situation, sir." After hemming and hawing a few more seconds, Gerry finally admitted, "She's pregnant, sir."

"Pregnant?" At Lawson's tone of disbelief, Gerry suddenly felt compelled to explain what Sam being pregnant meant.

"Yes, sir…ah…you know, like, she's gonna have a baby."

"I know what pregnant means. I have four kids of my own." Lawson sighed as irritation washed over him, for he could not believe Gerry was standing in his office over this. "Martinez, a woman being pregnant is not a medical crisis."

"But sir—" Gerry tried to interrupt but Lawson cut him off.

"I'm going to tell you what my wife told me with our first child. Mother Nature has gifted the females of the species to give birth, and they have done so for millions of years. They have it down pat. As humbling as it is to hear, my wife didn't need me then, and Sam doesn't need you now. She will be fine." Gerry's face fell when he realized, as Lawson continued, he was still headed for Germany.

Lawson heaved a sigh at Gerry as he told him, "Military wives are Atlas, Hercules, and Alexander the Great combined, and they conquer all. I've never met one that couldn't, for they are a breed all their own. Your request is hereby denied," Lawson announced, throwing his pen and pad aside with a flourish as he leaned back in his chair. "What I will do for you, however, is try to get you home in time for the birth. Congratulations, Dad." The slight smile on his face erupted into a broad grin as he devilishly chuckled, "Welcome to chaos!"

Gerry began to hover over Sam, incessantly. Vacuuming was too stressful, shopping was too demanding, and doing the dishes was too hard on her back. That final day, the day Gerry was due to leave for Germany within hours, he thought he would do one last thing…he decided to do the laundry. There are men who understand the concept of separating laundry loads, and are better at doing laundry than the women in their lives.

Gerry was not one of them. For him, there were only two colors, Army green and the ever-popular desert khaki or tan, what more did he need? While Sam was taking a quick nap, Gerry grabbed the laundry basket and dumped the entire contents into the washer, and decided hot water temperature would be good while he poured in the laundry powder, adding extra for good measure.

Sam woke up to the noise of the washer spinning off balance, and to Gerry sitting at the kitchen table filling out some paperwork.

"Thought I'd do some laundry for you," he offered as an explanation when he saw Sam's skeptical look toward the laundry cubicle. Stopping the cycle, Sam had peered into the basket and Gerry heard a gasp of *Oh no* from the backroom. The chair scooted on the floor with a screech as Gerry bolted toward the washing machine, and he found Sam standing with a look of total dismay. As she pulled out the items, they were all varying shades of pink. Shirts, underwear, socks, everything was pink. Standing with socks in one hand and dish towels in the other, Sam flung a look of disdain at Gerry.

"Gerry, you didn't sort the loads!" Sam disgustedly sniped at Gerry, who defensively blurted out, "Sort? Why does it matter if your stuff is mixed in with mine?"

As Sam pulled out what had been a white shirt used for teaching, now a less than lovely shade of muddy, dingy pink, she lobbed yet another glance at Gerry, this one peeved. "No...sort according to dark colors!" Gerry's impromptu lesson in laundry hit home when Sam gingerly pulled out his underwear, no longer regulation, but rather more of a mauve, perhaps even a dusty rose. Staring at the growing pile Sam was dumping on the floor, Gerry frantically muttered *No, no, no* as he raced over and began to pull all his stuff out. He had thrown it all in for one last wash; socks, underwear, T-shirts, everything he had.

Holding his T-shirts and briefs, Gerry stared incomprehensibly at Sam, "How did this..." as Sam held up the perpetrator, a maroon tunic whose hue was now muted from the hot water. The comical look on

Gerry's face caused Sam to giggle for a second as she told him to just grab extras and repack, but he couldn't. The socks and T-shirts were not an issue, but he was out of briefs. He had thrown in every pair he had in the load.

"Well," Sam said as she dropped the washer lid down with a bang, "guess you're going to Germany in pink underwear."

Checking his watch, Gerry started to run around, gathering stuff and yelling out, "If we hurry, we can pick some more up on the way."

"Pick them up on the way?" Sam scoffed as she reminded him, "Gerry, you can't buy those briefs just anywhere. I get those from that hoity-toity place in Chicago, remember?" His quiet *Aw crap* was heard when the realization of what Sam said hit him. Yelling out from the bedroom as she pulled out more clothing for him, Sam told him to decide.

"You are always harping about how being an officer is about making decisions. Well...you get to make one. You can either wear pink, buy regular undies, or not wear any at all. Take your pick, but make it quick! We need to pick up Stan so we need to get a move on— we leave in a couple of hours!"

He opted for pink.

The trio of Sam, Gerry, and Stan stood in the visitor area behind the fencing along with the throng of other family well-wishers saying their goodbyes. Looking to break the tension, Stan leaned in and hugged Sam, and then held her at arm's length, telling her, "Ya gonna miss me, y'know," his saucy grin growing ever-wider. Sam had long since become impervious to that smile of his, but he still struck a chord with her.

"Naw, I'm going to enjoy the peace and quiet without you strutting around as if you're in some Chippendale review!"

Stan did a slight chortle as he returned his quip. "Hey, I'm Mr. April..." His voice trailed off a bit. A sense of déjà vu came over the two as Sam and Stan both realized that they'd had this conversation before...on a dirt street outside of a *cantina* back in Arizona. Pleased that they had remembered that day, lazy smiles grew on their faces as Sam went on to finish what was to become a time-honored routine.

"Really? Oh please!" Sam had tossed out at Stan as she turned toward Gerry. Wrapping his arms around her in a bear hug, Gerry suddenly jerked her back looking at her midsection, afraid he had hugged her too tight, which only had Sam laughing, "I'm pregnant, not dying!"

Holding Sam by the shoulders, Gerry tried to say something more about the baby, but what came out were merely scratchy whispered squeaks. Sam cupped his face with her hand as she told him, "Hey, I'll be fine. We'll talk when you get back. All is good."

Nodding his okay and wrapping his arms around her for a final hug, Gerry whispered for Sam to stay at his place for as long as she wanted. He knew she was due in Missouri next month, but he was possessed by a nagging uneasiness as he and Sam stood there. As silly as it sounded, Gerry was more at peace knowing Sam was at his apartment in North Carolina, rather than hers in Missouri. Maybe it was knowing that the base community was there for her.

Brady and Mark, while each on their own path, were both only a stone's throw away if she needed them. Maybe it was that Lawson's wife Colleen had maternally announced she would be checking up on Sam regularly. While he couldn't quite put his finger on how to describe the feeling, he did know where it came from—the next time he would see Sam, he would be just weeks from being a dad. The thought made him draw Sam in even closer in a tighter hug.

Inhaling deeply, Sam took it all in, the smell of laundry soap, the smell of the duffel with its distinct Army scent, elusive to describe, an eclectic mix of gunpowder, dirt, sweat, machine oil, and a hint of something else, so vague and intangible that Sam hadn't been able to identify it. With surprise, she also smelled fresh aftershave.

Pulling back, Sam chimed, "You shaved?" in a shocked voice.

Gerry asked back, "You're surprised?" wondering why Sam would even notice.

"Well, yeah. You're going on a plane with a bunch of guys for hours at which, at the end, you will be grumpy, grungy, and downright nasty to be around," Sam's tone so matter of fact.

"Well, Hon," Gerry joked as he drew himself to his full height of mock self-importance. "I'm officer material now, I can't be looking like something the cat dragged in. Besides…" Gerry paused as he drew Sam back in against him again, "I wanted this last hug, and I know how you are about beards."

The moments where soldiers' families said goodbye before deployment were always somber. Stan had heard Gerry's remark about Sam not being fond of beards, and he seized the opportunity to poke some fun at her while lightening the mood.

Accentuating his southern drawl with a fake higher female voice, he swaggered a bit, imitating Sam's mannerisms, and then threw an invisible feather boa over his shoulder. "If I wanna cuddle up with a porcupine, I'll get myself a room at the zoo!"

A chorus of laughter and groans erupted from several of the nearby men, but the joking ended abruptly when someone shouted out in a terse business voice, "Yo people, incoming, three o'clock." It was Lt. Colonel Lawson arriving and the atmosphere lingering behind the fence shifted with a sense of finality.

As Lawson strode toward the plane, his booming voice bellowed out a sound wave, "Okay people, let's break it up."

Sam had been surprised at her level of disappointment. She had been eagerly anticipating it, and was saddened, upset even, when Gerry hadn't given it to her. She had been expecting to be given a book for them to read together, the "deployment book." After that first book, *Cosmos* by Sagan, there had been another tome to entertain them during their second rotation together—a fiction novel that they read together over the weeks and months apart.

Their worlds were separated by over 4,000 miles and six or more hours, but while each read on opposite sides of the world, they found themselves feeling the other's presence in the chair with them at a sunset, reading the same words. Within its pages, time and distance became manageable.

After reaching into his duffel, Gerry finally pulled out what Sam had begun to think he had forgotten. She wondered what he had chosen this time as she unwrapped the paper bag. *Science fiction, of course,* Sam thought laughing to herself as she read the book's title,

Timescape by Gregory Benford. Gerry had marked the page numbers with little dividers for how much she was to read each week so they would be in sync, and as he stood watching as Sam read the back jacket, her smile told him he had chosen well.

Taking his face in her hands, she tenderly told Gerry, "You are gonna knock 'em dead! No worries!" And with a curt nod of her head, she shooed him, "Now go on, get."

As he turned to motion to Stan and other members of his unit that it was time to get moving, Gerry murmured to Sam, "I'll call you when I can," but his attention was drawn over to where Lawson was reviewing and supervising an issue with the loading of the plane.

Sam, noting his gaze, silently leaned over and questioned, "Everything okay?"

Gerry pondered for another second as he studied Lawson some more before whispering conspiratorially, "No way he's wearing thong underwear. I'm going with boxers over briefs, what do you think?" his eyes dancing with laughter as he tried to keep a straight face.

Sam's astonishment at his remark had momentarily caught her off guard, but as Gerry and Stan shouldered their duffels, and worked their way through the crowd onto the tarmac toward the plane, she thought, *He's going to do just fine.*

They were already joshing and joking with other soldiers in that unique camaraderie that units have, and as Sam turned to leave the rail, she was expecting to be a distant memory before the wheels even left the runway.

Gerry settled in his seat, and patted the side pocket of his duffel, feeling for the edge of a legal pad. He had learned his lesson the previous year with his and Sam's first real goodbye. It had been more emotional than he expected, and he realized as the plane lumbered down the runway, that he had forgotten to say something in the moment. A subdued *Aw crap* escaped him, but had been loud enough for a nearby officer across the aisle to hear him, and sheepishly, Gerry glanced over and admitted, "I forgot to tell her about the bloody stove," not needing to explain who "her" was.

The officer had just chuckled a bit before advising Gerry nonchalantly, "Just write her a note and we'll post it when we land. No big deal. I'm always remembering things I forgot to tell my wife. I just drop a note in the mail bag when we land."

Reflexively Gerry wondered, "Wouldn't it be easier just to call her, sir?" The officer had smiled slightly as he shared a thought.

"Maybe...but it's better to write. You say more...and you say it better." The tilt of his head spoke of what the officer didn't say out loud. And that officer had been right, Gerry did find it easier to say things in a note.

Gerry needed to talk about the baby, marriage, everything it seemed. They had tried to discuss it over the kitchen table, but he was stymied as to how to describe the uncertainty and fear of something he had never experienced. Growing up he had no family, no parents or siblings, and he didn't really know where to start. There had been one sentence that Sam had said that chilled him to his bones.

You will now be responsible for something that will depend on you for everything. He was still comprehending the magnitude of that comment, which Sam seemed to accept so easily.

Gerry kept stalling for time by arranging the pens, making minute adjustments in the angle of the pad, pouring himself some coffee. He had so many fears, questions about the baby, about being a father and husband, and at first, he scratched out more than he wrote. He would rip a page out, crumple it up and start all over again, numerous times. The words were there just under the surface, he just couldn't find them and in frustration, he began to just jot down bullet points. When the plane landed on the other side of the Atlantic, hours later, Gerry looked down in dismay at what he had written—only three abbreviated paragraphs.

This wasn't such a good idea after all, he thought. He put the legal pad away, and forgot about it, until the weekend phone call home to Sam. Suddenly, across the ocean on another continent, he had a ton of questions and worries he hadn't realized he had. Now, with her on the phone, as in his apartment back home in North Carolina, he couldn't say them. At the end of that call, he dug out the legal pad with his three paragraphs and wrote.

Friday night…I called you today. You sounded so tired. I wondered if… It was only another paragraph or so, but the questions came forth and were written down. The following week, after he had called Sam, he pulled out the legal pad again, and jotted down more thoughts and questions as he added to the bottom.

After a month or so, Gerry mailed his first real deployment letter to Sam, now back in Missouri for the term.

19

THEY PLOTTED FOR WEEKS

On the drive home to Missouri, Sam reflected on her life's sudden change in direction, and with Gerry away in Germany, she had many alone hours to spend wondering. Her focus was now not just on teaching, or forensics, or preparing for the upcoming field season, or medical school, or graduate school.

The pregnancy had commanded her full attention as she wrestled with its implications. As she turned west along the back side of Charleston, West Virginia and began her trek toward home, Sam forced her mind to begin reviewing her current forensic case, and its impending court date next month.

The miles ticked by in tandem with Sam ticking off her mental checklist of procedures and protocols, inwardly making notes of what to double check and document, what facts and data to have at her fingertips. She ticked off her last box as she pulled into the parking lot of her apartment building.

[Gerald, 2001: Quoted Text From Letter

"But this is all my side of our story. Yours is utterly amazing. You seem so comfortable in so many areas whether it be field work, academia, or forensics. How one person can excel at all of them is beyond me but you rock them all. I loved watching you testify. I never knew that trial law was such a game of chess, game of poker, magic show with sleight of hand. Your tenacity to the details sometimes drove me nuts but it was what made you so solid on the stand. I'd watch as lawyers would try to trip you up, try to twist facts to fit their narrative.

"Remember that moron who after failing repeatedly to break you, had the audacity to ask if you were having your period while collecting evidence? Implied you women were incapable of function while so hormonally addled. That women were scared of dealing with tough men and thus easily swayed. You didn't miss a beat. In that amazing southern drawl you can slide into with such incredible ease [you said]—'I'm so sorry dear, you're going to have to repeat that whole thing—you know how us feeble minded women get—we can't hear a damn thing when our knees knock together.' The prosecutor later told me that moment won the case for them."]

Missouri, 1983, Weeks Later

Sam was running late. The fatigue and nausea of first trimester pregnancy still plagued her and that morning had been rougher than usual. Her forensic load weighed heavily on her mind, and she had been up all night documenting and preparing evidence to be submitted for a case that she was nowhere near ready for. Teaching obligations had been shoved to the end of the line and had begun to suffer. On the drive into campus, Sam frantically reviewed the lecture for that morning's class.

Sam loved teaching—she found it exhilarating. Growing up as a child, Sam's parents demanded her presence at the dinner table. Conversations around that table, where newcomers were welcomed, were polite but lively. Opinions were readily given and debates encouraged, but only if they were backed up with rigorous facts, and the skill of thinking fast on your feet served dining combatants well, for those who dawdled, were skewered. Those dinners percolated into

Sam's view of life, and into her way of teaching. While her course curriculums were well planned and executed, her lectures themselves, on the other hand, were often freewheeling events reminiscent of those dinners.

[GERALD, 2001: Quoted Text From Letter

"I loved listening to you give lectures. You can take the most complex topics and condense them down to the most simple common denominator. They become so clear you'd wonder how you didn't understand it before. I could never understand genetics until I sat in on your freshman class. Remember that day? You had this routine of using a common hobby or sport to illustrate the concept.

"You had asked a guy to pick a hobby. 'What was his favorite sport?' He answered guns. You were trying to get him to go with something more traditional but he wouldn't budge—guns it was. You hauled me up from the back row in front of all those kids. Made me explain all the different types of guns in this flow chart. I never knew how terrifying it was to be in an auditorium in front of 500 kids— how do you do it?

"You have a lecture pace—do you know that? You can't stand still, you pace from one side of the stage to the other and you don't lecture —you tell stories. How can you turn biology and science into a story? But you do and you don't even use notes. Oh every once in a while you just stop and realize you were sidetracked but overall it was just a monologue. You took my gun chart and used it to illustrate the basics of genetics. By the time you were done, even I understood and Hon, that's a miracle.

"Watching you tell those story lectures was a treat. You'd tell stories on yourself, of friends, family, colleagues, even me to make the concept real. I still laugh at you telling the story of your dad and the boxelder bugs to illustrate the power of selective pressure in evolution. How the students seemed to eat it all up—the stories, the jokes, the witty comebacks.

"Your classes were always full, always had a waiting list. Your classes were long—you don't believe in this short attention span bit but your students never seemed to tire. They were as engaged after 90 minutes as they were at the beginning. At the end of class many don't run for the door—instead, I found them gathered around the podium with you, telling their stories and jokes.

"And your students learned. I overheard a student once tell you that he had learned more in your one class than he had in all of the rest of his 4 years of college. Or the young lady in the restaurant in NYC of all places. She had been your student a decade earlier and recognized you, came over to say hi—remember? She thanked you for all you had taught her.

"I shouldn't have been surprised for I'd seen you do this a thousand times. What she thanked you for had nothing to do with biology or science. She thanked you for life lessons. These are no small feats Hon."]

THERE WAS a rumor that years ago, a class had pulled the ultimate joke on Sam Walker, one that the department still ranked as one of the best. Her 1983 class wanted that sought-after accolade for themselves, with their names up on that board, and today was the day. It was Halloween and the class had been plotting for weeks, orchestrating every element of their surprise.

The students had asked for permission to install the hydraulics and such, and Dr. Kent Fontana, the department head, was in on the joke. His task was to keep Sam busy and out of the classroom long enough to give the students time to set up. The students had pleaded for just ten more minutes as Fontana watched Sam wobbling down the hallway with an armload of boxes and files, getting closer and closer.

"Dr. Walker," Fontana boomed, loud enough for the students to hear, letting them know their final countdown had started. "Just the one I'm looking for." His overly loud voice shook the rafters and echoed down the hallway.

As he approached Sam, he put his arm around her shoulder and steered her away from her classroom. "How did testimony in court go last week? I'm interested in how the jury responded to our analysis. How well do you think they were able to follow the science?" he asked, trying to manufacture a sense of importance to his questions.

"Ah, Kent…it went well I guess, as expected really," Sam volunteered as she peered at her watch over the rim of the box of bones, files and a precariously balanced coffee mug that she barely had a grip on. A group of students coming out of a classroom momentarily caught Kent's attention and Sam spied her chance to escape. She threw out over her shoulder at Kent, "Sir, I really do need to get going," and bolted for her classroom.

The students had gotten the cables and props in place, and were now pretending to be bored while lolling about their lab stations. They had been excitedly whispering and conspiring amongst themselves, when Sam caught the handle to the lab door and raced in—just in time for the bell. The class was Human Osteology, the study of bones, and this week's lesson plan was the human arm and the pectoral girdle, also known as the shoulder girdle.

Bones had always intrigued Sam, and she found an innate satisfaction in their structure at the most basic level. Even their microscopic histological organization was beautiful. And this was Sam's favorite bone lecture—to her, the configuration of the human arm and shoulder was poetry in motion.

Easing into her groove and gaining speed, Sam launched into her lecture and a predictable pattern soon emerged as her voice carried over the lab—lecture, pace, quick sip of coffee, lecture, pace, quick sip of coffee.

With each pass of her lecture pacing circuit, she would pass in front of the skeleton closet, and her students would sit up a little taller, waiting expectantly if not impatiently, as Sam continued working her way through the skeletal structure of the arm.

"The head of the humerus articulates where?" she stopped to ask the class. "Anybody? What type of socket is it? Yes, ball and socket," she repeated as an answer floated up from the back of the lab. "It articulates with the socket of the scapula, which is called what? The glenoid fossa. Now, think people, where does the scapula articulate?" she asked an uncharacteristically inattentive class that morning, and the lab met her question with silence.

Patting herself on the back, she tried to engage the abnormally apathetic students. "Reach back and feel your shoulder blades," she intoned. "Feel the ridge running up to the top of your shoulder. What's it called? The scapular spine. Feel that knobby thing on the top of your shoulder there? That's the acromion..."

A sudden pirouette propelled her lecture pacing toward the skeleton closet, and once again the students were on high alert. Their fingers hovered in anticipation over the concealed switch box hidden under their lab table, but it was another false alarm.

While hydraulic cables that ran from behind the skeleton closet down to the third-row lab table had been carefully hidden, they were not invisible and Sam's relentless pacing had put her perilously close to the cords. The anxious students grew desperate for a diversion.

With cloak-and-dagger subterfuge, one student caught the eye of his classmate at the far end of the lab table, and clandestinely gestured for her to push her books onto the floor. Nodding slightly in acknowledgement, his classmate leaned forward surreptitiously and slowly pushed her binder onto the floor.

The sudden noise caused a preoccupied Sam to execute yet another course correction, and to the students' horror, she was now weaving up and down the very aisle where the cables connected to the switch box.

In a panic to avoid the impending disaster and divert Sam's attention, one alarmed student hastily called out, "Don't forget your coffee mug," while pointing to where Sam had left it on the windowsill. Astonished students watched in amazement as Sam, immersed in full lecture mode, merely nodded her acknowledgement, and absentmindedly stepped over the hump of carefully camouflaged cables to grab her coffee mug. She was so engrossed in her topic that she never noticed anything amiss.

Gazing out over the lab, Sam could see most students weren't even looking at the bones in front of them. *Geez, what gives with these guys today?* Sam irritatedly thought as she looked for an inroad to connect the class to the lecture. With a huffy sigh, Sam took a long slurp of her coffee, and then resumed her lecture, trying to emphasize the wonder of the human arm.

"What this means is that your arm, from your fingers to your collarbone, is attached to your body's core at only a single point the size of a dime. Think about this—think about the phenomenal range of motion this arrangement allows..."

Nothing Sam said or did seemed to make any difference—the students just sat impassively, staring at her with indifferent expressions. *Okayyyy,* Sam carped to herself as she inwardly shrugged her shoulders and pushed on to her next topic; the ulna and radius.

"One of the most remarkable features of the human arm is how the radius rotates and crosses over the ulna in your forearm as you twist your wrist inward. This is so awesome. Mother Nature was definitely on her 'A game' when she designed this joint. Let me grab the skeleton to show you what is happening inside your arm..."

Sam took another quick sip of her coffee while flinging open the door to the skeleton closet. The students threw the switches.

[GERALD, 2001: Quoted Text From Letter

"It was Halloween and some kids had rigged the skeleton closet with hydraulics and a mic. You opened the closet and that skeleton jumped out, arms waving and screaming."]

THE SKELETON WAS DECKED out for the holiday. The students had draped fake cobwebs with hanging spiders all over it, the pull-out track and both the arms and legs were all fitted with hydraulics, and a speaker had been attached to the back wall of the closet.

They also placed two buckets inside, that were to empty their contents when the hydraulics were deployed. One held plastic roller balls decorated as spiders that "walked" when the balls rolled on the floor. The final addition was the bucket of ghastly green slime that was to ooze down the sides of the closet.

The hydraulics performed flawlessly. When the door was opened, the skeleton rolled out on cue, screaming *BWAHHHHHHHH*, its arms and legs laden with cobwebs and fake spiders, waving and shaking wildly. Green slime dripped and oozed its way down the closet walls as the rolling spiders "scuttled" across the floor, running in whichever direction their roller balls took them.

In a single motion, an oblivious Sam screamed like a little child while jumping backwards, and then scrambled up on top of the main lab table. Sitting there gasping, trying to catch her breath, a dumbfounded Sam looked out over the lab room. The class was in total hysterics with students practically rolling on the floor.

Her coffee mug was nowhere to be seen, and her coffee was nothing more than a dark stain on the ceiling tile. *I'm going to have a hard time explaining this to the janitor,* she snarkily muttered to herself. "They say the pen is mightier than the sword. You all forget, I wield a mighty sharp red marking pen!" a flabbergasted Sam yelled out to a class that was still howling. They didn't care—they had plotted for weeks to pull this off, and it had been so worth it.

For the rest of her teaching career, each time Sam would approach a skeleton closet, there would be a moment's hesitation. The door would be opened more cautiously, and with reservation. They had gotten her good, and their effort won the class the coveted placement on the department board for years to come.

[**G**ERALD**, 2001: Quoted Text From Letter**

"You tried to downplay it but according to your students, you shot ten feet in the air, coffee sailing. I would have loved to have been there for that. The point is Hon that they didn't come to tell you stories— they came to say thank you. And not just a handful. Over the course of finals week, every year it would be fifty or so. Do you know how good you are? Just how special this gift is."]

2 0

WHAT'S DONE IS DONE

Sam's office suitemate, Linda, was all smirky when she arrived the following morning to find Sam at her desk, packing up her briefcase. Cackling over the joke the students had pulled, Linda playfully kidded Sam, who had begun to put on her winter coat.

"Man, they sure got you!"

"Yeah, they did, didn't they! It's going to take me forever to get over that!" Sam jested as the two chortled over the joke. Impatiently glancing at her watch, Sam grabbed her hat and gloves as she headed for the door. "Look, Linda, I'm sorry, but I've got to run. I'm due for a checkup at the clinic."

Linda peered over her reading glasses at Sam with a hint of suspicion before she candidly asked, "Are you going to tell me, or are you going to wait until you no longer can waddle through the door without turning sideways?" Sam's hand hovered over the door handle as Linda brusquely announced, "You're pregnant."

Amused at Sam's look of *How did you know?* Linda folded her arms over her chest as she needled Sam. "Hon, some women can hide it well, but you're such a skinny little runt of a beanpole. There is no place to hide it. Besides, what really gave it away is you not drinking at happy hour."

Linda had gotten up to get herself a mug of coffee, and was now perched against the window radiator. Her tone softened a tad, and over the slurp of the hot coffee, she quietly mumbled, "That, and you looking like death warmed over." Looking over at Linda's glib expression, Sam suddenly felt even more tired than she knew she looked, with dark circles under her eyes sapping whatever residual energy she had.

"Yeah," Sam said with a sigh. "I keep waiting for this 'glow' everyone keeps saying pregnant women have." Her tone was sarcastic.

The checkup had gone fine and all was good. Sam was past her first trimester, and the early pregnancy symptoms of nausea and the deep exhaustion were beginning to let up. Sam was elated when she only had to use two alarm clocks to get her up in the morning, instead of three, and then as an unexpected morning present, she had been surprised to feel the baby move, or so she had thought. The quickening, it is called, and a sense of optimism about the coming weeks began to creep up on her.

It was a shock that morning. Now into her second trimester and with a normal checkup behind her, Sam didn't expect it. She had just finished her lecture on adaptive physiology for her Human Biology class, and turned to put the overhead projector away. At first she thought she had thrown out her back, but then cramping seized her abdomen and as she stood there gasping, she felt fluid run down her legs. She was miscarrying.

The ward was noisy and drafty as Sam lay on the bed clutching the bed sheets in a death grip, trying to take in the last hours. A nurse stopped by her bedside.

"We would like to keep you for a bit longer to make sure you have expelled everything, and that there are no complications. OB-GYN will be by shortly when they are ready to examine you," she said, and Sam just nodded that she had heard. Tucking her clipboard under her arm, the nurse settled in by Sam's bed, smoothing out the bed covers, folding the edges around Sam's legs for warmth.

"Would you like me to call your husband for you?" the nurse gently asked, putting her hand on Sam's arm. Sam only shook her head no, not meeting the nurse's gaze. When the nurse noticed Sam wasn't wearing a wedding ring, she quietly asked as she leaned in close, "Are you married to the baby's father?"

Sam again only shook her head. The nurse kept probing with questions, "Where is the baby's father? Is he even in the picture?"

In a voice that was as far away as Gerry, Sam finally spoke, "In the military, overseas."

The nurse straightened up with understanding. "Ah…anyone closer you'd like us to call for you?"

"No," was Sam's simple one-word answer, still staring at the bed sheets.

The nurse shifted her clipboard to her other arm so she could pull up the blanket around Sam, and she reiterated, "Hon, you need to call him," and this time, Sam, still staring at the bed covers, tersely snorted.

"Have you ever tried calling the Army?" There was an odd chuckle to the nurse's voice, one that hinted at experience when she finally spoke after a pause.

"As a matter of fact, I have. Amazing, isn't it? How an institution that routinely handles hundreds of thousands of soldiers and complex logistics, can't handle the simple concept of a phone call. Mind-numbing incompetence combined with an operator who drips annoyance that you have bothered him." For the first time since the nurse stopped by her bedside, Sam looked up and saw a kind face.

"Oh, you have definitely dealt with the Army," she said, chuckling sadly. The nurse had been on the ward for many years and had seen the stinging ache of many a lost child.

"Look, I'm not going to tell you that everything is okay. I'm not going to tell you that you will forget this and have other kids. What I will tell you, however, is that you will get through this, but—" as she patted Sam's legs through the blanket and got ready to move on to her next patient, "you need to call him."

Her colleague Linda took Sam home, made dinner, and stayed a bit. The silence that followed the door closing after Linda left that night, was at first welcoming after the chaos of the day. But it followed Sam everywhere in the apartment as she wandered, unable to settle.

Sam sat down by the phone and started to dial the Army switchboard, but then hung up before the connection was made. She tried again an hour or so later, this time hanging up after the operator answered.

Sam didn't want to tell Gerry on the phone, she wanted to tell him in person. She had time to work up to it, she told herself, as she sat by the phone hugging her knees. She lost track of time as the hours passed, when she hesitantly picked up the receiver again. Dialing a colleague's number in Colorado, Sam whispered under her breath, *Pick up. Please pick up* as the line rang.

"Kati? Oh good, you're home. Ah…you got a minute?…um…it was a boy…"

Germany, Same Day

Sam didn't have time, not as much as she had thought, because over in Germany, Lt. Colonel Lawson sat in his office reviewing his latest headache. A panel of "powers that be" had reversed a decision and some units were being sent home, and as Lawson looked over the rosters of who and what, he remembered his hastily made promise to Gerry.

"Well, Martinez," Lawson muttered under his breath, as he signed the paperwork that would send Gerry home earlier than expected, "Today is your lucky day."

The soldiers had been relentless, and merciless, for Gerry's pink underwear briefs had not remained under wraps for very long. He would find pink cupcakes on his desk, with a pair of briefs drawn in the frosting.

Service members hung pink tights over his bed, complete with a ballerina tutu. Heartless, they had greeted Gerry for a first formation of the morning, lined up shoulder to shoulder in hot pink T-shirts and wearing high heels. Strutting, they teased him in high falsetto voices while making kissing sounds with lips painted fire engine red and cotton candy pink.

And none of it escaped Lawson. At the close of a staff meeting, Lawson gave Gerry a curt nod. "A moment please?" He then asked, "How's Sam?" after the door closed.

"Ah, doing good, sir, thanks for asking," Gerry said, somewhat pleased Lawson had remembered.

"And you?" Lawson asked offhandedly while casually mopping up a coffee spill.

"Ah, hanging in there, sir," Gerry answered as Lawson leaned forward over his desk to fix Gerry in a stare.

"I'd like an explanation," Lawson curtly announced, his face expressionless, and Gerry, not understanding, asked for what. "Oh, I'd like to know how the tighty-whities are doing," Lawson deadpanned, swinging his chair back and forth while sipping coffee.

Gerry hissed a muffled *Aww geez* before he cleared his throat and croaked out, "Still pink, sir," squirming as the office seemed to get suffocatingly hot.

"You do know you can get new ones at the PX?" Lawson stated with incredulity oozing in his voice. Gerry just bit his lip before admitting, "Yes sir, I do but…they're not the same."

Lawson continued to swing his desk chair back and forth for a moment, and while not sure he wanted to know the answer, he queried, "How are they different?"

Gerry hemmed and hawed. "Well, sir…um…Sam found this brand that fits really well and…um…I'd rather stick with them."

Lawson leaned forward with incomprehension. "You are wearing pink skivvies. How can they possibly be better than the Army's?" Gerry bit his upper lip as he uncomfortably admitted, "Well, um… they're…ah, really soft, sir."

Lawson's coffee mug hung momentarily in midair as he muttered a quiet *Soft?* in disbelief. A straight-faced Gerry barely contained his smirk as he asked Lawson if he would like Sam to call his wife,

Colleen, with the brand and such. Lawson declined but he did have something else to tell Gerry.

"Be sure to pack them with you," Lawson told him, smiling at Gerry's expression. "You're headed home." Gerry raced for the phone.

Missouri, Hours Later

The message light on Sam's answering machine was blinking as Sam returned home from work. It was from Gerry, but then so was the letter in her hand, the one from Germany that Gerry had spent months writing, and in the chaos of the moment, she slid it under a paperweight on her desk for safe keeping.

She didn't want to deal with it right then. He was so excited he hadn't waited until their weekly phone call to tell Sam he was coming home, but as she listened, the news wasn't welcomed. Her dilemma was now immediate; should she tell him over the phone or wait to tell him in person?

He would be home in weeks. It would be painful regardless of which way she went, she realized, and finally, she opted to tell him in person. The remaining weekend phone call was a game of cat and mouse, with Sam artfully dodging his questions about the baby, and how she was feeling. She felt like the American Revolutionary traitor Benedict Arnold for her out-and-out betrayal.

For the times when she tried to convince herself lies of omission were not real lies, a conjured image of Benjamin Franklin with his quote "Half a truth is often a great lie" stalked her.

At the arrival gate, Sam waited rehearsing in her head what she would say. She had thought about wearing a larger, heavier winter coat, but she couldn't. When Gerry appeared out of the tunnel, he walked up, laughing while pointing a finger at her. "I'm never wearing pink underwear again. Do you have any idea how much trouble it caused?" he said as he dropped his gear and gave Sam a hug.

It took him only a second or two after the hug, for it all to register. She wasn't pregnant any longer. All of Sam's rehearsing was for naught and all she could say was, "I lost the baby. I'm sorry," as she picked up his bag, leaving him stunned. Grabbing her shoulder from behind, Gerry stopped her in the crowded walkway, people pushing their way around them.

"I'm sorry," Sam blurted out again, but then began to tear up.

Through his shock, Gerry could only ask, "When?" and Sam blew out a heavy sigh before answering,

"A couple of weeks back." *That's not possible,* Gerry thought, as he took in the news. In his head, he was screaming, but it came out as a whisper.

"Weeks?" He bent over to look her in the eye. "Weeks and you, what, forgot to tell me? You lied to me all this time. I'd ask how you were feeling, and you lied?" Sam didn't argue. He was right—they had been lies of omission. Gerry's tendency to avoid emotional entanglements had worked in her favor, allowing her to avoid outright lying. She simply didn't elaborate, conveniently sidestepping the issue.

He was staring up at the ceiling, looking for words and was ready to say more when the look on Sam's face said it all for Gerry and stopped him cold. Wrapping his arms around her, they stood in the airport, a human kiosk that travelers weaved around, until both had settled and could speak again.

The car trip to Sam's apartment was consumed by only one question on Gerry's part. *Why hadn't she wanted to tell him?* "I didn't want to tell you while you were on deployment. You were overseas in a military setting," she said, while noticing how tightly Gerry was gripping the steering wheel. Every knuckle was white. "You had other things to worry about and I didn't want you distracted." There were a few moments where the only sound was that of the tires going over joints in the roadway, and then Sam heard a wooden voice.

"You didn't want me distracted? Samantha, I was already distracted. I've been nothing but distracted over the baby for the last couple of months."

The countryside streaked past her window as Sam stared, dully whispering, "Gerry, I had lost a part of you—of us. What if you had gotten hurt because you were preoccupied?" Gerry took his eyes off the road for a second to look at her as she turned to face him, and was crushed by her deadened eyes as she told him,

"There was nothing you could have done to prevent it. There was nothing you could have done afterwards. What was done, was done," she tonelessly said, barely audible.

As they tucked his bag into the cubbyhole that served as an entryway to Sam's apartment, Gerry ironically sniped as some of his anger from the airport began to creep back, "Well, my letter must have been a real laugh for you then." And was met with silence. Sam silently whispered to herself, *Oh my God,* as she realized she had forgotten about the letter in the turmoil of the miscarriage.

Watching the flurry of expressions flash over Sam's face, Gerry instantly knew, she hadn't even bothered to read it. Oddly, he wasn't really angry, just more hurt at Sam's dismissal of something that had been important to him. Sam quietly walked up to him and took his hand, asking,

"Can we read it now?"

Pulling his hand away from hers, Gerry sadly scoffed, "Now? Why? It was just a bunch of thoughts about us and the baby, that's all." Gerry's tone was sharp as he turned away from her to pick up his bag.

Sam stepped in front of him, blocking his path, "Gerry, will you read the letter to me like you read the book? At sunset? Hmmm… please? I need to hear those thoughts."

Sunset in the north in the winter was different than in the south. They didn't sit outdoors around a cozy fire, or sit on a cliff absorbed in the spectacle as the rays dipped beneath the horizon. They sat in front of a fireplace with the lights off, and Gerry read by fire and candlelight.

He read of all his fears of marriage and fatherhood. He read of his fears of failing his child and his child ending up on the streets like him. But he also read of his hopes for the future—for them and for their child to have a chance at something he had only dreamed of. There were so many questions.

Sam only sat and listened that night, not wanting to break the spell, but also not knowing how to answer. Days later, she decided to write back. Quietly, she took the legal pages of Gerry's letter and hid them in her desk, and when she could, she wrote answers to his questions, telling him of her hopes for the child along with her pain of losing it. When finished, she asked Gerry to join her after dinner in the living room as they had done days earlier, sliding in the chair alongside him. He was unsure of what she was doing until she unfolded a sheaf of pages and began to read.

Like Sam, when she hadn't said anything as he had read his letter, silence seemed to be Gerry's only appropriate response now, as Sam finished reading hers. Neither said anything as the logs in the fireplace crackled and collapsed under their burning, sending up a brief shower of sparks.

Sam heard the sharp inhale of air that told her Gerry wanted to say something, but didn't know how. She reached over and took his hand, curling her fingers around his and squeezed tightly, silently telling him she understood. Gerry gratefully squeezed her hand back and then wrapped Sam in a tight hug. The more they sat in silence watching the flames together, the more they seemed to be able to talk to each other—without a word spoken.

Sam had carefully folded her letter, placing it on top of Gerry's, but after a moment, she picked them both up and threw them into the fireplace, their edges furling as flames raced up in front of the paper, turning them to ashes.

"Why did you do that?" Gerry asked, more out of curiosity than anything else.

Watching the flames dance to a nonexistent breeze, Sam meditatively said, "So they live on in my dreams." As they watched the fire consume the letters, Sam quietly whispered, "Gerry, I'm sorry. I know I have disappointed you and—"

Gerry shushed her with a gentle, "*Shhhhh,* it's sunset. I'm imagining a sunset, so no talking." Sam stole a glance up at him and there was a faint smile beginning to dance at the corners of his mouth as he sat with his eyes closed facing the fire.

Snuggling in, Sam murmured, "I love you, you know that, don't you?" but was met again with a gentle *Shhhh*.

Just as she was drifting off to sleep, she heard a quiet, "I love you, too."

2 1

____

ONE-TWO PUNCH

*M*ISSOURI AND GEORGIA, *1984, M*ONTHS *L*ATER
Sam was getting ready for her routine health checkup before going back into the field and stopped in at the eye doctor for a new script. The *Uh huh, hmmm…*sounded ominous as the doctor looked closely at the back of Sam's eyes, first the right, then the left, and then switching abruptly back to the right.

"I see bone spicules on the retina. You need to see a specialist," the doctor commented while briskly writing out a name and referral on his pad. Ripping the note off and handing it to her as he got up, he left without another word.

The day of the retinal exam didn't go any easier. The battery of exams with all the pictures was exhausting, but it was the chat with the specialist that extinguished any shred of hope. He began with a lecture on genetics.

Sam taught the subject, and knowing as much if not more than the doctor, she cut him off. "Let's just cut to the chase, doctor. What's the deal here?"

Armed with suspicion, Sam had already done some research and had ranked the possible diagnoses in order of severity, from best possible to most likely to worst outcome. The news wasn't the best possible, or the most likely. Although she had steeled herself for the answer, a desolate Sam closed her eyes, heart sinking under a crushing weight, as she listened.

"You have a genetic condition known as retinitis pigmentosa, RP for short, and when coupled with a hearing loss such as yours, it forms a syndrome known as Usher's," the doctor passively said, and then went on to describe what they believed Usher syndrome was. The doctor's tone was rote and impassive as he explained.

"The disease is progressive, and will continually get worse. You should expect to be both blind and deaf, and most likely institutionalized by forty." Handing her some literature for institutions, he stated simply as Sam sat taking it all in, "I'm sorry, but there is no treatment. There is nothing we can do to even slow it down." He handed her the checkout forms as he left.

Sam's first response was to go to the medical library, to confirm the diagnosis and her prognosis. Sitting at a long table with a slew of medical reference books scattered before her, the stark realization hit home. There was no room for misinterpretation. She had Usher's.

It was an odd sensation for Sam, looking around the library at students working toward their futures, when the devastating reality hit home that she no longer had one of her own. The walk home was surreal as Sam took it all in. By the time she passed the ice cream shop, the lessons learned from a childhood dealing with her hearing loss, and from her parents, had made their way into her thoughts. Her parents had always said, "Histrionics never accomplish anything. Do your wailing, throw your hissy-fit, and have your hysterics, but then pull yourself up by your bootstraps." Sam stopped for a second, and then pivoted back to the ice cream shop, where she bought herself the largest, most indulgent ice-cream cone, with all the fixings. By the time she walked through her front door, she had begun to formulate a game plan.

The field season that she had been preparing for was still in play, and for the moment, she continued as planned with her preparations. With Gerry arriving for a long weekend from Georgia, where he had been transferred months earlier, Sam was at a loss as to what to do or say to him. So she put on a cheerful face and pretended nothing was wrong. Everything went as scheduled, all routines were the same, but Sam was on autopilot. When Gerry left to return to Georgia, his internal bells were going off.

The following weekend proved to be more of the same, and knowing Sam had been to several medical appointments, Gerry worried if there was a connection. Back in Georgia, it had been Stan, always attuned and able to see past Sam's shields, who had asked the obvious, *Could she be pregnant again?*

Although the urgency from that pregnancy was past, the couple still danced around the topic of marriage, and now the possibility of a new pregnancy gave it new importance.

On the flight into Missouri from Georgia, Gerry sat absorbed as he pondered, twirling the Styrofoam coffee cup in his hand. A pregnancy so soon after the miscarriage surprised Gerry, but he wondered if maybe this was a sign.

At first, the thought of having a child had been daunting, and after the shock of the miscarriage subsided, Gerry found himself actually relieved the pregnancy had ended. During the months since, however, Gerry had time to reflect, and the more he set aside his fears, the more excited he became.

Still mulling over the possibility of a new pregnancy, Gerry asked himself if marriage was as suffocating as he once felt, and he realized he was happy that Sam might be pregnant again, surprisingly so. In fact, he was beyond happy—he was ecstatic. He was finally ready to be a husband and a dad, and he couldn't wait for Sam to tell him. He had been so adamantly against marriage and kids. Now, it was all he wanted.

When Gerry's flight landed in Missouri, there was no Sam to meet him at the gate as she was still on campus teaching. Stepping out of the cab in front of the Hall on campus, he looked up at the old brick buildings and marveled at how the natural science buildings always seemed to be steeped in history, their old facades covered with vines and ornate edifices. As Gerry made his way through the corridors punctuated with dark oak trimmed doors, he located Lecture Hall 105 with its plaque of black letters edged in gold, complementing the décor.

As he opened the door, he could see the edge of the lecture platform down in the pit, the rows of seats arranged in tiers towered above Sam as she paced back and forth with the microphone in one hand and a coffee mug in the other.

A glance at his watch told him the class was essentially over, and Sam had begun the lecture's conclusion. Dressed in civilian clothes, Gerry passed easily for just another academic as he leaned up against the back wall, and none of the students who filed out, chattering away, gave him a thought.

Making his way down the center aisle as the last of the students passed him, Gerry caught Sam's eye as she packed up the last of her files and straggling students left the stage. She looked tired, but her face cracked a huge smile as he climbed the stairs onto the stage.

Geez, Gerry thought as he looked up at all the seats.

"How do you do this?" he asked Sam, in wonder of so many seats and no place to hide.

"You can face bullets, bombs and missiles, but you can't handle a bunch of freshmen? "Just what kind of Army do we have these days?" Sam laughingly questioned as she gave him a long hug. Gerry caught the longer than normal embrace and her tight squeeze.

When they broke apart, he held her at arm's length and looked at her questioningly, "You okay? All good here, Hon?"

Sam sat him down on the couch, not for a sunset, but to forecast a bleak future. She presented it like a lecture for non-academics, with easy to follow sentences, but with no padding. There was nothing to soften the blows, and he blanched at the news.

In WWII, there had been a decisive naval battle in the Pacific around a little spit of land called Midway. Gerry and Sam had often sparred over the logistics of that battle, a huge American victory, but they would question how big—how much had been luck, skill, fate. The Japanese Admiral Nagumo had played a gamble and lost—spectacularly. Japan had gone from being the dominant player to being on the run, with their most prized possessions burning in a span of mere minutes.

Gerry had often wondered how Nagumo, having lost everything, must have felt as he stood watching the burning hulks sizzle in the water as the Japanese retreated. Sitting on the couch that night, Gerry no longer wondered, for like Nagumo, he had seemingly lost everything in the blink of an eye.

As Sam explained the disease, its progress and its lack of treatment, Gerry was crushed by the fact that there was nothing he could do. Despite all of his training and experience, nothing had prepared him for this; all his knowledge was useless against a foe of this magnitude.

He felt he was shadow boxing an opponent that had no form or substance, with his punches landing only air, and an overwhelming sense of loss washed over him. Sitting on the couch in shock, Gerry struggled to contain the fear that there was not only no way to win, but there may be no way to even fight to a draw.

As Sam had been weeks earlier, Gerry was not content with accepting the diagnosis, and a shattered Stan had gotten in touch with a buddy whose wife worked at the Army medical facility of USAMRIID. The wife had offered to get ahold of a retinal specialist for a second opinion, a Dr. Collingwood, and Stan now stood in Gerry's apartment with the memo the wife had sent. Stan wished he hadn't asked.

"Ah," Stan began, "my buddy's wife said accordin' to Dr. Collingwood, the doctors here are right. The diagnosis is accurate." Taking a deep breath, Stan summarized what she had written. "'Cause it's rare and so few people have the disease, there's little research done on it. They're called orphan diseases. She said there's no treatment, nothin' even on the drawing board."

Watching Gerry woodenly stare out into space as he spoke, Stan swallowed a lump as he continued, "She said that since Sam was already showin' signs, she probably won't be functionin' well within ten years, and most likely hafta go to an institution or home then."

"Um…" Stan said, looking at the memo. His voice caught and he had to clear his throat again as he struggled to go on. Gerry vacantly looked up and, seeing Stan's pained look, he brusquely asked, "What else did she say?"

When Stan only stuttered about, Gerry angrily ripped the note out of Stan's hands, as he harshly spewed, "Just give me the bloody thing." Stan stood watching the color drain from a face that was already pale, and as Gerry read the memo, muscles in his jaw and neck flexed as he gritted his teeth.

His knuckles were white as he crumpled the note in rage. Looking at Stan, he announced, "We will beat this. They don't know me and they sure as hell don't know Sam." He grabbed his car keys to leave the apartment.

Stan watched his friend get into his car, parked on the street, and the light from the streetlamp illuminated the interior just enough for him to see Gerry repeatedly slam his fists against the steering wheel.

Not an emotional man, Stan fought to contain the single tear that had escaped as the final sentences of the memo ran through his head.

This is going to be ugly and it destroys both the patient and the families. Dr. Collingwood doesn't know of a patient whose family hasn't been torn apart by this disease, and he said the suicide rate for patients of diseases like this is high. The disease doesn't destroy their brain, it destroys their hope. Tell your friend, it might be best for him to cut her loose, while he still can. The longer he waits, the harder it will be for him to leave.

In boxing, there is the one-two punch. A devastating combination of two different punches forming a deadly weapon. It is led first by the stunning jab, which also functions as the range finder, allowing the boxer to gauge where to throw the second follow-up cross punch to the jaw. The cross punch is the lethal game-ender that carries all the weight.

All the times Gerry had coached Sam in the ring, play sparring as he taught her to box…she had learned well. The diagnosis had been the stunner of a jab, and what came next was the lethal cross, not to a glass jaw, but to the viscera, Gerry's gut.

Sam preferred to join Gerry at his home wherever he was stationed for that last weekend before a deployment, and she was careful not to deviate from the routine this time…except this time her return flight was in only a few hours. She had waited for that final weekend in Georgia to tell him, timing it for when he was leaving again for a stint.

She sat him down on a couch again, a different one, but with the same devastating news. Gerry could only stare at her in overwhelming shock as she starkly told him to leave her. He was in his early thirties, Sam had said, and she wanted him to move on to find someone else to share his life with. Sam's words were point-blank, and her tone was unambiguous.

As Sam got up to leave, telling him she would not be there when he came home, it was clear to Gerry that she considered the topic nonnegotiable. Sam had meant what she said—but then, she always did, and she was not there when he returned home from duty. Having taken a field position out of the country, she had told few where she was going.

When Gerry had returned, Sam's apartment in Missouri was empty, with a For Rent sign in front; she had moved and left no forwarding address. Gerry had tried calling her mother to no avail, as the woman couldn't, or wouldn't, tell him anything. He then appealed to Dr. Roger Belicampf, Sam's supervisor overseeing her work in the field.

The man was now caught between the two, a rock and a hard place, as he listened to Gerry plead for information, but Roger maintained his position. "If Sam didn't tell you, it's not my place." Her family and friends had circled their wagons.

Gerry did what he did best—in military terms, he reconnoitered.

In 1984, there were no digital footprints to follow, no online breadcrumbs, and closed-circuit cameras were scarce. The omnipresent digital age was generations away. While his own limited resources were slim, he had colleagues from his Arizona border days, colleagues whose resources were far greater, and whose breadth of authority and reach were expansive enough to help.

He pulled strings, and had strings pulled, and some perhaps were more under the table than not. But in the end, Gerry was able to locate Sam and he now had her destination; he didn't know where she was, but he now knew where she was going to be. He just had to wait and bide his time.

She had rented a small house, nothing fancy but it sufficed for her needs. It had been a long stretch, this last outing. Still reeling from the news of the diagnosis and what to do, Sam hadn't enjoyed it one bit, and all she wanted now was just a hot bath to soak out her misery.

Her mind was elsewhere as she put her key in the door, and at first, nothing seemed out of place. The house wasn't her home, and she didn't notice a disruption in energy. But something was off, and, in a flash, she recognized what it was. Aftershave. Gerry's aftershave. Just as this realization shocked her into action, and as she fumbled for the light switch, his voice came out of the dark,

"You missed the sunset."

An astonished Sam could barely register his presence while blurting out in disbelief, "How did you find me?" followed immediately by an even more incredulous, "How did you get in here?"

Gerry held her in a steadfast gaze as he took another swig of the beer, and then set it on the end table before answering, "Where else would I be? You forget who you're dealing with. I've been picking locks since before I could read, and I can pick one faster than Houdini." The discussion that followed, too civilized to be called a fight, was direct and intense.

In the end, it was Gerry's rationale that triumphed that night as he maintained, "I'm not leaving. Go ahead, call the police, have me arrested. Get a restraining order against me. Won't matter, and will not change what is." He continued his closing; he was an adult and could handle adversity, and he would decide what he could handle, not her. He ended his argument with a question for Sam, "Who are you protecting? Me from you, or you from yourself?"

As livid as Sam was that Gerry had circumvented her, there was one inescapable fact she couldn't ignore—she was elated to see him. Gerry had won the battle that night, but the outcome of the war was still pending. He would ask that same question of her many times in the coming years, each time after Sam once again had pushed him away.

The following night, when they sat to watch the sunset, Sam was at first stunned when Gerry pulled something out of his pocket, but then shook her head in amazement as she acknowledged she shouldn't have been. Gerry had written her a deployment letter. On that flight over the Atlantic, after she had told him to start a new life without her, he had written his letter.

He had spoken of the diagnosis, the fears, and of the anger. He had also made it clear the diagnosis didn't matter. He had spoken of what his life was like since he had met her. He then had compared that life to what had been his life before they met. Gerry had finished his letter with yet another question for Sam.

If you were me, which life would you want to live? Sam answered the question when she wrote her letter back.

[SAMANTHA, 2024: Quoted Text From Letter

"I fell in love with your kindness, hon. You accepted me with all my limitations, faults and foibles and handled my physical impediments without a thought. My mom had always made sure I understood I was different, handicapped. She also made sure I understood my relationships with people in general and with men in particular would be defined by it. She wasn't being cruel, babe, she was just preparing me for the realities of life. I am handicapped and am viewed by society as disposable. You never judged me for it as it didn't seem to matter. My medical issues were simply a part of what and who I was to you and weren't an embarrassment or a liability. And you didn't use them to bolster your self-esteem as many around me do. You simply allowed it to be what it was and never made me feel like a burden."]

SAM NEVER ASKED Gerry how he found her. She had been careful not to leave a paper trail and thought she had covered all her bases, but she had underestimated his resolve. She knew his compatriots from the various government agencies, the ones she collectively referred to as the Alphabets, had been involved, and she had neglected to factor those friendships and their willing participation into her equation.

A new understanding emerged out of that moment. Both parties knew there had been a fundamental shift in their relationship, from the more carefree youthful adventures to a now more mature recognition of each's hidden vulnerability—everything was now on the table.

2 2

THE HAIR ON THE BACK OF HIS NECK BEGAN TO PRICKLE

That vulnerability stared Sam and Gerry in the face as they tried to go about their business. In the coming weeks and months, they floundered, going two steps back for every three going forward. Sometimes, they were so overwhelmed, their momentum was a steady backward, with only an occasional step forward.

There was no lazy dance now, and Gerry only cringed as he watched Sam scramble to restructure her life, changing her focus within medical and graduate school. Field work became an anchor for Sam, one that provided a sense of stability without pulling her under.

[GERALD, 2001: Quoted Text From Letter

"I loved joining you in the field. Remember Alaska? Going from village to village dispensing medical care—you guys would treat anything. I watched you 'treat' a young girl's doll—[you] said it would be touch and go for a bit but thought it would pull through. You checked on that doll's condition every day. I watched you delight in learning native healing practices. I watched you join in native dances with total abandonment, no fears—just for the pure fun and joy of the moment.

"Remember Oaxaca? You working that archaeological site while trying to dodge cartel gangs and deal with the *policia*. It was there I really saw what you were made of. Those beautiful hazel eyes of yours would turn almost black when you would go up against them. Dicey season it was. I was ecstatic when you called asking if I could come down and help. Most others would have packed up early or passed on the assignment altogether. Not you. It wasn't until the flight stateside did I realize just how scared you had been. I looked over as we settled in our seats and realized your hands were shaking so violently you were knocking everything off the tray. I held your hands the entire flight home."]

[SAMANTHA, 2024: Quoted Text from Letter

"You mentioned Oaxaca. Let me tell you how I remember that moment. I should have passed on that job, but I let my ambitions and arrogance get the best of me and I undertook an assignment that put not only myself in danger but also my team. Bluntly said, babe, I was way over my head, and I knew it. My pride wouldn't let me pack up when I should have, for I had an ace up my sleeve and it gave me such confidence, even when it wasn't warranted. I took that job on because I knew you would be there to pick up the pieces and pick them up you did."]

COLORADO, 1985

Dr. Roger Belicampf sympathetically listened to Juan Santiago, his colleague from Oaxaca, México, describe his dilemma. "I've got the money and transportation," Juan was telling Roger, "but I need bodies. The site is too small and not very interesting so the *Museo* won't give me anything more than a junior archaeologist and a single worker."

"Why me?" Roger bluntly asked.

"I was hoping you could fit a crew in." Juan told Roger as he described how he needed a crew immediately, and then hopefully added, "Your people revel in being flexible." Roger was shocked to realize that Juan was thinking in terms of weeks, not months.

"Just how soon are we talking here, Juan?" he asked with skepticism, knowing how long it takes to clear red tape, especially when crossing borders.

Juan heard a quiet *Aw crap* from Roger when he revealed, "If I can swing it, I'm hoping in three weeks. What do you say?"

Shaking his head at Juan's optimism, Roger hung up, telling him, "I'll see what I can do, but to pull a crew together on such short notice...eh...I'll let you know."

COUPLE OF DAYS LATER

Sam was in a funk when she walked into Roger's office—she had a bone to pick with him. Roger was a forensic pathologist and the local coroner. He was also Sam's boss. Roger was on the phone when Sam entered his office and glancing up, he impatiently waved for her to sit down...and wait.

As Sam absentmindedly listened, she smiled warmly as her eyes wandered over his office. Pathology specimens in formalin jars dotted the shelves, a liver riddled with cancer sat next to a distended cardiomyopathic heart, and some eyeballs infiltrated by parasites. Rolls of maps and site charts were jammed into every crevice. Case presentation boards were tucked behind chairs and bookcases, and binders and reports were stacked on every horizontal surface. And any available nook and cranny held a skeleton, human or otherwise.

His office was as eccentric and messy as Roger.

But that messy exterior harbored an exceptionally shrewd mind whose passion for medicine and science showed through everything he touched. It was Roger who introduced Sam to the mystery and intrigue that was forensic pathology. It was also through Roger that Sam's independent streak found a home. She was just one of many who worked for Roger; it was an odd assortment of colleagues who were either retired, working part-time, or like Sam, simply preferred the freelance lifestyle. He was a gatekeeper of sorts for those who not only reveled in the unconventional, but also shared his love for adventure and freedom.

From the way Roger kept repeatedly shifting the phone from one ear to the other, Sam could tell he was talking to a prosecutor and from the snippets of overheard conversation, it was a homicide. "Just what the hell do you mean how'd he die?" he blustered into the phone. "He was shot, damn it!"

Geez old man, Sam thought as she snorted at the comment, and she got up to lazily wander about the office. Behind her she could hear him on the phone sniping, "I don't care if you don't like it—evidence is evidence—get over it!"

Photo frames filled every empty space on the walls and Roger's varied résumé was reflected in the grainy images within. It was hard to miss Roger in them, with his ponytail and beard, and he reminded Sam of Grizzly Adams—with an attitude. She was in many of them with him, doing field medicine or working at a historic archaeological site. She stopped in front of one taken in Texas, a paleontological dig excavating fossilized plants—and dinosaur footprints. She had been so amazed running her fingers along the imprint of a theropod foot. It had also been when she introduced Gerry to Roger. Sam worked to suppress a guffaw at the memory of those two personalities, of oil and water, colliding.

Her favorite hung just next to the door—it was of her, Roger, and another colleague, Kati, all disgustingly filthy, standing on the edge of a ravine overlooking a valley in Ecuador—grinning ridiculously with exhilaration. The picture summed it up—the hunger for adventure relentlessly driven by the thrill of a mystery.

Roger slammed the phone down, "Jerk, moron, idiot..." he spewed out.

"Ah, dealing with the prosecutor I see," Sam quipped, giggling as she sat back down in the chair.

Roger stared at Sam for a second before sighing—he knew the look. "What's on your mind, girl—what'd I do?" He was not just her boss, he was also her mentor, friend, and sometimes kick in the pants.

And Sam had no problem challenging him. "Why'd you pass me up for the site boss position?" she demanded, her body rigid while putting her elbows on the edge of his desk to fix him in a snippy glare. "What? I'm not supervisory material? I can't organize and get things done?"

Roger lightly laughed at Sam's mini temper tantrum. "Dearie, I gave that position to Chuck because you have never failed," he professed with an amused look on his face. "Look, girl, you are efficient, effective, and done. You go in and get out. There is no drama with you."

Wondering how being effective was a negative, Sam scoffed, "And that's a bad thing?"

"Honey," Roger scolded, "You can't lead until you know how to deal with failure—and you haven't—not really."

"Now," Roger announced, abruptly changing the subject, "I've got something you're gonna love!"

"Yeah?" Sam questioned, suspiciously looking at where Roger's finger was tapping a map.

"Oaxaca!" he exclaimed enthusiastically. "Bad location, time deadline, nasty politics, and rain—right up your alley!"

As Roger floated Santiago's Oaxaca project past Sam, he could see a flicker of interest. Like a fisherman who had cast and enticed his prey to take the bait, he now worked to set his hook.

"You've been lazy, child. You've been taking all those cushy medical research gigs and now look at you. Your field skills are getting rusty, your muscles shriveling as they atrophy. You need to get out there and muck in the dirt," he lectured as Sam sat, still smarting from his rebuke of her not knowing how to handle failure.

He lifted his eyebrows at her with a hint of amusement. "C'mon, where's my girl who swam with that little anaconda?"

"That was not intentional, Roger! And there is no such thing as a little anaconda!" Sam interrupted, chuckling at the memory.

"No, it wasn't," Roger joked, "but I swear you broke an Olympic record getting back to the boat!" Reminiscing, he kidded her, "Remember when you rappelled down that cliff to get to that burial cave and got hung up, or should I say upside down, when that piton came loose!" There was a daring smirk on his face when he leaned over at Sam and goaded, "Since when do you pass up an adventure?" When Sam's nose crinkled at his remark, Roger enticingly wiggled some bait. The field crew binder lay on a shelf near Sam, underneath a skeletonized bear paw and nodding toward it, Roger cunningly murmured, "Let's see who else is available, shall we?"

Sam caught herself saying, "Pardon me," to a skull missing its skullcap as she leaned over for the binder, and cracking it open, she was surprised to see Kati Banyon was available.

Dr. Kati Banyon and Dr. Doug Nievens were archaeologists attached to a small museum in Colorado and freelanced their services much as Sam did. The trio had met while on separate projects in Costa Rica, and quickly discovered they were cut from the same cloth.

As Sam sat deliberating Roger's latest intrigue, she knew he could easily find two more field hands, interns, to round out the team. Roger's hook was set—Sam accepted the job.

Missouri, Following Week

It was Gerry's turn to make the weekend trip and he stood in Sam's apartment, rigid as he listened to Sam excitedly describe her newest field project. He was not thrilled. It had come up quickly, and seemed way too fly by night for his tastes. He had numerous questions: Did she have all her supplies and gear in order? What about her medical checkup, any medications and vaccinations? Was she prepared for the police check-ins? Sam's glib dismissal of his concerns was as unsettling as her vague answers.

The hair on the back of his neck was beginning to prickle.

Sam was in the midst of complaining how grueling the process of getting the work permits had been.

"But I finally got it, authorization for six weeks of May into June and—" she was saying, while doing the dinner dishes.

Gerry cut her off. "Samantha, I can't go with you this summer. With me having just transferred to Georgia, there's no way I'm gonna get leave, not even for a few weeks."

Sam stopped and stared at Gerry as she scoffed at him. "I know that. I'm not expecting you to come with me to Oaxaca."

With a frown, Gerry forlornly asked, "Why do you have to take this job? It's not forensic." Gerry had worked with colleagues at the border, he knew firsthand of the dangers and caveats of working in México. His growing concern led him to add, "I just don't want you there by yourself."

"I won't be," Sam shot back, puzzled at Gerry's tone. "Kati and Doug will be with me. and we will be working with an archaeology crew from the local museum." Sam stood at the sink, soap suds dripping from the sponge as she gave Gerry a hard exasperated look. Gerry's hovering since the diagnosis was beginning to wear thin.

Sighing, Sam pulled the plug to drain the dish water and walked up to Gerry. Putting her hands on his chest, she softly asked, "What's going on here? Babe, I've been to México a bazillion times. Why are you so crabby about this?"

Gerry avoided looking at Sam and focused his gaze just over the top of her head. He knew what he wanted to say, but was not looking forward to seeing Sam's expression when he said it. "I don't want you going to Oaxaca," Gerry spouted. There—he had said it. "You are in no position to go anywhere. Samantha, you have Usher's." Sam's condition wasn't a hindrance yet, and Gerry knew he was being overly protective, but he fretted over every conceivable little thing and over-reacted over every insignificant problem.

"I'm the same person I was before the diagnosis," Sam solemnly told Gerry as she tried to calm his concern. "I know you're worried, babe, but...enough." Sam thought for a second as she struggled with how to say it in terms Gerry would understand. "I don't need you to fight my battles, hon. I don't need you to launch a front-line assault. I need rear support." Gerry had sat down at the table and was staring vacantly into his beer bottle trying to figure out what "rear support" meant, when Sam walked up behind him to wrap her arms around his shoulders. Hoping he could feel her assurance through the hug, she quietly whispered in his ear, "Just be there when I need you, okay?"

Gerry continued to pout as Sam shifted to a lighter topic—their planned vacation. The one positive aspect to the Oaxaca project was a shift in their eagerly anticipated ten-day adventure, now planned at the conclusion of the project. He wasn't listening.

Sam left him sitting at the dinette table, his expression sour as he stared into space. There was a shadow of something else on his typically impassive face, a hint of another worry, and Sam sensed there was more to this—something he wasn't telling her.

Georgia, Weeks Later

Gerry's apprehensions followed him home, and to bed. He had been tormented almost nightly by them—ever since Sam had told him of the Oaxaca job. Now, on the eve of her leaving for México, his worries played out a tale of chilling terror.

Awakening with a start, Gerry's fists had the bed sheets twisted in a vise grip. His heart was still racing, his breath was ragged and his shirt was damp with sweat. He listened to Sam's deep breathing of sleep as she laid next to him, and was grateful—not only that his nightmare hadn't woken her up, but also, that she was safe.

It was just a dream—he knew that, but it had been so vivid. His Samantha had been in trouble. He saw flashes of guns, knives and fear. He could hear her yelling in Spanish amidst chaos and dust clouds obscured his view, but in the dream—he knew—she was in trouble and there was nothing he could do.

In the darkness of the bedroom, he could make out Sam's duffle packed for her flight scheduled later that day, and the whiteness of the plane ticket tucked in a flap shone pale against the fabric. She had arrived days earlier, a shoe-horned "Our Time" moment, before she was to leave.

As Gerry steadied his breathing, he wondered if he should be more adamant about her not going to Oaxaca. *Should I stand my ground?* he asked himself, but he had nothing to point to, no real evidence that she shouldn't go. It was just a feeling…and he kept it to himself.

2 3

THE GODS OF ARCHAEOLOGY

Gerry gripped the steering wheel tightly as he drove Sam to the airport for her trip to Oaxaca. She would be flying out of Georgia to the Dallas Fort Worth airport, where she would rendezvous with the American crew. As he threaded his way through traffic, the heaviness he felt made him wonder, *Is this how Samantha feels when I deploy?*

Pulling into the next available slot in the passenger drop off lane, Gerry got out to retrieve her duffel out of the back seat. Sam gently tapped him on his chest and then presented him with a brown paper wrapped object.

"Did you think I would forget?" she asked, lightly laughing at his expression. Gerry traded Sam her duffle for the object, and gingerly began to unwrap the paper. She watched in amusement as he pulled out his jackknife and methodically cut the tape at the corners. It was their book—in this case, not a "deployment book" chosen by Gerry, but rather a "field book" chosen by Sam, *On Wings of Eagles*, by Ken Follett. She had tabbed the pages for him.

All that remained was the goodbye. Regardless of who was doing the leaving, Sam and Gerry hated this moment. After all the rushing to get packed and to an airport was over. After they'd opened their book, there was nothing left but the goodbye…and it never got any easier.

"I taped Roger's phone number next to your phone," Sam quietly told Gerry. "You call him for anything. He will call Juan Santiago, and Santiago will then get ahold of me."

Gerry snorted at her comment. "This…is why I am so nervous about this trip. What a rinky-dink system."

"Oh…opposed to your clearly efficient Army system?" Sam flung back with a bit of astonishment. "You know, the one where you are shipped off to some 'undisclosed locale' on maneuvers, and I can't get a hold of you for weeks. Hell…the Army won't even tell me where you are."

The snippy dig had surprised Gerry and he softly murmured, "Touché." He hadn't thought of it that way.

Leaning over with a knowing look, Sam lightly patted him on his shoulder as she verbally gave him a soft jab. "It's not so much fun when the shoe's on the other foot, is it?"

Gerry scowled while he struggled to control the worry, but he could hear fragments of the nightmare in his head. "No, it's not fun at all," he quietly said. "Not one bit."

Sam was not sure how to interpret Gerry's mood—she had never seen him like this. Finally biting the bullet, she asked, "Are you going to tell me what's bugging you…or am I going to have to use my thumbscrews on you?"

He tried to tell Sam about the nightmare, but all he did was fumble and stammer, finally confessing. "I know you deal with this all the time, this fear, but…" Gerry stopped, groping for words again. "I guess I just don't like having the shoe on the other foot." Embarrassed by his worrying, he rubbed his hands up and down Sam's arms as he awkwardly admitted, "I'm sorry. I'm being such a worrywart."

The roar of a plane overhead was deafening and Sam was aware of all the people jostling their way around them. Looking around for more privacy, she spied a pillar.

"Look," she told Gerry as she moved them to the side behind the pillar. "I know you're not happy about not coming with me this time, and I know you don't want me to go, but I need this gig. I need to find my direction again." Gerry's expression bordered on a pout and Sam tried to lighten the mood by joking, "Besides, how much trouble can I get into? I'll be with Kati!"

"I know, that's what I'm worried about," Gerry said dryly in such an unimpressed tone that Sam lightly chided him.

"Now that is not fair and you know it." Sam could tell from his snort and how his body had snapped rigid, that Gerry didn't agree.

He leaned back against the pillar, waiting for another plane to roar overhead. When its engine's rumbling faded enough for Sam to hear him, his tone hadn't improved any as he spouted, "Kati is a loose cannon and that mouth of hers got you thrown in jail."

Sam cringed at the mention of that moment. In a biker bar in Texas, Kati had provoked a fight. "Oh, only until they got things sorted out," Sam countered, her expression telling him she thought he was making a big deal out of it.

Just as he started to snipe a snarky comment, yet another plane roared overhead and he threw an annoyed look up at it. By the time the sound had receded in the distance, Gerry had mellowed and all he said was, "Hmph—she's not worth the trouble."

"Well then, I've only got two words for you," Sam touchily retaliated as she walked up to him and patted him on his shoulder.

"Yeah? And what are they?" he challenged. There was an inkling of a smirk behind her sharp tone as Sam leaned into him and reminded him of someone else.

"Stan Ibbotson."

Gerry started to laugh. "Now that was not fair...and you know it!" he teased, echoing a line she had just used on him.

They commiserated over their choice of friends as they said their final goodbyes. "We are so pathetic," Sam joked, but then she said regretfully to Gerry, "Babe, I gotta go, it's getting late."

Watching Sam gather her carry-ons, Gerry once again told her to call him when she could. Sam smiled at the reversal of roles as she reminded him, "I don't know if I will be able to call you regularly, but I will try. You know how the phone service is in rural México."

The dream still reverberated in his head and he uneasily looked into Sam's eyes as he held her face and pleaded, "Samantha...please be careful, okay?"

"I will," Sam promised as she shouldered her duffle and ran through the sliding doors. From over her shoulder she hollered out, "I will call you when I get to México." Her words drifted on the air just as the doors slid shut.

You better, Gerry muttered quietly to himself.

DALLAS FORT WORTH AIRPORT, TEXAS, HOURS LATER

A restless Sam parked herself on a bar stool at the eatery's counter within the Dallas Fort Worth Airport. She knew she needed to take the job, not for the money, but to get back in the saddle, as they say. The diagnosis had made her doubt herself, and she wanted her confidence back. She was also defiant—Usher's was not going to rule her life.

While grateful for a job that seemed to have fallen into her lap, Sam also realized she was dreading it. And the "what" she was dreading was disappointment. Gerry wasn't coming this time, and she had gotten so used to having him with her in the field—he was her warm comforter on a cold night. As she pulled up her chair at the table in the bar to wait for the crew to arrive, Sam sadly thought to herself, *I miss you already, babe.*

Apathetically waiting for her crew, Sam sat glumly staring into a beer while alternating between bouts of curses and self-motivation. She was trying to psych herself up for the long, grueling trip ahead. Going to new places and learning new cultures always left her with a sense of awe, but Sam detested the actual logistics of travel, and despite her thrill at working again with Kati and Doug, her mood was sour.

Kati and Doug, the pair of archaeologists who formed the core of the American team, had wormed their way through the tables, and now stood in front of a distracted Sam. Kati, mid-forties with dirty blond hair in a long braid, was a physically strong, rough-and-tumble sort of woman. Short and somewhat plump, her personality was straightforward, blunt, and in-your-face. And it demanded Sam's attention as Kati jovially quipped, "Look what the cat dragged in," piercing Sam's mental cheerleading.

"Hey, yourself," Sam joked, jumping up to hug them.

Dropping his duffel, Doug looked at her with a naughty grin and devilishly asked, "Ready to rumble?"

"More like me keeping you two out of trouble!" Sam teased back while laughing. In his late forties, Doug was the epitome of average. He was an average-looking man, with a nondescript face, with an average build and stature, and he easily got lost in a crowd. The dreaded male-pattern baldness had begun to claim vast swatches of the medium brown hair on his forehead. To counteract his plainness, his daughter had given him a pair of outlandish red checkered sunglasses that he wore proudly—they complemented his often off sided sense of humor.

Their reunion quickly descended into a rowdy and rollicking rivalry of competing travelogues.

Kati was in the throes of a hilarious caricature of imitating the haughty personality of a local news reporter at the very moment the woman had backed into an open excavation trench. The description of the woman's legs sticking straight up in the air, minus one stiletto high heel, while she screamed for someone to get her out of there, had both Sam and Doug doubled over in laughter. Doug suddenly sobered up when he stole a glance down the main walkway and muttered in amazement, "Oh lordy, what did Belicampf send us?"

In the distance he had spotted two young and impressionable men, and their attire was a blazing beacon that they belonged to the team. Bill and Dan, two undergrad interns from neighboring universities had spotted the veteran field crew, and were now laser focused on the astounded team as they threaded their way through the throng of travelers. Each was exuberantly hauling multiple bags that banged against their thighs and legs, threatening to trip them with every step.

Both interns were decked out in cargo everything: cargo bags, cargo pants, cargo shirts and cargo vests, and every compartment and pocket was stuffed. One had even rakishly slid his plane ticket and a couple of maps into the band of his field hat, giving him the air of a traveling salesman. Kati glanced up and at the sight of the two boys, almost snorted her beer out her nose as she cackled, "My God, they look like a couple of stuffed chipmunks!"

With huge grins that divulged just how thrilled the two young men were, they excitedly jabbered away as they introduced themselves to the crew. Their enthusiasm was cut short, however, when Doug stood up and while giving each a critical once-over, caustically announced they had brought too much luggage, and would have to pare down.

"And I would start with all of this," he sarcastically remarked, as he yanked the multitude of gadgets out of all their pockets onto the floor.

As they bemoaned the "joys" of field travel, the three field veterans sat over beers and quizzed the newcomers in an impromptu game show match. "What do you two know about Oaxaca?" Kati mumbled, stuffing a load of tortilla chips in her mouth. Dan and Bill looked at each other and reluctantly admitted not much. The three veterans put their beers down to do a round of rock, paper and scissors to determine who had to give the talk. Doug lost, and with a resigned sigh, he started to lecture the boys about Oaxaca.

"The state of Oaxaca, México," he wearily began in a droll manufactured travelogue, "is a beautiful region bestowed with three separate mountain ranges—"

Abruptly cutting Doug off, Kati snapped at him, "Oh—get to the point, will ya?"

Looking at the two boys, Kati emphatically gestured with her beer bottle, "Here's what you need to know. We are under the gun. We've got May for decent weather and after that, it's downhill and the gorgeous eighty degree temps dissolve into a muggy mess when the rain surges from two, maybe three inches, to ten or more inches per month. We get this done now, before the rain starts, or we don't get it done at all."

Kati's blunt stare at the boys drove home her unspoken point, she would be riding their tails to get work done. Satisfied the boys were properly indoctrinated, Kati turned to Sam with a smirk. "You got anything you want to add?"

Sam leaned over to pull a map out of her duffle and spread it out on the table, grabbing beer bottles to hold the corners. With a swizzle stick, she began explaining, "Our base will be this town here, Tlaxiaco, and from there we will be headed up into the mountains to this area here," tapping a small village several hours north. Making her way through the various topics, she underscored Kati's earlier point that they would be hustling. "A lot depends on the rain Kati mentioned," Sam continued. "This area is remote. The roads, which aren't the greatest under the best of conditions, can turn into a quagmire with ten inches of water. Road travel during the rainy season can be tough, or at times, virtually impossible. I will be pushing to be done before the rains start."

When finished, Sam ominously knocked on the table to catch everyone's attention.

"Um…guys, I'm going to be a wet blanket here for a moment and remind you of a sobering reality in Oaxaca. It's cartel territory. While there's no indication of anything of concern, we need to be on our toes down there, for the cartels run the show, and we're in their sandbox." Looking around the table, Sam said, "Let's keep our heads down, keep our mouths closed, and mind our own business. 'Nuff said?" Four heads bobbed in unison.

Over the din of travelers and the roar of planes, an announcement was heard. Their flight was ready for boarding. While short in terms of fieldwork travel, no one was looking forward to the trek ahead and a unified groan of despair erupted from the group.

Feigning an enthusiasm that none possessed, each of the three older team members downed the last of their drinks in their ritual field work prayers. Each would implore their respective patron gods of history and science to bless them and their project. They also pleaded that gods of chaos and destruction, who often plagued work sites, be held at bay.

Doug stood while raising his glass to the two ladies and with a faked air of sophistication, he twirled the ends of a nonexistent mustache and toasted ancient Roman and Greek gods.

"May the god Janus sanctify this endeavor and, if so inclined, may he shrivel the primordial god Chaos's balls," he melodramatically intoned, and then he guzzled the last of his drink.

Waving his hand at Kati that it was her turn, Kati cleared her throat and theatrically stood up. Raising her bottle, she began her appeal to Aztec gods, "May Quetzalcoatl drown and smote the mighty Chālchiuhtōtolin, while bestowing upon us honor and sparing our beating hearts." With a dramatic flair, she slammed her bottle on the table after draining. Then, she and Doug turned expectantly toward Sam for her to end their ceremonial sacrament of travel. Bringing up the rear, Sam hoisted her bottle and saluted, "May the gods Dagda and Ecne lead us to treasure, whether be knowledge or wealth, and send the god Balor to his realm."

Confusion clouded the interns' faces, and in a tone that barely hid his wonder if the boys knew anything, Doug leaned over and said, "They're Gaelic gods of time, knowledge and chaos." As Sam concluded her invocation with a final swig, the three then looked over at the two newcomers, awaiting their plea, but the boys didn't know what to say.

After an uncomfortable pause, Dan sheepishly stood and bravely offered his prayer, "May the Bears win the Super Bowl," which had Kati and Doug snickering with laughter.

"The Bears?! Oh, dream on!" they snorted as the group heaved themselves up off the stools.

2 4

A TYPICAL DAY IN THE FIELD

Tlaxiaco, Oaxaca, México, Following Day

By the time the American crew arrived in Tlaxiaco mid-morning, they were exhausted, bleary-eyed and in varying stages of grumpiness. Next item on their itinerary, however, was to meet the project archaeologist Juan Santiago along with his Mexican crew, a young junior archaeologist Augustin Cazar and Pepe, the field hand, at a local *restaurante.*

Outfitted in the cargo style apparel so typical of the field, Juan's round face was accentuated even more by his round wire-rimmed spectacles. His hair greyed and tousled by the wind, he came across as the quintessential field worker. Travel fatigue faded as the stately Juan positively beamed with excitement as he clapped everyone on their backs as they sat down. "*Gracias, Gracias* for coming," he gushed as he rushed to pour everyone coffee. "I am so anxious to show you the site! Would you like to see the site map? Yes?" he questioned hopefully as he comically began to pat his multitude of pockets searching for the one he had put the small map of the site in. Sam fought to hide her grin when he couldn't find his pencil which he had perched behind his ear.

His enthusiasm was contagious and soon everyone was impatient to get started. Before they could dig a single trowel in the dirt, however, the team needed to check off the next box on their agenda—the obligatory *policia* check-in, more of a courtesy call really, for work crews in the region.

Having none of the Spanish adobe architectural charm that so dominated the rest of the city, the municipal *policia* station was a disappointment. Bland with no personality, it simply was four walls and a roof. The crews stood staring at the dull building from across the street as they waited for a farmer, dragging a couple of stubborn donkeys resisting their halters, to cross in front of them.

Grins broke out among the group as they listened to the man humorously argue with his furry companions in a conversation, as if the donkeys could talk. Turning around in exasperation toward the animals, the farmer exclaimed loudly in Spanish at them, "No, I'm not walking too fast. You are too slow! Move, I tell you!"

The sight of the farmer waving his straw hat in frustration at the donkeys as they passed, trying to hurry them along, left the archaeology team giggling as they trudged into the station, but their disappointment followed them.

The *policia* station's interior was just as plain as its exterior. White-washed walls with maps and flyers and a few desks filled a windowless central room. Down a hallway, the metal grate of a jail cell could be seen. Aside from lamps and phones on the desks, there were few other amenities in the utilitarian space.

The commander of the municipal office of the *policia* was a standoffish, overweight, and overbearing sort of man who left Sam on edge. Initially there had been nothing specific in what he said or did, but the man seemed overly irritated and annoyed that they were there at all. Sam was mystified at the inordinate amount of time the officer spent inspecting their permits and stamps, as if in hopes of finding an error.

When the paperwork was finally verified with a satisfying chunk of the all-important official municipal ink stamp, the crews began to gather up their belongings. Impatient to be on their way, they were floored when instead, they were told, "You are now to be searched for contraband."

The two women stiffened as the officers ran their hands over their bodies, fingers groping and lingering, and when a leering officer's hands took the scenic route over Kati's ample bosom, an outraged Juan brusquely slapped the man's hands away as he forced himself between the two. Undeterred, the officers merely then dumped all the team's luggage and equipment, and set about leisurely inspecting every item as well, with one officer chortling as he twirled one of Kati's bras in the air about his head.

A routine check-in that was generally perfunctory, and by all accounts should have taken only twenty minutes at best, took well over two hours by the time the *policia* were done with them. Both the Mexican and American crews were not only offended by their rough treatment, but also unnerved by all the extra attention. But it was the project director himself, Juan Santiago, who had ultimately garnered the most attention, as every pocket was turned inside out.

At one point, Kati, still boiling from being manhandled, had leaned over and jeered sarcastically, "I'm surprised they haven't had him drop his pants for a cavity search." The comment had caused Sam to secretly glance toward the woman with a veiled expression that warned her to be quiet.

As the archaeology team descended the stairs from the *policia* station, tense friction erupted between the two crews, evident when the Americans went to one side of the avenue and the Mexicans to the other. The American men resisted the search and were treated crudely by the officers, being forcibly held against walls or desks. The Mexican men, while being inspected more thoroughly, it seemed, were handled far more gently, even politely at times, and the Americans took note.

All the goodwill and amity that Juan had worked to instill between the two crews over their introductory lunch had evaporated. He now stood in the street between the two groups, watching in dismay as camaraderie was replaced by animosity, and trust became suspicion—the American crew was close to a revolt.

Sam looked over at Juan's face and saw embarrassment for the crews, and disappointment in his countrymen. But, as the other four

American crewmembers spouted off how the Mexican crew had just stood there doing nothing, Sam saw something else on Juan's face—rage over what had happened.

Looking behind her at the foursome gathered angrily, Sam took the opportunity to tell the crew, "May I remind you all that it was Dr. Santiago who took the brunt of the search, far more invasive than ours? It was Juan who stood between those creeps and Kati—not you," she said, pointing her finger at Doug and Dan. Ambling over to where Juan was still standing, she loudly thanked him for his defense of Kati, but then gently gave him a hug as she whispered, "They'll settle down. They're just venting steam right now."

Telling the senior archaeologist she was going to take her crew-mates with her while she scouted for supplies, she asked him if there was anything in particular he wanted on the list. Juan merely leaned in and dejectedly whispered back, "A miracle, if you should run across one."

Desperate to find a way to mend the fences between the two groups, Juan made arrangements for the team to spend the night at a colleague's *hacienda.* There, he hoped, the two crews could relax and socialize, and begin to ease pent up tension.

The old-world charm that characterized the city center spilled out over the valley in little fingerlets reaching out for the foothills, and Juan's colleague's *hacienda*, situated in those foothills, exuded the magic and allure of the local culture.

Sam stood on the balcony overlooking a small neighborhood plaza, luxuriating in the solitude and view. Local children were glee-fully rehearsing in the filtered shadows of the afternoon for an upcoming festival, their billowing shirt sleeves and colorful skirts fluttering in the breeze that constantly seemed to race down the mountains through the valley.

With the children's laughter floating on the air, Sam turned her attention to the spectacle of the sun beginning to set. She sensed the warm colors more than saw them, and when she closed her eyes, she thought of Gerry, and of all the turmoil of the past year. Since the diagnosis, moments of silence were difficult as the uncertainties of her future were never far. To force those fears into retreat, she stood motionless, visualizing a different sunset, one where she was in a chair, wrapped in Gerry's arms, safe from the ravages of what was to come.

"Oh, babe, what I would do for you to be here," she whispered to the breeze that rustled her hair. Her daydream was interrupted by Juan's presence, and she opened her eyes to him standing alongside her, offering her a mug of coffee.

"You are worried, still upset by the *policia?*" he asked, misinterpreting the doleful expression on her face. Nodding her thanks for the coffee, Sam smiled lightly.

"No, I was just thinking of my boyfriend. We have a habit of watching sunsets together and this beauty—" Sam said, as she waved her mug at the sun, "reminds me of him."

"It is hard to be a boat that has drifted from its anchor, eh?" Juan asked as he studied Sam. "He is a good anchor? A solid one?"

"He is my Rock of Gibraltar," Sam answered with a grin, and Juan murmured a pleased *Bueno* as he took up a spot on the rail next to her to admire the view.

Sam turned to Juan, her face more serious as she asked, "Juan, I need you to be honest with me. I'm picking up a vibe that the cartel activity to the west is here as well. Do we need to be worried about…" Her conversation faded into the background as the two discreetly discussed the unnerving topic in solitude before rejoining the crews.

Sam's field boots echoed on the terra-cotta floor tiles as she made her way back through the atrium while marveling at the accented walls with their colorful mosaics of ceramic tile. Following muted voices and music, she wound her way through the sprawling *hacienda,* toward an outdoor patio where the two crews, while enjoying *cervezas,* were unwinding and getting reacquainted around a crackling fire.

Walking through the arched doorway, she was greeted by the image of both crews hunched over the project's site map, studying its features and arguing over what they would find. Juan and Sam were working hard to pacify any residual hard feelings left over amongst the team members. The good-natured ribbing that had broken out between Pepe, the Mexican assistant, and the two American interns, Dan and Bill, caused Sam to glance over at Juan with a relieved smile. The gods of archeology, it seemed, had smiled down upon them.

Growing excitement and anticipation greeted the archaeology team with the sunrise the following morning. All the efforts made at soothing the tensions from the previous day's *policia* duty call were evident as laughter and chatter could be heard between the two crews when they began loading their field vehicles for the trip up to the site.

There were two unexpected surprises, however, awaiting the archeology crews that morning—one was the weather and the other was Juan himself. Mother Nature was always an unknown variable in fieldwork, and she had lived up to her fickle reputation. The rainy season on average began in June, but the skies had delivered the grim, unwelcome news—the rainy season was arriving early.

The crews were busy buttoning up the jeeps against the impending deluge, when Juan issued a surprising last-minute instruction. "People, gather around if you would. I have something to tell you. Due to unforeseen circumstances, there has been a change of plans—I won't be joining you at the site as expected."

Augustin assumed, as the next ranking Mexican archaeologist, that he would take over. He was a slender, bespectacled, baby-faced young man whose loosely curled sandy-colored hair constantly hung in his eyes. Having spent most of his budding career in the lab, he had yet to experience the multitude of often eccentric personalities that exist in the field. And more importantly, Augustin had little experience handling the barrage of missteps and problems that crop up in the field.

Juan instead revealed, "Sam, I know you are not an archaeologist, but I would like you to be the project's leader." As he handed Sam the site permits and all other relevant material, he also gave her a slight smile with a wink—and some advice. "The villagers will try to get you drunk—do resist the temptation to embarrass yourselves…and me!"

As the crews climbed into their truck and jeeps, Juan handed Augustin a packed tool roll, not with shovels and picks, but with weapons. The unspoken words of Juan's look caught Sam off-guard. They had just been talking about the problems out west, where the cartels were becoming more entrenched, but Juan had assured her all was well. Sam casually leaned over and flipped the roll open to reveal its contents, several old rifles and a couple of handguns, all crusty with the rust of age. Without a comment, Sam threw a glance at Juan that caused him to murmur softly, "Just in case you might need it." For all of Juan's insistence of Oaxaca being safe, he also accepted the reality that sometimes trouble finds you. Scoffing, Sam silently nodded as she covered the roll back up and stowed it behind an equipment locker.

Excavation site, Oaxaca, Hours Later

The two hour or so drive from Tlaxiaco to the project site, made even more perilous by the rain, twisted through the hills to the north up into the mountains, and the rain chased them. At every turn up the mountainside, if they turned away from the downpour, it would follow or suddenly appear in front. It felt like being stalked in an odd rendition of "chasing salvos," a naval tactic used to avoid incoming shells.

Finally, they approached a small rural village of about five hundred people. Typical of the region, it boasted a lone winding dirt road through single story rural homes scattered along the valley. The pine-covered mountains that sheltered the work site they were soon to be working, loomed in the not so far distance. With no central plaza, a single domicile served as the village's mercantile and *cantina*, and its minimal utilities, limited supplies, and materials would serve as a source of respite and resources for the work crews during their stay.

The team's small convoy of one truck and two jeeps pulled in for the customary "last call," where everyone stocked up on any "necessities of life" they might have forgotten. Every crew had different priorities, but Twinkies, soda, and cigarettes were traditionally the huge front runners as "last call" favorites.

The final stretch of their drive was just a short five miles further from town to the farm of a local Indigenous farmer, Pablo Papaqui, upon whose land the site was located. Intrigued, the American crew wondered why the farmer had even bothered to report the site, let alone wanted it to be investigated, as for most farmers, archaeological sites were just not worth the hassle.

Their intrigue was answered when the farmer met them at the entrance to the farm.

"That explains a few things," Augustin observed as he studied Pablo. Sam, who had been traveling in the truck with him, was intently studying Pablo herself.

"What do you mean?" she questioned as she watched the farmer greet them.

Augustin sat up taller in the seat, trying to get a good look of his surroundings. "Look at his truck and what's in it. And look at his face, at the pride he has for the land—he owns this farm," Augustin remarked, admiration echoing in his voice. "This guy is not growing poppy like others."

Middle-aged, short, and sturdy with a solemn dark face, Pablo Papaqui was a no-nonsense man who kept a rifle at the ready. He strolled slowly around each vehicle in the little caravan, studiously inspecting each of its occupants. As he lifted the canvas tarps covering the equipment, Pablo ridiculed some of Doug's "necessities of life" paraphernalia while snorting *Americanos débiles*—or weak Americans —under his breath. Several minutes passed before Pablo decided they would suffice, and finally, merely nodding, he got back into his rattle-trap of a field truck and led them further up into the hills to the site.

The arrival at any new site, that first impression, was always a highly anticipated moment for field workers and the team eagerly craned their necks to catch their first glimpse as they cleared the crest of the ridge. A welcome site greeted Sam and the team—a small plateau area nestled amongst craggy ridges and swollen hills. Kati began her fussing before the vehicles had even come to a stop.

She was particular in wanting easy access to the work area, and in her eyes, that location trumped all other considerations. Having already "marked her territory," Kati, with hands clapping and fingers snapping, stood barking out her orders to Dan and Bill to clear the ground of debris as Doug unloaded the equipment.

Kati and Doug were polar opposites. Over years of fieldwork, the two had forged an improbable working relationship that, on the surface, seemed contentious, but those in the know recognized it was just a show. The running joke was that, as long as Kati and Doug were bickering with each other, all was right with the world. But if they weren't, then it was time to make out your will, say goodbye to the family, and grab your ankles—the zombie apocalypse was upon them.

Like clockwork, the ever-present bickering between Kati and Doug began, and the withering zingers flying between them were often accompanied by spirited hand gestures and exuberant body language. Kati was in the middle of bellowing instructions when she caught Doug, peaceably ignoring her, going about his business. Peeved, she snapped, "Damn it, Doug, are you paying attention to me?"

"Hanging breathlessly on every word," Doug sniped while sarcastically rolling his eyes for emphasis. Kati caught the roll.

Gesturing wildly, she threw back at Doug, "Really? Well, hang yourself on this…" Snippets of their mocking wisecracks rolled over the site.

"I'll have you know…" Doug retaliated, with hands on hips that he gyrated with every word. "And you suck the fun outta everything!"

"And I feel real bad about that too!" Kati shouted back at him as he complained.

"Like hell you do!" Doug bellowed, shaking a fist as he stomped off.

The two argued like cats and dogs, and provided constant entertainment, much like a soft radio playing in the background.

The team rushed as they fought to establish the camp and stake the work site in the waning daylight hours. While the work tables and equipment could be left for the morning, the site would be the team's home for the next month or so, and the instinctive need to establish a nest—a safe, secure place to bed down for the night, had the crews hurrying to set their personal tents up. Most would place family photos or tokens around their tents for a taste of home, but Sam merely laid her chosen "field book" with its tabbed pages, on her duffle.

She smiled as she looked at the title, *On Wings of Eagles*, the tale of a military style rescue mission that she hoped Gerry would enjoy.

Low hanging rain clouds obscured the sun as the front cleared the mountains the following morning. The filtered rays were enough to dry out the area, allowing the hard laborious task of working the site to begin in earnest. Sifting and bagging, photographing and sketching, all in an endless cycle.

It was a typical day in the field.

YOU JUST ROLL WITH IT

It was on their second day of work, however, that the beguiling tone of field archaeology was spoiled as things skidded downhill.

Flaunting their authority, the local *policia* arrived on site. There were four of them in two jeeps that eased to a stop, quietly as if sound offended them. They were not the same officers from Tlaxiaco who had rudely greeted them when they had first arrived. These officers were from the local station in the larger neighboring municipality.

Their uniforms were crisp, the metal buttons and insignias gleaming as if they had been polished for hours. One of the officers had a huge beer belly and he struggled to heave himself out of the passenger seat of the jeep. He strutted about, smacking a black leather riding crop in the palm of his hand. It was a sound the team would soon learn to hate.

"Stop immediately what you are doing," the pudgy officer announced, as if he was reading a proclamation, and then he posed on display in the center of camp. Pompously, he demanded, "Where are your permits and passports? You are to hand over to me all documents—immediately." His arrogant expression signaled he expected full compliance.

Sam stood glaring at the Mexican officers as they tempestuously paraded around the work table where the team had laid out all their journals. When Dan and Bill began to close up the journals, the pudgy officer slammed his crop down on top of them, claiming, "Those belong to me now." Dan and Bill, who had been working on cleaning some broken pot shards, slowly backed away and stood up, unsure of what to do or where to go.

One of the officers picked up a shard, inspected it a bit, then dropped it on the ground and pushed it into the dirt with his boot heel. The crack of the dried clay could be heard over the noises of their tents being tossed.

At the crashing sound of the water barrel being dumped, Sam whipped around and challenged the officers, "What the hell are you doing?"

The pudgy officer snidely announced with authority, "We're here to make sure you respect our laws and customs. Our inspections are for the community's safety as well as for your team." It was malarkey; everyone knew it, and the officer's overt lying only incensed the team even more.

"Enough!" Sam shouted when several other officers found her field bag and were dumping the contents, kicking them all over the ground. Fuming as she watched, she lashed out at the pudgy officer guarding them, "Just leave us alone." The officer just sneered at Sam as he ran his hand to the butt of his holstered handgun. His message was clear.

Hoping for a clue, Sam glanced over at Augustin and Pepe, the two Mexicans on the team. Their downcast expressions told her not to intervene.

Finally, the officers had their fill and left. As the dust cloud from their tires began to settle, everyone gathered around, confusion darkening their faces. Sam put Augustin on the spot when she angrily questioned him. "What the hell was that all about?"

The young archaeologist was as confused as Sam, and at a loss for words, he hesitantly admitted, "I don't know."

"This has never happened to you before?" Sam asked suspiciously as she studied Augustin's face to see if he was hiding something from her. What she saw was alarm, and it stirred up a sliver of trepidation in her as well. Still trying to grasp what had happened, Sam muttered absentmindedly, "This makes no sense. Why would the *policia* even bother themselves with temps like us? We have work permits—we're simply not worth the trouble."

Her confusion only grew over the week. Each day, Mexican officers would shout out for the team to stop work as they would drive up—sometimes two jeeps with four officers, sometimes only one with two officers. But the harassment was daily. Each time, the team would have to stop while they were interrogated and frisked. Hours were lost each day as the *policia* reveled in the intimidation.

They did not use physical force—they instead resorted to harassment...and profanity. The pudgy officer gloated over his skill of cursing in English, and took every opportunity to do so. The team would come to call him Pottymouth.

I have had enough of this, Sam spewed to herself as she watched the officers once again topple water barrels, scatter journals and tip over equipment. Discouraged, she openly questioned the veracity of her intel; clearly something wasn't right. The moment the officers' jeeps cleared the crest of the ridge, she roughly motioned for Augustin to join her in her tent.

"What is really going on here, Augustin?" Sam interrogated as soon as the tent flap closed. "What is it you haven't told me?"

Augustin was wide-eyed as he shook his head and confessed, "I haven't got a clue. I don't get this."

"Well then," Sam grumbled under her breath at Augustin, "It's time for Plan B. You up to coming with me to Tlaxiaco tomorrow? Juan and Roger owe us some answers."

Sam and Augustin didn't like what they saw on the trip into Tlaxiaco. The rains had turned the mountain roads into mud wallows, and in areas, a slurry mix had slid down over the roadway. "Aw, crap," Sam muttered while slamming on the brakes when they encountered a large pine tree down across the road. "Augustin, grab the chain will ya," Sam called out as she reached back to pull out the tool box.

Crawling under the front bumper, Sam scanned the chassis for the best place to anchor her end of the chain while Augustin wrapped his end around the trunk of the tree. The jeep groaned and slid in the mud against the weight of the tree as Sam shifted into reverse, but the tree slowly swung around, and finally was hauled to the side. To their dismay, Sam and Augustin had to repeat this procedure several more times before they made it to Tlaxiaco. The early rains were playing havoc with roads that were quickly becoming impassable.

They didn't much like the answers they got from Juan and Roger either. Undeterred and even slightly amused as Sam and Augustin reported what was happening with the *policia*, neither Roger nor Juan felt there was an immediate cause for concern. The two old veterans of the field had been subjected to similar behavior themselves in their day, and viewed such disruptions as part of the job.

"You just roll with it," they said. While the field veterans' assurances calmed some of their doubts, neither Augustin nor Sam was particularly impressed with what, in their view, was the dismissive advice to simply "roll with it."

Slamming the jeep's door shut as she got into the driver's seat, Sam bitterly spouted while glancing over at Augustin's cheerless face, "That was the biggest pile of crap I've heard in a long time."

She sat quietly for a bit, contemplating their next move, when she heard an odd gurgle from Augustin. He was sitting there, sarcastically imitating Juan's voice while laughing, "Just roll with it, just roll with it," mockingly shaking his head with each repeated phrase. Reaching over, Sam touched Augustin's arm.

"This coffee isn't going to do it for me. Let's find a *cantina* and talk over our options."

That evening, back at the site, a peeved Sam conveyed the information she had gleaned from Juan and Roger. She decided to ask for the team's opinion and took a vote—should they stay or go? To Sam's surprise, everyone voted to stay; no one, not even the youngsters, was willing to be bullied. But that boldness was short-lived when the second week on the job took a threatening turn, and shook their bravado.

What Sam didn't know was that during the interval between when the paperwork had been approved, and when the team arrived on site, a group of disgruntled and unruly youths had grown violent. A new and upcoming gang of "cartel wannabes," primarily young teenage boys who were inexperienced and greedy, wanted to be among the drug cartel big boys, but had yet to prove their mettle. The group had decided that spring was as good a time as any to begin, and when those cartel wannabes discovered the work site, the team became a classic case of being in the wrong place at the wrong time.

The cartel wannabes roared up to the site much more blatantly aggressive than the *policia*, their truck tires throwing up dust and gravel as they slid to a stop. Clamoring out of two older model rusty pickups, they shouted foul language in Spanish and taunted while wielding weapons.

A hard, mean-looking group, Sam counted nine of them that first time, ranging from fourteen to maybe seventeen years of age. She saw no gang colors but did see several with the same tattoo—a large, ragged starburst with a central weblike design on their left forearm.

Already on edge from her dealings with the *policia*, Sam yelled out in Spanish, "What do you want?" as she strode up to who she thought was the group's leader, and was met with a rifle in her face. Holding her hands up, Sam backed away and watched as the group motioned for the rest of the team to join her.

The cartel wannabes strutted around growling, brandishing their rifles and knives in intimidation, but nothing more—just words and posturing. "What are you doing, what do you want?" Sam repeated, but was ignored. The gang wildly ransacked and looted the camp, taking some shirts and jackets, a pickaxe, and all the beer in the camp cooler. They left as loudly as they had arrived, jeering and mocking.

The archaeology team was so shocked at the experience, that the rumble of the cartel wannabes' trucks' engines had faded before anyone spoke. A bewildered Doug walked up next to Sam and the two exchanged astonished looks. "Wow," Sam exclaimed as she looked over the camp, taking in the damage.

Behind her Sam could hear Kati, who didn't mince her words, spout off. "Shit…there is some really bad mojo going on here. Who were those creeps?" Leftover tension from the *policia* check-in began to creep back with her loosely disguised accusation. "Am I the only one here who thinks we've been lied to?" She was staring at Augustin.

Sam was listening to Kati's rant, but her mind was already in overdrive. "Enough, Kati," Sam grunted as she shut down Kati's outburst. She broke away from the team and wandered to the center of the camp, her hands on her hips as she scanned the disarray.

After a moment, she abruptly spun around toward the team and began issuing a flurry of orders. "Augustin," Sam barked, "you and Pepe start putting the camp back together. Begin with the tables and equipment." Pointing to the two interns, Sam instructed, "Bill and Dan, we need water. Take the truck and go get water from Pablo—and get double the amount." When the two boys just stood there, Sam snapped at them an emphatic, "Now."

Sam's mind was already working on what to do next as she distractedly told Kati and Doug, "You two—go gather up all the journals and notes. Locate all of our permits...and make sure you catch those that have blown away." Sam's job was food and the tents.

As she struggled with a shredded tent wall, an idea suddenly cut across her thoughts—it would be best to cache the supplies. And those guns from Juan. A new checklist began to form in Sam's mind as she ran for a lockbox she had simply hidden from view—she would now bury the essentials for safekeeping. The thought proved fortuitous.

Over the next twenty hours or so, different groups of cartel wannabes returned repeatedly, each a diverse assortment of boys, but all with the same attitude and demeanor. And each time, Sam watched in satisfaction as they stomped around, hell-bent on destruction, but never found her stash of essentials.

Between the daily morning *policia* harassment and now the cartel wannabes, Doug grew both more assertive and indignant, and in a tense confrontation, he forcibly demanded the wannabes answer him.

"Hey! No more," Doug shouted as he tried to muscle his way in between some of the boys. "You've taken everything we have, now leave us alone. Just what the hell do you want from us?"

A young boy, no more than maybe fourteen years old, sniggered while he gestured sharply with his rifle for Doug to move away. Doug's temper erupted. "No, damn it, don't you wave your gun at me," he yelled, his frustration at a breaking point. "What do you guys want? Answer me!"

The oldest of the boys looked over at the various gang members and called out for them to gather around him. They all cackled and snorted while talking amongst themselves for a few moments, and then…took target practice on the team's vehicles, parked about a hundred feet or so from the site. With rifles, semis, and handguns, the cartel wannabes unloaded into the lone truck and two jeeps, rendering them all inoperable.

The explosive sound of gunfire shocked the crews into action and everyone bolted for cover as they scattered. Sam and Augustin had dove into a work pit next to Kati and Bill. In the second pit, huddled Doug with Dan and Pepe, the Mexican helper, and the faces of the entire team registered shock and disbelief.

Doug lifted his head up over the edge to watch the boys have their fun, whooping and hollering while waving their guns about carelessly. The gang once again plundered the camp for whatever last remaining food and drink they could find, and then, swaggering as they drank and laughed, they drove off, leaving the camp in stunned silence. It was over in minutes, but for a team composed of academics unaccustomed to being shot at, it had seemed like an eternity.

Sam instantly whirled around and hissed when several members of the team started to shift. *Don't move until I say so*, she silently mouthed, gesturing for them to stay put. Crawling out of her pit and stopping every few feet to listen, Sam scanned the area, checking to make sure the gang had truly left. She saw and heard nothing.

Slowly, she crept to where she had cached the tool roll with the guns, and pulled out a handgun. When the *policia* harassment had started, Sam had made a point of cleaning and oiling that handgun. Now, carefully sliding it into her back pocket, Sam silently blessed Gerry, *Thank you, babe, for insisting on teaching me how to shoot.*

Crawling backwards toward the overturned work table for the binoculars that had been tossed on the ground, Sam then scrambled up to the top of the ridge to look out onto the dirt trail that led to the road. "Oh thank God," she whispered under her breath as she heaved a sigh of relief. The gang was gone.

While no shots had been fired their way, rattled, hysterical, and petrified all aptly described the team as they stood in shock evaluating the damage. The camp had been stripped and demolished, and not one vehicle was salvageable. Ideas and questions were thrown about as the team grappled with what to do next.

Doug stared incomprehensibly at the vehicles and then turned to look at Kati and Sam. Putting his hands behind his head, he unthinkingly asked, "Does anyone have car mechanical skills?" but realized as soon as he said it, it was irrelevant. While Doug knew his way around a car engine, there were no tools or spare parts. The team was now trapped with minimal food and water, no transportation, and no significant weapons.

Field workers as a rule were an intrepid lot, not easily discouraged, but the team's earlier sentiment of sticking it out was now being replaced by a determination to figure out a way to leave. Climbing into a jeep to inspect the damage, Sam asked hopefully, "Do you think we can cobble a working engine together by cannibalizing from the others?" It was also moot, since all the tires were flat, not to mention there was the problem of gasoline and oil as the precious fluids dripped out from underneath the vehicles, soaking the ground.

Pablo the farmer had been tending his crops in a field nearby when he jerked abruptly at the sound of a distant fusillade of gunfire coming from the direction of the camp. He had bristled at the news of the intimidation tactics of the *policia,* but admitted there was little he could do for the team. The enfilade had startled him, and the closer he got to the camp, the more his apprehensions grew. Easing his jeep alongside the bullet-strafed vehicles, he called out while he stared in amazement at the destruction, "Is everyone okay?"

To his relief, he was greeted by the sight of an angry, but safe archaeology team.

Waving Pablo over, Sam began questioning him. "Who the hell were those boys? Why didn't you tell us about them?"

Pablo just shook his head he didn't know. Still staring at the jeeps, he confessed to Sam he had heard something a few weeks back about a gang causing problems. "But that was over to the west. It wasn't here," he grunted. "How could they have been here and I didn't know?" Sam heard Pablo quietly ask himself.

Sam recognized the stern, impassive look on Pablo's face—she had seen it on Gerry's many times. It was anger mixed with embarrassment at not only at what happened, but also that he had gotten caught with his pants down. Pablo vowed he would go to the village to get the team supplies, notify the *policia*, and find out what was going on.

As he got into his jeep, Pablo only nodded curtly when Sam drove home her concern. "The supplies are wonderful and needed short term, Pablo, but what we really want are vehicles. I want a truck large enough to carry everyone to Tlaxiaco."

Good on his word, Pablo and his son made the trip that night into the nearby village, picking up desperately needed supplies for the team. While grabbing a *cerveza*, they took in the gossip flying around the *cantina*, and they were discouraged by what they heard.

The gang's violent behavior had spilled over into the village, but the local *policia* did nothing—they merely ignored the situation. After the villagers, who knew their way around a rifle, shook off the jolt of having been caught off-guard, they decided to take matters into their own hands—they took up armed watch. If the cartel wannabes came back, the villagers would be waiting for them.

The *cantina* buzzed over the gang's violence, but another snippet of news upset Pablo even more when he caught wind that many in the village blamed the presence of the nearby Americans for the problems. While taking on the *policia,* or even the cartel wannabes, concerned the villagers little, for they were used to fighting, they were keenly aware of the repercussions of antagonizing the Oaxaca cartel. If the Americans had aggravated the cartel, then the villagers wanted nothing to do with them.

Optimism faded as Pablo realized that while the village wanted the archaeology team gone, they would do little to help them leave. He definitely would not be able to procure a truck to get the team to

Tlaxiaco. As he scanned the crowded *cantina*, Pablo caught a glimpse of an old friend tucked away at a small table in a corner.

A friend who Pablo knew had a working phone in his business, and excusing himself, the farmer joined his comrade for another round of *cerveza*. After much heated bickering between the two as they negotiated at the back table, Pablo had found a way for the team to call out.

The archaeology team had been eagerly awaiting Pablo's arrival the following morning with excitement and hope, but their expressions fell as he explained to them what he had learned in the village. "They don't trust you and they are not going to help."

A wave of disappointment rushed through Sam at Pablo's news, and it only deepened when Pablo looked directly at her and hesitantly admitted, "I need to stay away, too. For *mi familia*. I will help you as much as I can, but they come first." His expression was a study of not only determination, but of acceptance.

Sam's mind had gone blank as she took in all the information, but a flood of despair rushed in, filling the voids. She had assumed it would be easy to get a truck to leave, and Pablo's frank news left her biting her lip as her mind whirled with the uncertainty of what to do next. Pablo went on to tell them what his friend had agreed to.

"He will allow only one person to make a short ten-minute phone call, and you cannot be seen by the village. You must come after dark, around midnight, and come in the back way from the hills." Pablo had agreed he would take one person by horseback to the phone, cutting through the hills, and Sam decided that one person would be her.

Kati and Doug apprehensively entered Sam's tent and stood by watching as Sam pulled back a section of her tent's floor to begin digging up a cache of buried money. Throwing the wad of money into a satchel, she then rummaged through her duffel for her contact book.

"Are you sure about this?" Kati asked as Sam cursed while roughly searching around the tent for a bandana and a pair of gloves. Doug reached down to pick up the gloves that Sam couldn't seem to find, and silently handed them to her.

"No," Sam snapped as she snatched the gloves from Doug's hands, and threw them in the satchel as well. "I'm not sure."

With her hands behind her head as she scanned the tent for anything else she might need, Sam professed while shaking her head, "I still can't believe we can't rent a truck. Making a phone call wasn't what I had in mind," she grunted as she began to pack her field vest with supplies, "but if it is all we can do, then…that's what we do."

Sam stopped long enough to throw a glance at Kati and Doug. She could tell, from the lack of bickering between them, just how upset they were. "Look guys," she said while trying to sound confident, "Juan got us into this mess, he can get us out. We have enough supplies to stick it out until he gets here, so let's just keep it together—we can fall apart later."

At night, the ride by horseback took hours, even though the village was only a few miles away. Riding double, Pablo, wary of both the cartel wannabes and the local *policia,* was careful to keep the horse on soft ground to minimize hoofbeats, stopping occasionally when he thought he heard something.

They traveled in total silence. At times during the rocky route, he would dismount to lead in single file and Sam, plagued by night blindness as part of her Usher syndrome, found herself hanging onto the horse's tail for stability and direction.

At last, a faint shimmer of light in the distance announced they were near the edge of the village and soon Sam was sliding off the horse's rear onto solid ground. They had ridden up to the rear door of what looked like a service garage, and the door opened to their soft knocking. Pablo's friend was noncommittal as he led Sam into a small office area with a telephone, but she could feel the heat of distrust coming off the man. He just wanted her to make her call and get out.

While she had been stumbling behind the horse, her feet sliding on loose dirt, Sam's mind had been sorting through all that had happened. Pablo had stunned her when she had asked how soon the mudslides on the roads would be cleared. He merely casually shrugged his shoulders when he told her, "Eh, they'll get to them eventually." Even if she had gotten a truck Sam realized, they weren't going anywhere.

Her mind spun as she reevaluated what she knew, thoughts rushing in and then darting to the edges of her subconscious. *What could Juan do for me? What information can I trust? And more importantly —who can I trust?* Her thoughts flitted between Juan and Roger...and Gerry.

Those thoughts were still with her as she moved to dial the operator for a collect call. But her finger stopped and hovered, momentarily motionless when she realized it wasn't Juan, but rather her own people that she wanted to talk to.

While she trusted Roger Belicampf implicitly, it wasn't Roger she called.

2 6

YOU KNOW WHAT YOU HAVE TO
DO, NOW GET IT DONE

*G*EORGIA, *MOMENTS LATER*

The rude jarring ring of the phone jerked Gerry out of a deep sleep, and he struggled to silence the blaring noise. Groping for the receiver, he woke up enough to turn on the light and look at his watch. *Who the hell calls at this hour?* he grumbled to himself. It was 2:37 a.m.

The woman's voice at the other end was heavy with an accent, "A collect call from Sam Walker, will you accept the charges?"

Still shaking out the cobwebs, Gerry mumbled, "Yeah," and Sam's voice immediately came on the line, only to be cut off by another voice.

The second voice, a man's with a Spanish accent in the background, warned her, "You have ten minutes, I wait no more."

For a moment, Gerry thought he was still asleep, caught in the grips of the nightmare that had been stalking him. But then, the voice came back on the line again, telling Sam, "You go in ten minutes… and be quiet."

The icy tone signaled trouble and an immediate electric jolt of alarm shot through Gerry, bolting him upright and instantly wide awake. And he knew…his nightmare was real.

The ten-minute comment had his full attention, and he instinctively pushed the timer on his tactical watch to begin a countdown. Gerry, however, had no clue as to what he was counting down toward. There was no lazily cheerful greeting of *Hi, Hon, how's it going?* His urgent questions were abrupt and spoken so quickly, that they were all blurted out as a single sentence. "Are you okay? What's wrong? What happened?"

As fast and as clearly as she could, Sam described what had transpired over the last week: the *policia* harassment, the gangs of youths raiding the camp, and finally the volley of gunfire they unleashed on their vehicles. She also mentioned the nearby village was on edge, and the community's sentiment was that the Americans were on their own.

"What do I do? Who do I call to get us out of here?" Her questions echoed over the staticky line.

The timer on his watch showed only seven minutes left, and Gerry rapidly interrogated Sam with a flurry of questions that ran the gamut —type of weapons, how many were there, time of day, clothing, tattoos, type of vehicles, ages?

"You have nothing to fight with," he said bluntly, and in an even more foreboding tone, grimly added, "and you will not win." Drawing on all his training, the man on the other end of the phone began strategizing a landscape he couldn't see. "Do you remember what I've shown you about defensive perimeters and attitude?" he asked Sam.

Precious minutes passed as he tried to remind Sam of all he had taught her over the past couple of years, and as the watch ticked past the one-minute mark, he chose his final instructions carefully.

"Hon, take care of business. You know what you have to do, now get it done. I will take care of this. I will find out what's going on and get you out. I promise you." As that promise was made, a guttural voice demanded that she hang up, and Gerry heard a struggle for the receiver. Pablo's friend wanted Sam gone. "Remember our code words," were the last words her shaken boyfriend spoke as the line went silent.

"No, no...Gerry don't ha—" But Sam was now talking to dead air— he had hung up on her. *Our code words? We have code words?*

Petrified that he had just made a promise he couldn't keep, Gerry sat on the edge of his bed doing mental gymnastics, working out who to call, and in what order. He started with Roger. The early pre-dawn morning call set the tone for Roger's day while he listened to Gerry's terse voice clip words as he described what had unfolded at the Oaxaca site. Roger admitted he had heard from Sam and Juan several days earlier, and that they had discussed some concerns, but nothing like this.

As he read out Juan's phone number and details of the site's location, he offered to contact the State Department for more information, but was rebuffed as Gerry curtly told him, "Don't bother, I'll take care of it myself." Gerry, instead, called a different number.

A few minutes later, across the country in southern California, narcotics agent Jared Romney had barely gotten into bed after a long unproductive night working a case when his phone rang. The disembodied voice on the phone abruptly ordered, "Tell me what you know about Oaxaca, México, the local *policia,* and the Oaxaca cartel."

Momentarily at a loss, Jared then recognized the voice, "Martinez?" Gerry briefed his former colleague on the situation, and as he listened, Jared told him, after a momentary pause, "I'm not the person, but I know who is. I'll call you back, sit tight." His sentences were as short as Gerry's. Through a series of back-and-forth phone calls with his contacts, Jared gathered enough information to assess what was going on and set a plan of action in motion.

Meanwhile, back in Georgia, Gerry had been making calls to his own people, notably the Musketeers of Stan, Brady, and Mark. Stan was stunningly quiet as Gerry brought him up to speed, and his tone grave, he somberly asked, "Whaddaya want me to do?"

Gerry, who had already been working on timetables and options, bluntly barked, "Call Brady and Mark. Start calling anybody and everybody. Get me ideas. Get me to Oaxaca. And find me some help."

Stan reassured Gerry as the call ended. "Ger, stop for a second and breathe. We got this. Ya concentrate on Sam. The rest of us—we'll take care of everythin' else. Okay, bud?"

"You're the best, Stan, " Gerry gratefully replied. "I can always count on you." Relief echoed behind his words.

His mind spun wildly as Gerry tried to think, and first on his list was, *How do I get to Oaxaca?* And as all his ideas and options twirled about, his phone rang—it was Jared.

One of Jared's calls had been to a colleague at the State Department who confirmed there were no advisories or warnings posted for the area, aside from the usual. Jared then conveyed what he learned about the cartels. He quickly assured his worried friend that, according to his contacts, this was not the work of cartels. "I was told, however, that there are reports of a youth group trying to make inroads into the drug trafficking trade. My contact says this new group is an unorganized mob with no goal or clear leader, and are operating on a false sense of importance."

Hope resonated in Gerry's voice when he asked, "So, this group— they're nothing to worry about?"

"No, I'm not saying that," Jared carefully pointed out. "This doesn't mean they aren't dangerous. What I'm saying is that they are not powerful. They have no resources or clout, and that makes them a different type of 'dangerous'—one defined by desperation."

Gerry sat trying to absorb everything Jared was telling him and then asked, "What about the *policia*? What's the deal with them?"

"Ah, that is a bit of a puzzle," Jared admitted. "I called several colleagues on that matter and none of them are real sure of what is going on there," he explained, "and our best guess is that the harassment from the local *policia,* and their refusal to intervene in the gang violence, are not related. The harassment sounds like an ego trip, but them turning a blind eye to the trouble those boys are causing is different. That feels more like the *policia* are either worried about cartel reprisal, or are in their pockets."

The information allayed some of Gerry's fears as he listened, but his blood pressure only skyrocketed again when Jared summarized their recommendations for the archeology crew.

"The seasonal rains have already begun," Jared went on to tell Gerry, "and mountain roads are already difficult if not impassable due to the mud and rockslides. Martinez, my people say the worst had probably already happened. They think, and I do, too, that this gang will simply move out of the area once they have stripped it of its resources. In other words, they will go to their next target."

Gerry, who had been listening in silence, had a sinking feeling when Jared cautiously added, "But there's another problem, and it's a mess. There is a growing protest movement among the Indigenous people, and it is making road travel treacherous, especially for foreigners. Our recommendation, one we all agree is the best option here, is for this team to wait this out in place."

Jared waited for the explosive objection from Gerry he knew was coming, and in a preemptive strike, he quickly interjected, "I know this is your girl, but you charging down there like some hot-headed John Wayne will only make matters worse."

Jared worked to appease his friend while outlining his plan for the immediate. He had located some associates who could make themselves available for a few days. "Martinez, my guys are already down there, and will be at the camp tomorrow," Jared revealed. "They are seasoned agents who can provide the much-needed eyes on the situation, and if necessary, they can handle whatever needs to be done."

The dead silence told the narcotics agent his proposal hadn't gone over well, and he pleaded with Gerry, "Please, let them do their jobs." Jared was genuinely surprised when he heard Gerry's resigned voice that had dropped to a whisper, agreeing.

"Okay, if that's what we have to do. Write this down and tell them to say this to her," he said as he recited a phrase.

That was way too easy, Jared thought as he hung up, knowing there was no way Gerry would have caved like that. He was up to something.

While intensely grateful for their help, Gerry was disgruntled by their "wait and see" approach as he hung up the phone. He had no intention of just sitting there.

· · ·

EXCAVATION SITE, OAXACA, AT THE SAME TIME

After the call, Pablo's friend had callously thrown Sam out the door. On the way back to camp, tears threatened as she sat perched on the old mare's bony hipbones behind Pablo. She was on an emotional roller coaster that peaked at despair and bottomed out in the valley of despondency. Everything had gone sideways in a flash, and she hadn't realized how much she had pinned her hopes on that phone call, but it had done little to subdue her panic. Scoffing at her naïveté, she viciously berated herself for having watched too many Hollywood movies.

Somehow, she had let herself imagine Gerry as some type of modern-day Zorro riding to the rescue, but instead, he had clobbered her in the face with a dose of reality. For a moment, a rush of insecurity flowed over Sam and she morosely bellyached to herself, *Where does Gerry get off thinking I can do everything he talked about? What do I know about defensive perimeters?*

She had no idea where to start, but the ride back to camp gave Sam plenty of time to dwell on all that had been said. And the first question she asked herself was, *Girl, just what the hell is wrong with you? Since when do you whine like this? Okay...so you don't have a game plan.* She badgered herself, *Get off your duff and make one.*

Gerry had been harping at Sam for years to pay more attention to defense. Not so much her personal defense, but rather to her overall defense in the field. He had wanted her to be more alert to her surroundings, to have a "just in case" game plan, and to make decisions based on that game plan. He had been so persistent and had droned on ad nauseam, that, after a bit, she barely listened to him anymore.

Now, Sam strained to recall all the things he had explained to her over the years and slowly, the pieces started to align themselves. They had been whirling around in a vortex, and to the rocking motion astride the mare, some of them had actually begun to settle into place.

It was in the predawn hours when she slid off the rear of the horse with the sunrise at least an hour away—an hour that the fortunes of her team hinged on. Walking up to the horse's head, Sam reached up and gave the old mare a hug around its neck while brushing its forelock out of its eyes. Holding the horse's head in her hands and staring into its eyes, she gratefully whispered, "Thanks, old girl, for taking care of me," wishing she had a treat for it.

Despite the darkness, Pablo could see the toll the night had taken. Sam's face was pale in the moonlight while she stretched up to give him an appreciative squeeze on his arm, but neither of them said anything as he nudged his horse into motion, the old mare's hooves clopping dully in the dirt. The farmer's tilt of his hat and curt nod communicated his silent *Buena suerte*, as the horse and rider disappeared into the dark.

Sam scrambled up the ridge and sat down heavily to study the area, her shoulders slumping in fatigue as she mentally readied herself for the task ahead. She could make out the camp below bathed in the fading moonlight, and the stark contrast of the tents against the surrounding hills startled her.

Suddenly it all made sense, and she made a short raspy gasp as she laughed at herself. *It's all here* Sam thought, as she viewed the landscape through a different lens. She began to smile as her perception changed. She no longer saw the beauty of nature with its majestic mountains and delicate valleys, but—as Gerry called them—their strategic assets.

Whispering *Oh my God,* she saw the elements described on the phone were now as plain as day. She had panicked when Gerry had hurriedly barked instructions about setting up a perimeter, finding high ground and defensible fallback positions, and caching supplies. *Yeah right. Look out world, Rambo is on the loose!* Sam had mocked to herself at the time, but there they were—the choke points, the defensible high ground vantage points. She gaped when she saw the grotto. "Build a blind and hunker down until help arrives," Gerry had said.

Sam giggled in delight and understanding...and in relief. The setting moon was just barely hanging on the horizon when Sam marveled—every time she thought Gerry couldn't impress her anymore, he did. Concentrating on the moon's glow, Sam gratefully sent Gerry a telepathic message, one she hoped he could somehow sense. "Thank you sweetie."

For that next hour before sunrise, Sam devised her strategy, and while incorporating as much as she could remember, she mapped out all the changes they would have to make, even subterfuge.

"Misdirect their actions, redirect their attention. Divert them from where you are to where you want them to go," Gerry had instructed.

When Sam finally stood up and dusted off her pants, she was oblivious to the chilly morning air for her attention was now focused on a single objective—she had a battle plan. The sunrise mirrored her mood and Sam chuckled at a growing confidence that erased the sweat of panic—gone were the wobbly knees. The echo of Gerry's voice, *Get it done*, brought a sense of calm to her heart, and she thought as she visualized her plan coming together, that it was going to be a good day.

As Sam stood looking over the camp, the sun's increasing rays illuminated features she hadn't seen in the dark—features that only bolstered her plan. As she scanned the surrounding area, a sudden flicker of light in Kati's tent focused her attention back onto the team, and once again, Gerry's voice flooded her mind. "Do not show fear," Gerry had said. He had oddly asked her to remember how she handled testy livestock, and then knowingly remarked, "They can smell fear. Whatever happens, Samantha, don't let them smell fear."

"I won't," Sam had promised, when she boldly told him, "I will look them straight in the eye when they show up."

"No," Gerry had corrected her. "Not the gang...your team. You're their leader, you are the boss, you are in control. Do not let them see indecision or doubt. You alone make the decisions. It's okay to have those fears—only a fool isn't afraid, but don't wallow in them—use them."

She had waited until after the jeeps from their usual morning *policia* harassment visit, had cleared the hills before setting her plan in motion. But this time, she had not taken a vote. This time, she simply had told the camp what needed to be done. The team scurried to abandon camp, bury supplies, erase all traces, and build the blind. Bill and Dan were tasked with leaving a trail of footprints leading out of the valley a ways, and then double back to safety, obscuring their returning footprints.

"Let them think you have run for safety. They are young and inexperienced, and will be too self-absorbed, gloating in their victory, to notice the irregularities," Gerry had stated.

His litany of directions kept repeating in her mind. *If possible, leave unessential equipment in the camp—it will be more realistic. Take only what you need and bury vital equipment you may need later. Mud on your faces and arms and no vivid colors, dress in earth tones only. Choose and build your blind carefully, but keep it within ear shot of the camp. Be mindful of metal, eyeglasses, and camera lens—anything that reflects or makes sound.*

Above all, he had begged her to remember two things: "First, don't panic and second...I will come."

The vivaciousness that characterized Kati was nonexistent as she watched Sam set the stage for the camp's transformation. Kati could not wrap her head around Gerry's advice, and candidly declared this was a mistake as she confronted her friend head on. Kati didn't like the man, and she let Sam know it. Thoroughly unimpressed with him, Kati had met Gerry a couple of years earlier and he had just sat there like a rock, quietly studying her as he dissected her. In her eyes, it was laughable to follow his advice when it was doubtful the dullard could even formulate a complete sentence, let alone a constructive thought.

The two women locked eyes physically—and horns mentally.

"Don't have time to re-explain everything to you Dr. Banyon," an acerbic Sam snapped, her use of the title telling Kati where she stood. Hoping to rally her friend to her side, Sam took a gentler tack and reiterated, "Kati, he's coming. Gerry said he would and trust me when I tell you, he'll be here. I don't know how or when, but he will be here."

Sam's faith in Gerry did little to soften Kati's scowl as she confrontationally stood with arms crossed while the two women opposed each other. "Suit yourself Kati, but I'm going to build the defenses whether I have your help or not." Banking on close to a decade of friendship to help sway her argument in one last plea, Sam put her hands on the woman's shoulders, and repeated again with total conviction as she looked into Kati's eyes, "He *will* come, and he'll get us home."

Until that moment, Kati would have argued Sam was incapable of such an unbelievable level of stupidity, one that was being eclipsed by her unwavering naiveté. "What makes you so bloody sure about this?" Kati defiantly asked Sam before flinging another accusation at her. "How the hell can you be such an asinine fool? How can you be so…" she blustered, her words falling off as she groped for words.

Sam studied her friend's harsh expression. "How can I be so… stupid?" Sam offered with a soft smile that caught Kati by surprise. "Do you remember when we got lost in Belize?" Sam asked as she reminded Kati of another uncertain moment. "When we were in a bit of a bind having taken the wrong turn, and then lost our supplies over that waterfall? We stood there trying to figure out which way would get us back to base. We all were convinced that one direction was the way, but you…you held steadfast that we were to head in the opposite direction, through rough terrain."

Kati softened at the memory as Sam recalled those days. "Everything pointed to heading downhill through the valley," Sam continued, "but you couldn't be swayed. Your conviction was so strong, so sincere that we all took a gamble…and we won. You were right."

There was a hint of a smile as Sam paused, her head tilted in remembrance of another moment. "Do you remember what you said when I asked you later how you knew, despite all the clues and our experience telling us to go the other way—you somehow knew?"

"Yeah," Kati scoffed at the memory and mockingly confessed, "I fed you some silly-ass line about how the jungle was talking to me and was telling me to follow a 'trail of energy'," Kati snickered when she quipped, "I couldn't believe you fell for that!"

Sam was grinning as she leaned forward and quietly told Kati, "That was no line. We all walked behind you, watching, as you followed an invisible straight path to safety—straight as an arrow. We still shake our heads over those days."

The anger between the two women ebbed away in the wake of

years of friendship as Sam continued. "Gerry and I…we have that same energy. I know my faith in him seems absurd, even irrational to you…but it is real. Just as you asked us to trust you then in Belize, I'm asking you to trust my faith in Gerry now. I know you can't see it, but this is my path. And Gerry…he'll come. He'll simply follow that trail of energy."

Doug had watched the scene play out and, strolling over to Kati as Sam went back to clearing out the camp site, he softly spoke to her.

"Kats, where are we going to go? The *policia* aren't on our side. The villagers won't help. We have no vehicle, the roads are out, and Pablo has said he has done all that he can. I don't know the guy, but I do know Sam, and she thinks this Gerry guy can help. Right now, that belief is pretty much all I have, and I think we should go with it." Watching Sam orchestrate things, Kati could only manage a slight head nod—she would help.

The cavern that was to be their blind left Sam dumbfounded. Providing what they needed—shelter and seclusion, it was a small natural cave nestled in a copse of trees and thickets with a narrow entrance naturally obscured in the shadows. All they had to do was finish what Mother Nature had started. She had been especially delighted to discover while exploring it, that there were small openings in its walls that could be used as observation points—she couldn't believe their luck.

They had carefully woven cut branches into existing branches of nearby trees to cover any hint of an opening. Large rocks and fallen logs were moved into place to erase any trace of a passageway. And when they were done, Sam stood back and grinned absurdly, for no one could see it—not even if they knew it was there.

Tucked in and hidden up in the security of that blind in the hills, an emotionally ragged team watched as their camp was visited three times over the next twenty-four hours. Several of the team were paralyzed with worry that their efforts would be in vain, and they would be discovered, others were more pensively fatalistic while still others were brazenly defiant with anger. Sam's worries took on the added weight of her having made the decisions, and she prayed they were the right ones.

The first visit came as a surprise that early afternoon just as they were putting the final touches to the entrance of their blind. It was the hopeful cartel wannabes with three pickups totaling seventeen gang members. In what had become their signature trademarked behavior, they wandered about the "abandoned" site, waving their rifles, laughing, and mocking the *Americanos*.

Inspecting the derelict vehicles and tents, the cartel wannabes tossed about the equipment left "behind," snatching a few souvenirs along the way. Sam could hear Augustin behind her in a hushed prayer, "Please don't find us. Please don't look up." She reached back and gave his arm a reassuring squeeze.

The track of footprints left by Dan and Bill going out up into the hills, triggered a series of victory whoops from the gang, and the cartel wannabes celebrated loudly as they left. The work crews took perverse pleasure watching the pickups triumphally spin circles in the dirt as the cartel wannabes fired their weapons haphazardly, before rocketing up the hills.

Watching the trucks disappear over the ridge, Sam began to chuckle faintly to herself. Soon, a nasalized snort erupted from Doug…and then Kati just plain lost it. Dan and Bill watched in amazement as the three veterans, while holding their sides in laughter, tried to muffle the sound by burying their faces in jackets. But then the two interns glanced over at Augustin and Pepe, who were fighting their own battle to contain their hysterics—it was in vain. The entire team rolled in the dirt of the cavern, their bodies shaking violently in convulsions as they stifled howls—it was the first good laugh the team had in days.

"Oh my God," Kati gasped as she wiped tears from her eyes, "that was better than a three-cheese, deep-dish, extra meat topping pizza!"

The mention of a slice sent Bill swooning. "Oh, what I would do for a slice right now!" he said, still giggling.

Doug's tone was mischievous when he asked with a smirk, "Will you settle for pizza flavored Cheez Whiz on a stale cracker?"

"You're kidding me!" Dan exclaimed in amazement.

Doug, who had pulled out a can of Cheez Whiz and was arranging crackers on a T-shirt for the group, teasingly shot back at Dan, "And you made fun of all my 'necessities of life' stuff!"

The joking was like a pressure release for Sam, and she soaked it all up. As the team dickered over the crackers, she gratefully thought to herself, *We're going to be all right.*

Later that night, gunfire was heard in the distance to the west—the cartel wannabes had found someone else to harass. Thankfully, the gang was gone, but the crews took no solace as the distant pop of gunfire portended a rough night ahead for someone else.

27

JUST HAPPENED TO BE ON VACATION

Not long after daybreak, came the second of their visits, the *policia* arriving on schedule to dole out the daily dose of bullying. Watching as before from the safety of their blind, the spectacle of officers angrily kicking remaining equipment in disgust as they stormed away, gave the team their second good laugh within twenty-four hours.

Sam had chuckled that the cavern that served as their blind seemed like Goldilocks. Not too big to be obvious and easily noticed, but yet was large enough to accommodate everyone. Not too small that it was claustrophobic, but yet small enough to promote a sense of calm. Their sanctuary was a cozy blanket.

Feeling safe, eyes grew heavy with exhaustion and fatigue crept over the team as all the stress and chaos of the past few days seized them. They fell asleep. It seemed like they had been asleep for only seconds when a few hours later, they were shaken awake by Dan, and there was concern in his eyes. "Guys," he hissed, "there is someone coming. I hear a truck."

Fear overtook fatigue and, in a flash, everyone checked to make sure the brush camouflage concealed the entrance of their hide-a-way. Then, they waited in jittery anticipation. A single small dark mud-splattered field jeep crawled its way over the crest of the hill, and pulling in next to the two bullet riddled jeeps, two men got out. Grungy, with long dark hair, dressed in ratty clothes and sporting tattoos, their gruff appearance only added to the team's misery.

In Spanish, one of the men called out, asking if anyone was there, but received no response. In the blind, motionless, the team didn't make a sound. The men wandered around the abandoned site, and Doug cautiously inched up to take a closer look at them through binoculars. Handing the glasses to Kati, Doug whispered with surprise and hope in his voice, "I think they are Caucasian, not Mexican."

Peering through the binoculars, Kati watched the new arrivals follow the footprints up the valley but quickly pivot to return back to camp. They were not as easily fooled, and Sam reached down to flip the safety on her handgun. With long shoulder length dark hair, a stained tank T-shirt, and faded jeans, the more imposing of the two stood in the center of the camp and bellowed out, *"Somhairlin, Chuir Gearóid chugainn."*

Stunned speechless when she recognized the words, Sam remained frozen as the man repeated the phrase for a second time. It was her name in Gaelic, followed by the phrase, *Gerry sent us,* also in Gaelic. They were the code words Gerry had told her to remember. Narcotics agent Jared Romney had been true to his word and sent two colleagues to help.

Relief flooded everyone as a visibly relaxed Sam reholstered the gun and stood up to make her way down toward camp and the agents. They all excitedly followed her down the hill, everyone talking all at once, and out of the din of voices, someone asked the agents where they had come from.

"We just happened to be seized by a ferocious need to vacation in Oaxaca and are taking a little side tour, that's all," the larger agent told them. The Cheshire grins on their faces clearly communicated that wasn't true.

Moving at a speed that mirrored their delight, the two ecstatic crews hastily gathered equipment, retrieved items from the blind and uncovered buried caches, all in the expectation they were now leaving.

Doug was holding all the journals and paperwork the team would need to clear customs, when he ran by Sam and shouted out over his shoulder, "That guy of yours really came through, didn't he! Remind me to buy him a drink when we get home! Better yet, how about you guys come for a weekend BBQ?!!" He was giddy with relief and expectation.

A warm flush of admiration for Gerry flowed over Sam as she watched the team enthusiastically gather up their belongings, and she paused the scene for a moment—a mental still photograph. Closing her eyes, she inwardly hugged Gerry and thought, *Sweetie, I don't know how you did it, but again, thank you.*

The voice of the larger agent broke Sam's private moment when he called out, "Which one of you is Samantha?"

Sam flicked a finger up in acknowledgement. Her enthusiasm overflowing, she gushed as she shook their hands, "I can't even begin to tell you guys how happy we are to see you. Just give us a few minutes here and we will be ready to go!"

"Um…about that," the smaller agent cautiously said as he began to explain the situation. "First, the roads are a mess. We had to off-road it at times just to get around debris and slides. Second, even if we could drive the roads, we can't take all of you. Multiple trucks grab attention, so we stuck to using only one jeep. There is no way we can fit all of you in it."

A grim feeling washed over Sam as what the agents were saying sank in. They weren't leaving. The larger of the agents then dampened Sam's hopes even further with his discouraging description of protests, and pockets of rioting with sporadic gunfire by the local Indigenous community.

Any residual hope Sam had of leaving was delivered a death knell when the same agent told her, "There are *policia* checkpoints set up along virtually every major road, and I'm not sure whose side they are on."

The smaller agent, seeing the crestfallen look on Sam's face, sympathetically told her, "I know we don't look like much, but we're unofficially here to help." With a small smile of encouragement, he then added, "and we'll be staying for a bit."

Her hopes dashed, Sam forlornly asked, "Why did you guys come if it wasn't so we could leave? Isn't that the whole point?"

"Actually, no. That's not the point," the larger agent bluntly told her. "Our job is your safety, not your comfort." Sam listened to them explain who the gang of boys were and that they shouldn't be returning. In the agents' view, the gang was no longer a concern. The roads and civil unrest were. "It is safer for you to remain here," the smaller agent added.

Kati and Augustin came up just in time for them to hear the agents tell Sam. "No one is hurt, so it would be best to make a stand here at the camp, and wait to leave when things get better." Sam, her face a picture of disappointment, looked over at Kati.

"You've got to be kidding me," Kati sharply barked, her voice full of raw incredulity. "Just what the hell do you think we're going to do here? We don't have anything—no supplies, nothing!" Kati spewed the words as she stood, hands on hips, her voice just below a scream. Murmuring some absent-minded *Uh huhs*, the two agents retrieved a couple of wrenches and, after removing some bolts, heaved the front seats of the jeep off their mounts. The jeep had been confiscated from drug runners and when the floor plates were lifted, there were hidden compartments full of supplies.

Straightening up, one of the agents gave Kati a good hard stare before announcing, "Now, I don't know about you people, but I'd like to get this place back together so I can have a beer."

Sam's first priority was coffee. As camp restoration occupied the crew, she scrounged around in the dirt for the coffee can, a pot and some mugs, and soon, the comforting smell of a percolating brew drifted throughout the camp.

Kati came and sat down, and the two women silently regarded each other. Looking for a way to break the ice, Kati playfully gave Sam a nudge as she said, "Looks like that path of energy you were talking about saved the day!" When Sam smiled over at her at the remark, Kati leaned over and whispered, "I'm sorry, I should've trusted you."

Kati's rebellion, first against Gerry and then against her, had left Sam feeling hurt, and she simply said, "Eh, no worries. You don't know Gerry like I do."

An uncharacteristically somber Kati ruefully admitted to Sam, "No, I don't—but I do know you. We've been through so much together, girl, where we've had to trust each other totally...and I didn't."

"This is a side of you I don't normally see," Sam teased, a bit surprised at Kati's apology, and after a moment, solemnly handed her a mug of coffee as a peace offering.

Kati, grateful the tension was lifting, raised her mug and murmured as she toasted, "To trust."

With a soft relieved smile, Sam clinked her mug to Kati's with a toast of her own, "To friendship."

The two women were sharing a gentle laugh when the agents came and sat next to them and asked, "Can we have a word with you?" They had a suggestion. "We've been talking...and we think you should continue the excavation as if nothing is wrong. We want it to look like 'business as usual.'"

Mulling it over for a second as she considered their request, Sam gingerly told them, "Let us think about this a bit, okay?" She called for a team meeting.

Conclaved in Sam's tent, the team deliberated. They could either stay as advised, or choose to disregard the agents' counsel and make an effort to leave.

Sam opened the discussion. "Okay guys, here's the good news: We're in no immediate danger. The gang is gone and they're not expected back. No one is hurt and the camp is intact. We have plenty of supplies for the moment. We're away from any unrest or rioting. From all accounts and information, we're safe here." The news was greeted by a round of applause and cheers of "Yay!" and "Awright!"

"Regarding transportation," she continued, "I've been told that

Juan has been informed of the situation here, and he'll be sending trucks as soon as roads permit."

Sam solemnly dipped her head for a second before delivering the bad news. "Now, for the not so good news. First, these agents can't guarantee your safety. There is no way to ever be absolutely safe in the field. You people know that. Next, the roads are out. The best hope is that they will be passable next week. I was told, however, not to hold my breath on that. Third, the village won't resupply us. We will probably be dependent on Pablo and the agents until we do leave. Lastly, the agents can only stay a few days. They will at some point have to leave us to our own devices."

Sam paused to study their expressions. Looking out over the group, she reflected on how everyone was always asking her what she thought, what they should do and whether she was scared.

She heard Gerry's voice float over from the side, telling her, *It's okay to have those fears—only a fool isn't afraid, but don't wallow in them— use them.* She smiled and started to make a joke that she had gotten it when he said it the first time, and then realized—Gerry wasn't there. She had only heard his voice in her head. A sense of calm wrapped around Sam as she told the team. "For myself...I'll be staying. For those of you who want to leave right now, I'll fight for a way to make that happen. This is a decision for each of you to make for yourself, and it is entirely up to you. What do you guys think?" Sam asked as she finished outlining the situation.

When Augustin wanted to know why she was staying, Sam didn't elaborate much, but instead simply answered, "I've been working the field for a long time now and I'm comfortable here. Besides..." Sam added with a serene, knowing look that explained her calm, "my Gerry's coming." Sam had thrown a look over at Kati at that remark, and Doug caught it. Alarm bells were going off in his head.

Hiding his voice within those of the team debating, Doug leaned over to Kati and whispered, "You've got to talk some sense into her. Sam needs to get real."

"Whaddaya mean?" Kati questioned with a sideways glance.

With blatant skepticism, Doug snorted, "Gerry's coming? Kats, there's no way that guy is going to get here. Did you hear what those agents said about the roads and such?" Lowering his voice even more, Doug admitted, "It's one thing to take his advice, it was good advice... but this?" Cynicism hovered in his voice when he said bluntly, "This blind faith of hers is scary."

Watching Sam and the team banter for a bit, Kati finally softly murmured, "He'll be here, you'll see,"

"*Et tú,* Kati?" Doug stuttered, amazed at Kati's change of heart.

After a few seconds, Kati spoke slowly in reflection as she recalled the conversation she had with Sam just days earlier. "Sam's not in denial, Doug. Remember Belize where we got lost? You guys reaming me a new one when I carried on about how best to get back to base?"

Doug's eyes flickered around at the memory as Kati plainly told him, "She's not worried because, like I did then, she knows."

It was a back and forth as the team weighed the instinct to leave against the desire to stay and finish the job. As Sam left her tent, she locked eyes with the larger lead agent, and her curt nod communicated the team's decision. They would follow the agents' advice and wait for the civil unrest to settle down. For the moment, they would stay and wait.

Secluded on remote private land, away from the village and the contentious hot spots of civil violence, and with the cartel wannabes gone, the site and the team that worked it were safe. So, they began to dig again.

As the site excavation continued, so did the restoration of the camp. Those hidden compartments were a motherlode of not only vital supplies, but also minor car parts and tools, including some gasoline and oil. The agents ambitiously set about cannibalizing the worst of the damaged jeeps in a dubious attempt to fix the other. In the coming days, they, along with Doug and Dan, would repair what they could, patch tires, and slowly return a bullet strafed jeep to functioning.

The arrival of the local *policia* the next morning was a surprise for the group as they hadn't expected them back. But this time, however, the surprise was on the officers.

There were only two officers that day and the pudgy one the team nicknamed Pottymouth was one of them. Pottymouth gave the agents' jeep, which was parked next to the bullet-ridden hulks belonging to the camp, a very long stare as he tried to figure out what was going on. And then the agents appeared.

Overnight, the agents had changed their appearance…and their persona. No longer grungy looking hoodlums, they had washed up, shaved and changed into clean clothing. They were now respectable looking law enforcement representatives.

"Ah, officers," the larger agent called out with fake enthusiasm as he strode up with his credentials in hand. "Thanks for stopping by—saves us the hassle of coming in to see you."

Pottymouth nervously inspected the agents and their IDs with suspicion and then belligerently demanded, "Why are you here? Under whose authority are you working?" Haughtily, he tried to intimidate the agents by getting into their faces. It didn't work.

"Naw, fellas—no need to get the knickers in a knot. We're not here in any official capacity," the smaller agent quipped, his eyes crinkling with enjoyment as he watched the officers back up.

The larger agent butted in, lazily joshing, "Yeah, we're just here visiting our friends. We were just down here on vacation and heard about some horrible trouble up this way."

Pottymouth slowly handed back the credentials as he flicked his eyes between first the agents, then Sam, who was standing just behind the agents, and lastly at the rest of the team who was on the sidelines watching.

Trying to regain his offensive edge, Pottymouth blustered, "I am the authority here and you will not interfere with our business."

The smaller agent burst out laughing, "Oh absolutely, officer. There's been a misunderstanding here." Leaning pointedly into Pottymouth's personal space, the agent firmly announced, "We just thought we'd pop in and surprise our friends, and make sure they're all right." Staring at the officers, his smile took on a rigid cast when he added, "We'd hate to have anything happen to our friends."

From the sidelines, Kati could barely contain herself as she watched the officers begin to shift their feet in discomfort. "Oh, get a load of Pottymouth!" she cackled. "He's dancing like a blue-footed booby!"

Despite the presence of the agents, the *policia* continued the harassment, but with a twist. Sam and Augustin still had to face off against the officers, but now, while the *policia* still huffed and puffed, they in due course, retreated without their customary vandalism of the camp. The ransacking had stopped, but in its place, a new routine of intense stare downs between the ranking officer and Sam emerged as the animosity continued. Nerve-wracking reminders, aimed at browbeating the team were continually issued daily, echoing the warning that they were not wanted, and were under watch.

At night, the agents took four-hour shifts, one on the prowl against the ridge all night while the other remained in camp. Another agent, also sent by Jared, ran the gauntlet of roads to roll into the camp a few days later. He replaced the larger agent and brought with him more vital supplies and information. Again, he just "happened" to be on vacation.

A few days after that, the fourth and last of the narcotic agents had also made his way through the mountains to arrive in camp, allowing the smaller agent to leave. Jared had promised Gerry the archaeology team would be safe, and he had kept his word.

With a prodigious command of the English language, Kati was never a woman at a loss for words, but now she was in love.

"You come here," she would order the various agents, giving huge hugs as she thanked them. She idolized them as they worked to repair a jeep, worshiped them when they were on watch, and spoiled them incessantly with fresh coffee and tasty tidbits. The smitten woman mother-henned them to death, hovering to wipe their brow should a bead of sweat appear. For Doug, it was an embarrassing spectacle to watch—his feathers ruffled and he pouted. Kati never fawned over him like that. The team just sighed, for the duo now had something new to bicker about.

The *policia* kept badgering the camp, poking, and picking, looking for that stray strand to pull on to get them to unravel. The team, however, now began to simply view them as an irritant.

As a routine was reestablished, Sam toyed with the idea of calling Gerry, but in a run to the village with an agent for additional supplies, it was clear that the edge remained. Glares accompanied tense verbal exchanges where the villagers insisted on only conversing in their native language, pretending not to understand the Spanish they had understood just weeks before. As Sam would try to purchase much-needed items, she was often told something wasn't available when it was in plain sight. Access to the phone, it seemed, was still out of reach.

2 8

———

THE ARMY TRIPLETS

*J*ust over three weeks remained on the work permit, and despite all the early disruption and chaos, the site was not only coming along well, but they were pretty much on schedule. The supporting agents had been there for about a week. And again, right on time, there was the sound of a jeep coming down the trail, and when it stopped at the edge of camp, a tall American stepped out.

He came! Sam mentally screamed to herself, not quite believing it, for she knew what it would have taken for him to be there. Gut instinct had always told Sam he would come, but...she still couldn't believe it. In a dead run, she vaulted over the worktable and hurdled a couple of camp chairs, enveloping the man in a ferocious hug as she leapt up into his arms. The two stood there, her legs wrapped around his waist as they embraced and Doug bravely went out on a limb, "I'm going to take a guess here and say that's Gerry."

With a look that dripped sarcasm, Kati caustically shot back, "Boy, your brain runs so hot, it sizzles!" Sam clung to Gerry, burying her head in his neck, and relief flooded her as she absorbed his presence. Her mind worked to process his scent—it wasn't a thing, a smell, but rather a concept. He smelled like her safe place. In a flash, the tension of the past few days had melted away.

Gerry didn't say much, but then he didn't have to—Gerry was a tactile man. Words didn't come easy for him, so he communicated through touch—a stroke of a finger on her face, a hand on her shoulder, or a caress of her fingers—they all spoke volumes. At that moment, Gerry's hug—its duration and strength, where his hands held her neck and ran down her back, even his swaying rocking motion—told Sam everything she needed to know.

Gerry closed his eyes and only hugged her tighter when he heard her say in amazement, "You came, you really came."

"Always, Hon," he softly whispered back.

After a moment, Sam hopefully asked, "How are the roads? Any chance we can leave?" although she already knew the answer. Looking out at the crews watching them, Gerry just shook his head and regretfully told her, "No, they're not passable yet...but maybe next week."

"I didn't think so," Sam muttered dejectedly, her face falling.

Gerry soberly offered in explanation, "It took me three days to cover ground that should have only taken one. You're better off here."

When they were finally able to have a quiet moment together, Gerry told Sam that more help was on the way.

"Have faith, Hon," Gerry encouraged Sam, as he detailed how Brady and Mark were working behind the scenes pulling together additional help for them, help that was probably only just a day or two away.

The "vacationing" narcotic agents left that following morning, although they stayed in the region, monitoring the situation and supplying information when they could. Concern still lingered in the air, but there was now a sense of assurance amongst the archaeology team. Gerry was as non-talkative as ever, and still scrutinized everything with eyes that missed nothing, but Kati now gazed upon him with fresh eyes of her own.

The following day, a jeep arrived with yet another "vacationer," this one retired Army. Brady and Mark had kept their end of the bargain, and had rummaged up a couple of Army veteran chums who, now in their late fifties, were finding retirement a tad tame. And again, like those before them, they inexplicably had an overwhelming desire to visit México.

The first to arrive was Terry Rainier, and the second, Lucas Michaels, came several days later, bringing even more supplies and information. More importantly, however, the arrival of Luke meant there were now three operating vehicles. They were just small 4x4 field jeeps, but they could squeeze ten people in, and their four wheel drive could handle the roads. The archaeology team had a way out. Now, fortified with the three vehicles, the team held one last meeting to take stock of the situation and discuss whether to leave.

Terry and Luke, the two new arrivals, joined Gerry as he sat with a mug of coffee, watching the shadows of the team members sway across the canvas tent wall. Luke quietly reached into a small hidden pocket and pulled out a note for Gerry from Stan, outlining the situation at home. Gerry had been expecting it since he had left the States abruptly—too abruptly for the Army. He was anticipating repercussions.

Gerry briefly thought back to how he had sidestepped Sam that first night when he had arrived. While soaking in the moment of their first sunset in Oaxaca, Sam's relief had been still palpable when she had asked him in wonder, "How on Earth did you get here? I can only imagine the look on Davidson's face when you explained this!" She knew Gerry's CO would have been difficult.

Everything she had heard about the man painted him as having a rather nasty personality. With awe that Gerry had come still evident in her voice, she questioned him, "And how did you find us?" She was expecting a wild tale of an unhappy CO, horrid airplane seats, tense *policia* checkpoints, and harrowing mudslides. Maybe even a comical donkey ride or two over a mountain.

Gerry, instead, just smiled softly as he mysteriously answered, "Oh, you know Stan, he can sell sand to an Arab," implying Stan had convinced Davidson, Gerry's CO, for an emergency leave. It wasn't entirely true. While Stan had been instrumental in getting Gerry to Oaxaca, the Arab—in this case, Davidson—hadn't bought what Gerry had been selling. Knowing she wasn't going to get much more of an answer, Sam had let the matter lie.

Luke studied Gerry's face as he read the note and then asked him, "Gonna tell her?"

"Naw," Gerry dolefully answered, "the damage is done. If I tell her, she'll insist on packing up."

Terry asked, "Do you think they'll leave?" His expression hinted that he hoped they wouldn't.

"Dunno," Gerry admitted, as he slurped his coffee. "But even if they decide to go, given the roads and unrest, it still won't be until next week."

The argument was two-faced. On one hand, if the road conditions were improving, the civil unrest was dying down and the cartel wannabes were gone, then it was safe enough to travel. On the other hand, if all that was true, then it was also safe enough to stay. Sam listened to them all debate—the danger was essentially over, they had supplies and transportation, they had been working the site and were pretty much on schedule.

In the crowded tent, the team continued to deliberate, but it was clear—no one was concerned any longer. Each member of the team had the underlying personality of those who work the field, and that quality, often described as determined, defiant, or just plain stubborn, enveloped the tent. Sam had already decided to stay, but for those team members who voiced concern and wanted to leave, she would get them home. It was unanimous—they would stay.

In the coming days, Sam and Gerry, along with the rest of the team, fell into an easygoing rhythm where loose joking replaced terse fears, and they even began to view the daily *policia* visits with amusement. The crews affectionately called the trio of Gerry and the two Army veterans, the Army Triplets, and an infatuated Kati mothered them all to death as well.

Late morning, about a week after the Army Triplets had arrived, the appearance of a single truck stunned the camp, which had grown rather complacent in the relative serenity of recent days. The drug cartel wannabes were back. There were six of them this time and older, late teens to early twenties, but just as cocky and bigheaded as those who had come before. And for a brief moment, the only sounds that could be heard across the camp were the resounding pound of heartbeats echoing in team members' ears.

The same unspoken question was on everyone's faces. *Where did these guys come from?* As recently as the day before, information from the narcotics agents showed the cartel wannabes were gone from the area, wreaking havoc on a village to the south. The six cartel wannabes strutted around and postured like peacocks as they approached the Army Triplets, all of whom had rifles and sidearms. The cartel wannabes clearly were spoiling for a fight and the Army Triplets were itching to oblige.

Doug and Sam had watched in alarm as the two sides challenged each other and in growing fear that the confrontation would escalate, they had come up behind the Army Triplets, in hopes of making a show of force. To their stunned horror, they watched the Army Triplets' demeanor shift.

Grinning broadly while laughing and casually joking with the six cartel wannabes as if they were best buds, the Army Triplets deliberately laid down their firearms on the ground, and pulled out their knives.

With only a blade in hand, Terry brazenly held his arms out to his sides as if in supplication, taunting the cartel wannabes with a flippant, "Wanna dance? I'll lead."

Sam silently screamed to herself *Are you insane?* as she watched in disbelief. She stole a nervous look at Doug, tilting her head toward a rifle on the ground, a silent plea for him to pick it up. Doug, equally stunned, merely slowly shook his head no. Tense seconds ticked by as the cartel wannabes' expressions betrayed an eagerness to take the Army Triplets on, and when their de facto leader laid down his rifle, the others followed.

Sam and the rest of the team, who had been watching, paralyzed, now all breathed a huge sigh of relief. While her eyes were still glued on the men in front of them, Sam whispered to a visibly pale Doug, "You okay?"

Doug, without a hint of humor as he swallowed hard, whispered back, "You know that phrase…first you say it, then you do it? Well…"

With knives unsheathed, the fight was now to be hand-to-hand, and appearances were deceiving as the two sides drew their battle lines. The six cartel wannabes sized up the older veterans and Gerry, and having deemed them easy pickings, they figured it wouldn't be a fair fight. They were right.

Sam had never seen Gerry "in action." In training sessions and in the gym, yes, but not in the field, and definitely not when it mattered.

As the two groups squared off, Sam was enveloped by an odd feeling. Once the rifles were laid down and it was hand-to-hand, she was no longer scared for Gerry. She knew how good he was at hand-to-hand combat. She had been told so many times about how Gerry was almost clairvoyant against opponents, and how quick he was during a match.

It was anticlimactic and over before it started. The Army Triplets had no trouble demolishing the mouthy group, disarming and disabling them in what seemed like mere seconds. It was a choreographed dance.

Gerry took out three, Terry handled two, and Luke deftly flicked off his target and then in a slick snatch-n-grab, had a rifle trained on the sprawled boys. In a delightfully refreshing turn of events, the obnoxious youths were now the ones held at gunpoint while Gerry and Terry restrained them, trussing them up like hogs in cute little back-to-back two-packs.

As Terry jerked the final knot, he snapped at the trounced posse on the ground, "No bathroom breaks for you, boys, so feel free to crap your pants."

Sam was experiencing a contradictory bout of Love-Hate, and was not sure what to make of it. She was beyond impressed, but she was also appalled. It wasn't the actual hand-to-hand that upset her—it was the fact that Gerry had laid down his rifle against the gang. In that instant, she felt he and the entire team had been needlessly exposed to the whims of the cartel wannabes.

In her opinion, while she had witnessed a level of skill and bravery that filled her with admiration, she had also witnessed cocky bravado. Gerry and the two veterans, she felt, were lucky that the boys had laid down their rifles.

After the commotion had settled down, she pulled Gerry into the privacy of their tent and was now unleashing a tirade. From the inside, the tent was secluded, but from the outside, filtered light from the skylight vent threw their shadows on the same canvas walls their voices easily penetrated.

Outside, the team listened uncomfortably to the argument as they watched the shadows play out against the tent.

Sam's shadow put a hand to her forehead before she snapped at Gerry.

"What's wrong with you? Were you out of your mind?" In shock over what she considered swashbuckling machismo, the shadow inhaled deeply to calm herself before evenly asking, "You laid your rifles down? What the hell were you thinking? You...you..." Her shadow sputtered as she looked for words. Struggling to hear Sam, Doug sidled up to the tent and leaned in closer.

When the team shot him a disbelieving look over his eavesdropping and gall, Doug was unapologetic as he silently mouthed, "This is the best entertainment we've had all month!"

He was suddenly joined by the remaining team queuing up next to him, and all six of them, plus Terry, leaned with a cocked ear, straining to catch every word as they took in the shadowy action within the tent. Luke, meanwhile, was on guard duty over the cartel wannabes and had to crane his neck to hear anything.

"Why do I always miss all the good stuff?" he whined.

Gerry's larger shadow had been waiting, and when Sam's smaller shadow finally broke her tirade, he interrupted, "Are you done? Just what the hell was I thinking?" he sniped sarcastically. "Oh I don't know...maybe saving your ass? Damn it, Samantha."

Sam's arms flailed to her side as she threw out a retort, "You're the one who said not to try and fight them, and then you go off and do precisely that!"

"Of course I said that," Gerry spat back, "but we know what we're doing. You people don't. You're a bunch of 'civvies' who couldn't find your asses in a bathroom if you had both hands and a map."

Dan the intern made a sudden gasp at the diss, and then wise-cracked, "Holy crap, is he fired up!" Enthralled team members just stood there, their eyes darting between the two silhouettes engaged in a shadow play, not wanting to miss a thing.

Gerry's shadow seemed to lean over Sam's menacingly as he spewed, his voice harsh with anger, "Well, since you know so bloody much, did they know hand-to-hand? Did they know basic defense moves and posture?"

Sam's shadow stood still, and she could be heard faintly parroting, "Posture?" her voice now uncertain. Gerry's terse voice threw out more questions.

"How about their guns? What type of guns did they have? Hmm? Did you see the magazines?"

Sam, her mind still stuck on Gerry's question of hand-to-hand, weakly murmured, "Their guns?"

The spellbound team watched as Gerry's shadow leaned in even closer toward Sam's and they heard him spit out, "Yes, guns, damn it! Guns. What were they? Were they AKs, ARs? Or perhaps CETMEs? Maybe M1908s? How about their RPMs, their fire rate? Hmm? Their sustained rates?"

Sam's shadow had stopped moving and the team could see her arms flutter about, before falling to her side as she reluctantly replied, "Um...I don't know."

The shadows were just inches apart with Gerry's larger silhouette standing with his hands on his hips. Kati was breathless with excitement when she blurted, "Oh God, this is so cool. What I can do with this!"

Doug slapped her shoulder, hissing as he shushed her, "Shut up, I can't hear them with you carrying on." Gerry's shadow had been walking in circles around the tent, but stopped in front of Sam.

"No…you don't know," Gerry could be heard saying, "but I do. It's my job, it's what I train for. Just what the hell do you think I do all day? Sit in a lawn chair sipping mint juleps?"

Sam's shadow's head jerked back for a second in realization, "I…I, ah, really didn't think…" Suddenly she was aware that she didn't know what Gerry did for a living, not really. The Army didn't allow civilians to watch training, so she didn't have a clear picture. She only knew what she had been told. She had filled in the blanks herself and casually viewed all the training as more of a game or sport that grown men indulged in, playing out war game reenactments and such.

Modern combat was carried out with tanks, high-powered rifles that can sight a target a mile away. Missiles flung at each other from over the horizon. Who fought hand-to-hand anymore? She knew what he taught and why, but hadn't fully appreciated the significance or value…until then.

"We weren't as defenseless as you think," Gerry's shadow was heard saying as he pulled up a shirt to reveal a pistol, "but it wouldn't have mattered. We were seriously outgunned, and not by just a little." The two shadows approached each other so close, there was only a sliver of light between them. Gerry's shadow waited for Sam's to look up, before his voice was heard. "If we had fought with bullets, we would have lost—so we fought with our brains instead."

Nebulous hands gripped Sam's shoulders as she simmered down and Gerry's words began to settle in her mind.

"Remember what I asked you when you called that night? Remember what you described to me, the type of weapons and how old they were? Do you also remember how I quizzed you on how they walked, how they were carrying the guns, where they kept their fingers? There was a reason I asked all that. It told me a lot. Told me they were inexperienced, didn't have much training, they were undisciplined. Now, how about these guys? What did their guns look like? Did they handle their guns the same way? These guys had themselves some significant firepower. By getting them to lay down their guns, I leveled the playing field by removing their advantage over us. I had to get them to fight me on my terms."

Sam's shadow stepped back and the archaeology team, hunched over as they tried to catch every nuance of movement, watched her head and shoulders shift as Sam took it all in.

"Guns are great equalizers," Gerry continued, "but they also give a false sense of abilities. I have seen it in combat, I saw it on the streets in Boston, and I just saw it a few minutes ago here in Oaxaca. Those boys had formidable weapons, but their abilities didn't match, something we call 'having too much gun.' I knew going in, before we even put down our rifles, they didn't know how to fight, not like us. They were brawlers. Rainier and Michaels may be older, but they have a skill set you don't easily forget. Those boys didn't have a chance against us."

Sam's voice grunted, "Let me guess, that skill set...they know how to fight."

The strident voices within the tent had lowered as the argument came to a close, the shadows no longer weaving about, and Kati and the rest of the team all groaned in despair, as they struggled to hear. Terry, who was as captivated with the drama within the tent as the archaeology team, whispered, "C'mon, Sam, give the man a break."

They could barely make out Gerry's shadow's soft comment, "Hon, I admit these guys were most likely all bluster like the others, but I didn't want to take the chance. I know I was probably grandstanding, showing off a bit. It's heady for us guys to be able to ride in on a horse and save the day for their girl, and Samantha, you're the most important thing to me." The team outside the tent held their breaths as they watched Gerry's shadowy finger hook Sam's chin to get her to look at him.

"You can't expect me to just stand by and do nothing. Not when I have the training, the skills, to end this. I know we scared you guys. I should have let you in on what we were doing, but...there just wasn't time."

Still shocked at how little she knew of his job, Sam was heard self-consciously questioning Gerry, "Do you do this every day? I mean, go up against people who can kill you?"

Grateful the argument had ended, Gerry's shadow merged with

Sam's as he drew her in for a hug, "No, Samantha, I don't. I train other soldiers every day how to go up against people who can kill them."

The tent flap was suddenly flung open as the couple left, and Gerry apologetically told Sam, "Hon, that crack about you guys not finding your ass in a bathroom, I didn't mean it."

Sam threw a self-depreciating grimace back over her shoulder at Gerry, "Yeah, ya did, and you're right." They had left the tent so abruptly, the team was caught still lined up along the side with nowhere to run. Sam tossed out a lighthearted, "Enjoy the show, guys?" when she realized they had heard the entire argument, but she then caught Terry's eye. Throwing a quick look over at Luke, still glum from having missed all the commotion, Sam turned to Gerry.

"How 'bout after dinner you guys teach us 'civvies' how to handle those guns?"

The following morning, the *policia* arrived right on schedule, and astonishment barely described the looks on their staggered faces as they gaped at the sight that greeted them. The Army Triplets went out to greet the officers as they stumbled out of their vehicles, staring at the bound boys on the ground.

Gerry and Luke, both fluent in Spanish, enthusiastically congratulated each of them for a job well done, clapping them on their backs while commenting on how proud they must be of themselves for apprehending the miscreants.

Gerry had been unnerved by the *policia* harassment when he first witnessed it the morning after he had arrived. Sam had made it clear —it was not his fight and he was to stay out of it. Those daily confrontations had left Gerry seething as he watched Sam go toe-to-toe with the officers during those morning shake downs.

Now, with the officers tripping over themselves while trying to save face, and the shackled cartel wannabes on the ground, Gerry seized the opportunity to drive home a point. Despite a smile that was from ear to ear, the tone of his sarcasm, his furrowed brow and intense angry glare all drove his point home as he congratulated the *policia*. Unspoken, Gerry's message was clear—there will be no more "morning visitations." The officers could only stutter that they would have to come back with a larger truck to pick up the gang.

The following morning, and for the remaining mornings in Oaxaca, the *policia* never returned. The intimidation was over. The Army Triplets worried about retribution from the cartel wannabe gang, but none ever came as reports and scuttlebutt in the village had them far away in greener pastures.

THEY JUST NOT BE NORMAL, GIRL

It had been a wild month and one night—with all the concerns of the *policia* and cartel wannabes behind them, the team went to the village to celebrate. The mood was light and gay that early evening as they all bounced in their jeeps toward the village. As they came to an exceptionally beautiful sight of the village in the valley below, Kati threw her hand across the vista and exclaimed with a beatific grin on her face, "And to think, we almost hightailed it home and would have missed all this!"

To an outsider, she probably sounded demented, but to the crews, she echoed their sentiment. It takes a certain personality to work the field, one that is often stubborn to a fault.

Sam had heard a phrase that government agency operatives in the field often use to describe themselves—*too stupid to quit*. It wasn't a derogatory snipe at their intelligence, but rather a comment on their drive. Their adrenaline, love for adventure, sense of duty, and training kept those operatives going forward, when anyone else would have cautiously retreated to live to fight another day. These traits are seen in field workers as well.

Coming around the last bend on the mountain road before spilling out onto the sprawling valley floor, a smile born of wonderment erupted over Sam's face, chuckling as she listened to her friends call back and forth between the jeeps. For better or for worse, they had been too stupid to quit...and like field workers everywhere...they were proud of it.

When the news of the fight had reached the village—they were impressed. Prior to the six cartel wannabes being taken down, the village had viewed the archaeology team as arrogant foreigners—weak and useless. Now, the team was viewed in a different light—people of good character who held their ground when pressed. The villagers were impressed because they valued the ability to handle adversity and to handle one's self under duress—and the archaeology team had done just that.

The turnabout in the village's opinion of the crews did have an unexpected consequence, however. Whenever the team would break for a *cerveza* at the *cantina*, the men of the village, who now viewed the crew as countrymen, would vie for who could buy the men of the team the most drinks. As a rule, the work crew men knew their limits and to the dismay of the village men, they would beg off. Usually.

That night, after much cajoling, the fellas threw caution to the wind as they joined the village men in celebration. Sam and Kati sat at a corner table and marveled at the sight. A contest of *cerveza* with tequila chasers, made all the more amusing with Petunia the pig oinking and snorting as she grubbed in the dirt at their feet.

"Aw, man, you've got to be kidding me," Sam grumbled at the sight of the men flopping over the tables, unable to sit straight—they were silly, slobbery fools. Luke couldn't hold his liquor at all. At the whiff of a bottle cap, he had begun a shrieking serenade. "What are we going to do with 'One Beer Louie'?" Sam asked Kati while grimacing in pain.

Sam had always appreciated that Gerry was not a heavy drinker. He didn't carouse at bars, but that night, he wasn't tipsy, he was soused. And Petunia the pig, a friendly, easy-going sow who weighed in at a svelte 400 pounds—easy—had her limits.

"What the devil is he doing?" Kati suddenly asked, eyes wide in amazement.

Gerry was reaching for Petunia and blubbering, "C'mere, Hon," trying to kiss her with a rubber-lipping sloppy smooch.

Kati teased at Sam's unimpressed look of *Yuck*. "C'mon girl, don't be so harsh! I can kinda see the resemblance—your buns are dead ringers!"

"Says the woman whose ass sank the Titanic," Sam dryly sniped, giving Kati an epic eye roll over her beer.

"Ooooh, that hurt!" Kati shot back, giggling. "I'll have you know, my butt is…shapely…and in some cultures, that's desirable!"

"Well then, you must be beating 'em off with a stick!" Sam jested while laughing, as she watched Gerry swoon over Petunia.

Leaning over to Sam, Kati joshed, "Ya know, I take back everything I said about him, he's actually kinda cute!"

"Would you like him? I'll even stick a bow on him for ya!" Sam sarcastically sniped, as she disgustedly watched Gerry carry on over the pig. "I'd be offended if he weren't so damn pathetic!"

"Aw, girl, he's just 'hamming it up'!" Kati quipped, hee-hawing at her pun. Sam erupted into a fit, rolling in her chair as she blurted,

"Oh, God Kati…that was so bad."

Suddenly, there were annoyed squeals as a tussle broke out between Petunia and Gerry, and Kati gasped in disbelief, "What the blazes is he doing?" The women watched awestruck as their amusement changed into astonishment.

Gerry was pawing Petunia, grappling as he tried to pick her up and pull her into his chair with him. "C'mon," Gerry pitifully whined as he strained against her bulk, "we're gonna miss our sunset." Petunia wanted nothing to do with him.

Sam just sat with her beer bottle frozen in midair as a flabbergasted Kati wondered, "Speaking of being pathetic—just what the hell is he thinking?"

With a heavy sigh, Sam exasperatedly muttered, "He isn't. That's the problem." Shaking her head as she stared at the men, a stupefied Sam toasted, "To us women, whose brain cells are located above the belt."

After the *cantina's* lights were turned off, the team's men, having degenerated into squabbling children, fought to get into the jeeps. The village men, honored at how well they had been matched, shot glass for shot glass, stood by and beamed in admiration.

Kati drove point, and as her jeep moved forward, the motion fueled Luke's symphonic desires and he began to bellow out what was music to his ears.

As the jeeps bounced up the mountain road, every now and then, the dim headlights of Sam's jeep would illuminate the back of Kati's jeep, and Luke. Looking up at the stars, Luke swished his arms in an ever-gentle arc back and forth, lucky hat in hand, as if he were the conductor of a stellar orchestra that only the truly "pickled" could see.

Caterwauling to an imaginary audience, he serenaded the stars about a girl he once knew but had tragically lost, and his screeching reached a high-pitched octave that no male larynx was built to withstand. The drive to camp was just shy of five miles, but for Sam and Kati, it seemed like fifty.

Pulling up at the work site, the women just stepped aside, and let the men ooze out of the vehicles onto the ground. Once safely inside their tents, the seven men were left to die with their boots on. The women gave up on Luke, who was energized and skipping around the camp, bowing to the chairs. He just had to tell his Amelia how forlorn he was without her, and he stood in the center of camp, enraptured by the glow of the moon. And he bayed...at the top of his lungs...all night. Sam sought refuge in the blind up on the hill, but nothing dimmed Luke's discordant yowling.

The excavation, dominated by panic at its onset, and then by a grueling grind as they strove to make up for lost time, had been one for the books, and was now, at its conclusion, a paradox. No one wanted to repeat the experience, but yet, no one wanted it to end either. Some final field sketches along with minor cataloguing of artifacts were all that remained, and the journals and notebooks would be then packed away.

The two women were unusually pensive as they sat enjoying their ritual morning coffee while watching the Army Triplets. Luke was almost vaudevillian in his exuberance while demonstrating to Terry and Gerry, some tactical move he had used on someone, somewhere, back in the day, and all three were grinning as his story seemed to get more outlandish with each uttered word.

Knowing the sentiment was shared by the entire group, the two women were positively giddy with an emotion they couldn't begin to describe. They were beyond grateful for all that had been done for the team.

After the weeks of watching first the narcotic agents and now Gerry with his Army cohorts handle things, the intractable and loud Kati, leaned over and admiringly whispered to Sam, "They have a screw loose, you know that don't ya. They get shot at, flambéed, crawl through mud, stay up all night in the rain, and they come back the next morning happy as a lark, looking for more." With emphasis, she wagged her head back and forth as she ended her unprecedented tribute, "They just not be normal, girl."

Tickled by her friend's offhanded compliment, Sam peered over the rim of her mug at the trio, and with a mixture of gratitude and pride, quietly murmured into her coffee,

"No, they're not normal. They're amazing—the whole frigging lot of them."

Oaxaca City Airport, A Week Later

Assembled at the boarding gates, it was a bittersweet goodbye. The two interns had already departed for their respective colleges, each with duffel bags full of stories and a few gray hairs. The remaining pairs—Kati and Doug, Sam and Gerry, and Luke and Terry—hovered, reluctant to give that final hug. They had become such good friends over the past weeks, a friendship that would endure for decades afterwards.

Sam fought tears that surprised her, she was not one to cry on a whim. Terry and Luke were flying out together and Sam was having a hard time saying goodbye. "Hey guys," she called out when it was their time to leave. "You two are phenomenal," she told them as she hugged Terry.

"Right back at ya," Terry chuckled and then he sadly confessed, "Damn, I'm gonna miss ya. If you ever need anything—you call me. I'll be at your door before the phone is hung up!" His grin was a mile wide.

"Aw, damn it Terry…ya gonna make me cry here," Sam blubbered under his hug.

Luke stood by with his lucky hat in hand. "I'm not going to say goodbye," he told her when it was his turn for a hug. "I'd rather say thank you."

"Thank me? For what?" Sam asked in astonishment.

"For this," Luke gratefully said as he looked around at the group. "I haven't felt this good in a long time."

Kati had one last zinger for Gerry. Now seeing him as her golden boy, Kati gushed, "You can darken my door anytime, doll," as she gave him a big smooch. Much to his angst, as she and Doug turned for the gate, she reached over and patted Gerry on his rear with a coy, "Be seeing ya, sweet cheeks." Her raucous laughter echoed up the jetway.

Sam and Gerry chose to return home rather than stay for their vacation. As the pair settled into their seats for their flight back to the U.S., the long weeks with all their drama of chaos and intimidation finally caught up with Sam. Struggling to contain the emotions she had kept bottled up, her hands began to shake.

A gentle swaying movement at the onset, but soon, they were a violent earthquake. While watching Sam try to open a package of peanuts, Gerry reached over and held her hands and did not let go. While both visited México many times over the ensuing years, neither of them ever returned to Oaxaca.

Georgia, In The Days That Followed

The impromptu trip to Oaxaca exacted a high price for Captain Gerry Martinez. The damage had been done, and they were waiting for him. Gerry's lobbying in those initial hours and days for an emergency leave had been to no avail, and Davidson, his immediate commanding officer, had denied his request. Gerry's options had been limited, as he could either obey and stay, or defy and leave. Gerry had chosen to defy orders and was officially listed as AWOL. Stan had enlisted the aid of former commanders Pernecki and Lawson, who were able to have a belated emergency leave issued for Gerry. Davidson, however, brought him up on charges anyways.

At the formal hearing, when asked why the request for emergency leave had been denied, Davidson's reasoning was that the woman was not Captain Martinez's wife or family, she was just a girl, and "I'll be damned if I'm going to jeopardize the unit's readiness for just a 'roll in the hay.'"

As the panel retired for a verdict, the officers were dismissed. Sam had been waiting outside on the plaza and she looked up hopefully when the doors of the building opened to Pernecki and Lawson, who had testified on Gerry's behalf. Following close behind was Davidson and he strutted down the steps past the ranking colonels as he made a show of adjusting his cap from his face.

He ignored the gathering of men mingling around, but stopped in front of Sam, posing haughtily as if he was waiting for something.

Glaring at her foe, Sam acidly sniped at him, "You seriously aren't standing there expecting me to salute you, are you? I'm not Army after all, I'm just a roll in the hay."

In the end, much was forgiven. The AWOL charge was dropped, and while there were reprimands and forfeiture of pay, there was no rank reduction.

His former COs, Pernecki and Lawson, while clustered with the group at a pizzeria table later that day, sternly warned Gerry, "That was your one and only Get Out of Jail Free card. There won't be another. From here on out, you are on a short leash, and you are expected to heel." Those were among the kinder comments that were lobbed his way that day.

The site did not yield a stunning cache of artifacts, but many interesting finds were made, and they now sit in the local *Museo* as a testimony to the area's enduring cultural history. As Sam turned in her field report for the project to Roger, she asked, "Is this a good enough failure for you?" The following year, she became site boss.

The cartel wannabes accomplished their goal, for they caught the attention of the local cartel, and through the grapevine, Sam learned the cartel resolved the issue in the same efficient manner they handled any other annoyance. The work crews had never been in any danger from the cartels in the area, who could not have cared less about their comings and goings.

The intense interest by the *policia* posed a more interesting question, as there didn't seem to be a rationale for their behavior other than a personal vendetta. The protests against the Mexican Army and government by the local Indigenous communities quieted down soon after, but reached a flashpoint again several decades later, before settling down into a low rumble that continues to this day.

Pablo Papaqui stayed true to his convictions and resisted the cartels for about seven years after that season, but in 1992, he was found shot to death on his farm.

The following spring after Oaxaca, as Sam began making preparations for her upcoming field season, she received a phone call from Luke Michaels, who wondered, with a hopeful lilt to his voice, if she would require their services again that summer.

Unfortunately, she told him, she was headed for Alaska that summer as part of a medical team. Her only worries, Sam sadly told Luke, would be an occasional marauding bear or a sporadic cantankerous moose, along with the ever-present B-1 bombers disguised as mosquitoes.

"Well, you know where to find us should you need us," Luke said with a twinge of disappointment echoing in his voice as he said goodbye.

Her field seasons were never the same after that phone call, for Sam knew the two men would always be tucked in her back pocket, and it was a good feeling. After Oaxaca, the friends made a point of meeting every year after field season, the two Army veterans, the Four Musketeers, Sam, and if lucky, the bickering duo of Kati and Doug.

They would all swap the most outrageous stories in a never-ending contest of the absurd and the ridiculous, and as Sam sat round the fire pit for that first get-together, she marveled at how lucky she was. Her Four Musketeers were now an eight-pack.

[SAMANTHA, 2024: Quoted Text From Letter

"I shudder at what might have happened, hon, if you hadn't been there for me. I called you in the middle of the week and you dropped everything. You rearranged schedules, called in favors, traded furlough days all to be able to help. You have no idea how relieved I was to see your colleagues from the Alphabets in the days before you showed up for those final weeks.

"You were, Gerry, quite simply said, my white knight in shining armor who did save me from the cartels. I kept waiting for the lecture. I kept waiting for you to yell and ask 'just what the hell was I thinking?' but you never said a word, not one. You took care of business, you took care of the team, and you took care of me. I figured you were waiting until we were alone before unleashing on me, especially when I came unglued on the airplane, but instead you just held my hands the whole flight home and all that night. Do you know how safe you make me feel? The world is a dangerous place for people like me, both physically and emotionally but with you, hon, there were no worries or fears, […]. I am so proud of you Gerry because you always had my back and never disappointed. I could always count on you for anything. You were my anchor, babe, my Rock of Gibraltar."]

30

THE ARMY'S GREEN WALL

Sam needed to talk about what had happened in Oaxaca. Sitting in their chair as the sunset finally gave way and slid under the horizon, their fingers intertwined, they each worked through the good moments, and the bad of Oaxaca. Sam apologized for putting him in a position that almost cost him his career, acknowledging he must be so angry with her. Gerry, still holding Sam's hand, merely brought it up to his lips, and kissed her fingertips.

"Angry—with you? No, Hon. I'm disappointed at how it all went down. But if you hadn't called me…" Leaning in close to Sam's ear, Gerry whispered, "I would have been beyond furious." Sam rolled over onto his chest and gazed expectantly into his eyes for a few seconds.

"Babe, I'm so grateful, honored even, that you came, but I have to ask—Why? Why did you come to Oaxaca when you could have handled it from here? Jared had sent the agents, Terry and Luke would have been there. You risked everything. Why?"

Wistfully, he softly said, "I risked nothing…but I would have *lost* everything if I hadn't gone."

Gerry knew she was waiting for him to say something more. "Samantha…I…" he murmured hesitantly. "I wish I could put it in words." Reaching over to stroke Sam's hair, he whispered, "I had to go. I lost you once. I was not going to lose you again, to Oaxaca or anyplace else."

What is he talking about? Sam wondered as she began to sit up. *He's talking in riddles.* Suddenly she knew. Just the year earlier, right after her diagnosis, she had ended their relationship.

She hadn't forgotten about it. The past year had been such a chaotic whirlwind of crises that they both had tucked it away for a bit. He spoke so little of that time that it appeared to Sam that it didn't bother him much anymore. The shock of hearing him now speaking of it with such pain sent an icy chill through her.

There was a hollow tone to Gerry's voice as he remembered the moment. "You didn't even say goodbye. You just told me not to think of you anymore, and to have a good life. And then you just left."

It had been a tough moment the couple hadn't really talked about. They had instead danced around it.

Her pangs of guilt and regret made Sam flush with shame—and she apologized. "Gerry," she said slowly, the memory of that day as vivid as yesterday. "At the time, I thought I was doing the right thing, maybe even being noble." She paused to scoff at herself. "I thought I was protecting you from the heartache, from all the pain. I was wrong."

Gerry was looking down when Sam finished, and a few moments passed before he finally confessed, "I have thought of so many things I had wished I had said then to stop you, but..." Gerry sadly looked at Sam and said, "you know how good I talk."

"Well," Sam said as she watched him, trying to catch all the subtle clues that told her so much. "Tell me now. What do you want to say?" Gerry thought for a second, and then leaned down, giving her a kiss. "Oooh, I like how you talk, sir," Sam murmured with a smile.

The smile brought with it a sense of gratitude for her as she snuggled back down into the chair and wondered.

What is it about the sunsets that makes everything possible?

. . .

[Samantha, 2024: Quoted Text From Letter

"You never failed [me], even when we didn't see eye to eye. Remember our biggest fight? I was always so grateful that we rarely disagreed, that we never had a need to have a true dust up. It was always a shock when we would get into it, have a skirmish over some silly reason. We had that routine with the sunset, remember? Began with our first sunset. No talking, just cuddling in the chair and watching it silently, immersed in the moment. When all was smooth the sunset was just that, a beautiful moment. But it was when all wasn't smooth that its true value emerged. That routine carried us through some rocky nights didn't it, babe? No matter how upset one of us would be, we would put everything aside for the sunset. Remember?

"We'd be so prickly. You'd sit down as tense as a rail, and I'd slide in next to you ramrod straight. You would put your arms around me as always, but your nails were like claws, both of us spoiling for a fight but the rules were the rules—no talking until the sun sets. As we would sit there, a miraculous thing would happen. After a few minutes, I would find myself not sitting as straight, your 'claws' would not be digging in as deep and by the time the sun set, I would be nestled against your chest and your arms would be so light. By the time the sun set, we would have forgotten what it was we were upset about and remembered why we fell in love in the first place. [...].

"Then there was THE FIGHT. The closest we ever came to the edge, remember? I fell in love with you in those weeks. Sounds like an oxymoron, doesn't it?"]

North Carolina, 1986

Lt. Colonel Alan Lawson stood flipping sizzling burgers on a charcoal BBQ. Light jazz music floated up over the chatter and hubbub of human voices and the thrill of a baseball game could be heard from the radio. An informal group of men stood gathered around with beers in hand, enjoying a rare moment of banal chit chat about seemingly nothing. The festivity and its lighthearted atmosphere were, however, ignored by a brooding Sam as she watched an unwelcome sight.

Her Gerry and Major Craig Thornton were clustered over to the side, huddled over a small patio table away from all the social activity. The two men were so deep in conversation that not even the roar of the crowd over the radio as they cheered the Boston Red Sox in the 1986 World Series, or the excited screaming of an announcer over a booming homer, caused a pause in their discussion.

They had met nine years earlier, Craig Thornton and Gerry, during the Pernecki days and a spate of transfers had briefly brought both men back together within Lawson's domain. Gerry in particular welcomed the friendly face, someone he could talk to and commiserate with. The past year since Oaxaca and his misconduct hearing had been tense, and until the transfer back into Lawson's realm, he had languished under the command of Davidson, the embittered CO who had brought those charges.

As male conversation often does, it eventually drifted to the women in their lives and Thornton, who had gotten married in the interim and was now the father of three, plied Gerry with an endless series of pictures of the trio. In the bathtub, at a birthday party, at Christmas—the man wore his family on his sleeve.

His attention turned to Gerry and the woman on the lounge chair by the pool. *Why weren't they married?* He wanted to know, elbowing Gerry with a huge grin on his face, *What was the deal?* Simple questions with long and complicated answers.

The explanation of Sam's medical condition wiped the smirk off of Thornton's face as he now understood the tremor of concern he had detected in Gerry's voice. A concern that revolved around promotion.

Prior to Sam entering his life, Gerry cared little about his future, for it was just him. Now, he worried specifically about something called mandatory retirement regulations. Gerry had sat describing it to Sam, explaining how he couldn't remain a captain for the rest of his career, and that he was expected to move up the ranks or be retired. The clouded look on her face raised an alarm in him as he began to realize its implications for him.

His elusive people skills were his Achilles' heel, and he was worried how it would affect his ability to secure further promotions. It was a skill set he knew he didn't possess, let alone understand, and he feared being promoted to the level of incompetence, if at all. A captain rank he could handle, but the higher officer ranks worried him.

He was also worried about pension. Gerry had no idea of what the future held, but a captain's pension wasn't going to provide that security blanket he felt they would need. Thus, he peppered Craig Thornton with questions in his quest for answers. *What is being a major like? The pension, the responsibilities, types of postings?*

Mandatory retirement also had Sam, deep in her own world, going down a different rabbit hole. She was surprised at how troubled she was by Gerry's revelation that he might be forced out if he didn't rise through the ranks. Lying on the lounge chair, she bantered back and forth in her mind as to just what her problem was.

While she had softened regarding the Army since meeting Gerry, she still rebelled against it, and by her reasoning, she should be delighted he would be kicked out, but yet there she sat, in a dither as it weighed on her. Gerry's discomfort in social settings was never far from her mind, percolating through her mental melee and the woman was startled when the realization finally hit home. What troubled her was that she didn't see how her ingrained Army man could function without that Army anchor holding him steady.

Lawson caught the gloomy countenance on Sam's face, clearly stewing over something, and he could tell as he followed her gaze over to the two men at the table, that she was worried about Gerry.

He didn't know her well—they had met only twice before. Once at the Officers' Ball four years ago, and then again last year at Gerry's misconduct hearing, but the host assumed Sam's sour mood stemmed from Gerry's anger issues. Excusing himself from his guests, suspicion crept over Lawson as he wondered if the positive changes he had seen in Gerry at the base were just an outward façade, and perhaps things at home were not so rosy. A quiet and sudden, "Mind if I join you?" jolted the absorbed woman out of her reverie.

For Sam, Lt. Colonel Alan Lawson was a breath of fresh air. Never blustery or standoffish, he was the most unmilitary military officer Sam had ever met. In uniform he was as crisp and tight as the next officer. Away from the base, however, despite being only fifteen years older than her, he came across as a warm, fatherly figure.

She hadn't seen him since that same misconduct hearing the year before, and knowing deep down it had been Lawson who had paved the way, she thanked him again. A huge barrel laugh erupted from the man and, leaning over to pat her on the knee, he quipped, "It was all worth it just to see the look on that idiot's face when you told him you were just a 'roll in the hay.' He was quite the SOB wasn't he?"

The memory of the moment gave Sam's turmoil a temporary reprieve, and grins broke out as the two giggled at the thought of that exchange.

When Lawson gingerly steered the conversation toward Gerry, Sam proudly admitted his transformation was dramatic, but not surprising, because she always knew he had it in him. The warm smile on Sam's face clearly told Lawson she was worried about something other than Gerry's anger.

"But that's not what's on your mind, is it?" Lawson asked, patting Sam's knee again. The tilt of his head caused the sunlight to glint off his black hair, and his dark eyes lit up like an old grandfather welcoming beloved grandkids. "What's the problem here?"

For the next few minutes, Sam threw out a slew of questions about army mandatory retirement, and Lawson tried to answer them as well as he could. Probing, he tried to see what she was hiding, but her scowl remained.

"What is it you are not happy about?" he leaned in and whispered.

Not quite sure how frank she could be with the officer—Lawson was after all, Gerry's CO—Sam just stared into her drink at first. She played with the straw for a moment before confessing, "Colonel, I'm grateful the Army gives Gerry a purpose and a sense of belonging." Stalling as she put her drink on the side table to sit up and look at Lawson, Sam took a deep breath as she continued, "But I'm not beholden to the Army nor do I care about the Army. I do care about Gerry. After the accolades have faded and the uniform is stripped, underneath it all, he'll still be that insecure little boy on the outside, with his nose pressed against the glass, looking in."

She understood the rationale, that the needs of the many outweighed the needs of the few. But Sam also understood what was good for the Army, was not good for some soldiers, and Gerry was not like other service members. His tenure on the streets had left a much deeper scar on his psyche than the ones on his back.

Growing resentment enveloped her, and her concern boiled over, scalding what had been a pleasant moment. She was being both unfair and one-sided, she knew it, but with a voice heavy with worry and sadness, Sam cut loose with a diatribe anyway.

"The Army will have used up his best years—his best ideas and energy—and will then toss him aside to fend for himself…and I'll be left to pick up the pieces as well as I can. But I'm afraid I will not be in the position to do so," she grimly added, referring to her medical condition.

The sudden chill in her voice held a level of disdain that took Lawson aback, causing him to defensively stammer, "Well…I wouldn't put it quite like that."

His remark was countered by a voice drifting up from behind him, "Oh, I would." His wife, Colleen, cynically had a thought or two of her own on the subject.

Balancing a tray of salsa, chips, and drinks on her hip, Colleen Lawson retorted, "That's precisely what the Army does, and that'll be precisely what she'll have to do," giving her husband an accusatory look while a coterie of wives gathered around her in a tight arc. Skewered by his wife on his left, Gerry's girl on his right, and a phalanx of wives behind him, an outnumbered and outgunned Lawson retreated to the BBQ for the safety of male numbers.

The cast of a shadow over her caused Sam to jerk in surprise as another wife leaned over to peer into her glass and astutely joked, "Oh, girl, you are going to need something *way* stronger than that iced tea." Mary, Craig Thornton's wife, was standing over her and reaching down into her beach bag. She pulled out a bottle of rum and poured a generous portion into Sam's iced tea.

The wives pulled chairs up around the lounger and collectively started both asking and answering questions at the same time. An impromptu counseling session took hold as the volley of questions and comments proliferated.

We've all been there, honey, we know the look. How long have you been together? referring to her and Gerry. Another comment, *I am guessing four, maybe five years,* floated overhead as Sam took a sip of her delightfully invigorated ice tea. The support of the wives enveloped her like a comforting warm blanket, and Sam could only nod an *Uh-huh* in affirmation as the women united in her defense. Another wife was heard chiming in with, *Yep, right on schedule. Most of us give it up right around that time, get tired of banging our heads against the Army's Green Wall.*

Bobbing their heads in commiseration and understanding, the wives listened as Sam vented about the Army in its entirety, men in general and Gerry in particular. She knew she wasn't making much sense, but the complaints just spewed out in a continuous eruption of weariness and exasperation. "The Army's all-consuming and he jumps at its every whim...I never know what I can count on and what I can't...even when he's home, he's not here...he's always training, either in his head, on paper, or in the gym...I feel like I'm an afterthought...I'm his secretary or worse, his maid..." She sounded like a whining broken record but couldn't stem her tidal wave of frustration. Mary just kept the rum flowing.

Every woman around the lounge chair had been there, and they knew to just let her get it out of her system. When Sam's inventory of grievances was exhausted, one of the wives lightened the mood with a sly comment that there was a saving grace to their husbands being on deployment, her voice dropping off in a gravid pause. All heads turned her way and expectant expressions waited in suspense as the woman clarified herself, suggestively cracking, "Yeah, it's tough when the guys are gone, but oh boy, you gotta admit, that first night they come home, *hoo whee*, they sure do make up for it, don't they!"

The sultry admission took Sam aback a tad and she sat there with her mouth agape for a moment, but just for a moment. There was a hitch before the snicker, one she tried to smother and would have succeeded had it not escaped and swelled into a contagious giggle. That giggle rolled through the group like a wave at a ball game and engulfed the women, erupting into such a howling laughter that when the men threw a look over at the ruckus, one husband was prompted to naïvely wonder what the ladies were laughing about.

Another dryly remarked with resignation in his voice, "Probably us." On cue, the women shot coquettish glances toward their husbands and once again dissolved into uncontrollable laughter.

The man followed up with, "Oh yeah, definitely us."

Colleen pulled her chair closer to Sam's lounge chair and surreptitiously tilted her head at the other wives to go join the men over at the BBQ. Colleen knew what a difficult man Gerry Martinez could be. She had witnessed his alarming volatility at the Officers' Ball first-hand years earlier, and while there had been a remarkable change in him since then, that didn't make him any easier to live with.

Coupled with the pair's other pressing issues, living apart for much of the year and Sam's medical condition, Colleen wondered how they had kept it together for as long as they had.

Colleen had seen a lot of military men and families for she was a military brat herself. Her dad had dragged the family from one end of the country to the other.

"There are two main types of Army men, have you noticed?" she softly asked Sam when they were alone. "The ones *in* the army—they do their tours, they have families, they have a life outside of the army. For them, it is army with a small 'a.' The other group—for them, they *are* the Army and Army is spelled with a capital 'A.' For them that commitment and devotion is, as you said, all consuming. To the Capital A's, being Army is not only their identity, it is their purpose. Being Army is how they take care of their family, and they can't separate the two."

With a flick of a finger toward the men at the BBQ, the long-suffering Army wife offered her take on things, one amassed from years of experience. "That group over there, they are all capital A's. Gerry is committed to the Army, that is a given. You need to decide if you can accept that commitment, and if you can, then you need to decide if you want to."

Getting up to join the others, Colleen leaned over for a final thought.

"You know, Alan told me about what happened in Oaxaca." Sam gazed upward, awaiting Colleen's point. "I know it is hard to see the horizon with a rain squall in front of you, but consider this. As committed as Gerry is to the Army, he was willing to give it up for you. Just some food for thought, honey."

3 1

PERMISSION TO SPEAK FREELY

*S*am didn't have much time to digest that food for thought. After that get-together, the couple drove to Sam's home in Missouri for the week—a week where their schedules had finally lined up. They finally had some quality "Our Time" together and she had it all planned out.

The sightseeing, the beaches, the lazy dinners, the furniture stripping in the garage. That week, however, the sanctity of their coveted "Our Time" was tainted. Gerry was recalled.

[SAMANTHA, 2024: Quoted Text From Letter

"You had only been back a few weeks, and I was so looking forward to our time together when you unexpectedly received orders to return. I exploded. In the car on the way to the airport we cut loose. Every frustration, every misunderstanding, even pet peeves erupted to the surface. I had had it with the Army, fed up with its bloody rules, that damn all-consuming sense of duty and oooooh, the constant absences. You countered with my lack of respect. How I hadn't met a rule I couldn't break and if I couldn't break it, I bent it until it shrieked for mercy. Remember all that? We held nothing back. In boxing parlance, babe, we hit below the belt and didn't pull the punches and by the time we reached the airport, we had crossed the Rubicon—there was no going back. No way to take back what had been said.

"You stomped off without our customary goodbye. Oh, you called on those weekends, it was part of the routine after all, but things were tense and awkward. We stood on opposite cliffs not knowing how to cross—we didn't have our sunset to smooth the waters, to temper the anger and neither of us knew how to move forward or even if we wanted to.

"In those weeks I contemplated our split, did you know that? Was this the life I wanted anymore, the life you wanted anymore? Was love enough? Was it even love anymore, or had we just become comfortable with the arrangement? I debated whether to even meet you at the tarmac and in the end, of course I would. While waiting on that tarmac I replayed our last conversation. We both were still steamed and I mulled over what had to be said, dreading what I felt was the inevitable conclusion."]

GERMANY, WEEKS LATER

The unexpected recall that had erupted into a nasty row between the couple, now settled into a cauldron of roiling bitterness. The ongoing resentment triggered a fuming Gerry to lash out at a young soldier for what he deemed sloppy performance. His simmering anger and irritation was not leveled at any one individual soldier, but rather at any and all comers, and it spilled over into a tirade that raged unchecked against the entire squad.

He was oblivious to the fact that he was just as culpable. Disheartened by the sight, an edgy Stan stood by watching as all of Gerry's gains in the previous years of controlling his anger were in danger of being unraveled. Gerry was returning to his old ways. And Stan knew why.

He had listened in on what passed as phone calls home to Sam over the past few weeks and they were painful to hear—abrupt, curt, and so distant you'd think he was talking to a stranger. He had even heard Gerry address Sam as ma'am several times.

Stan had heard Gerry's side of the argument and the man couldn't understand why Sam hated the Army. In Gerry's view, he owed everything to the Army and if Sam hated the Army, well then, she hated him, he had spouted. The man even unfairly thought Sam was embarrassed to be with him in public if he wore his uniform.

After listening for weeks, Stan finally had enough of Gerry's rambling blather and sat his friend down in what amounted to a shut-up-and-listen session. In his typical dramatic style, Stan emphatically ticked his talking points off on his fingers.

"One. Sam's grateful for the Army for what it's given ya. She doesn't hate the Army, she hates what the Army's doing *to* ya. Two. She's not ashamed to be out in public with ya in uniform, she just wishes ya weren't. She wants people to see 'Gerry,' not the bloody Army uniform ya spray-paint on."

A belittling roll of his eyes accompanied his next talking points as he worked his way to delivering his final coup de grâce, "If ya wanna break up with her, that's okay by me, I've been wanting to ask her out anyways. I think we could make a go of it, so lemme know when she's available. There's a couple of real swanky speakeasies I think we'd have a great evening at." Stan had said his piece and could only hope the taunts hit home.

Singing to himself, Stan left the room with a jaunty swagger and then loudly began to lay out how he would sweep Sam off her feet. Details of that first date he and Sam should have—the type of dinner and where, including some hopeful cozy after-dinner activities, all floated on the air and he made sure Gerry heard every word.

Gerry sat with a blank expression, shocked in a confusing jumble of disbelief and jealousy as he stared at Stan's retreating back. He couldn't tell if his best friend was kidding or not.

[SAMANTHA, 2024: **Quoted Text From Letter**
"You came down the stairs, walked over and dropped your duffle.

Walked up and asked, 'Permission to speak freely ma'am,' and then grabbed my face and gave me the deepest kiss. It was over. We learned from those weeks and [...] we never fought again. That was in January and once again, in just a few weeks, you were sent out again. This time just across the country to Utah for a few. You were in a small stone shop while there and found a small pink heart pendant, made of a type of stone that was connected to the heart chakra. Remember? You had these little mini military dog tags made, engraved with 'Permission to speak freely ma'am,' found a gold chain and gave it to me for Valentine's Day."]

THE FIGHT HAD BEEN a watershed moment. The miscarriage, the diagnosis and the Army were things out of their control, but the Fight had been theirs to own. For a moment, Sam and Gerry had forgotten that, while they couldn't control what life threw at them, they could control how they responded to it.

NORTH CAROLINA, MONTHS LATER

It was a "deployment widows" get-together where the spouses left behind during a deployment would swap stories and establish support lines. The usual lighthearted idle chatter and bantering were brought to a standstill when Nancy, a newer member of the group, blew her stack. In a fit of frustration, she slammed a baking pan loaded with breaded chicken tenders on the counter, sending the pieces flying onto the floor. And Nancy just stood there with a hot pad in hand, staring at the mess.

Colleen, Lt. Colonel Lawson's wife, quietly walked up behind Sam, put her hand on her shoulder and whispered more to herself than to Sam, "So, it begins again."

It had been Sam's turn at the BBQ over the summer, now it was Nancy's. Sam looked over at Mary, Major Thornton's wife, and silently asked where the rum was, and Mary just threw a head toss toward her bag; she was a woman who liked to be prepared.

Colleen, leaning close to Sam, murmured, "Why don't you take Nancy out to the patio? We'll join you in a bit." Mary handed Sam the rum bottle and a bowl of chips.

Sam looked at both of them with uncertainty as she muttered, "Me? I don't know what to say."

"Yes, you do," Colleen said simply, "probably better than most right now. Now go." She shooed her out the door while calling out to Nancy, asking if she would set up veggies on the grill.

A funny feeling of déjà vu washed over Sam as she settled on the lounge chair, the same one she had sat in a few months back when she had her own meltdown. Putting the grill lid down, Nancy dragged a chair over to the lounger and plopped down, heaving a heavy sigh.

"I suppose you're supposed to cheer me up by telling me I'm wrong." As Sam pulled the glasses of iced tea over on the side table and began to pour the rum, Nancy dryly asked, "How many glasses did it take you?"

"Oh…a few," Sam laughed, handing the glass to her. Sam sat for a second, not sure how to start but Nancy beat her to the punch.

"How do you do it? You and Gerry…Gerry's gone more than Tim. I don't get it."

"I trust him," Sam simply said after a moment. Nancy's expression was skeptical as she peered at Sam over her glass. "You asked how I did it, how Gerry and I make it. We trust each other. But it's more than that. I respect him, even though I don't always like him," she said with a chuckle, looking over at Nancy. "But I do respect what he does—his conviction and his beliefs. You can't change the Army—it does what it does. But you have control over how you deal with it. For us, we talk. Not in spoken words, but silently, through letters, the reading of books together. It's not the big things, it's the little—"

Her words were cut short as Nancy interrupted. "Tim and I talk all the time. "

"And what do you say?" Sam asked as she got up to flip the veggie kebabs on the grill. "Do you ever talk about what you and I are talking about right now? Or is it just the weather? Don't get me wrong, Gerry and I disagree. We can get into it like anyone else, but we also have a way to work through them. We use sunsets. I know it sounds silly, but it works for us. It's probably the routine more than anything, but we know while we're having a spat, that the sunset will allow us to see the other's point of view. What do you guys talk about?"

Nancy quietly looked at her drink a moment before she reflectively admitted, "Nothing."

"And that," Sam said as she sat back down on the lounge chair, "is my point. With Gerry, less is more, so we just hold hands during the sunset, we recapture the moment. The problem is still there, but having the sunset gives us time to settle down and get past the heat of the moment. We don't do this because it is the easy way. It's a choice, and we work at it. We work at carving out time just for us. A time where Gerry's not allowed to have his Army, and I'm not allowed to have my forensics. It's just us. It is so important, we even named it. We call it 'Our Time.'"

Nancy followed Sam's gaze when she stopped and looked up at Colleen in the kitchen before continuing, "A very wise woman once told me that I needed to determine if I could handle this way of life, and if I could, I needed to decide if I wanted to. I decided I wanted to. I love Gerry. I'm in awe of the person he is, and so, I decided to work at making it work. And it is work. For both of us. Gerry as much as me. Gerry works at keeping the connection going. He chooses a book every rotation."

Nancy interrupted with a tone of dismissal. "A book?"

A smile broke out over Sam's face at Nancy's expression. "Yeah, a book, a simple book. We read the same chapters together every week. Last week, I fell behind, and he spent his time on the phone reading the last chapter to me. It's important to him that we be on the same page, in more ways than one."

Nancy stared into her drink and sadly asked, "Has Gerry ever cheated on you while gone?" *Ugh,* ran through Sam's mind as she looked back over her shoulder at the kitchen, hoping Colleen would come out.

"No, he hasn't," Sam said with a conviction that Nancy couldn't quite believe.

"Are you sure? How can you be sure?"

Pouring more iced tea from the pitcher and adding a splash of rum, Sam casually asked, "What makes you think Tim has?" Nancy's face began to crumple as she took a sip from her glass.

"Oh, you hear things, you know," she solemnly responded. Suddenly, she jumped up and headed for the kitchen, leaving her drink on the side table. As Sam turned to watch, she saw Nancy make a motion of wiping away tears. *How do I know?* she thought.

[SAMANTHA, 2024: Quoted Text From Letter

"I fell in love with you sitting at a folding table in a field mess tent. Significant others and spouses would always get together after you all would deploy and we'd ruminate. I'd sit there and listen to the women go on about the behavior of the men in their lives and they'd talk about all the lies, the deceptions, the betrayals and catting about. They'd go on about how the men considered it a sport to go to bars to hook up with the flavor of the day and not just the single guys, the married ones too. It was the perfect set up for who's to know and the good ones, the ones who wouldn't have thought to stray or cheat? They were [the] most vulnerable of all to the vampire bitches, but I never had a moment's worry about you until that day in the tent.

"A few of the enlisted came in for coffee refills. They were joking, laughing about their past conquests, how easy it was to score and how to get away with it all—no one was the wiser. Out of the blue your name came up and in that instant my stomach dropped, I had been so naïve to think you wouldn't be part of all that. The men left and a young officer, his name was Josh—I only knew him briefly, but I did recognize him, came up and sat down, and quietly told me the rest of the story. Those young guys got their jollies by setting up the married men and they even had a betting pool going as to who they could get seduced by the VBs and how quickly.

"You had been a prime target, babe, and apparently worth a lot of points in that betting pool. Josh had said in all the years he knew you, while you reprimanded, it was never a personal attack, but once you realized what these boys were up to, you lit into them first rate, and you made it personal. Josh was quick to say you never as much as glanced at other women and he hoped one day he would be as solid as a 'husband' as you. I'm so proud of your moral compass Gerry for you never gave me cause to doubt and I can't even tell you how good that made me feel. How secure it made our relationship."]

3 2

THE TRUNK OF A SEQUOIA

Much had changed for the couple after the Fight—childish beliefs and attitudes faded. The miscarriage, the diagnosis, and Oaxaca all rumbled as earthquakes and a new landscape emerged. Loose shale and sandstone were replaced by granite and basalt bedrock. They jutted at times, their pinnacles presenting obstacles to be climbed or rappelled down, but Sam and Gerry were maturing.

Gerry vowed that, after the Fight, he would try to see things from Sam's point of view. He hadn't thought much of what it was like to be on the other side of the equation, of all the compromises and sacrifices she had made on his behalf. Sam had a career of her own and was insanely busy, but she was always there when he came home. Gerry pushed to find ways to incorporate himself into Sam's world—to be more present, rather than just be a comet making a planetary fly-by.

And learning to dance was one of those ways, for it was something Sam enjoyed. Secretly, he had taken dancing lessons, much to the horror of the instructor, and was looking forward to surprising Sam at the Memorial Dance with his new foxtrot.

Sam hadn't wanted to go that evening, but it had been one of those sacrifices.

. . .

[Samantha, 2024: Quoted Text From Letter

"I fell in love with you at the Memorial Honors dance. You were resplendent, so handsome. You do clean up well, hon, but it was your compassion that won the night. Do you remember? The night was so special for them—they had taken dancing lessons just for the event, a retired officer and his wife and were all dolled up for the occasion, but with nowhere to go. He had broken his hip the week before and was in a wheelchair for the event. They were still the center of the party and still were enjoying themselves, but you could tell they were so disappointed not being on the dance floor.

"You got up, approached them, and asked the elderly officer for permission to ask his wife to dance. When the wife asked why you would want to dance with such an old lady, your response was golden. 'I always like to dance with the most gracious and beautiful woman in the room.' She knew you were full of it, but she beamed anyway as you bowed and extended your hand asking her to dance. You were like a 17th century count in some historical novel—the consummate gentleman—and you made her evening and probably the week. You did mine too because it had been just another ordinary and compulsory event until that moment. I was so proud of you, and I must have looked like a fool sitting there watching you. Your kindness took center stage as you were so polite, so considerate of her."]

GERRY HAD SEEN the look of shock on Sam's face that night, as he and the officer's wife cut the rug, but he had also seen the look of pride and appreciation when Sam realized what he had done, and he wanted that look every day. And he worked at it. Gerry was aware of the sacrifices Sam made to insert "Our Time" into his Army world, and he likewise worked diligently to reciprocate, to insert a measure of "Our Time" into hers.

Sam's field seasons were central to his efforts. It wasn't always easy; the Army was a tough taskmaster and some years it was not just inconvenient or even difficult, it was a battle. The timing of field season and Gerry's furloughs rarely were in sync; last year, Gerry's leave was cut short and the year before that, chaos reigned in Oaxaca.

What Gerry relished most about fieldwork was the opportunity to be a part of Sam's world. His participation was a facet of their relationship that had evolved over the years and in those first few seasons, he didn't have a purpose or place within the team. He was the proverbial fish out of water.

Over the years, however, he worked hard to gain essential skills that he could contribute to a team, helping to run routine samples or assisting during blood draws. Now a proficient colleague, Sam viewed Gerry as a valuable asset, one whose absence was keenly felt. The time the pair spent together in the field was part of the interwoven mesh of their relationship and neither Sam nor Gerry could fathom any other way. They each waited impatiently for the season to begin.

For all the wonders of fieldwork, it was the last ten days to two weeks that Sam and Gerry waited for. It was just the two of them, on vacation. No jobs, no demands. They waited 355 days each year for those ten days, their ultimate "Our Time," and it made it all worthwhile.

The diagnosis of Sam's genetic disease while in medical school altered the trajectory of both her career and her life. She finished schooling and internship but declined residency. She was not a licensed practicing physician. Instead, she focused on the scientific and laboratory side of the field—it provided a more stable environment and offered her more control as her disease progressed.

She obtained her Ph.D. and continued doing fieldwork for as long as she could. It is said when one door closes, another opens and that was the case for her. Having a strong medical background, in addition to her forensic qualifications, positioned her for unique opportunities and it turned out to be a fortuitous combination as it gave her two avenues to chase. Some seasons she would join medical teams for village or rural evaluations. Other seasons had a more forensic slant with grave analysis. Sometimes the two collided.

Irrespective of whether medical or forensic, Sam loved fieldwork and it was her refuge from the world. It was in the field where she truly fit in, away from the chaos and demands of city life. In the field, her disability faded into the background, and she could be herself.

COLORADO, 1987

In 1987, the science of DNA was still in its infancy, but its promise was staggering. In recent years, science had advanced its understanding of genetics, and a revolution was on the horizon, one that would change the field in ways science was still grasping to understand. But today, however, Sam was mired in pre-DNA technology as she hurried to finish a case.

Dr. Roger Belicampf was impatiently hovering, leaving memos with numerous exclamation points, *Where is the case report?* Sam sighed when she found the latest one taped to her microscope eyepiece and exasperatedly muttered some unflattering references to Roger's persistent pestering.

The case had been a tedious one and she had finally finished all the preliminary processing. For weeks now, she had been sifting through dog feces. A man had allegedly killed his wife, chopped her up using a chain saw, put much of the remains through a meat grinder, and then fed her to their dogs.

Ironically, he hadn't believed in picking up and disposing of the evidence and the backyard was littered with the deposits left by four large mutts. Sam had picked up every one of those piles, pounds of it, and her diligence was rewarded, for she found bone fragments.

In the age before DNA examination and research, gross and microscopic analysis of bone were the primary tools available. Having sieved through fecal residue, as a forensic osteologist, Sam had hoped to find bone shards large enough to work with, ideally long bones, the bones of the arms and legs.

While most of the fragments were too small to be of any probative value, several showed promise as she had believed she could make out hints of muscle attachments found on the leg bones, notably the soleal line and the linea aspera, but regrettably, none of those features were unique to humans. She had set them aside to make ground thin section slides of those promising samples in the hopes of finding more clues from their microscopic histology. Finally, after days of laborious processing of the samples, they were ready to be viewed under the microscope.

Due to the small size of the bone shards, it was unrealistic to expect to be able to conclusively identify as human, so Sam's goal was to find features that would exclude humans. The best of these features was the presence of what is called plexiform bone. Adjusting the focus, she was looking for the telltale arrangement of osteons, which are the round microscopic structural units found in compact bone.

In plexiform bone, more commonly found in fast-growing animals and less so in human bone, these osteons were arranged in characteristic layers stacked on top of each other. Its absence didn't indicate humans, but it did put a check in the human column. She found none and regrettably the features she did find were not definitive, but rather merely consistent with humans.

At best, all she could note was the thinness of the cortical bone, a feature seen in osteoporosis which was common in older women. Consistent with the victim, but again nothing conclusive. There were no indications of pathological bone disease or of a chronic systemic one either. Disappointingly, the histology did not provide a smoking gun and while the results were discouraging, they were not unexpected. The recent advances of quantitative histology in osteology were decades away. But there was one more chance.

Sam's fingers tapped the X-ray. She had put a shard aside, one that to her had more of a story to tell. Examining it under a stereoscopic scope, which allowed for it to be viewed in 3D, the edge that caught her attention stood out like the Himalayas. A quiet *Unbelievable* ran through her mind. Sam had called Roger for the victim's X-rays, and then went to radiology to take an X-ray of the shard in question.

Now, the two sets of X-rays were up on a lightbox and she stood comparing. That edge wasn't a funky muscle attachment, it was a bony callus left over from a broken bone. She now knew where to look and as she compared the shape and position of mesh like trabecular bone patterns between the two X-rays, a huge grin of satisfaction broke out.

"Gotcha, you SOB. Thought you had gotten away with it didn't you?" The trabecular bone patterns were a match.

As Sam hung up the phone from updating Roger on her findings, she grew antsy. Today was her last day in the lab before field season—tomorrow she would be on her way to Montana to join a medical research team for the summer. But before Sam could leave for the field, she had one more crucial task to carry out: the vetting dinner of this season's interns.

As Sam entered Roger's office, he handed her three files and told her to pick one—the lucky student would be the intern for the summer. Summer interns were young college undergrads with an unglamorous job description that tasked them as gofers and manual labor, but the position gave them valuable skills and experience. Being an intern also introduced them to the realities of life in the field.

Regardless of its location, season of the year, or its purpose, field-work was not glamorous. There was not a Marriott around the corner, not even a Motel 6. Indiana Jones would not be swaggering through the jungle in his fedora and there were rarely majestic stone temples jutting through the jungle canopy. What there was, however, was plenty of rain in endless torrents, sandstorms, scorching sun and heat, dew points in the 70s, marauding animals, and snakes, both friendly and not so much.

There were also plenty of bugs—they were everywhere. Especially mosquitoes.

There was a circulating legend that told of mosquitoes being so dense that seventy-eight were killed in a single swat. Many locals laugh about their mosquitoes being the official state bird, but there was one site where Sam rebuffed the state bird analogy. She agreed with the running field joke that it was inhabited by mosquitoes which were in fact, a yet to be discovered species of prehistoric pterodactyl, and were just as nasty. These mosquitoes were so big and swarmed in such thick masses that they had been said to asphyxiate caribou as they ran.

Sam sat at her table at the swanky restaurant where she and the students were scheduled to meet. The combined aromas of a variety of different food cooking added an additional immersive layer to the vetting experience, one similar to the experience of surround sound in a movie theatre.

The vetting process was simple although to some, it could seem extreme. Every forensic program had its own style and Roger had come up with his version of vetting interns after an unfortunate incident where an intern had thrown up on a case. Vowing never again, Roger's vetting process was different, to say the least, but highly effective at getting to the heart of things. It weeded out those who did not have the stomach for forensics.

Sam made certain she had in her briefcase a wide variety of case files, covering virtually every type of dinner meal and once the meals were served, the final element of the vetting process began. The show-and-tell.

She would pull out case files, with color photos, that resembled whatever meals the interns were eating. If a rice meal such as risotto was ordered, then she would present a case with maggots. If the meal was a fettuccine or spaghetti dish, then a case with worms, *Ascaris* roundworms worked well. She would pull out case files with photos and lay them next to the appropriate plate...and watched...and waited. If the student turned green, it was yellow alert and caution was warranted. If the student ran for the bathroom, it was red alert and it was more humane to suggest a different vocation.

They have no idea what is coming their way, Sam chuckled to herself as she reviewed their curriculum vitae.

She remembered hers—Roger's vetting technique wasn't as refined back then. Rather than use photographs, he would describe in vivid detail various cases and she could still visualize him gesturing wildly as he animatedly told her about a case in all its gory detail. He would complete the image by ordering the messiest meal on the menu and in her case, it was BBQ ribs. With grease running down his chin into his beard, he would almost act out the squishy sound a dismembered head made when it hit a metal exam table. Sam never ate BBQ ribs again.

Of the three interns Sam vetted that night, it was Cory Frankopolous who was the surprise. With his meticulously manicured fingernails and dapper attire, Sam had presumptuously pegged him as a lightweight and figured he would fold on the first pass. He not only picked up his photo and scrutinized it thoroughly, he did so while enthusiastically attacking his enchilada. He further cemented Sam's revised assessment when he reached over and casually picked up the other photos and studied them with the same level of aplomb. Sam had her intern.

[GERALD, 2001: **Quoted Text From Letter**

"You are so at home in the field and there were so many moments. Remember that trainee that interned with you in Montana?"]

MONTANA, 1987

Of all of her diverse job descriptions, working in the field as a medical researcher was especially satisfying to Sam, usually. Today was not one of those days. Her karma was off today—an infant had peed on her boots, an older man had thrown up on her, and ants had gotten into the glucose. And the day was still young.

Keep it up, you old fussbudget, and I'll gut your wires, she muttered under her breath while disassembling the centrifuge. Sam was running serum samples, and the cantankerous centrifuge had a mind of its own. With its spindle gyrating wildly, the centrifuge simply would not cooperate.

Her forensic obligations to Roger fulfilled, Sam had been in the field for four weeks now. She was part of a medical research team in Montana, monitoring medical status, such as diabetes, high blood pressure, and cardiovascular, of local Native American reservations in the area. End-stage renal kidney disease also had become a significant health issue, and was the subject of Sam's focus that season.

Sam was assigned to two of the seven Native American reservations in Montana. Rugged and rural sprawling swathes of land, both reservations were against the stunning gorgeous backdrop of the Rocky Mountains with its stately pine covered peaks and picturesque turquoise lakes and lush streams. Although both spanned over a million acres, their population density was low.

In their valley grasslands, small tribal communities abounded, ranging from several hundred to several thousand inhabitants each. Looking very much like many simple rural towns throughout the Great Plains, these communities usually had a single main U.S. highway running through its center, with single-story homes and businesses dotting the surroundings.

In the more rural areas, Sam and her team would travel between these tribal communities, remain for a few days, and move on to the next. In the larger towns, the team would set up shop at the town central plaza or even a large museum parking lot, a homing beacon for those needing care.

Having arrived just two weeks ago, Gerry, the aloof city boy from the streets of Boston had slid seamlessly into place; the work, the land, and the people all seemed to agree with him.

Gerry watched Sam, huddled under a portable canopy tent in a corner of the large parking lot that served as the central plaza area of the town. Simply constructed utilitarian buildings formed a rim protecting the area from the wind. As she fought with the centrifuge, his heart dropped when he caught the slight hesitations, the almost imperceptible adjustments she was having to make.

The symptoms of her disease had begun to be more apparent. To the stranger, she was just like anyone else, but for those who knew her, they could see the subtleties, the changes in her demeanor and her self-assurance. It tore at his heart. At first, he was overprotective and hovered as if she was a fragile glass and Sam, while appreciative of his concern, booted Gerry out of the way. She told him she must find her own way and her own footing.

"If you try to keep me from failing, I most assuredly will fail, for I will have learned nothing. I must endure the frustration of defeat if I am to learn how to survive."

Gerry had always had a plan, a path forward, but now his carefully laid out Plans A and B were anchorless in quicksand. A Plan C didn't even appear to be a possibility. In the years since her diagnosis, he had struggled to unravel the underlying Why and How as he fought to find stability.

The gentle touch of a hand resting on Gerry's shoulder snapped him out of his trance and he discovered himself looking down at the gnarly face of Arnold, an ancient patriarch of the tribal community. When Gerry had first arrived, unsure how to relate to the tribe, it was Arnold who offered a handshake and with whom he had begun to form a solid relationship. Over the past weeks, it was Arnold's sense of wisdom, imminently greater than his advanced age would suggest, that Gerry was drawn to.

The old man had been studying Gerry from the steps of the town trading post and had seen the look of pain filter across his face, and the dark shadow it cast over his heart. Standing shoulder to shoulder with Gerry, Arnold gazed past the highway over the grasslands toward the snow covered peaks of the Rockies in the distance. His face was unflinching, but it radiated a warmth and harbored concern.

Sam glanced up and saw the two men, Gerry and Arnold, side by side, deeply absorbed in what seemed to be more than a simple chat. Pausing, Sam watched them intently. Tempted to wave, Sam then thought better of it, for whatever they were talking about, it had their full attention. There seemed to be a heaviness to the air and the somber tone was palpable from across the plaza. Gerry was a man who confronted life head on and usually on his terms, but today his body language radiated defeat, and this was not something Sam was accustomed to seeing.

"You seem like a man with a heavy burden. Such loads are lighter when shared," the old man gently said to Gerry when he finally spoke.

"It's complicated" was the younger man's short reply.

Arnold's gaze never left the horizon as he softly answered, "No, this is complicated. This—you standing here with a dark cloud smothering your soul is complicated." Briefly glancing at Gerry, Arnold continued as he waved a crooked finger between the couple, "But you and her—this is simple, as simple as you allow it to be."

Wanting to talk, but hesitant to say too much, Gerry haltingly began to explain and found himself weaving through the diagnosis and the long-distance careers. His voice quivered as he finished despondently, "I can't fix this."

Still looking out over the horizon, Arnold shook his head in disbelief, "Friend, what are you doing? You do not understand. Why are you trying to fix that which is not broken? Why do you worry about giving her a house? She already has one. Why worry about giving her a place in life? She has already found it."

It was like he was scolding a small child, gently but firmly, as Arnold's soft voice urged Gerry to view things differently,

"Yes, it is different from what you had expected, but it is hers, and hers to live. Why worry about giving her what she already has and doesn't need? Give her instead that which she lacks but requires. Do not tell her, show her. Show her that you understand and that you can deliver."

Arnold turned and locked eyes with his younger companion, and the two sets of brown eyes, one golden brown and the other the darkest of darks, regarded each other intently.

"She is smart, both here," Arnold continued, tapping his fingers on Gerry's forehead, "and here," now tapping Gerry's chest. "She does not need you to provide. She needs support to make her way on the road that is hers to travel and travel it she must. What she needs, son, is the trunk of a sequoia." He then suddenly left Gerry alone with his thoughts.

Watching Arnold's retreating figure, Gerry stood raking his fingers through his hair, trying to comprehend what the old man had just said and his appreciation slid into frustration, for it both made sense, and it didn't, all at the same time. The What was forming in his mind but the How still eluded him. Suddenly aware of people milling around him, giving him odd glances as he stood motionless in thought, he looked over and caught Sam standing watching him.

Waving him over, Sam gave him a hug as she looked up at him while asking, "I don't even want to know what you two were talking about, do I?" detecting a hint of the concern that still hovered on Gerry's face. Picking up the screwdriver and forceps Sam had been using to take the centrifuge apart, Gerry pulled up the stool and sat down.

As he scrounged around on the table for a washer, he was tempted to share what Arnold had said, but wasn't quite sure how to be that "trunk of a sequoia." He, instead, offered a white lie. With a sly grin, he exclaimed, "Our vacation...and how we are itching to get started! Arnold gave me the lowdown on all the best fishing spots!"

"I'm as anxious as you to get started, babe," Sam told him, lightly laughing at his enthusiasm. But then she teasingly reminded him, "We still have about a week's worth of work left!"

"Aw c'mon, "Gerry playfully asked, with a suggestive lift of the eyebrows. "Sure we can't leave...maybe just a little early?"

"That, sir, would be highly unprofessional, but I promise," Sam coyly murmured in his ear, "I will make it worth the wait!"

33

THIS GIG'S GOTTEN BETTER ALREADY

MONTANA, *Several Days Later*

In Colorado, Roger hung up the phone and pulled down his personnel binder off the shelf. Jokingly muttering an inward *Oh crap* as he looked at a map of where his teams were that season, he saw Sam was the closest, only an hour or so away on a Native American reservation in Montana.

Oh, she will not be happy, Roger chuckled to himself as he called the contact number on file.

Being freelance bestowed a certain level of freedom that Sam reveled in, for it allowed her to work whenever and wherever she found a position, and she had accepted a research position for the summer. With her on someone else's payroll, Roger knew he couldn't just assign Sam to this job. He would have to instead lay on the charm and hope to appeal to Sam's better, but often bullheaded, nature.

"Can you make a run for a quick prelim eval of a site?" a sanguine Roger asked, while explaining a rancher had uncovered some questionable skeletal remains during construction. "If this turns out to be Indigenous, we could really use your tribal contacts," he said as he described the site to Sam. Roger attempted to sweeten the pot by telling her the pluses—the site was close by, only an hour or so from where she was and if needed, he would make available the team, plus the intern she had vetted earlier that summer, Cory.

"This is a short and sweet side job and you'll probably be in and out within a few hours, a day max," he said cheerfully trying to keep the conversation light. Hoping to ignite a kernel of enthusiasm in Sam's otherwise dour mood, Roger pointed out that he knew she'd love the change of scenery and the chance to work in the mountains.

Saving his biggest gun for last, he dropped his voice to a whimper, and he laid it on thick, "You'd be doing me a huge favor, dearie. I'd be in your debt if you would."

The independence and flexibility of freelance fit her needs and personality like a glove, but Sam understood where her paychecks came from. The same unrestrained work structure that she counted on so heavily also carried its own set of problems.

At times, serving multiple employers resulted in a juggling act between competing positions and competing organizations, and a tug-of-war often arose between her loyalty and her obligations. Sometimes a tough decision would have to be made as to whom to disappoint. Diplomacy dictated Sam keep her thoughts to herself, for out of all of her chiefs, Roger was her cornerstone—she owed him so much. While agreeing to check out the site, Sam made it abundantly clear to Roger that she and Gerry had vacation plans. Their "Our Time" plans had long since been on the books, plans that could not nor would not be changed.

"Come hell or high water," Sam declared in a tone that left little room for misinterpretation, "I'll be off the site in a week. No discussion."

Gerry fumed at the abrupt shift in their itinerary that threatened their "Our Time" vacation. Characterized by a more relaxed and affable demeanor, Gerry found Sam's medical tours were both fascinating and fulfilling. They ignited an interest he hadn't known he had, and there was a rhythm to them that Gerry enjoyed immensely. There was no predictable rhythm to forensics.

Sometimes intricate precision work was required, whereas other times, it was more of a quick and dirty endeavor where the bulldozer approach trumped precision. Modern life had its constraints with budgets, time deadlines, politics as well as the weather and marauding animals to factor into the equation of determining which approach to use.

Permeating a forensic team's every move, issues of legality and chain of evidence would hang like a fog. With strict adherence to methodology being essential, crews that were gregarious off-site would become singularly focused on their task at hand and had little tolerance for interruptions. This terseness often triggered a shift in Sam's pleasant medical persona attitude into that of a strict martinet.

Not being trained or certified in any forensic capacity, Gerry was forced to the sidelines, quite literally, for he wasn't permitted within the site perimeter at all. In this setting, he was not viewed as a member of the crew, but rather his contribution was that of a gofer. It was a Jekyll and Hyde existence, and Gerry preferred to give the whole thing a very wide berth.

The few times he had been present for forensic gigs, he stayed out of the way by spending much of his time cleaning the firearms the team had brought into the field with them. Scowling, Gerry made a mental note to be sure to stuff plenty of extra cleaning rags and gun oil for this outing.

On their drive up to the site, Sam worked to placate Gerry. "This is nothing and is probably just a bear carcass, they have poachers all the time up this way. We will be back to normal by tomorrow morning."

She tried to soften his grumbling with the bribe of a quiet brunch out, maybe even some sightseeing. Upon arrival at the site, the two met up with the rancher and began to canvas the area. An excavator stood next to the gouge it had made in the bank as the rancher pointed out where he found the remains. He had been reworking a natural terrace at the base of an embankment.

To one side, the paleness of bone contrasted against the earth and Sam shifted from medical researcher to forensic osteologist. Pulling out her tool case and making a few trial sweeps of the brush, she flicked the dirt away from around the edges of the largest element and saw the edge of the tibia.

Moving over a tad, she inserted her probe and felt resistance and further examination revealed it to be the companion lower leg bone, the femur, and it was human. *So much for the quiet brunch out,* she grumbled to herself as her hope of pacifying Gerry with a calmer afternoon was dashed.

Standing up, she guessed where the skull might be and began a gingerly exploration along the edge of the bank, and finding a clavicle, Sam moved up a bit further and caught the bottom of the mandible. The skull was intact, and luckily, the surrounding dirt was easily dislodged and brushed away. Wanting to disturb the remains as little as possible and to keep everything in situ, Sam refrained from picking anything up. Instead, she knelt in the dirt beside it as she studied the skull, evaluating its ethnic characteristics.

It didn't look indigenous Native American to her at all, and the more she took in, the more it told her—this skull definitely had European characteristics. As Gerry flagged the locations of skeletal remains, Sam turned to investigate the adjacent area with a series of rockslides due to the excavator.

Spending the next hour scouring along the bank's edge, the pair located several more areas of interest, but more importantly, they were finding duplicates. These were skeletal remains of not one person but several. Quick and easy had just become long and dirty, and she would need a team up here to set up a full site grid after all.

The rancher, while taking the pair on a tour of the surrounding area, told them what little history of the ranch he knew, answering questions as they went. *Was this an old homestead? Could this be a cemetery? Was there a town here in the past?*

Regrettably the rancher had few answers—the team would have to dig for the clues. The couple spent the rest of the morning establishing and staking the site perimeter, flagging, and covering each of the remaining skeletal elements, all in preparation for the following day's dig.

It was hard to misinterpret Gerry's seismic vibrations as they were a ten on the Richter scale; he was miffed and the drive back down to the reservation was an uncomfortable carbon copy of the drive up.

Sam, still trying to appeal to his better side, assured him once again, "This is still nothing. We are just going to spend a day or so cleaning up the graves well enough to make an assessment—forensic versus historical."

Sam's observations of the weathering evident on the bones that she could see suggested the site was not recent, but also not incredibly old, causing her to say, "My gut says this is probably just an old pioneer family cemetery. That's not us, that's an archaeologist," Sam promised, flashing what she hopes was an encouraging smile over at Gerry.

That night, Sam called Roger with the update. "Okay Roger, here's the good, bad, and the ugly. First the good, the bones are human bones, and at first impression, they're Caucasian. The bad news is that there are multiple graves and the jury is still out as to jurisdiction."

She could hear Roger's sharp intake of air. "You think this is a homicide?" he asked, his voice full of surprise.

"Not likely, old man," Sam revealed. "I'm seeing conflicting information, but it may just be due to location—some graves seem to be far more protected from the elements than others. The bones in one grave look too degraded—they've been there a bit, although I'm not talking thousands of years of course...but centuries? Eh, maybe. Another showed very little weathering—if I had seen that grave first, I'd be leaning toward more modern."

Roger winced in dread as he asked Sam, "And what's the ugly?"

"Ah, you're not gonna like this," Sam answered, "but I need that team you promised me."

Sam could hear Roger mutter to himself as he rummaged through his personnel binder. "Okay," he said to her, "I can pull together Kati and Doug and have them up there in a couple of days."

Sam's grunt was followed by a blunt, "Sorry Roger—not good enough. A couple of days isn't going to cut it. I want them up here tomorrow—by noon at the latest." Roger began to bluster and Sam cut him off. "Oh, it's worse than you think, old man. I want John in forensics and that new kid, Cory as well."

Her demand prompted Roger to whine about how hard it would be to pull a crew together on such short notice.

Worried that this little side trip would encroach on her exalted "Our Time," Sam was unsympathetic to Roger's complaining, and pointedly interrupted him with a barbed, "Ticktock, Roger, ticktock."

The sun had just begun its daily arc across the sky when Sam and Gerry returned to the mountainside site. Having gotten permission the previous day from the rancher to set up a base camp and even do some fishing and small game hunting for dinner, the pair occupied themselves with the business of preparing the site while waiting for the team to arrive.

The two scouted the area more thoroughly, this time documenting evidence and the surrounding geography with film photography accompanied by line sketches, as well as flagging the perimeter grid. They also searched around for suitable bivouac sites for the pitching of crew tents and the base camp, which consisted of a main work tent with its worktables and their personal tent.

They had just finished arranging the last of the camp chairs around the campfire and had a pot of coffee perking away with a skillet of cornbread baking over the fire, when they spotted a cloud of dust off in the horizon.

Two pickups barreled across the open field, leaving huge dust plumes trailing in their wakes and metal equipment cases could be heard banging in their beds. The team had arrived. Led by Kati and Doug, the team was accompanied by a third member, John Doherty, the forensic tech guy. A professorial type, John's steady and focused demeanor offered a nice contrast to the chaos often surrounding the two archeologists, Kati, and Doug. Cory, the new and untested intern, rounded out the crew and was serving as its minion.

Kati, the forthright and irascible gal-Friday who could do it all, was barking out orders even before the truck had come to a full stop. Moving the crew in double time as they grabbed their gear, she spied Sam and Gerry lounging in their chairs by their fire. They hadn't worked together since Oaxaca, and Kati, the short, sturdy dynamo, tackled Sam in such an enthusiastic hug, that she knocked the wind right out of her.

"Jeez, Kati!" Sam squawked as she staggered about a bit, but Kati was undeterred.

"Damn girl, you look good!" Kati laughed as she turned her attention to Gerry when he stood up to welcome her. "Oh get over here, doll," carried over the camp as she greeted him by brusquely grabbing him by his belt buckle and hauling him to a nearby boulder.

Standing at only five-foot-two, she couldn't reach his face otherwise, but now perched on the rock, he was all hers. A startled Gerry was taken aback when Kati gushed, "Oh sweetie, you are a sight for sore eyes," and gave him a big smooch on the cheek. Jumping off the rock, a giggling Kati then slyly patted him with both hands on his rump and chirped, "This gig has gotten better already now."

Sam had forgotten Kati's fondness for her boyfriend, and now bristled with annoyance over the woman's blatant forwardness toward him. Accompanied by a wagging finger to drive her point home, Sam shouted out at the tornado that had descended on her camp, "Kati! Hands off the merchandise. You are a married woman for crying out loud!"

With a coy Cheshire grin, Kati only teased back, "Yeah, girl, but yours is a delicious bar of eye candy. Mine? He's a dried-out piece of sour lemon found years later under the fridge!"

Looking around, Kati shrugged and gestured to Sam, silently asking where to put tents and followed Sam's toss of a hand toward some flat terraces on a ridge, just above base camp. Kati again dispatched a series of orders at a blistering pace. John and Doug, however, just continued pulling out their equipment, seemingly oblivious to the rantings of their boss. The two men had long since learned to shrug off the mayhem that often followed Kati's commands and took everything in stride.

Poor Cory, on the other hand, was caught up in the crossfire of orders and was not sure which one to follow first, and Kati, watching Cory just blithely standing there, was compelled to bark out at the lad,

"Boy, did you forget to pack your brains? I said…" The woman, a natural drill sergeant, was born to bellow.

While tending to the cornbread, Sam watched the rest of the team pitch their tents and the experience and efficiency of the veterans was clear—they had their tents up in a matter of minutes. In contrast, Cory's rawness was front and center as he struggled with the poles of his tent bending in every direction except the one he wanted.

Lean with delicate features, Cory's black wavy hair constantly fell in his eyes as he fought with the fabric of the tent and his exertions were often punctuated with the colorful, volatile language of his Greek forebears. Being a city boy from Chicago, Cory didn't have much experience in the woods. In fact, he had none, and when Cory's dad first heard his son was going to spend the summer out in the dangerous expanse of the wild, wild west, he was concerned. There were dangerous animals to fear, and he was scared of every little snap of a twig, with a bear around every boulder and a snake under every log. Cory's dad had given him a rifle to have as protection against such threats; the rifle was a Daisy pellet.

Watching Cory carefully unpack the pellet gun as if it were a priceless artifact, Sam and Gerry exchanged amused looks with each other, trying to contain their mirth. The other three members were not so gracious.

"Damn boy, that won't do squat. What are you going to shoot, a bug?" In the high country, field teams routinely carried firearms and were proficient in their use and this neophyte's ignorance grated them. Deflated by the outright disdain from the rest of the crew, Cory tried to hide his embarrassment by busying himself with his tent. Gerry, meanwhile, was sympathetic to Cory's pain and tendered an offer to show Cory how to handle and shoot a rifle, a real one. At last, Gerry felt useful in the forensic setting.

With the pitching of their tents finished, Sam, as site boss, assembled the crew to run through the basic summary of the site, its conditions, and what to expect for the next few days. Outlining her timetable, she explained what information they were looking for and how she wanted it collected. Desperate for her vacation with Gerry to remain on track, Sam also impressed upon the team how quickly the job was to be completed.

"There will be no dawdling," she warned. She also emphasized the need to remain vigilant and mindful of their surroundings. "While we are only here for a few days, bear, cougar, and the prairie rattlesnake are out and about—be aware." Leaving the veteran crew to pull their equipment together and set up their stations in preparations for the following day, Sam motioned for the new intern Cory to follow her for a more personal one-on-one regarding some basic fundamentals of field life.

"It's not just the big critters you have to watch out for," Sam explained. "Evenings are cool up in the mountains at this time of year," she told the raw intern, "and the little creepy-crawlies, snakes and bugs, are looking for a warm place to spend the night. If you aren't careful, they can give you a nasty bite. To avoid this, there are some basic dos and don'ts you should follow." She began to recite a list. "Do pick up and secure all foodstuffs, don't leave duffel bags open on the ground, don't leave clothing on the ground. If you do, shake out and inspect before putting them on. This was the same for gloves, shoes, and boots…"

An impatient Cory nodded *Yeah, yeah, yeah*, but she could tell he wasn't paying attention.

The rest of the early evening was uneventful and pleasant, and while sitting around the campfire, the team all swapped stories and caught up on each other's lives. As the sun began its descent, the couple excused themselves to find a view to watch the spectacle. It was time for their sunset.

When they had first met, Gerry had scoffed at what he considered one of Sam's looser qualities—her love and appreciation of nature. He was a city boy, and nature was just something to be endured, tamed or defeated depending on the circumstances. No matter how many times he had witnessed it, he was shocked at her connection to nature. Sam seemed to become one with it and he swore she almost became transparent while she drank in its energy, a gossamer veil on the wind. Every time he would sit mesmerized by what he saw on her face, and he found himself tempted to reach out to see if she was solid.

Gerry's earlier disgruntled demeanor had mellowed as he glanced down at Sam leaning against his knee, her beer in hand. Totally immersed in the beauty of the mountain view, a shimmering blush of pink, orange, and yellow hues reflected on her face. He knew she was solid—he could feel her—but an aura seemed to glow about her, and he leaned forward, wrapping his arms around her as he perched his chin on her head.

A soft smile formed across his face as he wondered, if he closed his eyes, could he feel the same energy as her?

All they could hear was the call of the birds saying good night, an occasional bugle call of an elk in rut, the low gurgle of the stream below them, and the sporadic howl of a coyote in the distance.

Maybe forensics wasn't so bad after all.

34

NOW THAT'S SOMETHING YOU WILL NEVER SEE IN THE ARMY

The night's calm was beginning to give way to the daily arboreal background noise and the sounds of the forest awakening for the day began to crack through Sam's fog of sleep. With the sun having yet to fully breach the horizon, the morning broke with a slight haze floating over the camp.

Sam's stirring caused Gerry to roll over and stare at her; they loved this time of the morning, just lying there, spooning, listening to each other breathe. His fingers began a well-traveled path down the woman's back, prompting her to quietly whisper, "'Fraid not, big guy," as she tilted her head back with a soft smile to give him a kiss on the chin. "We're not alone here. There are four tents lined up on the ridge just thirty feet or so from us."

Undeterred, Gerry just murmured, "We'll be quiet." Shaking her head, Sam slid out of the sleeping bag and began to get dressed for the day.

"Sorry, babe, no can do. No matter how discreet you may think you are, in the field, there are no secrets. Everyone knows everyone else's business," Sam explained with a tone of regret, while lacing up her boots.

With an air of no-nonsense, she grabbed her utility bag and

glanced over at her paramour's clouding face, and curtly told him, "I have no intention to be fodder for Kati's barbs and jokes." Leaning over with a gentle smile and for one last kiss, she quietly asked, "Where's the Army stoicism, the stiff upper lip you are always spouting off about? Suck it up, sweetie," as she patted him on his hip.

Making one last perusal around the tent for anything she might have missed, the workload of the day began to weigh on Sam's mind and her attention became more focused on her job, than on the man lying in the sleeping bag.

Distracted, Sam absentmindedly muttered while sighing, "Besides, I need to get the coffee brewing before Kati gets to it." The standing rule of the camp was whoever arose first, started the ever-present coffee pot. Kati was an early riser, and her coffee was like her personality, strong and bracing, and it would take the lining right off your stomach.

Sam made it a point to beat Kati to the coffee pot. While arranging her clipboard, she briskly announced, "It's time to get up! We've got things to do," and thus, effectively put an end to any residual hope on Gerry's part of a leisurely start to the day.

The metamorphosis had occurred in the blink of an eye, for while gathering her paperwork and journals into her field bag, the orders had begun to fly around the tent. In a span of seconds, Sam shot off to Gerry a flurry of tasks to be completed, where they were to be done and when she expected them to be done by. He had no need to ask why they were to be done, that part was obvious. Because she said so.

Heaving a disgusted sigh, Gerry shot a mock salute accompanied by a sarcastic, "Yes, ma'am," at Sam's retreating back as she exited the tent. Grumbling *Shit,* he pessimistically flopped back down on the bed roll as he recognized her mood. Sam's forensic alter ego, Attila the Hun, had emerged and it portended a long, crappy day for him.

With Gerry still brooding as he lay in the sleeping bag, Sam stuck her head back through the tent flaps and hissed at him, "Will you get up and get moving?" He was not moving fast enough for her Attila persona, and rolling his eyes in a huff, Gerry threw his T-shirt over his face. Kati's coffee was preferable to Sam's personality today.

Sam had been up for just over a half an hour or so, going over the order of business and making breakfast for the team when a petulant Gerry eventually made his way toward the campfire. In the field, the two main meals of the day were breakfast and dinner. Lunch was a haphazard affair with crews snacking on their own at will.

Sam's breakfasts were large and complete, and she had the requisite beans, sausage, eggs, and hash browns all in various stages of cooking, bubbling, or sizzling away over the fire. Warming himself against the early morning chill while enjoying a cup of freshly perked coffee, Gerry was silently wondering what he would be doing that day and how best to stay out of Sam's way.

He was still caught up in his thoughts when the serenity of the predawn calm was shattered by a piercing scream from Cory, the intern.

[**Gerald, 2001: Quoted Text From Letter**

"You warned him not to leave his shorts on the ground at night. Winter was approaching and critters liked to find warm places to cozy in for the night. He blew you off. That morning at sunrise we hear this blood curdling scream and there he was—running along the ridgeline, stark naked trying to kick off his shorts while silhouetted against the rising sun, screaming like a lunatic."]

The rest of the team bolted out of their tents in varying states of dress. Doug had been in the midst of shaving and stood there with shaving cream dripping off his face, John was missing everything but his pants, and Kati came barreling up a second later still trying to get her boots on. The three of them, plus Gerry, just stood there in awe, mouths agape at the sight of Cory lurching across the top of the ridge.

Clipboard in hand, Sam had been fixated on the excavation paperwork, but looked up just in time to see Cory slide to a stop and frantically gyrate a heebie-jeebie dance, trying to get out of an underwear leg wrapped around his ankle. As Cory resumed his flight into the woods, his rear end in full view, Sam just unsympathetically shook her head in amazement.

[GERALD, 2001: Quoted Text From Letter
"You didn't have one lick of sympathy for him. Looked up and deadpanned 'Damn, his tush is so pasty white, could use it for a signal flare.'"]

IN UNISON, the dumbfounded quartet of Gerry and the crew, turned to collectively give Sam the most astonished looks. "What," Sam disgustedly snorted at the team as they stared at her. "Oh, enough with the look! Did I not warn him?" With a flick of a finger toward the ridge, she added, "Will someone please go run him down before he hurts himself?"

Momentarily speechless, Gerry watched in awe as the two men, John and Doug raced after the bouncing circle of Cory's rear end fading into the brush of the forest.

To the sound of blackbirds announcing the dawn, Gerry leaned over to Sam and dryly whispered, "Now that's a sight you'll never see in the Army."

The excitement over, Kati returned to her tent, yelling over her shoulder, "Well...bug or snake? I've got dibs on it being a snake."

Sam shook her head. "No way it was a snake, it's gotta be a bug," she called out. "That underwear jig he did—I'm thinking maybe ants!"

"Ain't ants girl," Kati yelled back. "With ants, you spin around like a top, you don't run. That's gotta be bigger. I'll bet ya a case of beer it was a snake."

Gerry stood between the two women as they had bantered, joking over Cory's downfall. "I can't believe you two," he uttered to Sam in disbelief.

"Oh, this happens a lot. He shouldn't have blown me off," Sam cackled as she turned her attention back to her clipboard.

Both Kati and Sam were wrong.

Cory's description of the culprit was astounding as he explained how he was attacked by a humongous spider.

"It was this big, black, and hairy thing," Cory insisted as he held his hands out to indicate a spider the size of a boulder. "And vicious, too!" Sam just stood there with an amused, *Uh-huh,* as she thought, *Yep, Montana has tarantulas the size of a dinner plate.*

Later that morning, the skies presented Cory with the realities of fieldwork as a series of squalls unleashed torrential lines of rain, threatening to wash the entire site down into the ravine below. The two women pushed the men to continue. Sam was on a deadline and Kati, well, the nastier the conditions, the happier Kati became. Kati was in her glory.

Sam and Gerry took on new roles that morning, ones of civil engineers, and they tried to keep the site as dry as possible. The erection of tarps, the digging of trenches to divert the runoff and the setting up of wick buckets to mop up water that did get into the pits, consumed most of their energy and time. By late afternoon the crew was exhausted and so apparently was Mother Nature, for the storms faded out, their greyish pallor punctured by struggling rays of sunlight.

Happy hour came early that afternoon. A beleaguered and embarrassed Cory had been relentlessly hammered by the crew throughout the day over his morning escapade. Under the guise of continuing with the intern's firearm training, Gerry took it upon himself to give the young lad a respite from the barrage by inviting Cory to go with him on the hunt for small game.

In addition to bagging several rabbits for the evening stew, the experience gave Cory a much-needed boost of confidence. With their soggy clothing strewn about the site, hung on poles, on lines between trees and on the backs of chairs in hopes of being merely damp by morning, the camp took on an eerie derelict cast. The enticing aromas of the dinner's stew tantalized the crew's taste buds and they gradually began to assemble by the campfire, still wet and grumpy from the day's weather.

Humiliation from the morning's events still poked at Cory and he was uncharacteristically quiet.

"I'm really, ah...sorry for this morning," he said apologetically to the group and a guffaw exploded from Kati.

"Oh, boy, that was nothing! You should have Sam tell you about Ecuador and the beetle!"

Oh geez, Sam thought as she cut Kati off. "He doesn't need to hear about that!"

"Oh, we do!" Gerry and John both enthusiastically exclaimed in unison. This was news to them.

The story was a sensitive one for men and Sam struggled to use delicate wording. "Well...let's say, like you, Cory, an intern had left his shorts on the ground, and a beetle—a very large beetle with pinchers, had settled in for the night." Sam cleared her throat. "Ah...apparently the little guy didn't care for the view coming at him when the intern pulled his shorts on that morning. And it clamped down—really hard —on a rather sensitive part of the male anatomy."

At the men's aghast expressions, Kati quipped, "Here's the best part! Sam had to pry it off with a knife! Just imagine! Sam standing over the 'family jewels' with a knife in her hand! Talk about every man's nightmare!" On a roll, Kati leaned over and poked Doug. "C'mon, tell Cory about the chiggers!"

"You would bring that up," Doug snorted in jest as he recounted his misstep during a call of nature in the bush. The moment had led to a massive army of miniscule arachnid-like chiggers feasting on his privates and the tale left the campfire circle doubled over in convulsions.

Cory's panicked eyes were as big as saucers. *Chiggers? What were chiggers?* The perils of the woods were far greater than he ever could imagine.

Cory then asked Gerry about his most embarrassing moment and Sam did a quick review in her head. While smiling to herself, she thought, *Peru, maybe Costa Rica, no...definitely Peru.* Gerry's answer left her speechless.

In the years they had been together, Sam could never get Gerry to talk about his tour in Vietnam. She could count on a couple of fingers the short simple answers he had given in response to her inquiries about that period of his life. Even his Army buddies, the Musketeers, could not get him to open up about those days. Now here, on a mountain in Montana, with a group of people he didn't even know all that well, Gerry was recounting his first firefight in Vietnam. His baptism by fire.

Gerry stared at the fire, not sure where to begin, but after a moment, he threw a glance over at Cory before he began to softly speak.

"I was eighteen and the new guy—fresh out of basic training. I thought I knew what a gun fight was." He paused long enough to shake his head in a scoff. "I had seen things as a kid. I was from Boston's back streets, but they weren't anything like that day." Staring into the flickering flames, his voice was so quiet that those on the other side of the fire had to lean in to hear him over the crackling of the logs. Even the night noises of the forest were gone; no owls hooting, no coyotes howling, nothing but silence came from the dark.

"You know, you don't hear bullets coming at ya. You don't know until they hit. I was so scared I wouldn't hear it coming over the pops of our guns," Gerry said matter-of-factly as he described the sounds the rounds made, both incoming going overhead and outbound. "The guy next to me. I never heard it, I didn't know he had been hit until he jerked."

Gerry stared at the fire so intently. He was no longer talking to the crew, he was no longer in Montana. He spoke of the smells, the spent gunpowder, the bracing human smells of sweat, blood, and urine. And he spoke of the leaves.

"Jungle leaves have a smell when they're cut. It's like when you mow a lawn, that grassy smell, but oily. The bullets would turn leaves to mush and the smell..." Sam gritted her teeth as she imagined the moment, its chaos with its fear. She could almost feel the desperation as she visualized a young Gerry, crouching there, with pieces of leaves obliterated under the barrage of bullets, pelting his face as he had turned toward his buddy's jerk.

A small shudder ran through Gerry, his voice heavy and distant, as he dully admitted, "I can still smell that stench." A small gasp bubbled up from Sam and she involuntarily twitched when she suddenly realized why Gerry always held his breath every time they would walk past a freshly mowed lawn.

Sam could barely make out the expressions of Doug and John across the fire, but she could feel the energy that ran through the circle. No one moved. No one even took a sip of a coffee or beer as they sat hypnotized. His unit was pinned down in an unexpected firefight.

Gerry knew he was supposed to fight back—he knew what to do, but he couldn't seem to make his hands and head work together in unison. The fire's spell over him finally broken, Gerry looked up at the group and ruefully admitted, "I was so scared, I tried to load the bullets in my rifle backward." Shaking his head with a crooked smile, he answered the unspoken question Cory's expression asked, "No, they didn't fit, but I was trying."

When it was all over, Gerry was still alive as was much of his unit, but Gerry had voided his bladder during the fight. He had peed his pants. His sergeant had been a crusty soul who, perhaps in a bout of tough love, nicknamed the youngster Private Pee Wee, and the boy felt the sting of that moniker for the rest of his tour. The story was Gerry's way of telling Cory he understood. If Sam harbored any hopes that event marked the beginning of Gerry's sharing of those days, they were quickly dashed for she was sorely mistaken. Gerry never spoke of Vietnam again.

The following morning, Sam's trowel's edge scraped away a bit of dirt as she thought of Gerry's Vietnam story, trying to take it all in. Needing to avoid stepping in the grave itself, she had crouched next to it, but her awkward lean only caused pain to screech throughout her body.

The gawky position was beginning to take its toll on Sam's back, and she realized it would be best to work the grave over boards. Whenever possible, Sam preferred to dig out ledges along a grave's two long axes, from which boards could be laid to provide a scaffolding that she could lay on suspended over the grave, leaving it undisturbed.

Heaving herself up, Sam glanced at Gerry, who sat over at the main table, out of the team's way, unhappily cleaning Doug's rifle. While the site was still a work in progress, enough had been cleared that Sam was no longer seriously entertaining the notion it was a forensic case.

They would continue to work the graves that had been disturbed by the excavator, verifying that they were historic, but the earlier issues of legality and maintaining strict forensic procedures, were no longer of concern. The tone of the job had changed, and Sam's Attila the Hun persona mellowed a tad.

"Hey, babe?" she called out and when Gerry looked up, she tossed a "come here" look with her head. "Are you at a stopping point? I could really use a hand here." Delight erupted over Gerry's face as he eagerly dropped the rifle, mid-cleaning. Sam reached over and pulled her tool roll toward her, tossing it so it flipped open to reveal its contents. Gerry loved Sam's tool roll. It was old-school, a coyote brown canvas with leather straps, worn dull and smooth from years of abuse. He watched as Sam's fingers flitted over the tools in the holding tabs, choosing a larger trowel for him. As an afterthought, she pulled out a compact geological pick hammer as well.

Standing next to the grave, Sam explained to Gerry, "I need you to dig a level ledge, between four and six inches wide on each side of this grave, from here to here." She pointed to where she needed them, handing Gerry the tools. Pulling a bucket over toward them, Sam explained not to discard the dirt, but rather put it in buckets, telling him with a sly grin, "That'll be your next job!" as she left to retrieve the wood planks.

When Sam returned, the ledges had been dug, and Sam then handed Gerry a wood skewer from the tool roll. "Metal probes can leave marks on bone so we use these," she said as she explained how to probe the dirt with them to locate points of resistance. Handing Gerry a cup filled with fluorescent markers, similar to bingo chips, Sam told him to place a chip on top of every point where he met strong resistance, either bone or rock.

"How do you tell the difference between the two?" Gerry asked.

Sam grinned, already envisioning Gerry's *Ewww* when she quipped, "Me? I just do the lick test. If it's bone, it often sticks to your tongue. Rocks don't!"

With Sam at one end and Gerry at the other, they began to gently insert probes in a grid pattern, placing a pink chip at contact points. When they met in the middle, Sam and Gerry stood back to see the chips making a vague outline of a skeleton. Laying the planks on the ledges, Sam sprawled above the grave on her stomach and using picks, brushes and trowels, began to remove dirt from the edges, using the chips as a guide for where the bones might be.

As Sam would fill a bucket with excavated dirt, Gerry would dump it into a sieve and shake the dirt through ever decreasing mesh screen sizes. Sorting excavated backdirt from not only Sam's grave, but from the others as well, Gerry worked for hours, finding nothing but tiny animal bones, twigs, or pebbles.

But after several hours, Sam heard an excited gasp and looked up to see Gerry holding something in his outstretched palm, a button from the backdirt of the grave Doug and Cory were working on. Activity stopped as everyone gathered around, watching Doug examine it closely. Rusty and encrusted, an eagle could still be made out on its metal surface. At the center, near the eagle's feet, was a crest with an I.

"It's an infantry button," Doug announced, "probably from the mid-1800s." An hour or so later, Kati called out she had something as well and pointed out a thin discoloration of the soil with the point of her trowel.

"That looks like coffin residue," she told Sam as John collected samples to be examined later.

The site did indeed pan out to be an old pioneer cemetery. State historical records confirmed that it had once been the location of an extended family homestead. The indications from the graves themselves—there were eleven in all with several more thought to be hidden further back—were consistent: All were of European descent, all were oriented in the same cardinal direction, and all were positioned in a similar burial manner.

There were mixed ages and genders, and the button, the wood coffin residue, along with other artifacts found alongside several remains provided additional confirmation. The site was turned over to archaeologists and the crew was on their way home; they had been there five days.

Cory survived his rite of passage in fieldwork although the crew still had their entertainment with him; he was the "butt" of jokes for the rest of the week. Each morning was heralded with yet another team member reenacting Cory's epic "Dance of the Spider" along the ridge.

After each had their fun, Sam pulled them aside, admonishing them, "No more," as she waggled a pointed finger at them. The boy had paid his dues.

On their last morning, the crew rose with the sun as usual and began the task of breaking camp. All was safely stowed, the tents, the gear and equipment. Sam also safely stowed, much to Gerry's relief, her Attila the Hun alter ego as well. Gone were the tensions and the edge that had dominated much of the previous days and while gathered around the campfire for one last get-together, the camaraderie and geniality returned. The full disc of the sun had barely cleared the horizon, its reddish glowing rays illuminating the dark forest, when again, as in the last four mornings, there was a piercing shriek.

On that last morning, however, it was Cory who performed his glorious run along the ridge. In a hilarious parody, he sashayed across the ridgeline, stopping every few steps for a dramatic kick of a leg and swish of the rear, all in a perfect rendition of his "Shaking of the Booty Prance."

Sam even put aside her clipboard for the show. In the field, perhaps the most important quality of all to have, is a good sense of humor.

[GERALD, 2001: Quoted Text From Letter

"My absolute favorite moment in the field, Hon, was the leech. I'm sorry—I can still see the totally stunned look on that agent's face when you whipped out that leech. Remember? You were part of a swamp dive for homicide victims and was covered in muck. In all fairness you weren't the picture of authority at that moment. That agent was chewing your head off, hell bent on kicking your behind, making sure you knew your place. You held up your hand as if to say —hold that thought and then shoved your hand down the front of your pants—rummaged around for a few, pulled out this humongous leech and chucked it. Only you Hon."]

[**SAMANTHA, 2024: Quoted Text From Letter**

"I fell in love with your sense of humor. Quirky, dry, sometimes incomprehensible but always true. After I pulled that leech out of my pants in Louisiana, that agent had blown a gasket, remember? He had screamed at me that I was a disgrace and there wasn't enough booze in Louisiana to deal with me. You made it a point to track down his address and sent several cases of whisky to his office with the note "Wouldn't want you to run out, you will be dealing with Dr. Walker for the rest of the summer." Ouch.]

[**GERALD, 2001: Quoted Text From Letter**

"I have so many memories of you in the field. Some funny, some scary, some inspirational. All are totally you."]

35

THE ALLURE WAS LIKE CATNIP

*U*ntil Montana, Sam and Gerry had been going with the flow, experiencing the excitement of adventure, and allowing the winds of fate to carry them, much as a leaf drifts as it floats to the ground. Montana drove it home.

Standing in that plaza back at the Indian reservation, the realization that the diagnosis was real hit home, and that life and time were marching forward. The adventure Gerry had asked Sam if she wanted to go on, back in the *cantina* in Arizona years ago, was ending.

But oddly enough, the spate of crises of the past few years—the miscarriage, the diagnosis, the Fight and Oaxaca—all brought about a new adventure. The new adventure wasn't an action thriller dominated by exploration that had so characterized the couple's lives up until then, but rather was more of a people story distinguished by maturity. Those tough moments ushered in a time of choosing for both Sam and Gerry—choices that young people, such as they had been, often can't even see, for it takes life's trials to pull back that curtain.

The simple necklace Gerry had given Sam after the Fight, with its pink heart-shaped pendant, became the symbolic heart of their growth toward the future. The couple transitioned from frantically trying to make the youthful adventure work, to steadily building the base that allowed the roots of a mature relationship to take hold, one based not on excitement, but acceptance.

Their relationship was still an "independent, but together" affair. They still carved out "Our Time." But now, when they united, there was a deep private chuckle between them as they acknowledged all that they had weathered together. It would be a moment of "us against the world" when they'd raise their glasses in victory to the sunset, proud that after everything, they still stood hand in hand.

Their relationship was coming of age.

[SAMANTHA, 2024: Quoted Text From Letter

"I fell in love with your maturity and your ability to grow. It now had been a decade into our pilgrimage, and you were no longer the young CO but now the older guard, the mentor. We were getting into the car to go to dinner, and you glanced up to see the new training officer dealing with a recruit. You excused yourself from me to call him over, asking him what he was trying to achieve. When the sergeant explained he was merely showing the boy how to do something, you didn't say much, just nodded and went 'Hmmmm,' but as you turned to get back into the car, you said to him 'From where I'm standing, you weren't trying to show him as much as trying to show him up and that there was a difference. One is benevolent and constructive whereas the other is destructive and detrimental. You need to choose which path you want to be on.' You got into the car with one last comment – 'Oh son, best you choose wisely for it not only determines your path but of those around you.' The wisdom of the ages my dear."]

THOSE COMING-OF-AGE choices led Gerry to take a leap of faith with his promotion to major. At his promotion ceremony, as had been with his captain's ceremony, Sam was there. When she brushed smooth the edges of his lapels afterwards, she congratulated him, but also complimented him on being willing to move forward. Gerry jokingly had told her he didn't have much choice, since the youngsters were faster than him now.

Sam had only smiled with a philosophical air as she joked back that she was slowing down too. As Sam's medical condition worsened, she began to make changes. Her field seasons were now closer to home, in environments she knew and could navigate, and were with people she trusted.

She began staying in one place longer, as the coping mechanism of memorizing environments became part of her daily existence. Her time in the classroom and on bases took on a different flavor, not only from the challenges of Usher's, but also from that the young people now seemed just that—young.

It had been a shock when a student had called her ma'am and when Sam had asked why, he simply stated that he had been raised that way—you call old people ma'am or sir. Only in her thirties, Sam was unprepared for the rude transition from being the young free-wheeling professor and colleague, to that of the more steady role of mentor and advisor.

Georgia, 1989

Bored with nowhere to go, Sam was held captive. It was Friday afternoon and the only available flight she could get put her in way too early in the day. Arrival times determined where she waited, whiling away the few hours before Gerry joined her.

As a rule, Sam avoided staying on a military base whenever possible, preferring to wait at his home instead or simply to meet up at a local eatery. There were times such as today, however, where staying on base was inevitable. The couple had dinner reservations at an exclusive restaurant that was all the rage and its distance meant they would be leaving straight from the base. As Sam eyed the cocktail dress perched on a door frame, she checked her watch once again and saw she still had several hours or so before she would have to change.

That day, a stack of omnipresent paperwork commanded her

attention, and its monotony was building as the endless exams and report papers to grade not only proved tedious but were testing her patience. The ingenuity of students bluffing their way through an exam answer with the latest cock-and-bull story never failed to amaze her, causing her to carp with exasperation. *Do they really expect me to fall for this?* she thought as she carelessly tossed an exam on a pile.

And then there was the noise. The base seemed unusually active, with shouts and machinery noise everywhere, assaulting her senses from every direction. Sam excelled at the ability to isolate herself from her surroundings and normally would have been safely cloistered behind her abstract wall by now.

While many have achieved the ability to partition their mind and work in total chaos, Sam had refined hers to new heights. Her ability was such that while she was "in the zone," her crew mates laughed that you could land a 747 next to her and she would never budge.

Today, however, that ability was exasperatingly elusive. Every time, just as her focus and thoughts would coalesce into a point of single-mindedness, voices would penetrate, disrupting the construction of her fortress.

The clomp of boots on the ground, stepping in unison, followed by the sing-song of a marching cadence, would poke holes in her wall's foundation and then it would crumble.

Waiting, she began anew as the sounds of the marching faded and the raising of her mental ramparts resumed as she cleared her mind and concentrated. Once again, the sound of clomping boots accompanied by a sing-song cadence grew in the distance.

Argh…this was not working. Sticking her head out the door, Sam peered to the left. Yet another column being drilled in the distance, or maybe the same one that had been driving her to distraction all afternoon. Front and center, a building was being framed for construction, a new command post she'd heard.

Then, off in the distance were the on-base obstacle courses. Obstacle courses were, for Sam, a tantalizing draw. She had run many in her day, but they were law enforcement, search and rescue, various government training courses, never the Army. She had never been allowed to walk, let alone run a military tactical course.

There were many types of military obstacle courses depending on their level of difficulty and their purpose. Some went by colorful names such as Red, White, and Black, while others just by their objectives—Confidence, Conditioning, Leadership, etc. The design and flavor of these courses often reflected the sadistic nature of the training officer for the crankier he was, the meaner the course. Their construction also reflected the changing tides of war. Regardless of their type and purpose, the training grounds were not user-friendly.

Base life was not conducive to civilians lingering; many areas were restricted, and some were downright dangerous to wander in. On every base Sam had ever visited, she was issued the same stern admonition—the obstacle course grounds were off limits, no exceptions. Today the obstacles were silent. *What's the harm? I'm just out for a stroll,* Sam thought as she decided to check out the area, ostensibly to stretch her legs and to clear her head. The allure was like catnip and as she approached, the course was empty, yet she was hearing voices far off to the right. Climbing up the embankment, she overlooked a large group of soldiers in a wooded strip along the gully. And an obstacle course.

Off in the distance, several officers stood off to one side bordering the course, one she could make out was medical. The other two, probably the safety officer and the officer in charge, she figured as she shifted to get a better view.

Why the separate course? As she studied the obstacles, she could see this course was different. Far longer than an average course, this one was more complex, difficult and the distance between the obstacles was shorter than she would have expected. Not only that, many were also in a combination of two separate challenges to be negotiated as a single obstacle. Embankments, rocks and trees had been positioned everywhere, adding to the difficulty. There were also man-made barriers, such as walls, or derelict trucks, for the soldiers to contend with. *Ooooh, this course is menacing!* Sam chuckled deliciously to herself as she enjoyed her distraction.

Sitting down on the top of the bank, Sam broke out her snack and coffee thermos and cheerfully hunkered down to savor her unexpected diversion while watching the men, in competing teams, negotiate the course. Clad in the usual T-shirts and fatigues, the soldiers were on a muddy course dotted with wallows the hogs back home would covet.

Crawling under nets, up ramps, jumping down inclines and over walls. The more she watched, the more she was impressed.

The course was designed to train the negotiation of obstacles with weapons in hand, and focused on transition. To emphasize moving from one position to the other while firing, going from standing to kneeling to prone back to standing. With each subsequent obstacle, the ante was upped, all with the purpose of learning to handle weapons under duress.

The last obstacle put all of it together as one.

Composed of multiple elements, the final obstacle began with a flank vault over a low vertical wall with a four-point landing, and progressed into a forward shoulder roll. The soldier was expected to retrieve a pistol, placed on the ground in a marked square, as he came out of the roll, and once stabilized in a crouch, shoot a target down range. The soldier was also expected to hang on to his rifle during all this. *Who dreamed up this gem?* Sam wondered as she admired the abilities of the soldiers to execute this maneuver. *This takes talent.*

A flurry of commotion up on the bank caught the attention of Sergeant Jack Billings, the officer in charge of the course, and annoyed by the interruption, he snappishly halted the exercise. Likewise, Sam sensed motion behind her and heard the crunch of boots on the grass. She had been caught by a team of no-nonsense MPs.

Ominously having growled for her to stand up and present her ID, the two MPs now stood unamused as Sam frantically rummaged through her backpack looking for her surprisingly absent identification card.

A man who did not tolerate disruption well, Billings stood by impatiently as the minutes ticked by and his temper approached the critical maximum pressure before leading to a blown gasket. He paced in an oval circle, hands on his hips, glowering as he watched the woman empty her backpack looking for her identification while gesturing at the MPs. The more the sergeant fumed, the tighter the circle got and each revolution brought him closer and closer to that critical pressure point. His pacing tightened to just a few steps each way and he was a livid ballet dancer doing a pirouette.

Disgusted with how long the MPs were taking to apprehend the intruder, Billings stomped across the gully in a huff, only to recoil in shock when he realized he knew the woman.

Is that who I think it is? Billings wondered, as he got close enough to hear the woman tell the unimpressed MPs, unmoved by her explanation, to call Major Martinez. As soon as Billings heard Gerry's name, the light bulb went off and he signaled for the MPs to bring the lady down to him. After all the ruckus of verifying her identity and credentials settled down, a tickled Billings turned in astonished disbelief toward Sam, giving her his version of the Army hug.

"Ma'am, I can't believe it. My lord, I haven't seen you in ages. How long has it been?"

The two had met years earlier when Sam had participated in a seminar he was teaching at a local law enforcement training camp. They struck up a conversation, and a friendship. Billings had taught her much of what she knew about running courses and much to his chagrin, the student had risen to match the teacher.

Whenever possible, Sam would participate in one of his training camps and every time, she and Billings would run a challenge. Billings would beat her every time. Their last meeting, however, Sam had bested him, barely, but a win was a win. Billings blamed his bum knee as he had sullenly watched a triumphant Sam do a passable touchdown victory dance.

Sam always had liked Billings; he was a complicated man who was a contradiction. On the surface he was stern and no-nonsense, a man who stood ramrod straight with his hands always on his hips, you'd think they were glued in place. His eyes would scan every element and detail while dissecting a soldier's run for any weakness.

But behind that imposing demeanor, if you looked closely enough, you could catch the glimpse of a twinkle in the eye. The man had a devilish sense of humor. Having asked about the course, Sam was told it was called, tongue in cheek, the Loaded Potato. As in a loaded baked potato with everything on it or in this case, everything in it.

The Army ran on the clock, and the exercise must continue its inexorable timetable.

"I'd love to stay and watch. Do you mind?" Sam pleaded as Billings grew antsy to get back to business. Finding a perch behind the sideline, she settled in to watch the boys go through their paces, and Billings resumed the exercise doing what he did best, bellow.

As Sam found a roost, Billings looked over at her and raised his finger at her, a silent "behave yourself." It began with a groan of commiseration. A young soldier was tripped up on the trip wires, and Sam's groan was not only for the lad's embarrassment in dropping his rifle, but also, because she knew firsthand what it was like to be skewered by Billings's caustic wrath.

She could almost see the bolts of lightning from Billings's eyes harpoon the fella and Sam covered her eyes as she, louder than she intended to, murmured in pity, *Oh, sweetie.* The medical officer who was standing to her side had heard her groan, and chuckled while throwing a grin over at her. The disruption only caused Billings to shoot them both a peevish look.

The young soldier was not having a good day. His rifle was completely hung up. And so was he, and the more he struggled, the hotter Billings's lightning bolts became. And the more Sam cringed. When the soldier finally got himself untangled and moving again, Sam impulsively jumped out of her seat and yelled,

"Yes! Now ya got it!" Several soldiers stifled giggles as Sam flinched and gingerly sat back down when Billings turned to shoot Sam yet another withering look.

She would applaud good performances and groan when they would miss. Initially startled by Sam's presence, the squads began to enjoy her running commentary and every now and then, a soldier would call out, "How's that, ma'am?"

"Looking good, hon," was the hoped-for response, but if the effort wasn't up to par, a soldier would hear a groan followed by, "Oh sweetie, my grandmother could do better." After one less than admirable effort, Sam jokingly called out, "Am I going to have to get in there and show you boys how it's done?"

Turning to Billings, she teased, "You really need to light a fire under their backsides."

Billings, hands still on his hips, showed a rare smile while he feigned indignation and shot back, "Oh, really, Ma'am? Care to give it a go?"

Sam cheekily returned fire as she countered, "Oh sure, I could run that course so slick I'd have you crying for your mama!" The trash talking exchange continued between the two and the only things missing were bleachers and the hawking of a hot dog vendor.

As the last team cleared that final obstacle, the safety officer called the range and course cold, and seizing a rare opportunity, Sam shamelessly begged, "Do you think I could walk the course?" Billings couldn't see the harm. He always enjoyed shooting the breeze with Sam and their chats were a veritable potpourri that ran the gamut of topics; from the new non-lethal ammo to history to holiday recipes— you never knew where the conversation would end up. He was excited to show off his creation to her and diligently explained each obstacle, its purpose, goal and how to approach, drinking in her approval as she asked questions.

As Sam inspected each element, she began to point out how many obstacles were eerily reminiscent to indigenous training regimens she had studied or even endured herself in the field. After one particularly vivid description of a pre-battle ritual endured by a warrior tribe, the horrified squads begged for Sam to stop.

"Please don't give him any ideas!" they playfully pleaded.

"Well done, Billings, well done," Sam said, thanking everyone as they finished her tour. "This has been quite the treat. I've never been on one of these courses close up." Several of the soldiers looked quizzically at each other and then at her, asking,

"Well why not, ma'am?" The die had been cast and the squads now formed a growing chorus for her to run. As it began to sink in that they were serious; this was a bona fide challenge, Sam began to object with a litany of excuses,

"You have got to be kidding. I'm twice your age, on the cusp of middle age here, and out of shape. Get real guys, I haven't run a course in years. I'm rusty, my timing will be off." Having run out of excuses, she finished with, "And me judging distance? Oh please," as she pooh-poohed them with a dismissive hand gesture. She expected that to be the end of the whole affair.

Instead, a raspy, "Ah, should have known you'd be chicken and cop out," rumbled up from the sidelines. Billings knew exactly which buttons to push and despite all of Sam's protesting, the venerable master knew his old student was just itching to try.

A conference between Billings and the other officers rendered a verdict: Sam could run the course but was not to handle any arms or munitions of any sort—she would carry a decoy in lieu of a rifle. The medical officer then dictated his conditions: He insisted on gloves and a helmet, and since Sam was wearing sneakers, he also wanted Sam to wrap her ankles.

"If there had been elbow and knee pads, the man would have insisted on them, too," Sam muttered to herself. And then there was the question of what to do about that last obstacle.

"I've got just the ticket, sir," a soldier chimed in, looking at Billings. "How about a paintball gun? My son and I played last weekend, and I still have it in my trunk. Will that be okay?"

Sam negotiated for extra time with a growing sense of dread. *It is preposterous to think I can complete this,* she thought as the squads begrudgingly agreed to give her an extra two minutes, which was very generous.

With a stopwatch in hand, Billings shouted out, "Ready Ma'am? Now!" Handling the early obstacles easily, Sam cleared the trip wires and the "jump and land" without a hitch. She scampered across step-pingstones just as smoothly and even handled the rope ladder with aplomb. With a growing cockiness, Sam began to tell herself *I can do this* as she continued to negotiate the course.

Mentally reciting, *Just keep it slow and steady girl,* as her confidence grew with each new obstacle she cleared, Sam actually began to believe she may be able to complete the course with some semblance of dignity intact.

Anyone who had ever run an obstacle course had a nemesis. It was not necessarily the most physically demanding obstacle, just the one that gave you the conniption fits and stymied you at every attempt. The Irish Table mocked Sam. It was simple enough, just two uprights and a horizontal plank, but depending on the height of the uprights and the width of the horizontal plank used, that puppy taunted her. And it was coming up.

As she knee-bent to gain power for her jump, an injury from years earlier made itself known. Searing nerve pain shot through her hip and down her swing leg and she missed the horizontal plank altogether on the first try. Wrestling to hoist herself up onto the horizontal, Sam finally caught a foothold, pulled herself up and over to collapse onto her back. Waiting for the pain to subside, she groaned silently *Aw, geez…did that smart.*

"Are you okay?" wafted up from the worried spotter below.

"Just peachy," came her terse reply as Sam's voice squeaked an octave higher than normal. "Just having me a Hallmark moment here, hon."

Upcoming, were the net crawl followed by the zig-zag balance logs. It was at the net crawl that things truly began to crumble. The ground under the net was a boggy swamp, and while shimmying under the ropes, mud flowed everywhere, even down the inside of her pants. She was dressed in blue jeans with a belt and while preparing for the run, she had removed a utility case clipped to the belt but left the mounting clip on. That clip snagged on one of the ropes, trussing her up like a chicken. Squirming to disengage herself only forced more mud to find its way to places she had forgotten she had.

Then loomed the balance logs. Sam was often teased for her long torso and even longer legs—gazelle legs, many called them. Long legs were not advantageous on the balance logs. Unlike the short compact form of a gymnast, diver, or figure skater whose center of gravity was mercifully stable; long appendages and torso meant the center of gravity precariously wobbled unchecked. In bipedalism, being upright was all about the center of gravity and ignoring this basic principle inevitably led to a painful catastrophe. Those graceful gazelle legs of Sam proved to be her undoing.

The zig-zag balance logs were an upgraded version of what Sam was used to. There was no ramp up onto the logs and it was set higher, about four feet off the ground. While changing directions, the log zigged one way, but her body continued zagging the opposite—she lost her balance.

A decidedly ungraceful dismount from the balance logs resulted in an inglorious plop in the mud below, which was in turn met with a resounding if not mournful *"Oooooooh"* from the sidelines. If there had been a judge's table, she would have barely scored a two.

An embarrassed Sam rolled over and sat up in the mud. Not what she had in mind at all, but determinedly, she hauled herself back up onto the logs and continued onward. The squads were no longer just spotting her and several members had begun to pace alongside her, offering tips on the best way to approach each new obstacle.

It had now become a group event.

36

IS IT TIME FOR DINNER YET?

*G*erry was trying his darndest to get his paperwork done in record time. He had been looking forward to getting away for a quiet evening at dinner with just the two of them, he and Sam. Involving considerable wheeling and dealing just to get the reservation at the popular restaurant, the tables had been nearly impossible to get, with wait times generally two to three months out.

A young staff officer stood tentatively at Gerry's door. "Ah, sir, you may want to come and see this."

Closing a file and tossing it into the Out bin, an irritated Gerry looked up over his glasses and tersely questioned, "And what, pray tell, would I want to see?"

Hesitating, the young man answered, "Best you just come with me rather than me explain it, sir." As he got up, a put-out Gerry muttered under his breath a thinly veiled warning at the young officer that it had bloody better be worth it.

Bouncing along in the jeep, Gerry learned that there was an issue down at the new auxiliary obstacle course, an issue he could clearly hear for the cheers and calls grew louder as they drove up. *What the hell?* Gerry curtly grumbled to himself as he got out of the jeep and forced his way through the men gathered to the side.

At first, he didn't recognize the figure on the course, but then Sam turned to tackle the next obstacle and the surrounding soldiers had stepped aside enough for Gerry to catch a glimpse. Stunned disbelief consumed Gerry when he saw the cause of all the commotion. Initially speechless, his incredulity morphed into roiling blustering annoyance.

Why does she do this? What is so bloody hard about following protocol? Gerry quietly spewed under his breath as he stared incomprehensibly at the scene before him.

Sam stopped in her tracks as she eyed the last obstacle—the formidable low wall vault combination with its drop, roll and shoot. The stopwatch had long since been relegated to insignificance—she was so far behind that time was no longer a factor. As she grappled with how to approach, the squads on the sidelines began to cheer her on, shouting out encouragement while clapping.

It began well. Sam vaulted over the wall with ease and even did a commendable forward roll, but her effort unraveled on the back half of the exercise. She fumbled the retrieval of the paintball pistol, entirely.

The unexpected weight of the paintball gun had seemed off-balanced and awkward, causing Sam to clumsily bungle her snatch as she came out of her roll. Unable to check her forward momentum enough to eruditely grasp the pistol, it had flipped uncontrollably out of her hand, spinning while tumbling to the ground.

The misstep had forced her to fall back hard onto her rear as she reached backwards to recover the pistol. Using a rocking motion to propel herself back up into a crouch, a struggling Sam fought to regain her equilibrium as she fired the paintball gun. But now, totally off-kilter, she missed the target—completely.

"Aww, ma'am. What an effort!" barked one soldier. Another rushed in to help her up, telling her, "Oh that's nothing. First time I tried this, I dang near shot myself in the arse! Nicely handled, ma'am. Sir would be proud," the second soldier sympathetically remarked as he took her arm.

Somewhat deflated by her performance, a dejected Sam could only look up and dryly reply, "That remains to be seen, son." Mud oozed out and ran down her face in rivulets as she removed her helmet.

Sir was not proud, and his familiar but irate voice cut through the chatter as he spat incredulously, "What the *hell* are you doing?"

Sam glanced over and saw an apoplectic Gerry standing on the sidelines, his hands on his hips, body rigid and face an unbecoming color of maroon red. She was covered completely from head to toe with mud and muck, and even had some caked in her hair. In her zeal of the moment, she had forgotten why she had been waiting on base in the first place, dinner reservations. It now all came rushing back with crystal clarity at the sight of the towering figure whose fury was on full display.

"Oh, hi, honey, is it time for dinner yet?" was all she could think of saying.

At first, words failed Gerry and he said nothing. He just studied the scene through narrowed eyes, but then slowly turned to skewer Billings with a penetrating glare.

"What is a civilian doing on the obstacle course? It is against regulations." The tenor of his voice signaled, without discussion, that he viewed this debacle as clearly Billings's fault. Beneath the rage on Gerry's face, Billings could see he wasn't just upset over protocol being broken, and in a flash, the sergeant realized in disbelief, he had forgotten about Sam's medical condition.

It was the reason she had stopped coming to his seminars—she couldn't judge distance anymore. Sam's comment from earlier ran through his head, "*And me judging distance? Oh please.*" He stood, furiously kicking himself in the rear as he wondered how he could have missed that.

Billings snapped to attention and desperately rattled off all the safeguards that had been taken, not only in the frantic hope of fending off Gerry's ire, but also to persuade himself that he had not put Sam at risk.

"Sir, we took all the precautions. Ma'am wasn't allowed anywhere near a service pistol. She used a paintball gun, sir. All ammo and arms were in lockers, sir. Medical took measures as well and we spotted her on every obstacle. She was never in any danger, sir." Billings came to a halt as he caught a peculiar expression on Gerry's face. Gerry was no longer glaring at Billings, but rather was now looking out over the course at Sam.

As he had composed himself and took stock of the situation, Gerry noticed Sam did appear to be fine. In fact, she seemed to be more than fine as he watched the unit surround her while high-fiving and wiping the mud off her.

"Alright, but damn irregular Billings. Damn irregular," a distracted Gerry said vaguely as he continued to watch the unit joke with Sam. His tone was less strident when he turned back toward Billings and pointedly told him, "We do not allow civilians on an obstacle course—period."

Billings offered in his defense a line that would later give Gerry pause for thought, "But sir, she isn't a civilian. She's Ma'am."

Now on her feet, Sam turned and bowed to the squads. "Well fellas, I yield to a superior opponent," she said, acknowledging her defeat, and was answered with the sharp crack of a shouted "ten-hut" piercing the air.

"Well done, ma'am" floated out over the course as the mud-splattered squads snapped to attention in unison and gave the astonished woman a salute. It wasn't the most polished salute ever given, but it was one of the funniest. Many of the men were so covered in muck themselves that when they had saluted, they flung the sludge on their faces as well.

Sam apprehensively wandered over to the side where Gerry was standing, his hands still on his hips. The look on his face said it all and she knew she had wreaked havoc with his orderly evening itinerary. His Plan A was shot to hell, Plan B was circling the drain and Plan C, well she was fairly sure this wasn't in Plan C either. Gerry's time-honored creed of A + B equaling C had just been torpedoed. Sam leaned in and softly whispered to him,

"It's not as bad as it looks—it's not like I sat on a cactus." With a deliberate turn of his head, Gerry stared at her for a moment, their faces only a few inches apart and gentle knowing smiles broke out over their faces simultaneously at the shared memory.

As the couple walked away, Gerry had begun to pick off the remaining mud clods from Sam's clothing and hair, and he could be heard saying, "Hon, even after all these years, you still can't hit the broad side of a barn."

37

BUT SHE'S NOT A CIVILIAN, SHE'S MA'AM

As proud as Gerry was of Sam, her penchant for getting into things irked the hell out of him, and the car ride from the obstacle course to his home off-base grew increasingly tense. In a tone of voice dipping in anger, Gerry fired off a slew of rapid-fire rhetorical questions.

"What is it with you? How long have we been together, and you still do not understand this basic principle? Did you ever think about how it reflects on me? On the base? On top of it all, we had dinner reservations, one that took months to get—"

Sam, trying to get a word in edgewise, started to interrupt him, "I didn't think—" but she, likewise, was cut off mid-sentence as Gerry plowed ahead, nonstop with his tirade.

"No, you didn't. That's the point—you never do. You shoot from the hip." His sarcasm oozed throughout the car as he pulled into his driveway. "Oh of course, how silly of me—you don't ask for permission. You only ask for forgiveness." As he shifted the gear into park, Gerry leaned over the car seat to scorch Sam with a withering look as he evenly told her, "We are the Army...and the Army doesn't forgive."

The argument had spoiled the mood, and Sam bolted inside to take a quick shower and get ready. If she hurried, they could still make dinner.

"That woman could drive a man to drink," Gerry muttered in disgust as he poured himself a stiff double. But as he settled into the recliner in his study, he quietly began to reflect as Sam showered off the mud and muck. He thought back to what Billings had said earlier.

But sir, she isn't a civilian. She's Ma'am.

It was amazing how a single statement, simple in its complexity, could instantly and completely transform one's perception of things. The squads had fawned over Sam while complimenting her on her effort as they brushed off all the dirt and mud; they were so proud of her. Just as filthy and muddy as the rest of them, she, in her own way, had become one of them.

In his latest report, Billings had commented on how the unit wasn't unifying as well as he would like and there were still several lacking in the concept of solidarity. But now, even if it was just an obstacle course, they were functioning as a cohesive entity; collectively as one, they had her back.

Yes indeed. She is Ma'am, Gerry caught himself saying.

His racing thoughts were commemorative as he began to think back on other incidents over the years. There were so many, it seemed.

[GERALD, 2001: Quoted Text From Letter

"I want you to know how much you mean to the units Hon. Most of the other spouses just stop in briefly, a nonevent. Not you. You know they call you Ma'am. None of the others, just you. Want to know why? Maybe it was the time you took the guys up on the obstacle course challenge and then stood there dickering with them as to how much extra time you should be spotted. After all, you were middle age and it wasn't fair to be up against guys half that and in good condition you argued—got them to spot you an extra two minutes. Damn, you gave them a run for their money—they were impressed. Although Hon, even after all these years you still can't hit the broad side of a barn.

"Maybe it was the time in the mess hall where Masters was obsessing over being a new dad—didn't know how to change a diaper. You grabbed a loaf of bread off the rack, a knife off the table and turned that loaf into a 'baby.' Fashioned a diaper out of some napkins and gave him a diaper lesson complete with the warning that if he had a boy 'best to stand aside—you boys like to pee' you said. Warned Masters that he was a big target and his son wouldn't miss. Next thing I know there are four guys, all with bread loaves and napkins in a contest as to who could diaper their 'baby' the fastest. Only you Hon.

"Or maybe it was the time at a pub and several of my guys got into it with a couple of tadpoles from a neighboring base. You not only stood up and forced your way between them all, you dressed those youngsters downright proper for being rude and arrogant. You didn't just stand up to stop a fight, you stood up for my guys. Word traveled fast Hon—don't mess with the CO's lady. Only you. Or maybe it was the time I caught you out on the grounds showing the guys how to boogie down 1970's style. I don't remember what song was playing but I do remember 20 some guys having a great time without a care in the world.

"You have their backs. You always stand up for them in a world that increasingly despises them. I'm their CO but it's you they want to see. They wait for when you visit. As soon as I post your flight info they start gussying themselves up—can't be looking shabby for Ma'am. You are their mom, grandmother, wife, sister, girlfriend, girl next door and sometimes mama bear all rolled into one and they love you for it. It was not all fun and games. You had no problem scolding them when necessary. Oh, you don't yell, bellow—that's my depart-ment. You have the dreaded 'look.' You know the one I'm talking about—there isn't a hole big enough to crawl in when you flash it at someone."]

· · ·

OR MAYBE IT WAS WHEN…GERRY'S memory flitted around other moments and he zeroed in on one that still caused him to marvel.

GERRY'S MEMORY FROM A FEW YEARS EARLIER

Old Man Winter had unleashed a snow blizzard on the southeastern United States that many were still digging out from and the weather was still brisk enough for Sam to take a short cut down through a side passage to get out of the cutting wind. At his post, the MP glanced up just in time to catch Ma'am cutting down the alley. As he was about to turn his attention back to his clipboard, he saw another form follow her down the walkway and this one seemed even more out of place. The sneaky gait hinted at something not being right and the guard was now on the run across the compound.

Private Isaacs was steamed. A new recruit, in the few weeks he had been there, he had been harangued by just about everyone, including some lady everyone called Ma'am. Feeling insulted and disrespected, the angry Isaacs fumed, *Who does she think she is?* as he cornered Sam when she took the short cut between the buildings.

The two stared each other down as Sam, vaguely recognizing Isaacs from last week, icily inquired, "May I help you?"

Strutting up to her, Isaacs blocked all attempts by Sam to sidestep around him. "Where do you get off calling me a boy?" he spat with contempt as he stood over her. "You think I'm stupid?"

Sam routinely taught large freshmen classes—seventeen- and eighteen-year-olds full of energy and ideas, but at that age they had yet to be dealt many of life's stark lessons. Eager to make their mark on the world, young students often were impatient, belligerent, and quick to take offense.

Lecturing freshmen was not for the faint of heart. At times, it required intestinal fortitude and Sam often wondered if teaching freshmen prepared her for dealing with the Army, or if dealing with the Army prepared her for teaching freshmen. Either way, it was from this environment that the "look" was born.

As she confronted Isaacs, Sam recognized the posture; she knew this bluster all too well and had dealt with it many times over the years.

"No, I refer to you as a boy because that is how you behave," Sam lectured. "How old are you? Eighteen, nineteen?" Sam didn't bother to wait for Isaacs to answer as she, barely pausing for a breath, continued on with her diatribe. "You strut around thinking you have the world by its tail. You've heard the analogy of the world being a snake? Well, it is. And the problem is when you focus on the tail, it leaves the head to whip around and bite you in the…"

Ever the student, Sam had watched everything over her years on different bases, including how the various drill sergeants handled incoming recruits, and she had picked up a couple of pointers from them along the way. With each phrase, she would take a step forward, leaning into Isaacs as she kept talking.

"Being an adult, man, or woman, isn't about age, size, position or accomplishments. It's about how you handle yourself, how you respond to life. We all have been bitten by that snake." The gap between them had closed to a mere foot or so, and Isaacs had no choice but to back up with each step she took forward. Undeterred, Sam continued the lecture unabated.

"We've all had our keisters handed to us on a plate and we all have been knocked down. It's how you get back up that matters. Being a man is about your principles, your priorities, your morals. It's about your strength of character or lack thereof."

Now, within inches of his face, she gave him a question to ponder, "You are born a boy, but you must earn the privilege of being called a man. I know fifteen-year-old men and I know seventy-year-old boys. So, what's it going to be? Which are you?"

Isaacs didn't say much; he didn't even move for the frozen stony demeanor of Sam's face called forth emotions he wasn't accustomed to feeling. Nervousness, with a twinge of *Oh crap*.

The sound of running boots from around the corner signaled the MP had caught up with them just in time to see Sam harpoon Isaacs with a look that could turn Medusa's head to stone. When the MP had first arrived at the base, he had heard gossip about the woman called

Ma'am, and her "look." One glance at Isaacs's rigid stance caused him to wonder if what they said about Ma'am's infamous stare was true. Inquiring if everything was okay, the MP was startled to hear Sam answer,

"Why sure, hon, Private Isaacs and I are just laughing about the joys and pitfalls of growing up." Patting the MP on his shoulder as she turned to make her get away down the alley, Sam was surprised by a sudden ragged gasp as she exhaled—she had been holding her breath throughout the exchange. As Sam turned the corner out of the alley, she gratefully blessed the drill sergeants of the Army.

[GERALD, 2001: Quoted Text From Letter

"Someone once asked you if you had gone to a class to learn that look. You shot back you didn't have to—us men gave you so much practice."]

THE RUMOR MILL on the base was operating on overdrive and news of the altercation had spread throughout the barracks, if not the entire base by Monday's first light. Retribution was swift. Months later, Isaacs ran to catch Sam leaving for the night. He had been rehearsing, trying to use the most respectful words he knew.

"Pardon ma'am, but may I have a word please?" Under a surly and churlish glare from Gerry, Isaacs removed his patrol cap and squared off facing Sam as he delivered an apology that was straightforward and brief. "Ma'am. I do wish to apologize for my horrid behavior a few months back. I was out of line and woefully disrespectful. For what it's worth, I am terribly sorry. Just wanted you to know. Have a wonderful evening, ma'am."

The crack of a car door being opened for Sam punctuated Isaacs's apology and holding his gaze, she thanked him for his words as she slid into the front seat. The sharp snap of Gerry slamming the passenger car door caused Isaacs to jump and as the major slowly stalked his way around the front of the car to get into the driver's seat,

Isaacs fought not to wilt under his withering scowl. Almost as an afterthought, Sam leaned out the window and called out to Isaacs, telling him not to worry about it too much and saying,

"You're eighteen, and you men don't wear that age well." A final, "Pleasant evening to you too" hung in the air as the car departed. Disappointed, Isaacs had hoped his apology would be better received, but as he sullenly headed back to the barracks, Sam's words sifted through, taking a few moments for their meaning to sink in. She had said *you men*. Isaacs had to work to contain the urge to skip like a little girl at hopscotch.

GEORGIA, 1989

A chuckle escaped from Gerry at the memory of the look on Isaacs's face when he had apologized, a look that hinted that he had begun his trek from child to adulthood. The smile then broadened when Gerry thought of how far along that path Isaacs had traveled, when years later, Isaacs confessed to him, that he wasn't sure which had surprised him more at that moment; that Sam had forgiven him for his indiscretion, or that it was so important to him that she did.

Ironically, years later Sam also confessed to Gerry that Isaacs had grown to be one of her favorites. Gerry sat, shaking his head in amazement as he recalled, how every now and then, he would catch a glimpse through his office window of the two—Sam having taken Isaacs's cocked elbow, just leisurely strolling around the base, chatting casually about life in general and laughing about "the joys and pitfalls of growing up."

The smile on Gerry's face widened as the list of remembrances grew. *No, that woman just marches to her own drummer. Bless her heart.* Sitting there in the recliner, Gerry had an epiphany. What he had long considered one of Sam's greatest faults, one that had rankled him for years, was in fact one of her greatest strengths.

While Gerry sat in his study mulling over the afternoon's events, Sam was also reviewing those same events. Hurriedly showering to get cleaned up and dressed in time for their dinner, Sam was in the midst of thoroughly chastising herself. *Gerry is right. I do know better. We've been together for how long? I know the drill,* she disgustedly sneered at herself as she threw the shampoo bottle in the holder.

She had decided years ago after the Fight, that make-or-break watershed moment in their relationship, that she would have to accept Gerry's commitment to the Army, and along with it, its rules.

Getting out of the shower, Sam grabbed a towel and began rubbing her hair dry, mentally cussing herself out as she exasperatedly wondered, *Why do I keep poking the bear?* Having rehearsed her apology, she wandered out into the hallway and stopped in the doorway of Gerry's study; he was staring out the window, seemingly lost in thought as he nursed his bourbon. Sam knew her apology wasn't going to smooth the waters much, but she foraged ahead anyway.

Sucking in air and in a winded rush, Sam admitted, "You're right. This was entirely my fault, and I should have known better."

There was no response. Not even a twitch came from the direction of the chair and resolutely, Sam pushed forward hoping to calm tensions.

"No one was in any danger, including me—there were safety and medical officers present. Precautions were taken and everyone thought all was in order. Billings was only trying to please me out of deference to you. It won't happen again." With his elbow perched on the arm of the recliner, the glass of bourbon remained suspended in air, and Gerry remained mute, staring at a fixed point beyond the window on the horizon.

Dismayed by his attitude, Sam tried again, this time louder, "Hon, are you listening to me?"

Sharply swirling the recliner around toward Sam standing at the door and with overly dramatic manufactured shock, Gerry sputtered, "Umm, what? Did you say I was right?" The smile on his face that had begun a few minutes ago in reflection was now a full-blown grin, catching Sam totally by surprise. She hadn't seen this coming. While glad the tense moment had passed, she was baffled by the sudden about-face in Gerry's mood but didn't want to push her luck.

"Oh you...smartass!" she scoffed, snapping her towel at him as she scurried back to the bathroom while trying to figure out what had just happened.

Smiling as he shook his head, Gerry reached for the phone and dialed.

"I apologize for the short notice, but I'd like to cancel my reservation for dinner."

[Gerald, 2001: Quoted Text From Letter

"I teach them how to be soldiers, differences in weapons systems, how to navigate minefields. You teach them how to be men not boys, the difference between doing something because you have the right to do it and doing it because it is the right thing to do. You teach them that keeping a promise or their word is far more powerful than any assault strike I could teach. Don't ever underestimate or forget how much they appreciate you. The military is in constant motion—that's its very nature. Throughout all my transfers, commands, the different bases, it was always the same. Years after we all have moved on, former unit members will ask 'how's Ma'am'? They don't ask how I'm doing, they just want to know how you are. As I sit here writing this, as the guys walk up and down, they'll ask 'you writing to Ma'am? Tell her I said Hi.'

"I'm so very proud of you. I'm so honored that you have spent the last 20 years with me. I admire your brilliance Hon but I am blown away by your backbone and your strength, and this ability of yours to see beyond what is, to what can be—it is for me your most amazing superpower.

"Yes, I'm telling you all this in case I don't come back. I want you to know I remember all of this and I cherish every amazing moment."]

PART II

1991-1998

3 8

—————

USHER'S TIME

*G*erald, 2001: **Quoted Text From Letter**
"I'm also telling you all this for when I do come home. I want you to remember what things were like before you moved back to Ohio."]

CARGO TRANSPORT OVER THE ATLANTIC, AUGUST 2001

It had been seven hours since Gerry's flight lifted off on his last overseas deployment. Despite its spacious interior, the transport plane jammed with troops and cargo was claustrophobic and with three hours left in their long flight to Germany, restlessness besieged the younger men of the unit.

Books were finished, tapes and CDs had been played over and over, and jokes and stories were now an afterthought with no one left to tell them to. Confined to their seats and small aisle walkways, youthful energy had got them going stir-crazy and they started to goad Private Taylor for the last of the cookies his mom had baked. They were desperate for some activity, any activity and round two of comedy hour began as Taylor passed the tin around.

He had been writing for close to seven hours straight and Gerry had come to the hardest part of what was to be his last "Five Paragraph Order" home to Sam. Not one for internal reflection, this was proving far more difficult than he thought it would be and he was grasping at straws for an idea. Leaning back against the bulkhead, he tried to compose what to say next while subconsciously rubbing his hands trying to ease the cramps seizing his fingers. A voice hovered from above,

"Still writing Ma'am, sir? How's it going?" It was Taylor with the cookies again, flashing an impish smile. "Come on sir, you know you want another one!" Laughing, Gerry shook his head in mock horror,

"No, Ma'am will kill me!" The amused Taylor merely shrugged his shoulders as he turned to leave, only to have Gerry unexpectedly reach up and snatch one last cookie; his sweet tooth had gotten the better of him.

Munching on the cookie, an exhausted Gerry was frustrated as he struggled to find a clear path for this next part, and he absentmindedly began to lightly bang his head against the bulkhead, as if to jar an idea loose.

His mind was suddenly awash with the memory of Arnold, a Native American tribal elder, who in Montana, fourteen years earlier in 1987, had given him some valuable advice about being supportive. The image of the old man's craggy face staring out over the horizon filled Gerry's mind.

He had been watching Sam struggle with a centrifuge from across a plaza area of a tribal town, when Arnold had come up beside him. Both men had stood, staring in silence over the horizon as if they were waiting expectantly for something to appear and Gerry could hear Arnold's gentle words come back to him across the span of time.

But you and her—this is simple, as simple as you allow it to be...give her instead that which she lacks but requires...she does not need you to provide... what she needs is the trunk of a sequoia.

As the old man's voice whispered in his ears, Gerry whispered back.

"Arnold, you craggy old goat, Thank you." Gerry now clearly saw what he needed to say and how to say it, and it was as simple as he allowed it to be. It was time for him to be that trunk of a sequoia for Sam to lean on.

With one final shake and flex of the fingers, he polished off the last of the cookie and picked up the pad and pen again. He couldn't vanquish her demons, but he could help keep them at bay.

[GERALD, 2001: Quoted Text From Letter

"Hon, you are miserable there and I feel I'm losing the very essence of what I love most. Ohio is not a safe haven for you. You are languishing and it is draining the life out of you. I know the diagnosis has just shattered your world. I can only imagine how hard it's been to lose all that you've worked for, your identity. I can't even begin to fathom how scared you must be—I'm terrified."]

OHIO, 1991-1998

At the time of her diagnosis, knowledge of genetics in general was limited and her condition was barely understood. Sam had been expected to be incapacitated and institutionalized by the age of forty. Medicine and its doctors had been wrong. In just the decade that followed, scientific techniques improved, and the overall under-standing of genetics grew at an exponential rate, and with it, that of her degenerative condition.

Her prognosis had changed as well. It was still stark, but with a softer blow. It was still progressive, just slower. The sword's edge was still sharp, but the cuts were not as deep.

Every day, she was the best she was going to be, for tomorrow she would lose a bit more. "Functioning, but failing" became Sam's new daily motto. There still was no treatment, not even a band-aid on the horizon.

The career Sam had pursued and chased for so many years was over. By 1991, her vision and hearing had deteriorated to the extent she was no longer an asset in court. She was a liability in the lab as well. In both law and forensics, perception was everything, for all a legal team had to do was to merely suggest that mistakes were made due to her condition, and all would be for naught. The field, her sanctuary away from home for so long, wasn't as welcoming either and she was no longer comfortable there. It was time.

With her lab station packed up and files cleared out, Sam turned for one last look at what had been her life as she climbed into the U-Haul. She had said her goodbyes—Roger, of course, had been the hardest. Ohio was where Sam hailed from, born, and bred, and she slinked back there with her tail between her legs.

Although outwardly stoic, the pain and the burden of the disease had also tattered the edges of the family portrait a bit. Her family didn't know how to handle the uncertain future any more than Sam did. Sam told herself it was just a brief stopover and that she wouldn't be making this permanent, but down deep, she knew better. She simply didn't know how to start her life over again within the new ever-changing limitations.

Tentatively, Sam began to cobble together a facsimile of the life she once had. When Sam first began setting down roots in Ohio, she bought a cute, little blue vinyl over brick cape cod with a small back-yard and cherry tree along the front walkway. She procured a teaching position at a local college and began helping her mother, also a small business owner, out at her shop. Once again, the old saying of one door closing and another opening rang true. This time it was technology that threw her a lifeline—technology and Roger, her old field boss.

The digital technology age had begun, and email and computers were soon to be in every home. Times had changed for Roger as well. Budget constraints meant staff had to be cut but the workload was as heavy as ever. A cheaper alternative had been needed, and the answer was consultants. It was an option that appealed to Sam's independent streak, and when Roger had reached out floating the offer that she could work for him again through email, no longer on the front lines, but still could have her fingers in the pot, she took it. Sam found herself working from home long before COVID made it popular.

Life kept her busy, but not fulfilled.

For Sam and Gerry, the couple's relationship evolved once again. Gone were their impromptu adventurous jaunts and the long, glorious field seasons with commemorative vacations, and in their place were reunions on the weekends and scheduled leaves, with Gerry coming to Ohio. Sam no longer joined him wherever he was posted; he now had to come to her.

They had always been reading the same book, not necessarily on the same page sometimes, but always the same chapter. Now...ideas and priorities clashed, fueled by an existence fractured by two sets of alternating realities. Sam's and Gerry's increasingly separate lives were now defined by her retreating into the background, as she dealt with her loss and limitations, and him charging forward, becoming more immersed in an Army life. Gerry's new rank of major brought with it greater responsibilities, and a greater confidence in himself. While his social uneasiness remained, it would always be a factor, Gerry's life was fuller than ever within the Army.

When they did come together, they strained to adapt to Sam's ever-progressive disease. Her field of vision grew more narrow, cataracts clouded what remained and her hearing grew fainter with each passing month and year. Sometimes the loss would be so gradual it was hardly noticeable, but other days, she would awake to a deterioration of such magnitude, she could not do what she had been able to the day before.

No sooner would they adjust to the new conditions, than Usher syndrome would arbitrarily move the finish line once again, and they would have to start over again. To add more strife to the situation, there were times, as calm had finally settled over Sam's and Gerry's world, the Army would stir the pot with transfers and reassignments, causing the pot to boil again.

Respite came for Sam when she and Gerry came together for "Our Time," and she didn't have to fight as hard to get through the day. For those few days or weeks, Gerry would take up the slack, provide support and her life would be eerily reminiscent of "before."

With Gerry's presence, there would be a fleeting mirage of how things used to be, but then Gerry would pick up his duffel, walk out the door and go back to the Army, and Sam would suddenly find herself in an alternate reality as life abruptly flipped back to her "after diagnosis" existence.

In those competing realities, where Sam's world was ever-diminishing and Gerry's was ever-increasing, the common ground upon which the relationship had flourished, was now dwindling. Having provided the couple with a well of strength and understanding that had carried them through much, their common ground was being supplanted by a wall. A wall that was transparent where they could see each other, touch each other, but not seemingly understand each other. Their coveted "Our Time" was being replaced by "Usher's Time."

The old gang all helped. When Gerry and Stan were on assignment, whether that be stateside or overseas, the gang pitched in—on the sly, of course. They would "just happen to be in the area." Terry and Luke, the Army veterans from Oaxaca, would arrive in a camper, beer in hand, wearing straw hats and Bermuda shorts. Roger and his wife Marion would jokingly take wide detours on sudden trips east from Colorado to visit. Then there was Hurricane Kati, who swept in with a tidal surge that cleared away all the fears and anger in her wake. The word 'no' was not in her vocabulary. And Brady and Mark visited whenever they could.

Brady especially would make the effort with every furlough, stopping by even just for a day. Brady stopped by to surprise Sam. Gerry had warned him that going out for dinner wasn't comfortable for Sam anymore, so Brady came up with the excuse of making the famous beef stew that always had everyone raving.

Sam couldn't believe it when she opened the door to a brick filling the doorway and to Brady's gravelly voice.

"Oh, don't you give me that look. I know you're thrilled to see me! I was jealous. Gerry was telling me that you guys were making your beef stew this weekend!" Brady rolled his eyes melodramatically as he exclaimed, "And he gloated *soooooo* much that I had me a powerful hankering for some of it!"

As Sam held the door open for him to enter the foyer, Brady prattled enthusiastically on, "If you promise me you'll save me some, I'll help you with the prep," holding up a bottle of Sam's favorite brand of Cabernet as a bribe. Sam could only smirk, as she knew better.

"Ah, Brady, you abhor wine! You call it 'boxer's piss water,' I believe." Brady just grinned mischievously when he pulled his other hand out from behind his back, with a six-pack of beer. Sam explained that they would have to go shopping since she didn't have the fixings for the dinner and Brady erupted with an eager, "Well, let's get moving, they only gave me a four-day pass, and it takes you forever to trim meat."

Grabbing her coat and bag, Sam threw a pretended scowl over at Brady. "Oh, it does not."

Enjoying the back and forth, Brady yelled over his shoulder at Sam, "You are pathetic! I have never seen anyone be so picky about a little gristle or fat on meat!"

Their bickering continued as Sam laughingly shot back as they got into the car to go to the store. "Yeah, yeah, yeah…Brady, you poor thing!"

She hadn't seen the man come up behind her for Sam had been so focused on Brady and the vegetable bin. His presence startled her and she jumped backwards into him, knocking his shopping basket out of his hand and its contents spilling on the floor.

The man instantly turned and raged about how she was incompetent and was a stupid clod, yelling at her, "Are you blind?" Brady muscled his way between Sam and the man, and stuck his face in the man's with an Army lean that was spot on, a credit to Army sergeants everywhere.

"As a matter of fact, she is," he said, moving Sam out of the way while staying between the two. "There's no harm done here, so let's just be on our way shall we?"

The man sputtered as he stared at Sam in disgust, "It's blind? What the hell is it doing out? Put it in some retard house where it belongs."

Sam was used to the words—she had heard them before and often. Brady, however, had not and he went ballistic as instant hate filled his eyes.

"Did you just call her an 'It'?" Moving at a speed that belied his bulk, he shoved the man hard enough to send him to the floor on his rear, taking out the Valencia orange display and sending the avocados rolling, their uneven shapes causing them to ricochet as they bounced over the floor. Humiliated, Sam, with a hand on Brady's arm, tried to calm the situation.

"It's okay, let's just go," she pleaded as she scrambled to try to pick up all the oranges strewn about. Brady was still in a rage as he stood over the man.

"Don't you dare pick those up," he snapped at Sam as he snatched the few oranges she had out of her hands, and heaved them at the man still sitting on the floor. Taking Sam by the hand, Brady led her out of the store, pausing only long enough on their way out to yell at the cashier, "Yo, clean up on aisle 5 in produce," while tossing a thumb in the direction of the back of the store.

Sitting in the car, the sounds of Brady's ragged hyperventilation filled the interior as he struggled to settle his breathing. Sam was beside herself. She was ashamed over what had happened and was horrified that Brady had witnessed it. But as she sat watching Brady regain his composure, Sam was even more mortified to realize she was smiling, and she reached over and gave Brady a hug and a kiss on the cheek.

"Thank you for that, but promise me you'll never do that again." When Brady shook his head, muttering that he didn't do well with promises, Sam grabbed his collar, threatening, "Promise me, Brady, or I swear, I'll make you drink that wine you brought!"

Brady started to smirk at the thought and as Sam lost her battle to contain her giggles as well, the two sat in the car wiping tears of laughter at the image of the avocados bouncing along the floor in front of the astonished man. No longer hungry, Sam said, "Could we just go home? Let's order a pizza instead, okay?"

They never did get the ingredients for the beef stew that night.

Gerry had known Brady planned on taking Sam shopping. He had been so keen for the stew dinner all week that he was practically salivating on the flight into Ohio. As he laid his head back on the head-rest, he could smell the hearty aroma.

When he arrived at Sam's home that night, he thought he would get a jump on the meal prep as Sam washed up for the evening. But there were, however, no ingredients and when confronted, Sam just shrugged nonchalantly, saying she and Brady hadn't had the chance to get to it. They could go shopping tomorrow, she had said with a weak smile.

As Sam went up to take a shower, Gerry knew "just not getting to it" was only part of the story. He called Brady. She was drying her hair, coming down the staircase in her bathrobe and slippers, when she stopped short midway, the towel hanging in midair. Gerry was sitting in the recliner, a beer in hand, waiting and Sam knew even before he spoke.

"Why didn't you tell me?" His voice was harsh with disappointment. Sam didn't want to talk about it, not just because the humiliation of that day was still fresh with its sting raw, but also to hide it from him. Gerry had always joked that Sam was his "Mama Bear," and she had been protecting him from society for over a decade, careful to shield him from its widespread bluntness and frequent ruthlessness. It was instinct.

Trying to placate and deflect, Sam defensively muttered a flippant, "It was nothing, the man was having a bad day and took it out on me." Sitting on the coffee table next to the recliner, Sam tapped Gerry on his knee to get him to look at her. "We can pick up the stuff tomorrow morning, first thing. It'll give us a reason to go have breakfast at that diner you like so much," she said, her small smile hopeful.

Gerry only stared at her for a moment, not swayed, before he commented with a sarcastic edge, "For someone who doesn't have much use for excuses, you sure have a lot of them these days." His voice was heavy with the realization of how precarious things had gotten for Sam. He had been shocked it had happened while Brady was with her.

Sam worked diligently to keep her growing dependency on Gerry hidden, keeping it cloaked in routines and coping mechanisms. Gerry, regrettably, hadn't recognized how much Sam was concealing from him. Misinterpreting how well she seemed to function when he was there, he did not fully comprehend the extent to which things fell apart when he left. At times, he would even allow himself to forget there was anything amiss, but then Gerry excelled at not seeing as much as Sam did at hiding.

Gerry's coping mechanism was avoidance. He noticed the subtle changes, the loss of function when he would return, but he pretended. He pretended he didn't see them and that all was well. It was a welcomed pretense for it was a cocoon that both he and Sam gravitated to in hopes of hanging on to what had been.

He pretended the deterioration wasn't real, and that she was just having a bad day, but when it would become obvious she wasn't, then he pretended they didn't matter for they were little things. But those little things added up. He pretended the losses weren't a problem since Sam adapted; she always did. He pretended that there wouldn't be a day of reckoning on the horizon.

For Sam, these years haunted her not only for her own physical challenges, but for what she saw they were doing to Gerry. It had become distressingly obvious to her, as she was no longer able to do many activities, just how limited his life was when he was with her. He would turn down invitations, not going to events he normally enjoyed because he didn't want to leave her alone.

She would remind him he left her alone all the time. After the incident at the grocery store with Brady, Gerry became obsessed with protecting Sam, and on the rare occasions when they did go out, he would be velcroed to her hip. The constant vigilance was exhausting for Gerry and suffocating for Sam.

Their social circle shrunk and they became more reclusive as the "what we can't do" overshadowed the "what we can do." Activities centered around what they could do in the safety of Sam's home. Saddened to see Gerry so constrained and diminished by her restrictions, Sam had found herself one week actually hoping he wouldn't come for the weekend. She hadn't wanted to see the ache on his face.

Solitude and reclusiveness became the focus of Sam's social circle.

She spoke on the phone constantly, or via email, but didn't physically interact much anymore. Her western colleagues in Arizona and Colorado were a thousand miles away, and while she loved to hear about their exploits, to hear about what she could only experience vicariously, hurt. Sam no longer participated in the present, but rather was fixated on controlling a future that she didn't look forward to.

Physically in Ohio, she mentally existed in the netherworld of the past. Sam's soul remained entrenched in Arizona and Colorado, and in her old life. She was not accepting a new life in Ohio, and Gerry began to worry—a lot.

ANOTHER FINE MESS YOU'VE GOTTEN US INTO

Sam eventually made good on another decision she had made when she had moved to Ohio—to get a dog, and a German shepherd, husky, golden retriever mix puppy soon found its way to her. An animal abuse case, she took it in, hoping it would help ease the passage of time and fill those empty spaces. She named him Gabe.

Privately, Gerry was worried about Sam in a way he never had been in the past. Now, void of the circle of friends and colleagues she had so relied on, she was in his eyes more alone than she had ever been, and he worried for her and her safety. The dog was an excellent choice he felt as it would provide both some social interaction and a measure of protection.

New routines with unfamiliar problems soon dominated the couple's conversations and Gabe the dog soon became the center focus. Gerry was pleased to hear about the puppy and their conversations abounded with tales and laughter of training mishaps and housebreaking woes.

Prior to that year's duty rotation, the couple had an uncomfortable discussion where once again, Gerry had stepped in it, when over dinner, he took the opportunity to work into the conversation his opinion of Sam's move to Ohio. The meal the couple traditionally made every year before he rotated out had cast a contented glow about the kitchen. The comforting routine and smells soon had the pair laughing in anticipation and as Gerry added some dry red wine to the stock, Sam had playfully tilted his elbow, adding another healthy splash to the mix.

"Never can have too much," she joked as she scraped the vegetables off the chopping block into the stock pot and replaced the lid.

Gerry had argued vigorously and loudly against Sam's move to Ohio for he viewed it a huge step backwards with few positives. Once again, he pushed for them to get married, and for her to move in with him. From her perspective, Sam couldn't believe they were rehashing the same worn-out conversation yet again.

Recorking the wine bottle, she dismissively flung at a dismayed Gerry, "Why bother?" as she pointed out that she needed help to navigate a future that at best was going to be difficult and he was never there. Struggling to make him understand, Sam searched her mind as she sought for new and different words to describe the same old tired argument. "We're already married, just not on paper, and being legally married won't change anything. You still won't be here. So again, why bother? How does being married help anything?"

Gerry had been sitting on the bar stool across the counter and when Sam looked over at him, he was holding his head in his hand, his eyes closed. Frustrated at the wall that was malignantly growing between them, he knew he had blundered from the sarcastic bite that had entered Sam's already bitter tone.

"Oh, let me guess, you want me to follow you everywhere. You want me to join you on some godforsaken base somewhere? Have to relearn everything all over again every time they yank you to some-place new? At least here, my home environment is constant. I have stability here and I have family here. I know you don't get that, but it is important to me, because babe, it's all I have left."

Gerry had tried to tender a counterargument that when he wasn't deployed, he would be home during the week and could help, but Sam wasn't having it, and she cut him off with a derisive snort.

"When you're home? Oh please! Even when you're stateside,

they've got you willy-nilly somewhere." Her sharp retort was made all the worse when Sam sadly let him in on a secret she had never told him; he was gone so much, whether stateside or overseas, that at times, he wasn't real to her anymore and perhaps he didn't exist. Sam's cynical view of his presence in her daily life was cutting but telling for Gerry, and her blunt and brutal honesty hurt deeply. The fact that it was true made it all the more painful.

The argument had been a rehash, and as Sam stood in the entry into the living room, she studied Gerry pretending to read the newspaper. She could tell from the cadence of the turning pages, he wasn't seeing anything.

Kneeling before him, Sam reached up and lowered the newspaper as she asked, "Permission to speak freely, sir?" She looked up at him, trying to catch his eyes. It was a phrase rarely used and for the couple, its significance was huge. For them it meant, I have something to say and as painful as it is to hear, you need to listen. Permission to Speak Freely meant listen with the heart, not the brain. Sam gently rubbed Gerry's knee as she sought words to begin.

"It doesn't have to be today, or even tomorrow. We have time, but it does have to be on the horizon. There has to be a game plan, Gerry. You can't just say 'Oh, we're good today,' and sweep it under the rug for later. This has to be confronted and dealt with. Gerry, you always have a plan. Why can't you have a plan for this…for us?

"You're so competent in the Army, so capable. There must be something in the Army you can do that you would enjoy, that would fulfill you—a transfer that doesn't have you traipsing to hell and back. I know…you'll die behind a desk, you're not a paper pusher.

"I'm not asking you to give up the Army, I'm not asking you to give up training. I'm asking you to stop running. I used to think you were running toward something, always wanting something more. And you may be, Gerry, but you're running *from* something, too, trying to escape something…and I can't follow you anymore." Gerry bit his lip as Sam's words hit home and kept his head tilted down, eyes closed as Sam talked.

"You are the strongest, most intelligent, capable and accomplished man I have ever known." Sam reached up to take Gerry's face in her hand to make him look at her. "And you act as if this is beyond you. Right now, we're spinning our wheels in opposite directions.

"I know what I'm asking and I know you don't know any other way. But I'm going blind and deaf in a world that barely tolerates dealing with those who have only one of those issues. If you are blind, you use hearing to compensate, if deaf, you use sight. I have neither and the world doesn't know how to—and to be blunt—it doesn't want to deal with me.

"I don't have to stay in Ohio, but I do have to stay in one place. I need stability. I need to find some place where I can build the support system I'll need to function. Are you avoiding making a change, transferring, because you think it'll be too hard for me to handle? That you're doing me a favor? At least if we stay put, if you pick one spot...I can accommodate. I can learn what I need to. I can help you with the social stuff, or do you think I can't do that anymore, either? I can still help, but as long as you keep jumping around, I can't do much."

Gerry had been sitting quietly, folding and refolding the newspaper, playing with the creases as Sam talked. When Sam got up to leave, Gerry looked up and nodded, and she made one final plea.

"I know this isn't what you signed up for, but I'm asking you, Gerry, to give us a fighting chance. Right now, we don't have much of one."

Gerry hadn't liked the way that conversation ended as he left for overseas, and while there didn't seem to be any residual bitterness between the couple and their weekly calls had been funny and easy, he wanted nothing more than to erase that moment. Thus, Gerry was in a hurry to return home to Sam.

Normally there was a lag when he rotated back to the States, a period of time after he returned stateside before he'd formally taken his leave and made his way to Sam's home. This time, however, the troubled waters left an uneasiness that kept nibbling away at the corners of his security blanket, and he arranged to return straightaway. Having scored a spot on an earlier flight, Gerry was eager to surprise Sam and meet the new pooch he had heard so much about. He had even bought a stuffed squeaky toy for the little monster.

Marriage, Sam's disability, and Gabe the dog were not the only concerns weighing on Gerry's mind as he flew into Ohio that night. There had been an odd vibe to the phone calls with Sam over the past weeks, where in between the jokes of Gabe the dog, Gerry found himself fielding a lot of questions surrounding a new staff aide, a woman.

To Sam, Gerry had sounded so happy in those phone calls as he would tell her what he had done that week, a joy that Sam didn't feel in him when he was home with her. While she had been telling herself for years that he wouldn't be fulfilled in a world defined by her limitations rather than by his possibilities, she was now beginning to believe it. She had misinterpreted the joy she heard in his voice that was simply from being able to share his week with her, even if it was just on the phone.

Those phone calls home had cracked open the vault door of the cavern that contained the devil that had once danced on Sam's shoulder over a decade ago, the devil that had prompted Sam to push Gerry away and leave him. That devil had awakened, and now loose to perch on her shoulder once again, it had begun its dance. Sam found herself painfully thinking that just maybe, Gerry would find someone while on rotation.

Women of the Army had become more commonplace in the field, and Sam actually began to hope for his sake, he would find someone else who could share that part of his life with him.

On his end, Gerry had not sensed the devil had crawled out of its cave and he misinterpreted Sam's interest in the female soldier. Erroneously, he thought Sam believed he was having an affair, and it was a belief he wanted to nip in the bud. More than anything, Gerry thought as the plane landed and he grabbed his gear, he was desperate for he and Sam to have their sunset. A sunset where all the misgivings, insecurities and misunderstandings that seemed to be piling up, could be banished.

The house was dark, no lights were on. *It's two a.m., of course she'd be asleep. She's not expecting me,* Gerry realized as he made his way up the walk around the cherry tree to the front door. As quiet as Gerry thought he was as he put his key in the door lock, he was no match for the sense of hearing of a dog. The rattle at the front door alerted Gabe and he took his newfound job seriously; the house was to be patrolled and defended. The rattling continued and Gabe got up from his dog bed and padded over to the foyer, standing at attention by the door, ears erect and hackles up, in full intruder alert mode.

The door squeaked ever so much as it swung on its hinges. Laying the duffel bag down on the tile floor, Gerry tiptoed into the foyer and pushed the door closed as quietly as possible. There was no warning or preamble. A flurry of white teeth accompanying loud growling was followed by a male human voice roaring out of the dark, "Shit—the dog!" Snarling and snapping, Gabe forced the intruder into a full retreat, backing him across the family room in a maelstrom.

Awakening to the sounds of all hell breaking loose but still half asleep, Sam stumbled down the stairs to be greeted with the sight of Gerry perched on the top of the couch, using his jacket as a shield. Gabe the dog had him cornered. While grabbing the dog's collar, the chaos of the moment finally dwindled to the sound of Gerry's thundering bellow, "That is NO puppy," rattling in Sam's ears.

The following morning established Sam's control over the situation with Gabe as his chocolate-brown eyes followed her everywhere, and he obeyed her every wish. But Gabe regarded this new human as an interloper; he had found a new home with a purpose, and he was not going to share. Gerry was of similar mind. He had been expecting a cute little roly-poly puppy, but he had been gone for months, and that fat little puppy had grown into what was before him now, a nearly full-grown adversary. Gerry regarded Gabe with the same animosity as the dog did him. The battle of the males had commenced.

In Sam's presence, all was well. The dog would lie at their feet, allow Gerry to take his lead while on walks, even brush him. But it was all a ruse, and it was when his mistress wasn't home that Gabe's true intent surfaced. Sitting in the living room recliner, Gerry was perusing the evening newspaper when Gabe walked up, lifted his leg, and sent a stream of hot yellow urine down Gerry's pants and onto his shoes.

In the ensuing days, wherever Gerry went, sat, or slept, whatever he touched in the house, the dog felt the need to reclaim. The bed, chairs, shoes, clothing, coats, uniforms, and the duffel bag, especially the duffel bag, which endured numerous dousings and was beginning to suffer from the barrage. The harder Gerry tried to make amends, the more Gabe marked his territory. They were caught in a vicious feedback loop.

The showdown had come to a head. It was movie night and Sam had disappeared into the kitchen to grab some popcorn and beer. True to form, Gabe pushed himself up off the floor and snuck up behind the unsuspecting man in his recliner. Biding his time for the perfect opening where Gerry was absorbed in reading the newspaper, the dog waited and he found it. Seizing the moment, Gabe the dog whipped around to the front of the chair with the urine flowing before the leg was even fully up. And with a full bladder no less. As the warm sensation crept over his skin, Gerry exploded and in a fit of rage, he did what Gabe the dog was never expecting.

Oblivious of the bedlam that had erupted out in the living room, Sam shouted out as she came back around the corner, "Babe, I found an Oktoberfest tucked in the back of the fridge. Would you like tha—" She stopped, dumbfounded at the sight before her. Gerry, an intelligent, capable grown man, had unzipped his pants and was urinating all over her dog. Not quite sure how to respond, the stunned woman merely turned on her heel and retreated back into the kitchen.

By the time she had collected her wits, the two urinary combatants had each retired to their corners, glaring at each other with narrowed eyes and set jaws. They were a couple of mismatched pugilists locked in an uneven battle of an interspecies war.

Having had enough of the two, the object of their affection shot blazing daggers at a disbelieving man, who couldn't see what she was so upset about, and an anxious dog as she stomped around the family room. Her ire had both males on the run. Attempting to defend his actions at first, Gerry whined a pathetic, "He started it," at Sam, but instantly reconsidered when she speared him with "the look" while she spat out at him, "I'm not spending the night with you reeking of dog piss. Get up there and take a shower."

Tempted to make a stand and plead his case, Gerry wisely reconsidered when Sam shot a second searing look his way, sending him in a hasty retreat to the bathroom. Likewise, Gabe the dog cowered behind furniture, desperate to find any place out of his mistress's line of fire.

Just as the water in the shower had gotten warm, the shower door was abruptly flung open, and Gerry looked down to see a brown shape hanging on to the door frame for dear life. The claws of all four paws were locked precariously on a raised edge of the shower door frame, Gabe did not want to join the fun, but with one final kick, the pooch was unceremoniously tossed into the shower stall.

A bottle of dog shampoo flew through the air as Sam snapped at Gerry, "You made this mess, you clean it up," and then slammed the shower door shut with such force, its shaking hummed with the cadence of the water spray. The two males, one human and the other canine, had been left to duke it out. Gerry looked down at the bedraggled-looking dog, now clearly out of his element. His tail tucked, the mutt was huddled in the corner of the shower stall, peering out from underneath squinty eyes, trying to stay out of the water spray. Hyperbole and irony were not lost on the man as a line from Laurel and Hardy skits flitted across his mind. *Well, this is another fine mess you have gotten us into.*

Whether it was Gerry's act of retaliation or a dubious moment of male bonding during their mutual water punishment, Gabe the dog stopped marking Gerry the human. The short routine weekly absences did not tax the relationship between the two, but the extended deployments overseas were another matter. Whenever his competitor would return, Gabe would test the waters. There would be the tense long five- to ten-second stare down, each daring the other to blink, but it was always the dog who folded, lying down on his dog bed with a huge huff. The Great Ohio Pee-Off had ended. Neither male, regardless of species, was willing to risk being put in their respective doghouses again by the lady of the house.

While never bosom pals, the two had made their own way with each other and Gerry went on record saying he was grateful for Gabe; he never worried about Sam's safety again. As for Gabe, his marking prowess proved to have an unseen benefit. He simply didn't tolerate any male in the house, and while having some remodeling done, the work crews would drop their tools and tool belts where they stood at the end of the shift.

Every night, Sam would come home and have to pick everything up before letting the dog out. One night, she was simply too tired and confronted with all the stuff lying about, she told Gabe to go for it. Happy to oblige and as Sam admired his ability to measure out each precious drop of golden liquid, he lifted a leg on each and every tool.

The work crews never left their tools on the floor again.

In the coming years, Gabe the dog not only provided solace for the couple as they struggled, but also adopted a deeper role as his light-hearted antics gave the couple something to laugh about, something they could share. By becoming the caulk that filled the cracks in their crumbling "common ground," he restored it to a solid surface upon which Sam and Gerry could stand together.

[GERALD, 2001: Quoted Text From Letter

"But I know this—we will get through this. Yes Hon, it's we. You have stood by me for the last two decades. It's my turn now. It's my turn to take charge of things for the next 20 years. Don't deny me that privilege. Don't deny me that honor. You never gave up on me, never once doubted. Are you giving up on yourself? Not on my watch lady. Don't you dare doubt your abilities, your strength. Don't you dare lose that fire, don't you dare push me away. How many times have you told me when I'm wallowing in self-pity—'you don't like it, tough shit, suck it up and get over it.' Well Hon, forgive my crassness here but it's time for you to suck it up. You are the one who has taught me that retreat is rarely the best option.

"You of all people know how to fight and win in the face of insurmountable odds. Yeah, the odds aren't good right now—they downright suck. What was it you said when that crime boss lawyer tried to take you down, tried to destroy your career and credibility? You looked that lawyer straight in the eye, leaned over his desk—'by all means' you said. 'let the games begin.' You didn't back down then. Don't back down now—let the games begin. I will be with you the entire way. Nothing that is to come will ever change how I feel about you, how much I love you and how much I want to be there for you."]

4 0

EVERY MAN CHOOSES HIS HILL
TO DIE ON

*O*HIO, *1999*

After the excitement of Gabe the dog, the years rolled by as life settled into a predictable routine for the pair where demons of Sam's future and Gerry's past ruled the roost. Loss of independence and her reluctance to accept her new life were the main specters of Sam's Luciferian pantheon, with her loss of purpose serving as its supreme king.

For Gerry, vampires from long ago roamed at will the castle he had so diligently built from Boston's red bricks, and they satiated their lust for blood by feasting on those still lingering childhood insecurities of worthiness, belonging, and trust.

In 1999, Gerry, now a lieutenant colonel, was understandably startled when the staff officer told him his mother-in-law was on the phone. He didn't know he had one. Knowing Sam's mother would only be calling in an emergency, he picked up the phone and asked with some trepidation, "Is everything okay?"

Reassuring him that all was well, Sam's mother Betty said she was calling for another reason. "Will you be coming into Ohio this weekend to Sam's house? Can we meet for coffee over the weekend?

At the coffee shop at the corner by Sam's house perhaps? Just the two of us?"

As he sat across from the older woman, normally an effervescent warm individual who instantly put everyone at ease, a nervous Gerry could sense this was not to be a pleasant conversation, and he would be proven right. Easing gently into things, Betty said she needed to have an honest discussion with him regarding Sam.

As Betty began telling him that she thought the world of him and that he was a wonderful man and all, Gerry could feel the weight of a huge "but" coming his way. Betty's words were well chosen and delivered kindly but still stung and rattled his cage.

"You are never here for her. I'm not criticizing you or the Army, but this isn't working anymore. How many years has it been since the diagnosis? And nothing has changed, and face it, nothing is going to." Gerry tried to hide his discomfort from the blunt words by chasing crumbs from his scone around on the plate in front of him, and Betty, knowing her words couldn't be easy to hear, simply put her hand on his arm as she continued.

"Don't misunderstand me. I'm immensely proud of my child, but as strong as she is, she can't weather this storm alone."

Although afraid to hear her answer, Gerry looked at the solemn expression on the woman's face and tentatively asked what he needed to do. Betty was candid and to the point.

"My daughter needs something more stable, and more importantly, something more tangible. You need to be here—not on the other side of the country or the world. She needs more than a weekly phone call or a letter in the mail. She needs you to physically be here, not some promise on the horizon."

Trying to soften her next sentence, Betty took Gerry's hands in hers as she looked into his face, imploring, "You need to make some decisions. You need to decide whether to transfer to a new position, a permanent one here in the states, or leave the military for the private sector. If you can't do this, then you need to let her go."

For the second time in a short timeframe, Gerry heard the same words. *Had Sam been right?* Was he so intrinsically linked to the Army that he couldn't leave? Was he afraid he couldn't stand on his own two feet without it? He enjoyed Army life. He enjoyed being assigned for training maneuvers and being a part of forward units. Could he give it all up for her?

After her meeting with Gerry, Betty tactfully began to work on Sam as well, trying to push things to a conclusion. Betty was an old-school traditionalist and did not understand this long-distance romance between the couple, certainly not one that had gone on for this long. The concerned mother also didn't believe Gerry had it in him to change, and she wanted her daughter to face up to that and move on.

Orchestrating a series of heart-to-heart meetings held at that same local coffee shop, she worked to prod her daughter to move forward toward a different life. A life without Gerry.

For Sam, the tipping point had arrived. Her condition had progressed to that moment that had always been on the horizon but no longer, and she needed to make decisions about her future—painful ones.

The weeks flew by as mother and daughter met and talked about the realities of Sam's future in the neutral territory of the coffee shop.

While hard to swallow, many of Betty's points were valid, and her mother's opinions began to take hold. Sam had argued, "You're asking me to just throw away eighteen years of love and commitment." Concerned that as long as the man was in the picture, Betty, who wanted Sam to be open to alternatives, had counterargued,

"He may be the light of your life, daughter girl, but he's no longer your pillar of strength. Surely, you can see that." Reluctantly, Sam had to agree.

She conceded that even decades removed from the streets, he was still in its grips.

Aside from his social issues, those childhood streets of decades past also held yet another stranglehold on Gerry. Despite all of the man's accomplishments, Gerry was still fighting the ghost of a little five-year-old street boy back in Boston, the bad boy from the wrong side of the tracks.

Convinced he would be judged by the past that hung over him, Gerry was driven to erase it; it was always as if one more rank, one more ribbon or medal or commendation would even the odds for him and he would be accepted. He had never questioned his value as a soldier, but he was still fighting to find his value to society as a person.

As Sam reviewed Gerry's own list of difficult challenges that he had to confront daily, a heavy weight settled in her stomach as she began to accept a reality she didn't want—the status quo between them would never change. Gerry would never stop running and she couldn't chase him anymore.

One morning, weeks after those café shop détentes with her mother, she was woken by the incessant ringing of the phone. A groggy Sam answered to the loud, excited yell of her mom exclaiming, "You won a free trip to Paris!" Through her small business shop, Betty had won this event, and the prize was an all-expenses-paid, ten-day trip to Paris. Sam's mom's tone was adamant as she declared that she not only wanted Sam to go, she was insisting that she go—and that Gerry should join her. Betty wanted her daughter to get out again and shake out the doldrums. She was hoping for the trip to Paris to be a time of reckoning between the two.

As Sam made all the travel preparations, any excitement that the trip to Paris may have held for her was dashed. She was imprisoned, in a sense of sorrow and heartache, by the weight of the decision to finally end the relationship that had defined her entire adulthood. Feigned enthusiasm became her shield as she hid her true intentions from Gerry while pitching the unexpected trip. Coinciding with spring break in teaching, the timing was perfect; even Gerry was available, for he was in Germany that rotation. It was as if the trip was ordained from above, and it hammered the final nail in the coffin.

On the flight over, Sam thought of nothing but of what her mother had said, and her heart and head were at odds, but reality was winning. She had called Roger, her forensic colleague and old field boss, before leaving to let him know she would be gone for a bit, and they had gotten into a philosophical discussion regarding Gerry, marriage, and Sam's future—without Gerry.

Roger couldn't believe what he was hearing and had bluntly asked why she wouldn't marry Gerry. "Marriage isn't the answer, old man—changing is." Sam had candidly told him, "We need to change how we're handling things, but Gerry just can't seem to see that. He can't seem to settle down."

Mystified, Roger had demanded that Sam explain. "Girl, you are going to have to explain this new way of thinking you young people have these days. You need him home. Are you telling me that if you asked him, Gerry won't leave the Army?"

There was no misinterpretation when he had defiantly answered his own question. "Bullshit, I don't believe that." Bone-weary, Sam sighed deeply as she defended her position to the one person she thought would understand.

"Of course Gerry would, but that's the problem. If I asked him to, he would leave the Army in a heartbeat, but it wouldn't be his choice. He would do it because of that damn sense of duty of his...and his commitment to me. There would be resentment as he would fester, it eating away at him. C'mon old man, you know Gerry as well as I do. I can't force him to be somewhere and somebody he doesn't want to be...or to fit into a world that doesn't understand him anymore than he understands it. And it is a very unsympathetic world, Roger. Trust me, I know."

Roger could feel the burden of Sam's sadness ebb over the phone as the two old friends exchanged their opposing views, each digging at the other. Sam held her ground.

"I don't need him to leave the Army, in fact I don't want him to, he needs it," she had said, her voice crackling. "I want him to put in for a transfer to a different position, one where he comes home at night and weekends."

Sam had paused for a second before whispering, "And you and I both know, he isn't going to do that."

For a moment, Roger held the receiver to his forehead as he struggled with his emotions, but brought it back up to his ear to Sam's voice sadly admitting, "He's a lieutenant colonel now, did I tell you that? He's got all these new responsibilities in new social settings and

I can't be there for him any longer. And what's worse, old man, it doesn't matter. Gerry doesn't need me anymore. I can't even remember the last meltdown he's had."

Roger had known when Sam had called, it wasn't going to be an easy call—he had caught the hints that things weren't good. Still, he hadn't been prepared for the defeat in Sam's voice and his heart sank.

"It isn't that we don't want to make it work, we want that more than anything," Sam continued as she expressed their frustrations. "We just don't know what to do, and if we do, we don't know how to do it. It's a moving target that never stands still long enough for us to catch up. Every time we find a way forward, old man, every time we find our peace again, the goal posts are moved and we are back to square one.

"It's the fight, Roger, not the blindness. Once I go blind, it'll be bitter, but at least it will be over, and I can work on acceptance rather than the fight. But now, every day is a battle to maintain what little shred of dignity there is left. I just want it over…we just want it over. We are gasping for air in a lake with no oxygen and we are exhausted. We don't have any energy left," Sam said, her deadened tone catching the old man off-guard.

There had been a feeble attempt by Roger to interrupt with a supportive phrase when Sam had paused for a second, but nothing came to mind, so he just quietly listened to a voice that echoed surrender.

"We thought we could beat it, Roger. We thought we could just push our way through this, but there are so many things ending, things around which we had built our lives."

Roger sat, overwhelmed in stunned sadness. The conversation had been one he had never dreamed he would have. He had been there at the relationship's beginning. He had been there when it took hold and became something that he marveled at. He had never imagined he would be there at its end.

He struggled to find words. "There's joy in even the smallest of acts. Sometimes you just have to dig a bit deeper than you thought to find it, but it's there. Your fear is greater than your disability."

Sam wavered a moment, in part trying to compose herself, but also Roger's remark about fear had left her wanting to reach through the line and knock him on his caboose.

"Fear, Roger—you want to know what I fear?" Sam's tone stiffened with an edge. "I wake up every morning wondering what I'll be able to see that day," she said, her voice catching on a sob. "Every time he leaves for a stint, on a rotation, old man, I try to memorize every detail of him, of his face—just in case I can't see him when he returns."

Grateful she couldn't see him through the phone line wiping away his tears, Roger announced in the most cheerful voice he could muster, "Girl, I want you to do two things while you are in Paris. Don't think. Just experience the moment and trust. Trust yourself and Gerry."

"I do trust him, Roger, you know that." Sam's tone was defiant.

"Yes, child, but where is your trust *in* him? Where's your trust *in* yourself?" Roger's question left Sam wondering where it was, too, and then she thought to ask, "What's the second thing? You said two things."

Roger began to chuckle as he dramatically exclaimed in jest, "Drink lots of wine. You can't be in Paris and not drink French wine!"

The joke managed to get a momentary shy smile out of Sam but her somber tone returned as she ended her call. Stoic but fatalistic, Sam had whispered so softly that Roger had strained to hear her,

"Things are already tough, old man, and they're only going to get tougher yet. Much tougher. What we're doing isn't right and it's not fair, for either of us. We're already headed for divorce, we're just too stubborn to admit it. This has to end."

Roger had sat with the phone receiver still in his hand, unsure of what to do next, when his wife Marion's voice cut through his thoughts,

"That didn't sound good." She was standing in the doorway of his study with a dish towel in her hands, watching and while she couldn't hear Sam's side of the call, her husband's haunted expression told her everything she needed to know. Marion and her husband were never able to have children and over the years, Sam had become the daughter they never had. "Well, what are you going to do?"

After forty-some-odd years of marriage, Roger knew that tone of his wife's all too well, it was her way of kicking him in the rear, telling him to do something. Roger only silently shook his head, causing his wife to huff at him as she threw the towel over her shoulder and left, but after a moment he called out,

"Marion? Do you know how to dial an Army base overseas?"

GERMANY, *1999*

The trip to Paris was also the catalyst for a contentious flashpoint conversation between Gerry and his longtime best friend Stan. The coffee shop meeting with Sam's mom, Betty, had left Gerry unsettled and he began to dwell on the topic of marriage again. Every time he brought up marriage to Sam, she always turned him down, saying he wasn't ready to be domesticated. He had even tried the traditional on-bended-knee approach in a restaurant, positive she wouldn't turn him down in public. He had been wrong. But the more he mulled it over, the more convinced he became that marriage was the key to solving all their problems.

Fuming, thinking, *Gerry's such an idiot,* Stan sat in the chair of Gerry's office, as he, in a fit of disgust, threw pencils at the dart board behind the closet door. He loved the man, but right then, Stan wasn't liking him much.

He could hardly believe his ears when Stan had listened to Gerry once again start talking about marriage—with, as usual, Sam making all the concessions. Gerry had prattled on how well Sam was doing and how easy it would be for her to adjust whenever he was transferred. Stan had been speechless as Gerry refused to, or couldn't, see that the zero hour of dealing with Sam's condition had finally arrived.

Stan had been surprisingly quiet regarding the topic, it was, after all, Gerry's decision to make. But he was fed up with the guy hiding his head in the sand, and when Gerry finally showed up, Stan got in his face as he unleashed years of frustration.

"Dude, we're talkin' Paris here, the most romantic of places, and you've been handed it on a platter. It's time, but if you're going to propose *again*, then damn it, mean it this time." Grabbing a fistful of darts for the dartboard, he began to forcefully throw them at the target as he continued to argue. "C'mon Gerry, these past years—you make it out like Sam's the one dragging her heels and digging in. This isn't on her—it's on *you*. Ya sit there and expect her to take care of your problems—like she always has."

Hostility bubbled as Stan, throwing his last dart with such force it stuck through the dartboard into the door, turned and sneered at Gerry in a withering voice,

"Just what the hell's the matter with ya? Why are ya such a prick? She's the one who has done all the adapting, has started over. She doesn't have a choice—ya do. When they offered ya that spot out west, where ya wasn't travelin'—what'd ya do?—ya passed. Like always, ya did what was best for *you*. What's the matter, it woulda been too borin' for ya? Too claustrophobic for ya? For once, stop bein' such a spineless wonder and step up."

The two men, lifelong buddies who could say anything to each other, suddenly found themselves with too much having been said.

"You want Sam to marry ya? Then lose the pathetic on-the-go mentality of always havin' to be part of the spearhead." Stan's raw anger boiled as he scornfully repeated his question. "You want Sam to marry ya? Then be a part of her life, rather than her havin' to be a part of yours." And he repeated it again. "You want Sam to marry ya? Then stop expectin' everythin' to be on your terms."

Gerry had crossed the room to stand in front of Stan, inches from his face. It was taking every ounce of his being to control the anger he had spent years mastering. Hackles raised as shoulders tensed and each glared with steely eyes as the confrontation raged on.

"Sam doesn't need some friggin' marriage license," Stan snapped, "she needs *you*. She needs ya to grow up and be there for her."

An angry Stan roughly shoved the office chair aside as he curtly spewed at Gerry. "Are you willin' to lose her? Because you're gonna. Sam's done—there's not gonna be any more chances. You can see it on her face, and hear it in her voice. You're already losing her—and ya should—you're a moron."

Standing chest to chest with his friend, Stan contemptuously jabbed Gerry in the shoulder as he continued to spit his words. "Ya know, that street kid you're always struttin' around tryin' to prove you're not? He died a lifetime ago. You're just too stupid to see it. Look at everythin' ya have, damn it, everythin' you're so eager to throw away." Stepping back, Stan snorted, "If brains were leather, ya wouldn't have enough to saddle a June bug."

The fight was one-sided, for like always, Gerry hadn't said a word...and Stan couldn't believe him.

He stood at the office door, his hand on the door handle as he glared at Gerry. "I dunno why Sam hasn't dumped you. You don't deserve her...ya never have." He abruptly jerked the door open in blind disgust as he muttered, "Do whatever ya want, bro. Every man chooses his hill to die on." His words disappeared behind him as he slammed the office door shut.

The door to Gerry's office closed so forcefully and with such a sharp crack that the young aide stationed in the vestibule jumped, almost spilling her coffee over the jumble of files on her desk. The young soldier had tried in vain not to listen to the argument, but the walls were so thin and her desk was so close.

As Stan worked his way around her desk, he knew she had heard everything and without breaking stride, gave her a mock order, "Talk some sense into that jackass." Wide-eyed and stunned, the aide's fingers flitted nervously over her desk looking for something to light on as she hid her face behind her coffee mug until Stan left.

Heat had risen through Gerry's face at the accusations, but as his adrenaline from the fight ratcheted down and he could focus again, he reluctantly had to admire Stan's ability to cut to the chase. For the third time in a brief period, Gerry had heard the same words; first Sam, then her mother and now Stan.

Maybe they all are right, a melancholy Gerry would later wonder. *Maybe I should step back and let her go.*

The aide out in the vestibule was in a quandary as to how to approach Gerry. There had been little noise from his side of the door since the disagreement with Stan hours ago, but he had a phone call and wasn't answering his page. The voice on the phone was initially courteous, but turned nasty when the man rendered his opinion of the military and its rules, and her ears still rang from Roger's tirade.

"I'll make this easy for ya, sweetheart. Is he off in battle somewhere getting his ass shot off? Is he in a meeting with God Almighty himself? No? Well then, honey, get him on the phone. I'm family and it's important!"

I deserve a Bronze star for this, The aide snidely thought to herself as she cautiously knocked, and was rewarded with a gruff *What?* thundering through the door. She guardedly opened it to stick her head in.

"I'm sorry, sir, for the interruption, but you're not picking up the page, and you have a phone call."

Sitting at his desk studying paperwork, Gerry didn't even look up when he answered caustically, "Could it be that I don't want to be bothered?"

Carefully, the aide relayed, "Ah, yes sir I know, but he says he's family and it's important, a Dr. Roger Belicampf from the States."

The name brought Gerry up short and in a single motion, he dismissed the aide to answer the phone. In all the years, Sam's crusty old field boss had never called him anywhere but at Sam's home and he expected the worst when the call connected, and Roger's voice came over the line. He was surprised by the rather cheerful tone.

"How's Germany, son?" Roger greeted him, his voice hoarse from chronic bronchitis. "I know you are busy and all, but I would like to run something by you if you have a moment. It won't take long."

The man's ability to switch between vernacular and dialects had always amazed Gerry. Roger had a razor-sharp mind and was very articulate, but often sprinkling his words with salty language, he could easily slide into the crass, rough and rude. And Gerry had observed over the years, Roger's words were often crude when making a point, but he became excessively polite when incensed.

Roger's current forced politeness ran a warning flag up Gerry's flagpole and he interrupted as he cut the doctor's next sentence off, "Is Samantha okay? Is something wrong?"

"Is Sam okay? No, she is not. Is there something wrong? Hell. Yes," Roger snapped, his cheeky personality reappearing. Gerry could envision the man staring at him from across the ocean, lasers for eyes as the words were spoken.

Roger settled back into his chair in Colorado as he began a paternal lecture to a man on the other side of the world whom, over the years, he had begun to view as a son.

"Remember when Sam first introduced you to Marion and me? That paleontology dig in Texas? I was so appalled when she first brought you around. Lordy, her shacking up with some trench monkey." Gerry chuckled at the memory of that first meeting, oddly pleased to hear the crusty old man's rude disregard for social graces creep back into the conversation.

"You know what I saw at that gig? Our Sam, she always had that cement wall of hers, but then she's always had to. Had to deflect all the crap thrown her way. Called her cripple, dumbo, they did, if she didn't hear some snarky crack they threw at her. And all the garbage about her being a girl in the good ole boys club. Hell, that defensive shield of hers was like some frigging UFO." Gerry murmured in agreement as he reflected upon how well knew that shield.

"You were the weirdest thing back then. I did not like you, not one bit," Roger spewed out over the line and Gerry shifted uncomfortably in his chair at the blunt and free flowing criticism. "You weren't like-able—just stared through people. You didn't even have the sense to laugh at my jokes, and I'm damn funny. Hell, a cardboard cutout had more personality. Well, boy, for the first time since I'd known that girl, that defensive shield was down. What I saw that weekend wasn't just happy. I saw peace. And son, not just on her face, but yours, too. I don't see that kind of peace when you go on about that Army of yours. I hear you're some highfalutin colonel now."

The misuse of the rank caused Gerry to correct Roger, "Ah, it's Lt. Colonel, colonel is the next rank up."

But Gerry's remark only caused the old man to retort, "The only people who give a hoot about that difference are your Army cronies. The rest of us don't care. You are Gerry to me, son, not some colonel. You will always be Gerry, and you will always be part of us here, no matter your rank or where you came from."

A flash of insight flickered and Gerry asked, "We're not talking about Sam anymore, are we?" A wry chuckle escaped from Roger and it floated up the phone line as he, pleased that Gerry had made the connection, toned down his crude, loose talking rhetoric. He was now a soft-spoken, genial old man.

"No, son, we are not. I'm just an old coot who has been blessed with a phenomenal life and central to that is my wife. I marvel at what you and Sam have—amazed even by you two. You have a connection that seems to be able to cross vast distances of time and space. I don't understand it, I probably even fear it somewhat, but son, it is special. Do you know what a chimera is?"

Gerry thought for a second before responding, "A mythical monster?" with a level of doubt in his voice that caused Roger to smile.

"Yes, that's one definition, another is the biological definition of a combination of cells from different genetic origins within one organism. That's you two, you and Sam. Same vessel, separate origins but drawing energy, strength from the same well." Roger's voice dropped to a whisper as he told Gerry, "You two defy description."

The line went silent and for a moment, Gerry had thought Roger had hung up. The voice that came back on the line was so grave, so serious, that it didn't sound like Roger's. "Don't you go throwing it all away because things are different."

A pregnant silence engulfed the two men as Gerry sought to explain, and finally he spoke, "Samantha doesn't think I can do it. She doesn't think I can handle things anymore."

Roger only uttered a reflective *Ahhh…*before ending the call with a final thought.

"That is where you are wrong, son. Sam doesn't think you can't handle things. She knows you can. She thinks, down deep, you are convinced you can't. It's not good enough to accept that you can handle the upcoming challenges you two face. If you have to tell your-self that you can do this, then you don't believe it. If you genuinely trust in something, then you know it in your gut and there is simply nothing in the way. You must honestly have faith, for it is that convic-tion that carries you through the hard times. Until you believe, with absolute certainty, until you know with all your heart that you can face this—Sam will be right."

Gerry heard a heavy sigh as Roger whispered, "Prove her wrong, Gerry. Prove her wrong."

The affirmation gave Gerry much to think about as he hung up the phone.

41

PLAN A + PLAN B

Paris, 1999

Sam didn't need headphones to hear the conversations playing in her head on the long flight over to Paris. Their reception was loud and clear. In a last-ditch effort to preserve what had been, Sam was grasping at straws in the hopes of seeing something left in the nearly two decades-long relationship to save, but there wasn't.

As she replayed over and over in her head, the conversations with her mom and that phone call with Roger, Sam sadly thought *Mom's right*, as the flight attendants began the cabin cleanup in preparation for landing. In the decade and a half since Sam's diagnosis, Gerry had remained steadfast in his approach to life, and its challenges. Her mom had said it best; what they both wanted was no longer what they both needed, and Sam knew something had to give. It was time for her to take a stand and move on, not just for her sake, but for his, too.

People with normal vision and hearing took all the little things for granted while traveling. In a single glance, they could determine where they were, where they were going and instinctively avoid obstacles, but for Sam, traveling had descended into a hell on earth.

While in the States, assistance from gate agents was available, but in foreign countries, it was a rare commodity. The chaos of an airport, with the roar of announcements that echoed in the vaulted open spaces was disorienting and overwhelming. The plethora of languages, spoken with heavy accents, made simple conversation hard to follow. Face masks, often worn by those who interacted with the public, made lip-reading impossible and muffled any chance at understanding.

Visually, a simple short distance from A to B was a different type of obstacle course for Sam, as curt impatient travelers with luggage, children running to and fro, and go carts all would suddenly cut across her field of view. She might see the person, but the little wheeled luggage bags that trailed behind them, now all the rage, were a nightmare and she often tripped over them. Harsh glaring lighting with shadows played havoc with her cataracts, and her loss of depth perception impaired her ability to judge distance.

To compensate, she would take up a spot along a wall and scan, watching the flow of people to get a feel of the layout to know which direction to head. She would pick a family and use them as a guide, following them through customs and luggage pickup. She would scan the customs agents, looking for the one she felt she could understand the best.

All the little tricks of navigating came at a price. Sam's limited field of vision and hearing meant she had to expend tremendous amounts of not only physical energy, but mental and emotional energy as well, just to take in her surroundings to navigate. What would take able-bodied people only minutes to traverse, would take Sam hours.

Sam's arrival at the Charles de Gaulle airport in Paris found her bleary-eyed and weary, and slogging her way through customs, through baggage claims, and finally hailing a cab, she arrived at her hotel and collapsed. The room was a nice corner unit with a turret that had bench seating for a beautiful view of the river. The view, however, was the last thing on her mind. She was exhausted.

With Gerry not due in for two hours, Sam laid down for a nap.

As Sam had done just hours before, Gerry now sat in a plane aisle seat with his mind and heart also at odds. The conversations in his head were curiously similar to the ones that had filled Sam's, and the words echoed.

I'm asking you to give us a chance…If you can't, then you must let her go…She's the one who has done all the adapting…she doesn't have a choice— you do…Until you believe…Sam will be right. He had also been thinking about that word. Change. It was only a word, but what a terrible word for him. It seemed to possess a power to instill fear, to command his actions, that extended far beyond its dictionary definition.

They had all been right, Sam was the one going blind and deaf, but he had been the one who couldn't see what was in front of him. She had always been the stronger one and she never had needed him, wanted him perhaps, but never had needed him, until now. Gerry had never been needed before. He never had to be the bedrock for anyone before and not knowing how to be that person, for the first time in his life, Gerry was truly scared. He worried he wouldn't just fail, he worried he would crumple.

He tried to visualize a future without the woman he had been so linked to for the past eighteen years, and what he saw terrified him. Gerry knew, like it or not, change was coming, and he needed to determine how he was going to deal with it. Gerry thought back to the deployment letter he had written the year Sam had left him after her diagnosis. The one where he laid out what his life had been like before they had met, and then what his life was like afterwards.

On the short hop from Germany to Paris, the single question he had asked Sam in that deployment letter years ago hung in his head. He had asked her which life she would choose to live. The answer, Gerry realized, had always been clear.

Arriving at their Paris hotel, an expectant Gerry stopped and chatted with the concierge on duty, asking for directions. He was looking for a particular item and was given a card with an address to a nearby jewelry store, for a custom engagement ring. Not a fan of fancy jewelry, Sam would be a hard sell for traditional rings, and he needed someplace that could make a simple but defining statement on short notice. This time would be his last proposal and the ring had to be different, so he wanted it to reflect his commitment.

Deep in thought as he returned to the hotel and entered the elevator, Gerry had been only half paying attention to the lift operator who was asking him which floor. Muzak was playing and there was this song; the words broke through his thoughts, and he just stood there listening. When the elevator stopped, the lift operator held the door open for him as he stood there engrossed in the music.

"Monsieur? Your floor, *Monsieur."* The words of that song still clung in the air as Gerry exited the elevator, but as the doors were closing, he stuck his hand in, stopping their movement. "Do you know the name of the song playing?" he asked, while pointing to the ceiling. The operator apologized that he had not been listening, but he would see what he could find out, and inquired what the song was about. Something about wind being beneath wings, Gerry reflectively said as a smile grew across his face.

Gerry had let himself into the room and quietly set his bag down when he saw Sam asleep on the bed. While cheerful in their weekly phone calls, he had detected an undercurrent of fatigue in Sam in recent weeks and now, as he studied her sleeping form, he could see just how drawn she was.

Dark circles under her eyes marred her face and accentuated her exhaustion. Pulling up the duvet on the bed up around Sam, Gerry slid onto the bed and leaned back on the headboard as he watched her.

A presence beside her had caused Sam to wake with a start to find Gerry propped up against the headboard, having dozed off himself. She had slept through his arrival and hadn't even stirred when he had lain on the bed.

Some greeting, she laughed to herself as she leaned over and stroked his face, causing him to stir.

"Why didn't you wake me?" she whispered to him.

"Because I love just watching you—now go back to sleep. We'll talk later," he told her, kissing her on the forehead. Wrapping his arms around her, he felt Sam's tension and fatigue dissipate as she shifted, snuggling in deeper, and he contently held her as she slept.

Smoothing Sam's bed-tousled hair, Gerry sadly saw all the stresses of the past few years reveal themselves on a haggard face that seemed paler than usual. The words from the song in the elevator ran through Gerry's head again as he marveled at the woman beside him, his fingers caressing hers and his gaze fell upon the necklace, with its pink pendant, around Sam's neck.

It's been thirteen years since I gave it to her and she still wears it, Gerry thought in amazement as his fingers stroked the polished surface that was beginning to show some wear.

He had stood in the jewelry shop describing the ring he had envisioned when a ragged flash of fear had suddenly raced through him. Fear he thought was from being forced to change. Now, as he softly ran his fingers through Sam's hair and looking at the necklace, he realized the fear was not of changing—but of not. He had made the right decision. Gerry leaned over and whispered in Sam's ear, "Hang on, lady, 'cause I finally get it. Don't give up on me yet."

When the pair finally made their way out, the same concierge from earlier ran through the lobby after them, "*Monsieur* Martinez? I have that information you requested." He handed Gerry a card with the lyrics to the song playing in the elevator. Pleased, Gerry could only smile as he nodded a curt thank you. His plan was coming together.

Paris in the spring was as beautiful as rumored, and it worked its magic. The couple reconnected all over again and any lingering misgivings that Gerry might have had over his decision, the week all but banished them. It was day seven of their ten days in Paris. The ring was done but Gerry also had another surprise for the woman he considered his soulmate. As he wrote a short note on a smaller separate card, he fished out a pin from his pocket and pinned it to a larger one.

While he was beginning to understand that, for Sam, the card's and pin's accolades weren't a deciding factor for his life-changing question, he still hoped they would make her proud of him. He put them, along with yet another card and the engagement ring in a small wooden box with an embossed flowery flourish top. It was perfect.

The early morning had been misty, and the sunshine was bravely struggling to break through, portending a beautiful day as the pair strolled down along the banks of the Seine River. They had been chatting about what to do that day, delighted in not having an itinerary and every moment scheduled.

Ah, let's just see where the day takes us, they decided.

Gerry did, however, have a destination in mind, an extremely specific destination. Upon waking that morning, he knew that day was the day and the concierge had suggested the perfect location, the very location where he himself had proposed to his wife many years previous. On a map, the concierge pointed out to Gerry a small, often overlooked park along the Seine, Square Barye on the eastern tip of Île Saint-Louis. Assured it was quiet, private, and a botanical oasis, Gerry's anticipation and anxiousness had been building throughout the morning as he worked to keep the box hidden from view in his jacket pocket.

Sam had also been becoming increasingly more anxious, but for a different reason. She had avoided bringing up the whole reason for the trip. The week's joyous and jubilant mood had been marred by a growing sense of foreboding, for there were only a few days left and she had yet to find the way to bring things up without hurting him. When they first arrived in Paris, it was a déjà vu of those early weeks when they had first met, only the love was deeper from shared memories.

But as glorious as the week had been, Sam tried to shake the feeling off, knowing it was only temporary. As the week wore on, her time was growing ever closer to that moment she had been silently dreading but knew was coming. Several times a sense of apprehension crept up on her when she caught Gerry starting to say something and then watched him back away. She could tell he had something on his mind, too.

Their meandering path along the riverbank led them to that perfect spot. The view was beautiful, the ground was soft grass and it was private. Laying down jackets on the damp earth, Gerry spoke first, saying there was something he wanted to talk to her about, and Sam's stomach lurched while she stiffened up; she knew that somber tone of his all too well. She was grateful that it was he who was starting the conversation.

His grim expression signaled how serious Gerry considered the discussion, and a despondent Sam sadly thought he also agreed that it was time to end their relationship. In an effort to keep her composure, she focused her attention on her coffee cup, fumbling with its plastic lid. As he began to talk, she bit her lip and closed her eyes while she kept twisting the lid.

Inwardly, she pleaded, *Oh please, Gerry, just get this over with.*

Sam was caught completely off guard when he placed a box on the ground in front of her. She had been so sure of his words and their impending conversation that she hadn't really been listening. A quick glance at Gerry's typically stoic face offered few clues when he had to prod her gently, "You need to open it, Hon." There were several cards and a small rustic wooden box inside. Picking up the top card, it was a poem to which a pin attached a brief handwritten note.

I love you more than words can describe but these are pretty close. The card had what she thought was a poem at first, about her being the wind beneath his wings. But then she recognized it as lyrics to a song, a song of gratitude and appreciation. Through its words, Gerry spoke of Sam's unwavering support of him, and of the strength and guidance she has given him.

As Sam read it, the significance of the pin sank in—it was the eagle collar insignia for an Army colonel, the next rank up the ladder. The second card, as it was unrolled, announced a promotion ceremony, thus confirming her suspicion, but the date and location were To Be Determined.

Seconds ticked by as it all registered and her astonishment subsided before she could vacantly stutter,

"You've been promoted?" At that moment, it seemed everything from the last eighteen years hinged on Gerry's next sentence.

He studied her face for the slightest hint of her thoughts as he said, "No, but I'm on the list and more importantly, I have put in for a transfer to a stateside position, a permanent stateside position. It won't be quick, but it is in the works."

There was an instantaneous flash of anger as Sam was consumed by the malignant thought that perhaps, this was just some kind of ploy. But everything about Gerry, the soft smile, the gentle intent gaze, the sincere timbre of his voice, said it wasn't. This was for real. Stunned at the words and what they meant, Sam desperately stalled for time while watching river tour boats float by, oblivious to the drama on the shore. The gears in her mind groaned with exertion as they labored to grasp the idea that after all the years, the status quo had finally been broken. He had stopped running.

There was no immediate response from Sam as she mulled over what she was hearing and for Gerry, hope crashed into the hollow pit of his stomach. He quickly launched his Plan B, what he would say if she wasn't impressed. He deliberately and carefully laid out the details of how he and Craig Thornton, his friend with whom he had sat at a table at a BBQ years earlier, had spent those years working out a promotion path.

The crooked grin that Sam had fallen for all those years back in Arizona creased his face as Gerry held her hands and told her, "I'll be home—*our* home. Only a few more years, and I will be home for good."

He spent the next half hour outlining, in his typical meticulous bullet-point fashion, a summary of his plans for their future, complete with an exhaustive list of pros and cons. His presentation was so honest and candid that a smile of delight broke through Sam's disbelief, and she laughed at Con #7—apparently she was a bear before her morning coffee. The how, where, when, why and the who were all laid out and carefully addressed, providing the groundwork for Gerry's Plan A + Plan B to come together for Plan C.

Opening the small wooden box, the ring was as simple as it was practical...and she said yes.

[**Gerald, 2001: Quoted Text From Letter**

"Been thinking about the honeymoon Hon. How about we go to Scotland and Ireland? I would love to see where your heritage is. Your mom has talked so much about the McFarlands and their islands off

Scotland—I would love to see what it is all about. Who knows, maybe find some long-lost relatives still living in the area? Thought it would be nice to see that Giant's Causeway you've mentioned, never have seen something like that. Maybe even see if we can get tickets for that new group you like—what are they—the Irish Tenors? Does any of this sound like something you'd like or are you thinking someplace warmer? Maybe someplace with blue water, warm sand, you in a bikini—Oooooh, now that would be nice!"]

Cargo Transport Over The Atlantic, August 2001

Hitting a patch of turbulence, the cargo plane shuddered and bucked as it interrupted Gerry's thoughts, and paused his flow of words in his letter to Sam. He stretched his muscles in the cramped seat and then leaned back again as he wondered how best to approach the topic of her mother. Sam's mom, Betty, was initially thrilled to hear about the engagement when they returned from Paris, but over the past year, she had become increasingly distant with him. Betty acted as if she didn't believe they would follow through with the wedding and there had been no happy announcement to the family. In fact, there had been none of the excited making of plans that his Army brothers had warned would drive him crazy.

Just weeks after returning from Paris, Sam's father was diagnosed with terminal cancer and Sam and Gerry became a dismissed afterthought, as Betty shifted her attention and focused on more serious matters.

Even taking into account Betty's disapproval of the wedding, Gerry had been surprised at the animosity of her tone on the phone when he called that morning looking for Sam. He needed to be careful how he worded things as he danced around what was said during that call.

[**Gerald, 2001: Quoted Text From Letter**
"Speaking of your mother, I'm sure by now she has told you I

called their house looking for you and got her instead. Hon, we need to talk. I'm truthfully not sure what is going on but your mom has thrown me for a bit of a loop. Your mom is understandably upset over your dad—I'm hoping I just misunderstood, misinterpreted the whole conversation but I keep replaying it and I don't think so. Your mom said if—if we get married, not when. Hon, I have waited 20 years to marry you. I love you to the ends of the earth and can't wait to be your husband. I don't know how else to convince you I'm sincere—which begs the question—do you even want to get married? The impression from your mom was that you didn't think I would be around. Do you think I will leave when things get tough? Do you think I will get tired of you?

"Forgive me Hon but Stan was standing there during all of this, heard it all and he brought up something that I guess I hadn't wanted to see. You've not been yourself Hon for quite some time, since we got engaged. Oh, you go through the motions, try to hide it but there is a deep sadness in you now. The eyes don't twinkle as bright, I'm not hearing that laugh much and your smile is not as broad. I thought you were just tired over your dad but now I'm not so sure. You don't even seem excited about the wedding. I know you love me. I truly know that at my core. I don't want to talk about this on the phone—needs to be in person. I do want you to think about all this. I do want you to confront these demons—with me, your illness, and perhaps most of all yourself. I need to know what is causing all this. I need you to tell me why you are so concerned, so fearful of your future with me. I need to know what I have to do to ease those fears. Know whatever this is all about—we can handle it. I'm not going anywhere."]

4 2

THE APPROACH SIGNAL HAS GONE OFF

*L*ANDING IN GERMANY, AUGUST *2001*

It had been nearly ten hours of continuous writing in a confined airplane seat when Lt. Colonel Gerald Martinez finally put his pen down. He scanned his opus, all twenty pages worth, and then carefully folded the sheets, for they barely fit into the envelope.

In addition to her address back home, he prominently wrote another directive: *Samantha, read this now, don't wait until I come home* and then deliberately put the bloated envelope in a side pocket of his duffel bag. He felt good.

As the plane was maneuvered into position, the units got up, groaning as their stiff muscles rebelled against the sudden activity and grabbing their gear, they began to disembark the plane. For the second unit that had boarded the plane back in the US, Germany was the end of the line for them. But for Gerry and his unit, Germany was just a stopover en route to their final deployment base station elsewhere in Europe.

Filing through the base buildings, a smiling Gerry was at ease and happy as he made his way to post his final "Five Paragraph Order" home. As hard as the letter had been to write, he was surprised to realize he wasn't tired—a huge weight had been lifted, and he actually felt rejuvenated. With a start, he recognized, as this phase of his life was coming to a close, he was not just happy, he was eager to see what was over the horizon.

OHIO AND EUROPE, A WEEK LATER

Leafing through the daily mail, a serene smile broke out over Sam's face as she recognized that distinctive block printing of Gerry's, a smile that changed to wonder. Two things had jumped out at her. First, how thick it was. *What had he sent her?* Secondly, the note on the outside for her to read it now—both were out of character and a break from their routine. She would read it at sunset.

She poured herself a glass of wine, picked up the envelope, and headed for their chair out on the patio with Gabe the dog following at her side. The letter's expected opening of *Somhairlin mo ghràdh* caused Sam to smile happily in anticipation, but when she had finished reading it almost an hour later, her fingers trembled, causing the pages to flutter. Sam sat lightly shaking her head in stunned silence as she read his last line, *Permission to speak freely ma'am.*

This was a man that you needed the Jaws of Life just to get out of him how his day went. His "Five Paragraph Orders" were on average barely two pages, maybe three with a tail wind. *And he wrote twenty pages?* she thought incredulously. It had been those last few pages, however, that shook her, and it hurt her to know that her behavior had made him even entertain the thought she didn't love him. And that last line. *Permission to speak freely.* He was asking her to listen.

Gerry and Stan had been arguing good-naturedly over a soccer match while crossing the base compound as they returned from the dinner meal when a shout rang out with a message. *Martinez's fiancée was looking for him and she wanted him to call home,* ASAP. Stan had begun to snicker pathetically when Gerry cut his argument off mid-word and immediately pivoted toward his office.

Stan's tease of Gerry not even being married yet and Sam already having him on a short leash earned the kidding sergeant an up-yours look from his friend. When the couple finally connected, Sam had only two things to say to Gerry.

"First, never doubt I love you and I apologize that I made you do so. Secondly, what the hell did my mother say to you?" The one-sided conversation was interrupted only by an occasional, "I see" from Sam, each time her expression growing darker and darker as she listened to what her mother had said.

Despite the tension, they ended in good spirits and the couple hung up with assurances on both sides that all was well, but they also had acknowledged that there was an 800-pound gorilla still in the room. Gerry had been right to have said in his letter what he did. Sam did have issues to confront, and they would face them together when he came home.

The unpredictable personality shifts, the emotional outbursts, the sudden irrational behavior; none of them were her mom. All of that was irrelevant, however. Appalled at Betty's behavior as she hung up the phone, Sam cared little about the What anymore, and nothing about the Why. Incomprehension had descended into fury and en route to her parents' home, all of Sam's justifications of her mother's behavior over the past years were thrown to the wind.

By the time she barged into her mother's kitchen, her rage had been consumed by unprecedented flames of disgust. Sam regarded her mom not only as generally the smartest person in the room, but as a true friend and one of the best people she had ever known. The mother-daughter confrontation that followed would be their first, and only, real argument.

As Sam demanded an explanation from her mother, it was clear that the woman had changed and Betty did not deny saying those things. When asked why, a coldly detached voice that belonged to a complete stranger, impassively noted that she simply had told Gerry what needed to be said: that Sam and Gerry were not meant to be and it was her job, her duty in fact, to prevent this. Sam's final words to her mother as she left were simple.

"You stay away from me and you stay away from Gerry."

Sam's mother's erratic behavior was a warning bell, one that went unheeded. Unrecognized at the time, her mother Betty had dementia. Excuses and rationale had predominated Sam's perception of her mother's disposition and its cause, as she overlooked and justified all the behavioral changes. They were due to her mother dealing with the stresses of her father's dying, Sam had told herself.

It would be several years later before Betty's condition was officially diagnosed, and ultimately determined that she had three separate degenerative neurological diseases—Alzheimer's, frontal temporal dementia, and vascular dementia, all working against her. But in the meantime, mother and daughter remained at odds with each other as they cared for Sam's father in his final days.

[**GERALD, 2001: Quoted Text From Letter**

"The approach signal has gone off so we will be beginning our descent soon. I have saved these last ones for the end because they are the hardest for me Hon. They are also the most important to me.

"If I should die, know that I did not leave you willingly. I began this life just a street kid from Boston who often rued the day he was born. Had no future for all I knew was distrust and hate. Had no vision for all I could see was a world where fighting was the order of the day, the only way to survive. My ability to fight served me well for it took me on a path to you. I never understood why anybody cared how they lived or even if they lived at all, until I met you. I never had a reason to care about anything or anybody until I met you. There is simply a before you. And an after you. Before you, life was bleak and pointless. After you, life was a wonder.

"We have talked about this. No mourning, no grief, no anger, no what ifs. I died doing what I was put here to do, what I needed to do. Know that if possible, just as my first thought of the day was of you, so will it have been my last.

"Well Hon, I'm out of time. We've been given landing clearance so I guess it is time for me to close and get this in the mail bag. The guys are beginning to josh me about how long this letter is saying you will be still reading it when I get home. It's just that I had so much I wanted to say, so much I wanted you to know.

"I love you and I can't wait until I come home. Will call as usual this weekend. Till then.

"As always,

Permission to speak freely ma'am"]

43

TO CONQUERING MALE STUPIDITY

*E*UROPE, *2001, 2 MONTHS LATER*

The drudgery of the last several months of being overseas and away from home had begun to eat away at Gerry as he entered the final leg of his final rotation. A growing excitement began to take over his thoughts and much to his chagrin, he caught himself, more than once, peacefully daydreaming of his new anticipated future.

Standing at attention before the desk of his immediate superior, Colonel Craig Thornton, he fidgeted like a schoolboy at the principal's office. Thornton, preoccupied with his paperwork, had barely looked up as Gerry entered his office, but the dismissive stance was an illusion; the two men had been friends for years.

The career orbits of the two men had intersected periodically over the years, and Colonel Thornton had become both a critical career resource for Gerry, and an avid personal participant in the couple's lives. Ever since that day at Lawson's BBQ, when Gerry had first told Thornton about Sam's medical condition and of his own worries of handling the higher ranks, the two Army friends had spent many a happy hour over drinks, discussing Gerry's options and how realistic they were.

It had been Thornton who had paved the way, sponsoring and

supporting Gerry when he first began his quest to transition to a permanent position stateside two years prior. He even had finagled Gerry's last overseas posting to be safely within his chain of command, thinking it would make a nice wedding gift.

Gerry's report of a routine surveillance run earlier in the month had made its way through the channels and was now sitting on the commander's desk. All business, and with not even a hello, the staid Thornton briskly updated Gerry on the current status of the area's additional surveillance reports, and concluded the meeting by assigning him to escort a couple of civilian contractors the following day. The two contractors wished for a more thorough review of the sites indicated in Gerry's report. The assignment was a waste of time in Gerry's view, and he said as much while he pointed out that he had included the GPS locations of pertinent areas in his report. They didn't need him, he felt.

Treading that fine line between being both a friend and commanding officer, Thornton leaned back in his chair as he patiently explained in a tone that made Gerry feel like a child,

"Martinez, it is your surveillance report they read, and it is you they want to talk to—in person. More importantly, it is what you didn't put in that report that they are really interested in." Heaving a sigh that spoke volumes, a more congenial Thornton cautiously remarked, "These people are our allies—find a way to work with them and please—" He crinkled his nose as he pleaded, "Keep it cordial."

As Thorton swung his chair around to dispose of the report, Gerry's knack for bluntness caused him to stop and think twice, and after a moment's reconsideration, he commented as an afterthought, "Better yet, take Ibbotson with you."

With their business at hand concluded, a relaxed attitude flowed over the office, one signaled by Thornton's use of first names, and lazy smiles that reflected their deepening rapport broke out between the two men.

"Gerry, I know this isn't to your liking, but you are a short timer now—you only have seven weeks left." While reaching into his desk for a bottle of whisky and two glasses, Thornton changed the topic.

"Have you two lovebirds set the date yet? I still haven't gotten my invitation," he chided with a crooked grin as he poured a generous couple of fingers in each glass.

As Craig Thornton pushed a glass forward for Gerry, he admitted, "I know how hard this has been for you and I've been wanting to tell you something. I not only support your decision, but I also agree with it." He clinked his glass to Gerry's in toast.

His warm smile hinted at how happy he was for his friend as he further confessed, "This is the right thing you're doing, not only as an Army officer, but as a man, and I for one, am proud of you on both fronts." The kind words from a typically undemonstrative and reserved Thornton were unexpected, and they provoked an overwhelming sense of gratitude to flow over Gerry as he fumbled about trying to thank his friend for everything.

Not just during the latest transfer and promotion process, but for the decades of support. His effort was cut short by a rather annoyed and curtly uttered, "Oh nonsense, I am delighted to have done so," from his superior and the glint in his eyes indicated that Thornton considered the subject matter closed.

Toasting to their friendship and to change, Thornton nodded as he tipped his glass, "To you, to that wife of yours, and all that is to be for you both."

Gerry sat quietly in thought for a moment, pains of regret streaking across his face. When he finally looked up at his friend, he softly confessed in a voice laded with sadness, "I should've done this years ago, Craig."

Their conversation slid into remembering all the times over the years, the two friends had argued over how best to handle Sam's inevitable decline. Craig poignantly reminded Gerry, "You wanted to make a certain rank for its pension. No one, not even Sam, can fault you for trying to secure the future." But his words only caused Gerry to shake his head in disappointment.

While sipping his whisky, he scoffed while thanking Thornton for the sentiment, but said they both knew that wasn't the only reason he had dragged his feet for so long. Leaning over Thornton's desk for the bottle, Gerry poured another round of drinks for the two men and with a sigh of resignation, raised his glass and somberly toasted, "To conquering male stupidity."

Chuckling at the toast, Thornton jokingly quipped, "If we're tackling male stupidity, we're going to need another bottle."

Gerry glanced at his watch as he finished the day's reports and saw it was perfect timing to call Sam back home. With this chapter of his life ending, he had thought he would be more apprehensive with a sense of dread. He had expected to be melancholy, but instead, he found himself impatiently waiting for the next chapter to begin.

The tenor of the calls back home promoted a sense of peace that flowed through everything. It wasn't just the peace that surprised Gerry, but the feeling of satisfaction, and they both grew stronger as his time in the field drew to a close.

Picking up the receiver, Gerry X'ed out another week on the countdown he kept under his desk blotter—only seven more phone calls, and the thought caused a huge smile to break across his face as he dialed. A pleasant and comforting routine, the call was filled with updates on the family and of course Gabe the dog. The running joke of how much Gabe moped around, missing Gerry kept the couple entertained, but privately it pleased Gerry to hear how Gabe actually would go into the closet and sleep on his spare duffel.

When reluctantly asked about her dad, Sam confirmed he was in the final stretch of his cancer, but thankfully, pain meds kept him comfortable. It was now just a matter of time. As the conversation drifted toward the touchy topic of her mom and how she was dealing with the stress of it all, an uncertain Sam didn't know how to answer, making a few vague comments, but finally, just sighed deeply.

It sounded like mother and daughter were still just treading water and Gerry quickly changed the subject to something more lighthearted. As he filled Sam in on the latest gossip and weather, he described his drives up into the surrounding countryside in a cheerful travelogue fashion, portraying the people and villages. He especially hammed up his account of Stan's latest mishap involving getting lost, a young lady from the local village with her less than impressed father, and a truck's engine fan belt.

Flinching, Gerry reluctantly told Sam he had been assigned for another surveillance run up in the hills the following day and he knew she wouldn't be happy. The closer the red-letter day of him coming home drew, the edgier Sam became and underneath it all, Gerry knew she privately wished they would just bury him behind a desk under a mound of paperwork.

Trying to soothe the unease he heard in her voice, he lightly laughed while telling her it was nothing dangerous, and the area was quiet, with no current activity. Quipping that there was nothing to worry about, except of course, Stan getting lost again, he hoped he allayed some of Sam's apprehension.

Just as the couple was saying their goodbyes, Stan, with his uncanny impeccable timing, arrived for dinner mess, and realizing who Gerry was talking to, snatched the receiver out of his hand. Bawling it out in his heavy southern drawl, Stan's wisecrack, "Hiya darlin,' ya missing me?" garnered a huge laugh from the other end of the phone.

Over the next few minutes, Stan recited his interpretation of his latest escapade of being lost, then found, and the beautiful young lady from the village; his version was far more entertaining than Gerry's.

"How's she doin'?" Stan asked, looking over as he hung up the receiver.

A wistful Gerry answered, "A tad off if you ask me," as he cleared his desk. "I think she is far more rattled over her dad than she lets on." Nodding pensively, Stan reached back over for the phone on the desk. Next to Gerry, the woman was Stan's dearest friend, and he knew just what to do to cheer her up as he dialed her number.

On her end, Sam had just hung up and hadn't gone more than a few steps when the phone rang again. Answering, she was greeted not with words but only with song as a rich male tenor voice reverberated over the line. It was her Stan singing one of her favorite songs, "Amazing Grace." All seven verses.

The symphonic timbre of Stan's voice echoed as he stood there serenading the woman on the other end of the phone. Heads popped out of office doors into the hallway and activity had all but stopped while everyone within ear shot just listened, with some quietly singing along. For those four minutes or so, time seemed to have taken a pause, and when finished, Sergeant Stanley Ibbotson, one of Sam's most treasured friends, simply hung up without saying a word to her. It was to be his final gift to her.

The following morning, Gerry and Stan were en route to meet up with the two independent contractors in the next village over and set out on a northwesterly route up into the hills. Stan had been driving and Gerry, in the passenger seat with the map, would have been reviewing landscape features, landmarks, and points of strategic or intelligence value.

They might have been aware of motion, a sense of something amiss from off to the left. The incoming round would have been accompanied by a flash of light. A loud explosion would have followed as the round tore through the cab of their truck.

44

OCTOBER 2001

While on a routine, non-combat support excursion in the European Theater, the vehicle in which Lt. Colonel Gerald Martinez and Sergeant Stanley Ibbotson had been riding, was struck by an RPG.

The round pierced the left rear passenger side.

Colonel Martinez and Sergeant Ibbotson were both wounded, but survived the initial impact.

They each were subsequently dragged out of the vehicle by persons unknown and Sergeant Ibbotson was shot and killed shortly thereafter.

Lt. Colonel Martinez was taken some distance from the vehicle and beaten before being executed.

No group claimed responsibility.

4 5

THIS WAS GERRY'S MOMENT, HIS AND SAM'S

It was early morning in the American Midwest when the phone rang, just a little after dawn Ohio time. It was Brady, the gentle giant and fellow Musketeer, who was the one who made the call—he had wanted Sam to hear it from a friendly voice. She could tell from the awkward silence with its muffled sob cut short, and she knew instantly. His voice breaking at times, Brady told her what little he knew, and said an official notification would be forthcoming with more information.

There was nothing left to say or do to fill the void that hovered in the air, so they hung up. While trying to comprehend and process Brady's words, Sam's phone rang again, and she answered to momentary silence before she heard a quiet, "Sam? It's Craig." It was Colonel Thornton, Gerry's commanding officer, making a personal call, not as an Army officer, but as his friend.

This was not his first loss as a commander, but it perhaps was Colonel Thornton's most personal. In the years he and Gerry had spent working out Gerry's transition stateside, Thornton had developed a deep fondness for the couple and their twenty-year saga. Hiding it well, Thornton choked up as he spoke, providing more details of what they believed had transpired that morning, and of their last moments. Details that Sam absolutely needed to know, but had caused her to stagger nonetheless, and would have preferred not to have heard.

He told of his last conversation with Gerry, the warmth of their friendship so clearly evident in the words so carefully chosen. He recalled the drinks in the office, the joke about male stupidity that at the time struck both men so terribly funny, but now rang so hollow as neither Sam nor Thornton could see the humor.

Most of all, Thornton called to tell Sam that he was sorry, and he was the one to blame. It was he who had sent Gerry and Stan out that day and he was responsible, Thornton repeated. They both knew he wasn't. After hanging up, a shell-shocked Sam gathered up her notes for lecture that day and left for campus.

Those days of October and November 2001, the days just after the deaths, were an empty blur for Sam, and the two remaining Musketeers, Brady and Mark, mercifully took care of most of the details—all except the last. The memories were excruciating as Sam sat in the aisle seat on the same route she always took to Boston. The trio of friends—Sam, Brady, and Mark—met at that same café, the scene of so many moments. Except this time, there were no jubilant bear hugs, only sorrowful embraces with few words.

Chartering a tender from the pier, it was midmorning when they arrived one mile from the lighthouse, due east out into the Atlantic. Brady reverently carried Gerry's ashes as Mark helped Sam out onto the boat's fantail, while dodging divebombing seagulls hoping for a free meal. Stan was not with them that morning; he was to be buried in his hometown back in Georgia. This was Gerry's moment, his and Sam's.

At its finality, Sam turned to see the boat captain, himself a veteran of the Navy, standing at attention alongside Brady and Mark, saluting while his boat flag flew at half-mast. It was a fitting end to the moment.

· · ·

[**SAMANTHA, 2024: Quoted Text From Letter**

"I need to apologize Gerry for not having written this letter to you a long time ago. I should have written it when I returned you to Boston, but I was so numb and in so much pain. That day in the harbor was in the 50's, sunshine with a mild breeze as I scattered your ashes past Graves Lighthouse. I watched as the water turned murky, opaque and then you were gone from me. I stood there in stunned silence, not knowing how to go forward or why I would even want to. I've never been back to Boston, the scene of so many of our memories, nor will I until I go to join you. Never made it to Scotland either, babe, never have gone anywhere we talked about for that matter—waiting for you I guess."]

SAM HAD WAITED weeks before telling her mother about Gerry's death. Going through her own nightmare, Betty was torn up and worn out from taking care of Sam's father, in his final weeks. When an opportunity finally presented itself, Sam arranged to meet her mother at the corner café, ground zero for so many poignant conversations over the past year or so.

Over coffee and scones, and with tears rolling down her face, she desolately described to her mother what had happened, and the two women sat there grieving for lost husbands: Betty crying her pain and Sam hers.

Betty's grief was not for Gerry, however, and her reaction was not at all what Sam was expecting. From Sam's point of view, her mother was stunningly cruel as Betty was openly relieved that Gerry was now out of the picture and thus, her problems with him were solved. Sitting there, Sam fought not to recoil in shock as she tried to reconcile the woman before her as her mother, but could not. When she got up to leave, Betty grabbed Sam's hand and told her to remove the engagement ring and be done with him. This was all a good thing, she promised her daughter.

By the end of 2001, the topics of Gerry, his death, and Sam's grief all became taboo, and they were not brought up again by either woman for years—a silent wedge and sinking anchor between the two. The family was focused on the crises of the living, and that was where Sam directed her energy as well. Her grief was internalized with work, caring for her parents, and teaching.

PART III

2023-2025

4 6

SEEMED TO HAVE BYPASSED
THEM ALL

*O*HIO, *NOVEMBER 2023*

The sun bore down on her back, but the air had a crispness to it that foretold the coming of colder days as Sam Walker, on her hands and knees, pulled weeds out of the flower bed. It was November of 2023 and the fall season was in its glory.

She used to love the fall—the colors and cool air were welcomed after the heat of the summer, but now, she dreaded its appearance. Gerry and Stan had been killed twenty-two years earlier in October. Then, six years later, Brady, retired from the Army at the end of his tour, had been shot and killed in a drive-by shooting while going out for cigarettes, in October. Mark, who left the Army the following year when his tour was up, succumbed to prostate cancer ten years ago, in October.

She was now without her Four Musketeers. All four were gone, and through the fickleness of fate, they all had left her in October. She hated the month. Each year she would tell herself she would not go down memory lane, that she would not dwell on what she had lost, but rather, on what she still had, and every year, she failed.

October remained a bitter month.

This year, this October, had been especially rough for her as she fought with an errant weed that refused to be yanked from the ground. Roger, Sam's friend and former boss, had passed away during the summer, and he was the last of the core group of her life forty years ago. A very strange sensation came over Sam as she acknowledged Gerry would not be proud of what she had become. She now lived a life that not even she recognized, and she wondered, *Had it all been for naught? Had any of it been real?*

It had been twenty-two years since her world shattered, two decades where time had little meaning. For the last twenty or so years, time and life trudged forward for Sam—dragging her with it. She never left Ohio—after Gerry's death, there was no need. Now, in her late sixties, her Usher's had continued its relentless deterioration without pause, and Sam's vision and hearing were both extremely limited.

Her motto from years earlier, "functioning but failing," still applied, but now the words were reversed. Her new revised motto was "failing, but functioning." Technology and the social trends of the day proved to be her saving grace. Online deliveries, a mere convenience for most, became Sam's lifeline for they allowed her to still have some semblance of independence.

November of 2023 brought in its wake other symptoms unusual for Sam. Edgy and agitated, she could not seem to settle down nor could she sleep. As she continued pulling weeds and clearing the beds for fall cleanup, one of her dogs came over to offer its mistress her interpretation of help, digging a hole with dirt flying everywhere.

The act of putting down her gardening knife to shoo the first dog away only allowed her second dog to snatch the tool, and scamper off to hide with her new treasure. Their antics caused Sam to smile. Ebony and Ivory, two labs, one black, the other yellow, both with a knack for getting into trouble. They also had a knack for knowing when she needed a diversion, but the diversion was to be temporary and superficial, for there was a storm brewing beneath the waves.

Sam's father's cancer had ultimately triumphed, and he passed a few months after Gerry, and Gabe the dog passed a few months after that. Betty, Sam's mother, was diagnosed with Alzheimer's within a few years, and had succumbed to its ravages seven years ago. For Sam, life revolved around what she was physically capable of doing. No longer able to teach, forensic consulting remained her sole passion for as long as possible, in addition to caring for her mother.

Now they were both gone as well.

Grief is composed of five main stages: denial, anger, bargaining, depression, and acceptance. Some scientists add two more stages that address the complexities of guilt, and Sam seemed to have bypassed them all.

While still grappling with the loss of her career, and with it, her identity, she was confronted with the losses of Gerry and Stan, and then, with her father's death, a third grief cycle began on top of the current two cycles that were still active. These three cycles ran concurrently, one on top of the other, but each on its own timetable.

The deaths of Brady and Mark, along with the Alzheimer's decline and death of her mother, brought forth additional grief cycles, numbers four, five and six, and with each new subsequent death or crisis, a new cycle was added to the growing pile of heartache.

In an effort to cope, Sam began to truncate cycles, combining and shortening the stages and ultimately halted the grieving process altogether. Like a computer with too many open programs running simultaneously, Sam's internal hard drive froze with the interminable blue screen, and its circular arrow spinning on an endless path.

Numb, Sam was stuck in this limbo, safe from the past, but not moving forward toward the future. And she stayed in this suspended state for twenty-two years, able to function and outwardly doing well, but never having dealt with Gerry's death. She had worked her way through cycles two through six, but Gerry's still loomed.

His was the first death and she had encased her emotions, telling herself she would process them later, but later had never come. In his last letter, Gerry had asked that she confront her fears and demons of her illness, and of the future, saying that they would face them together when he got home.

With his death, they never had that conversation and Sam never confronted those issues. Instead, she had packed up all those fears and demons along with Gerry, and put everything in boxes, drawers, closets, and safes, hoping the saying, *out of sight, out of mind*, would lead to her salvation.

[Samantha, 2024: Quoted Text From Letter

"I didn't know how to handle this new existence that was thrust upon me. So, I did the easy...I bundled up all the pain, emotions, memories. I put them in a box, and I locked them away in the deepest recesses of my soul where they couldn't hurt me anymore. Or so I thought. In the ensuing years I, in the vernacular of today's youth, 'ghosted.' I did just enough to exist and function but not live."]

As November rolled by week after week, a normally solid Sam was on an emotional roller coaster that seemed to have no end. The earlier agitation and edginess grew even more fierce, and she at times, seemed a caged animal pacing to and fro.

On a morning in mid-November 2023, while making the bed in the master bedroom, she had a profound experience, one she was not prepared for. The depth and intensity of what transpired in that moment were of a level she had never encountered.

DO YOU KNOW HOW PROUD I AM?

*S*am had been in a hurry when she glanced at her watch. She hated being late and was quickly tidying up the bedroom when she was gripped by what was not a dream, not even a daydream, but a waking vision, and it was all-consuming. For the duration of the vision, she was not aware of her surroundings and there was no time. She was stunned to see, when she finally could move and glanced at her watch again, that she had been standing there, motionless, for only a few minutes. It had seemed far longer. The power of the moment almost prevented her from breathing.

It was like she was watching a movie, in vivid detail, starkly blunt in its message, and in third person. She was watching a vision of her and Gerry, at a time and place that could not be real. She was aware of everything, the smells, the heat, the humidity, the sounds. She was aware of the crunch of fabric and boots, as she and Gerry moved. She had felt a bead of sweat roll down her arm, and as she stood there afterwards, she reached down to flick a fly off her arm, a fly that didn't exist.

They were crossing a clearing in an unknown jungle-like location. Maybe Vietnam or maybe somewhere else. They both were in their prime, thirties perhaps, and Sam could feel the breeze and smell the vegetation. There were no other people in the vision, just Gerry and her. They both were in olive-green combat fatigues, T-shirts with tactical vests, helmets, and M16 rifles. Gerry's helmet was pushed too far back on his head and Sam noted his hair was longer than it should have been. Her helmet had mesh with twigs inserted between the strands.

As Sam watched the scene, she instinctively knew they were just coming off a sweep or firefight. They approached each other from opposite sides of the clearing, passing near its center, and they both were gesturing and pointing to each other with their rifles in a careless manner that no soldier would ever do.

Their laughter was jovial and deep, with a cocky behavior seen with ball players after a big game, a "you the man" attitude. Huge grins dominated their faces and they were deliriously happy, almost indescribably so, just to see each other. The joy each had in seeing the other was eclipsed only by their immense pride in each other.

Nothing about the vision was real. It could not be a memory. Sam had never been in the military, and Gerry's uniform was mismatched, not tallying with where he had served or with his age. The only reality of the moment was the range of emotions that engulfed Sam, and that her numbing fog of the last twenty years had lifted.

All the grief, pain, and turmoil of the last twenty years had somehow been condensed down into a single point, much the way a black hole condenses matter. The emotional pain was crushing, but through it all, she could see clearly.

[**S**AMANTHA, **2024: Quoted Text From Letter**

"Fast forward 22 years, babe.

Then November came. Why now after all these years? I never saw you in my dreams in all the years since you died. In memories yes, in thoughts and daydreams yes, but not in dreams. I had put you away. I put you in boxes in my closet where you were out of sight. I put you in boxes stored in the depths of my conscious for safekeeping. How did you escape? What changed? Hard to describe what I've been experiencing let alone explain it.

"It began with the Clearing Vision; a singular event that has changed everything. It was not the scene that was so intense, it was the emotion. In a microsecond, the extent of my unhappiness was exposed bare and impossible for me to ignore any longer.

"That vision was not real, not a real place or time or event, yet it is more real than the grass beneath my feet. It has been the catalyst that has driven these last three months. Three months. It feels like yesterday and eternity have collided."]

THIS VISION, which Sam began to call the Clearing Vision, was followed by intense dreams that were forceful and full of memories of her past that shook her. In her earlier years, when confronted with confusing or even disturbing dreams, Sam would always bounce them off her mother, but that, of course, was no longer possible.

Sam had always been a follower of dreams. Dream analysis had been handed down through the women in the maternal McFarland lineage for generations; her mother, grandmother, and great grandmother all contributed to her comfort with dreams. Some colleagues questioned how Sam, as a scientist, could even subscribe to dream analysis, but for her, they were not mutually exclusive—they complemented each other and each added substance to the other.

She used dreams to better understand her inner self and relied on them to provide a compass direction in times of turmoil. The insights received from those dreams were honest, not swayed by the conscious daily worries and that made them a valuable tool that Sam thought foolish to dismiss.

She was a firm believer in the saying, *Let me sleep on it.*

The dream process had all but shut down for Sam after Gerry's death. While the dreams had never left her, she had left them. She no longer journaled them or gave them any thought and, resenting their intrusion, she prevented them from invading her realm. For the past twenty-two years, her dreams had been relegated to the same dark place as Gerry's memory.

In an effort to digest what was happening, Sam began to do something she hadn't done in over twenty years—she began to journal her dreams again. And as she did so, she realized she was lacking a critical element, her sounding board. Some of her most treasured memories with her mother were of the two of them, Sam and Betty, over a pot of tea or a glass of wine, laughing hysterically while analyzing each other's dreams. Sam made a portentous decision.

At her mother's church, there was someone who was also well versed in dream interpretation, and Sam reached out to her friend in hopes she could be used as that much needed sounding board. In the weeks that followed, the process of discussing and analyzing the dream images with her friend, Carol Matthews, permitted a sense of control to reemerge, but also brought forth more questions than answers for Carol. And a renewed sense of trepidation for Sam.

Ohio was a sharp divide in Sam's past, one the size of the Grand Canyon with many deep hidden gorges and towering cliffs, and each held a secluded memory. She had never shared that past, of Arizona and beyond, with those in her new life in Ohio, for they were different people on different paths. Sharing her stories of those days meant sharing Gerry, and that was someone Sam had gone to great lengths to bury.

As the years went by, she had transformed the man from a living person into a nebulous shadow residing in a box in her safe. She had learned how to keep the pain under control and contained, and she was determined not to drag all of it back up again.

Carol, unaware of Sam's life before Ohio, listened throughout December and learned much while offering insightful comments and suggestions, but she was puzzled. Military themes cropped up in Sam's dreams, and not grasping their source or significance, Carol probed and urged her for more information. During those weeks in December, Sam began to disclose her Arizona past, the past that those in Ohio knew nothing about.

As Sam dragged Gerry out of her hidden recesses and started to recount some of her memories that were so fresh, the tears began to flow. She hadn't cried much back in 2001, twenty-two years ago, or in the years after his death, but now she seemed to be making up for lost time; she simply couldn't stop. Gerry's death wasn't twenty-two years ago. It was yesterday for her all over again, and this time, with the pain as raw as ever, the grief wasn't pushed aside. The slightest hint of a memory, good or bad, would send her into a tailspin; she cried for months.

Through the tears and emotional turmoil that dominated December, a singular thought would emerge to invade Sam's mind—the letter, Gerry's last letter to her. Any and every silent moment was filled with the letter. It consumed her, and she was driven to read that letter again, something she hadn't done in decades. It was still there in the safe, where it was put all those years ago, and the thickness of the office walls did little to dampen its beckoning. Finally, Sam stood in front of the office safe, took a deep breath, and entered the code.

The sight of the box caused a slight gasp that surprised her. *Had she thought it wouldn't be there?*

Inside, the mementos of those years had been kept safe from the ravages of time, and the tears flooded everything as Sam pulled out each item; cuff links, his Army coaster that sat on his desk on top of those waiting letters, the engagement box from Paris and more were all there.

She stared at the bottle of aftershave she had saved and wondered if it was any good after all these years. And then along the side of the box, laid the envelope. She focused on the rubber Army P.O. stamp on the outside, the air mail stamp in the corner and Gerry's distinctive block printing for an address long since forgotten.

Willing her fingers to work, she lifted the flap and took out the yellow pages. The legal pages seemed so thin and fragile as she unfolded them—*had they always been like that?* It was all a lifetime ago and it didn't even seem to be her past anymore—it belonged to someone else, a someone who no longer existed.

.   .   .

[**Samantha, 2024: Quoted Text From Letter**

"It drove me to pull you out of those boxes, out of my closets and out of the chasm in my soul. I read your letter again—something I hadn't done in 22 years. All the pain, hurt, loss came roaring back—it was yesterday all over again."]

SHE RECALLED the day she had gotten his letter in the mail; she was so happy back then. It had made her day, and while it was not Gerry's voice, it was his presence, and she had found it soothing. Its reading destroyed her as she sat on the floor of her office in front of the safe. *This is a mistake,* Sam thought as uncontrollable tears just poured out. Hastily, Sam threw everything back into the box and quickly closed the office safe door, but the letter, now awake, wouldn't be silenced.

The vision and continuing dreams gnawed at her, poking at every hidden crevice in her psyche and all through December, the letter and Gerry, haunted her.

The letter, now back in the office safe, had a life and voice of its own, and as she carried on through the weeks, its pull spurred Sam into action once again. Her eyesight had gotten much worse over the past years and suddenly she was racked by the fear that one day, she would not be able to read the letter at all—a fear that seemed to strangle her. Sam decided to digitize the letter, to enter it into the computer so it could be read back to her. She began on January 2, 2024, fittingly enough, a new year for a new beginning she hoped.

For two decades, Gerry's twenty-page opus had sat quietly biding its time, and now, it tormented Sam's every waking thought; a raging fire of pain and energy. At first, hoping quick meant painless, she read impatiently and hurriedly, not contemplating the words or their meanings. The faster she got through the letter, she reasoned, the less painful the words would be, for they were just ink on paper. After a few days, however, she found she had begun to savor the words and their meanings. At first, it was just a sentence here or a paragraph there, but she worked her way to reflecting on whole pages and sections.

She typed rather than scanned, and it forced her to weigh and absorb every page, to think on every paragraph, on every sentence, and on every word. Every agonizing detail jumped out at her and subtle nuances she had missed twenty-two years earlier now screamed at her at the top of their lungs. She laughed at the coffee ring on page nine, in the upper right corner, made by the thermos she had given Gerry for Christmas several years prior to his death.

She could see all the hesitations as he paused to work out what he wanted to say, and she saw the words for what they were, not ink on paper, but a snapshot in time of his feelings of the moment. Words perfused with worry, words full of pride, even words bristling in anger, but all written with love.

[**Samantha, 2024: Quoted Text From Letter**

"The letter, babe, why did you write that letter and how did you write that letter? From where did you find those words? My God, hon, what I would have done for you to have read that to me like you did the others. I've never said this but thank you for somehow finding the strength to pen those thoughts. They have torn my heart open again with anguish, but also with joy and pride."]

The ordeal of transcribing the letter took a week, and Sam viewed it as torture therapy, a way to excise those demons of yesteryear that had such a grip on her present. The cyclone that the vision had unleashed was still raging, but she hoped her confrontation with the letter would cause the tempest to lose strength, and thus its grip on her.

It was odd to hear Gerry's words spoken in someone else's voice, computerized with no personality, emotion, or inflection. But listen she did—repeatedly, while waiting for the moment when the scabs weren't ripped off as she heard it, and she no longer cried through the whole thing. The transcription of the letter was finished, but its author wasn't. Gerry the man began to creep into Sam's thoughts and dreams. The same dreams she shared with Carol, her friend from the church. Carol was perplexed by the continuing military references and just who this Gerry was, and Sam found herself struggling as she tried to explain a ghost. She made another crucial decision—she gave Gerry's letter to Carol to read.

Throughout the following weeks, Carol goaded and badgered Sam to write a letter back to Gerry. At the time she was unaware of the couple's tradition revolving around the letters. Carol just thought it would be good therapy, and every time Sam declined. Writing the counter-letter, her yin to Gerry's yang, was of a magnitude Sam didn't think she could yet handle.

[SAMANTHA, 2024: Quoted Text From Letter

"I began to see you again in my dreams. To my horror, I began to see your death again—you being dragged from the truck, you being beaten and tortured, you being shot. I see you on your knees and fall forward into the dirt. Repeatedly. Over and over as if stuck in some tortuous feedback loop. All I could think of: Were you scared? How much pain were you in? What was your last thought? For weeks I could not function as I grappled with all the emotions, pain, and despair. I know I wasn't responsible for your death, that I wasn't the instrument of your death but...what if? I railed against the higher powers for once again putting me through the agony.

"Then it changed. I would still see you but now you would be still moving after you fell. I was shaken to think you hadn't died quickly, that you were still alive after you were shot. That was replaced by a new dream, hon, one that was balm on the open wound. You still were shot, you still fell forward into the dirt, but now, you rose again. You stood up, dusted the dirt off your pants and had a big smile on your face. You were OK, no longer in pain, no longer in fear."]

THE WEEKS that followed the Clearing Vision of November 2023 had been replete with dreams. Many were of Gerry, and they filled Sam with a sense of peace that began to calm turbulent waters. Sam had awoken to one dream with a smile, as the dream hovered in that space between realities.

She and Gerry were in a jungle, but across a valley from each other. Sam was far in the valley below with a group of people, perhaps as their guide, while Gerry, with his unit on a cliff top above on the other side of the valley, worriedly looked for her. He had gone to the edge of the cliff and intently scanned the valley's green foliage for any movement, but he couldn't find her.

His unit came to join him on the cliff's edge, and they all stood frantically surveying the jungle terrain. Concern had grown to fear when Gerry suddenly took a deep breath and broke out in song. "Amazing Grace" echoed over the valley. One by one, the men of Gerry's unit joined in, and the chorus resonated over the treetops.

Deep in the jungle on the other side of the valley, Sam's group was making their way down a jungle path when a woman in the group stopped. Turning to Sam, the woman touched her arm while asking, "Do you hear that? Can you hear him?"

Sam listened and, in the distance, she could hear Gerry's song. Standing there, Sam knew she was to sing back so they could find each other. Sam awoke just as she took a deep breath to begin singing.

[**SAMANTHA, 2024: Quoted Text From Letter**

"I began to see your smile everywhere, to feel your presence everywhere; on mountain tops, in elevators, in living rooms—always with a sense of peace. I feel as close to you now as I was 22 years ago. In some ways closer."]

OTHER DREAMS, however, were explicit with a different purpose and they began to guide with a common theme; medical settings and the making of doctor's appointments. In the stress and chaos of caring for dying parents, Sam had predictably put off the routine general medical checkups, using the inevitable excuse of *when I have time to get to it,* and in the immediate years afterwards, COVID made a convenient evasion as well.

Amidst her emotional upheaval, she brushed aside vague physical symptoms as the dreams nagged, coming nightly and sometimes multiple dreams per night. All with the same purpose, to go to the doctors. Many of these dreams involved a man.

Since December 2023, the weeks following the evocative Clearing Vision, Sam had been seeing a reoccurring figure in her dreams, a man in military khaki uniform. Given her history with the military, having dreams of soldiers wasn't all that unusual, but this one was different. He felt different.

The first time she encountered him, she was in what seemed like a VFW hall, and she was in a wheelchair. The man in khakis leaned over so close, so intimately that it was clear he was no stranger, and quietly told her he would be waiting for her in the car when she was ready. He then turned and walked down the hall toward the exit. At that first visit, she only saw the back of him. He seemed older from his walk and build, but somehow, Sam knew this man and what was more, her confidence in him was absolute.

What shocked her to her core was the overwhelming flood of admiration, a sense of pride in the man as she watched him walk away. She would see him repeatedly in dreams over the coming weeks, always waiting, always supporting, and most were in medical settings. She saw him in a hospital hallway pacing outside of a recovery room, and she saw him sitting in waiting rooms, always nearby, always watching. There was a sense of fealty, of devotion that was not just his to her, but hers to him.

In one particularly vividly prophetic dream, just after the first hints of an issue, this man in khakis stood before an X-ray and studied it for a bit, mapping out his approach. Sam was on a table, lying on her back. The man in khakis eventually came to her side and reached into her abdomen, he scooped out material. He would go back to the X-ray and study it some more, and then come back to Sam on the table and scoop out more.

After a particularly powerful and graphic series of dreams vehemently drove the point home, Sam finally made the appointments. The vague, almost nonexistent symptoms that were chalked up to getting older, erupted soon thereafter and rapidly escalated.

After months of blood work and biopsies, an appointment with an OB-GYN delivered some unwelcome news; Sam most likely had cancer. The following weeks leading up to the end of February were a whirlwind of tests, and she found herself in the office of a surgical oncologist, staring at a CAT scan of her pelvis while the surgeon spoke. She heard his every word but couldn't tear her eyes away from the screen. Trained as a pathologist, Sam knew what it meant both for the immediate, and for the future. Stage 3 ovarian cancer with multiple sites.

Surgery was immediate and there were only days to put the last of her affairs in order. Projected to be long and complicated, there was always the risk she wouldn't survive the surgery, and Sam sat in her office organizing her papers for an "In Case I Die" folder for the family. Gathering up her legal and financial folders, her eyes rested on the box of mementos and Gerry's letter within.

She had so much to do in such little time. So many arrangements that had yet to be made with so many finalities yet to be tied up, but the letter was a blazing beacon to her, and Sam was driven to finish what Gerry had started twenty-two years ago. She simply couldn't risk dying and leaving it all unsaid. Despite all she had to do that weekend, her letter to Gerry became paramount, and it overrode everything else. Having crumpled herself up into a chair, Sam reread that last letter from Gerry, and once more was overwhelmed by the need to answer it with one of her own, the one she never wrote.

With time of the essence, Sam chose to dictate rather than write. She thought, no, she knew, Gerry wouldn't mind. Sam had no clue as to where to begin, for so much had happened and so much had changed, but her feelings, she realized, hadn't.

In a sunlit room with soft blue walls, fireplace and country accents, Sam and Carol sat in a melancholy moment. During a hand-holding session as Sam looked through the last remnants of mementos of Gerry, her friend Carol had asked a couple of simple questions.

"How does it make you feel? What do you feel when you look at the mementos?" Sam answered immediately because she didn't even have to think.

Pride. She felt pride. Sam was so proud of Gerry, of all that he had accomplished and who he was. She had forgotten just how much until right then.

Deliberating for a few moments as to the whats and hows of her letter, Sam then picked up her cellphone, set it up for dictation, slid it into her shirt pocket and began to compose her letter back to her Gerry, one that was twenty-two years in the making. She began slowly as words and feelings swirled without direction, but soon a rhythm set in and the words flowed, as she went about making her final preparations for surgery.

Sam wondered if she could remember Gaelic.

[**SAMANTHA, 2024: Quoted Text From Letter**

"Gearóid mo Anam Cara (Gerry my soulmate)

Haigh leannan, (Hi Love)

"It has been 22 years since you left me. I don't even know where to begin for like you, I have so much to say and so much I want you to know and remember. I know we talked about you not coming home but…damn it Gerry, you had seven weeks left. The last two decades without you have been beyond difficult. I miss everything about you, hon. You implored me not to hide, retreat, give up and I have done all those things. We agreed I wouldn't mourn, grieve, be angry or wonder what if and I have done all those things.

"I have stumbled through these last two decades, a shell of what I once was. There has been no joy or peace as I merely go through the motions of getting through the day, waiting for tomorrow. I have raged over you being killed, over how you were killed and why you were killed. The days are just so empty, and I have grieved over the loss of my future with you. I once read somewhere, maybe in a poem, about rain mirroring mood, it being as if the heavens were crying with you. I understand that now, for there is sunshine but no warmth and I actually enjoy rainy days as the heavens seemingly are weeping as much as me. I have tortured myself with a thousand what ifs…

- Missing Excerpts -

"…They say unrequited love harbors the most painful sting. I would argue so does a love cut short, with all its promise lost. Despite all the pain and misery of these past years, I would do it all over again —every minute. You worried that you were boring, predictable and I would get tired of you—I did like my adventures after all. You never failed to amaze me, surprise me Gerry for there was always another facet, another door to explore. Hon, I didn't just have adventures with you—you were my most amazing adventure."]

REACHING into her pocket for her cell phone, Sam paused its dictation and reflected, as she pondered over what to say next while standing before the coffee machine, waiting for another cup to brew. The answer wafted up with the aroma of coffee.

She had made Gerry his morning coffee that last day home, as she had every morning they were together. Each morning Sam would get up before him to make the coffee and take it to him as he washed up. And every morning, Gerry would thank her in the most appreciative voice, as if he hadn't been expecting it.

She had lightheartedly teased Gerry that last morning, asking why he was so shocked she brought him coffee—she had only been doing it for the last twenty years. Sam wiped away her tears as she smiled over the remembrance of him telling her that he was not shocked by the coffee, but rather that she was there with him at all. Every morning, he had said he had to pinch himself because he couldn't believe that she hadn't walked away. That after all the years and everything he had put her through, she was still on his arm.

· · ·

[SAMANTHA, 2024: Quoted Text From Letter

"You said you couldn't for the life of you figure out why I chose you. How could I not? You and I orbited each other like binary twin stars where neither of us could escape the gravitational pull of the other. Perhaps it was that we were both deemed disposable that bound us together. Perhaps it was fate. Or simply Anum Cara [soulmate] as we have joked about so often. Whatever the reason, thank you for following me to that *cantina* that day.

"We had a wonderous, magnificent life together, hon. But there are things I am sorry for. The biggest? I'm sorry I didn't marry you sooner. I'm sorry you didn't get to experience belonging to a family and all that it encompasses, both the good and bad. You never got to be called a son, and it would have been son, not son-in-law. I denied you all that and it has caused me much remorse. Things would have been rocky in the beginning, but they would have loved you for you loved me. My mom adored you and spoke of you highly. After you died, we went on a trip to South America, by then my dad had passed and there we were, two miserable widows, and it was there I saw she regretted how things had gone with that last phone call. She openly referred to you not only as my husband but her son and was proud of what a good man you were. I have never forgotten my mom's behavior or her words during those last years, but I have long since forgiven her for I know it wasn't the real her. I hope you have too...

- Missing Excerpts -

"...The sight of you, your presence was so comforting and reassuring, but I began to wonder why. Why were you here with me now? I have wondered, Gerry, if all I've experienced with you in these last months was in preparation for me to pass. The cancer had asserted itself at this time. Were you here to help me through this or to take me home? Either way, I've been grateful for you joining me on this adventure.

"Well, babe, I'm also out of time. The approach light has gone off for me as well and I will be going for surgery tomorrow morning and things are not looking promising at the moment. I've made my peace and have gotten my estate in order. I will burn this letter along with yours tonight—their ashes to be put with mine when the time comes. People all say how brave I'm being, how stoic and that I don't seem to be upset or worried over the diagnosis or the surgery, but why would I be? Just like Oaxaca and all my adventures, you will be there with me. In many ways I'm looking forward to seeing you, hon.

Till then… As always, *Is tú mo ghrá.*

I will close my letter as you began our story,

Permission to speak freely."]

THERE IS ALWAYS A LOGICAL EXPLANATION

FEBRUARY 2024, NIGHT BEFORE SURGERY

Sam stood before the fireplace with the letters in her hands, staring at the crackling fire as she waged an internal battle. The flames seemed to dance about the logs as if they were jumping in anticipation, eager to devour the paper. It was the last physical remnant of him, Gerry's handwriting, and she fought with herself to burn it. Running her fingers over the ink on the pages, feeling the crinkles and pen divots made from writing, she entertained the notion for a moment of burning a copy, but then had an odd thought that if she did die, she wanted the letter with her.

The writing of her letter back to Gerry had opened the floodgate of emotions, and while the magnitude of her loss crushed her again, the urgency of preparing for her surgery in the morning yanked her out of her sea of memories.

"All right girl, enough of this crap," Sam muttered under her breath, sucking in a huge breath before heaving it back out in a sigh. She scolded herself for being so sentimental. "You've been daydreaming, and you need to get back to work."

Gerry had been so real, so vivid during the recent weeks, but the real world was beckoning and as it pushed the past aside, Sam knelt before the fireplace to toss the pages on top of the logs. Orange-yellow flames erupted over their surfaces as the pages succumbed to the fire, and Sam, with tears threatening, watched the letters turn to ash.

"Bye, luv," she whispered, as the last of the ash fell between the logs.

"Wow...that was one hell of a trip down memory lane." Sam ruefully chided herself as flashes of her life with Gerry seemed to fight for one last memory—the gun range, the cactus, the Officers' Ball, Oaxaca, the obstacle course, Boston. Sam roughly shook her head trying to clear those flashes, and then heaved herself off the floor to head for the kitchen. There were last-minute instructions to write for the dog sitter.

Day of Surgery

The days leading up to the surgery were a blur. For months, Sam had been slogging through an overburdened medical system, trying to get appointments and testing done. Although test results suggested cancer, forward momentum was agonizingly sluggish, and the weeks rolled by as further testing refined that suggestion of cancer into a definite. Appointments remained an elusive commodity. If appointments were available at all, they were weeks if not months away.

Finally, after three months, at the end of February, she had made her way through to the oncology appointment desk. When told the consultation would be yet another month out, at the end of March 2024, Sam pointed out the results of the blood work and scans, saying she didn't have a month to wait. The woman on the phone was kind when she stated it was the best they could do for her.

Waiting until she knew for sure what she was dealing with, Sam had chosen not to divulge any information to her family, but by the end of February, the cat was out of the bag, and the somber call was made.

Grasping at straws, her family had asked, "Could they be wrong?"

"Yeah, but not likely," Sam had said while explaining the blood test for the 125 cancer marker, showing a sky high level of 520 versus the 35 upper limit of normal, had been repeated several times. The ultrasound that showed a large mass had been verified by other scans. "One could be a mistake," she admitted, "but in their totality ...No. I have cancer."

In the midst of that call, as Sam's family was making travel plans to come back to Ohio, her phone call waiting cut through. It was the hospital, and when she answered, a male voice came on the line.

Sam had no idea who this man was, but her file was on his desk, and he had questions. He was a surgical oncologist who was both confused and displeased, and he wanted to know why she was waiting until the end of March to come in. In the brief, but fervent back-and-forth exchange that followed, this doctor insisted she move forward quickly and curtly outlined what he proposed for her to do, all of it immediate. Interrupting, Sam explained there were no available appointments, that she had been told the March date was the best the system could do for her, and the additional testing was even further out yet. Without pausing, the surgeon tersely spoke words that Sam will in all likelihood never forget.

"Well, it is not the best *I* can do," he said, and then he summarily hung up on her. She sat on the couch listening to a dial tone, wondering what had just happened. That was a Thursday. Monday was the CAT scan, Tuesday the pre-surgery consultation, and surgery was scheduled for Wednesday. Sam had gone from ten to 100 miles per hour in less than five minutes.

The day of surgery was quiet as the family braced itself for the reality of what was to be. In the pre-op waiting room, the handing over of legal papers and last-minute instructions were accompanied by the uneasy stilted chitchat people do when trying to fill awkward silence and allay fears. Everyone spoke in hushed muted murmurs, as minds were both whirling and blank at the same time. There were no hopeful adjectives sugarcoating things.

Everyone had seen the scans, the blood work, and all the other testing, and privately, all wondered if Sam would even be alive come Christmas. The truth was searingly clear as science and medicine painted a grim picture. The surgical team as well as Sam, and her family, understood the focus of the surgery was simple mitigation or damage control. The surgeon would do what he could, but expectations were low.

The primary tumor's mass had been large, the size of two bricks side by side, and when she awoke the following morning, Sam could tell immediately it had been removed, because the pressure and pain were gone. Probing with fingers, she did an immediate incision check, checked for whether there was a colostomy bag—there wasn't—and was stunned when she realized they had not inserted a port for chemotherapy. She had been prepared for both, and then she checked out the whiteboard that hung on the wall in her recovery room. The words didn't make sense, they must have the wrong pathology report. But they didn't.

Verification came during surgical rounds that morning, as Sam dumbly repeated questions she already knew the answers to, but she still couldn't quite wrap her head around. As the team left the room, Sam caught the eye of the young resident who had taken her history during the intake consultation; the doctor was grinning from ear to ear. Stage 3 Ovarian Cancer, but Grade 1A—there would be no chemotherapy, and the team was cautiously optimistic, perhaps even confident, that they had gotten it all. It was an extraordinary turn of events.

A month almost to the day after Sam's surgery was March 28th. Despite the optimistic results, cancer was cancer, and it had a way of coming back. Wanting to make things as easy as possible for the family, Sam had set about clearing the house while putting the last of her affairs in order. The tedious, often laborious tasks of clearing out a lifetime of debris and clutter from her house, and the shredding of documents occupied Sam's energy since the surgery, dominating her thoughts.

There was one day, a day that was just another day in a line of similar days since the surgery. March 28th didn't start out any different or more portentous than any other day. That day, Sam's two impish Labrador retrievers, Ivory and Ebony, tore into a garbage bag of shredded paper confetti set aside from the last of such shredding sessions. It was something they had never done before, nor have since. The contents of that bag were strewn everywhere, and as Sam came down the stairs, little paper chips glittered on top of everything, floors, furniture, even lights. There were even some on their square heads as the two irreverent clowns looked up at her with glee, there was no remorse on their ends.

Cursing and muttering as she began the cleanup process, Sam ultimately made her way to the dinette area with its hard vinyl floor. There was one spot that just wouldn't pick up, despite being vacuumed over and over and finally, she gave up and bent over to inspect the object. The moment floored her.

It was just a trinket, the object Sam was holding, but it was something she hadn't seen since 2007, seventeen years prior when she moved to Cleveland. Nestled in her palm was a pink heart-shaped stone pendant, the one that Gerry had given her thirty-eight years earlier, but had been lost during the move. About a month before moving, she had noticed the little ring attaching the dog tags to the chain was loose, so she had removed the tags and stored them in the jewelry box as a precaution—they had never been lost. As for the chain and pendant, Sam continued to wear them, but realized one day during the week of the move, they were gone from her neck.

It was only the pendant in Sam's hand, as the chain was still missing. The bail that held the pendant on the chain was intact and undamaged, and the pendant itself was as pristine as the day Gerry had given it to her. She stood motionless, afraid to break the moment, and was positive she was having another vision, for in her mind, this simply could not be real. She went and got a glass from a cupboard, put the pendant inside and placed the glass on the counter. Like the moth relentlessly drawn to a flame, Sam returned to that glass at least twenty times during that day, convinced each time, the pendant wouldn't be there, and that it had all been a mirage.

There was always a logical explanation for everything Sam postulated, but this one was escaping her. There was no way the pendant had been in the garbage bag; it couldn't have gone through the shredder. Seventeen years had passed, with carpets replaced, floors redone, rooms repainted, vacuum cleaners thrown out and replaced. Every explanation she came up with was rejected. Yet there it was, on the floor in her dinette. It was another inexplicable coincidence in what was to become, in time, a lengthy list.

Months earlier, back in the beginning of 2024, Sam had enlisted a friend, a talented artist, to try and render a drawing of her Clearing Vision. At the beginning of May 2024, Sam hung it on a wall in her office. While hanging that picture, she dropped a nail and spent considerable time on her hands and knees looking for it on the floor, combing every inch of the carpet at the base of the picture. It was a momentary irritation that became important the following day.

Carol, the friend behind all the dream analysis, was excited to see the picture in place, so Sam went about tidying up the area, vacuuming the rug in front of the console table along the wall under the picture. A glint caught her eye as she ran the vacuum, and she bent down to pick up whatever it was. It ended up being the missing chain for the pendant, in a room it had no business being in, at the base of the drawing of the Clearing Vision she had just hung. Sam had been on that floor looking for a nail just the day prior. There was no way that chain was there then, but yet here it was now, not damaged with the ends joined at the clasp.

Questions abounded regarding the necklace. How did the chain get separated from the pendant? How did the two pieces end up where they were found over a month apart? How could neither piece be damaged, but yet separated?

The pendant, dog tags, and chain have all been reunited as one and Sam wears them once again.

[SAMANTHA, 2024: Quoted Text From Letter

"…I wore that pendant for decades, babe, and it helped carry me through the dark days of your death. When it was lost during the move to Cleveland, I felt like I had lost you all over again."]

. . .

AFTER THE SURGERY, it wasn't Gerry's letter that was on Sam's mind. It was her own letter back to him that now taunted her and she kept rereading it, trying to see what it was that her mind wouldn't let go of. As earlier with Gerry's letter, after a great deal of trepidation and soul searching, she ultimately gave her own letter to Carol to read.

When Sam's mother had passed, parishioners and colleagues sent condolences that were pages-long eulogies. Carol, who had a close relationship with the woman, only wrote two words—*Well done*, referring to the home care Sam had given Betty. Carol had a way of cutting to the chase.

When Sam asked what Carol's thoughts were regarding her letter, she was expecting her friend to say any number of things—that she was overreacting, she was being overly emotional, she was giving significance to things that weren't real or simply was making something out of nothing. Carol, sitting in the rocker with her fingers tapping the pages, enigmatically said, "This letter is not done with you."

Over time, Carol prodded Sam to write of her experiences, not just the last few months since the Clearing Vision and the cancer, but of the last forty years. "Nonsense" was always her reply, no one was interested in the rantings of an old geezer's memories, and sadly, everyone had dealt with cancer one way or another. There was nothing of interest here.

Gerry continued to visit Sam in her dreams, sometimes just to say *Hi Hon*, but other times, he seemed to want something, and he dropped hints and prodded. She began to see dream images of manuscripts, title pages, and of her editing typewritten pages, and Carol just kept digging at her about writing. She dismissed them both, for writing was simply not something she had ever aspired to.

Then one night, Gerry dropped in for a visit, and spent the night sitting at a small desk writing. Just him on a blank background, no longer dressed in khakis, but in a cream fisherman's sweater over a faded blue denim shirt. Chinos for pants. He would carefully put each page when finished on a growing pile, but he never stopped writing. Nor did he look up.

That was April 16th. On April 17, 2024, Sam sat down, opened up her laptop, created a file, and began typing the first line of the first chapter of this book. Arguing with Gerry, she reminded him she was trained as a scientist, not a writer, and her idea of conveying ideas was in outline form, abstracts with punctuated sentences and bullet points. Not prose. Drafting a book was beyond her abilities, she asserted. Gerry had an answer for that too, one that caused Sam to laugh when she woke up the following morning. He had stood before her on a blank background, just him, and told her, A + B = C. It was as simple as that.

There was no outline; none was necessary because the book, forty years in the making, was already written. All Sam had to do was put it to paper, filling in some blanks. The two letters formed the framework, and where they took the story, the words and pages followed. Sam doesn't remember writing that first line, but according to her computer logs, she did. Nor can she tell you what the final impetus was that drove her to put pen to paper. She just knew Gerry wanted her to, or perhaps more accurately, needed her to.

The last twenty-two years had been difficult, and were not what Sam had wanted for herself, but the ten months since November 2023 at the time of this writing, exceed description. She would be lying if she said the pain of those twenty-two years was gone, it's not.

Sam is astounded at how easily the tears still welled up, even after ten months. She still mourns her loss, but the deep hole in her heart now has some warmth to it, the kind of warmth that comes with peace. She has no idea what caused the Clearing Vision to appear that day in mid-November of 2023, or why. She only knows that in that moment, everything changed.

Nothing was visibly different from the outside. Her appearance of course was the same, she lived in the same house. She still had the same problems, the same memories with the same pain. She still had the same emotional baggage. Nothing had been miraculously solved.

What had been altered is how Sam looked at them. In the oft-quoted phrases, in the blink of an eye and the wave of a hand—the fog had lifted and there before her was a path. Not a physical one, but rather a mental or emotional path. In that moment, clarity lit not only the path in front, but the trail of misery that was behind her. In that moment, she realized the path she had been on was not the same path that was now in front of her, and she could see the way forward. At that moment, for the first time in two decades, Sam could see a glimmer of daylight on the horizon.

The ever-vigilant scientist in her still looks for the rational, large hormonal swings from ovarian cancer causing the vision and dreams perhaps? Might explain the vision and dreams—the human brain has been known to perceive things in odd ways, and there is much that neuroscience has yet to learn. But physiology does not explain the necklace, or the list of other inexplicable occurrences that just happened to fall into place. Some may argue that this all has been nothing but daydreams or emotions fulfilling fantasies—we see what we want to see.

And yes, there is a logical medical explanation of the tumor's Grade 1A status, as benign tumors have been known to be precancerous and undergo malignant transformation. While the 1A status is remarkable, and as welcomed as it is, it is not a miracle. The outcome, while being unexpected and uncommon, is still not all that unique. Sam's cancer outcome per se is not the miracle here.

Part of the miracle is how all the pieces, spread out over months, came together, seemingly orchestrated to fall into place, thus allowing the cancer to be caught as early as it was. Another part of the miracle was how the outcome itself came about. How a change in Sam's perspective allowed her to appreciate and understand the dreams that goaded her into action.

Had it not been for the Clearing Vision, Sam might not have paid attention to a different type of dream, a dream weeks prior to all the testing. In this one, she was drawing something on a sketch pad, a shape, kind of an irregularly shaped square contained within another larger structure. At the time, the shape meant nothing to her, but it hinted at something important and was connected to her other dreams, so she had taken note.

Sam merely drew it in her journal, not fully recognizing its significance until she saw the CAT scan weeks later. Holding the image of the primary tumor from the CAT scan next to the image drawn in the journal, there were some small discrepancies, but the two images were stunningly similar. The larger structure lined up with her abdominal walls.

Each element standing on its own, warranted an offhanded comment of *Oh wow, what a coincidence,* and could be easily dismissed or written off. Some could be explained through a series of what ifs; if this happened, and that over there happened causing this over here to happen, then maybe…a seemingly endless list of remarkable coincidences not brought to light here and occurrences that just happened to fall into place.

Dumb luck can only explain so much. Sam was lucky she listened to her inner self to make appointments when she did. She was lucky that she had a young surgeon whose passion shoehorned her into an already impossibly tightly packed schedule, and she was lucky that they caught the cancer just as it was on the edge of exploding.

Both "miracles" culminate from that single, crystal-clear moment in time, back in mid-November 2023. It is hard to say what would have happened, but most likely, if Sam had not experienced the Clearing Vision, things would be very different. She never would have tackled that last grief cycle so deeply buried and there would have been no dealing with her past. She would still be mired in a rain squall that obscured the horizon.

There would have been no dreams pushing her to seek medical help and the cancer most likely would have been found much later, with a much less favorable outcome.

Occam's Razor comes to mind. In science, one is a coincidence, two is suspicious, three is a pattern, and four is a conundrum. Anything more than that falls into the realm of mystery. Even in medicine, one is taught when presented with a myriad of symptoms, you always look for the one condition that explains them all. Perhaps a combination of Arthur Conan Doyle's famous Sherlock Holmes quote in *The Sign of Four,* "When you have eliminated the impossible, whatever remains, however improbable, must be the truth," and

Occam's Razor, "The simplest solution is almost always the best," holds the answer.

Whether improbable or simple, Sam has no tangible or verifiable explanation for what has happened over the past year and no one is more shocked than her. If anyone had told her ten months ago, just before the experience of the Clearing Vision, that she'd challenge the demons of her past, resurrect the ghost of the man who was her reason for being, confront ovarian cancer, pull herself out of an emotional quagmire, and then write a book of those times, she'd still be laughing as they read these sentences.

Ten months ago, all of that was not even a pipe dream.

Critics say the words miracle or miraculous are used too liberally and argue that everything is a mystery and resembles divine intervention, until science explains it. It is an argument that appeals to Dr. Sam Walker, for she prefers facts over fantasy and data over delusion. But it is an argument that is pending review. An examination of various dictionaries for the definition of miracle yields four common understandings of the concept.

The first one: *something that is sensational or outstanding.* Words associated with this definition would be rarity, phenomenal, surprise, and wonder; all apply to this story. The second definition: *A beneficial thing for which one is grateful.* Exemplified by words such as blessing, stroke of luck, godsend, or fluke, it also applies to this story. Third is the definition that a miracle is *the achievement of an aim or goal* and success, triumph, victory, and favorable outcome are terms that also apply here, making the count three for four.

The fourth and final definition is probably the one most people assign to the word miracle. *An extraordinary event that is not explicable by natural or scientific laws,* and here the descriptions are more ambiguous, being harder to pin down. Definition number four is described as a sign, divine intervention, heaven-sent, or perhaps a mystery. Definition number four is open to interpretation.

Sam will leave the hypothesizing and guessing to theologians, philosophers, physicians, even astrophysicists, and others whose expertise in the area far exceeds hers. What she does know is this: She never wants to go back to how things were before that fateful day in mid-November 2023.

Many ask how things have gone these past months and when Sam relates the outcome of her surgery, all of the elements leading up to it, and the inexplicable occurrences and "miracles" since, to the person, she hears the same sentiment, *Someone is really looking out for you girl, you have a guardian angel up there.*

And she nods and says, "Yes, I do, and I know who it is."

Sam wonders if, with the chaos of the cancer having receded to a backburner, will Gerry still be around? A question she frets over a bit because she has gotten used to having him with her. He is.

He still comes in dreams, still supporting in his own way. Many women wear their husband's or boyfriend's shirt as a source of comfort. Sam wears one of Gerry's for the same reason, and she never wears it outside of the house.

A test result had raised a red flag, and she was called back in for further diagnostic testing, rattling the cages once again. Dreams told her to wear his shirt out to the hospital while going for those tests, something she ordinarily would never do. And she did.

Those tests showed new cancers. They were different types of cancers, but as with the ovarian cancer, Sam was "lucky." And through it all, all of the testing and treatments, Gerry was with her.

On September 6, 2024, Gerry once again visited Sam in a dream after she finished the chapter before this one. Eighteen weeks earlier, he had sat at a writing desk in a different dream, writing page after page. Now, at the same small desk, he sat finishing the last page. As before, he put the page on the pile to his right, but now, he laid the pen down, and while leaning back, he stretched his shoulders and back. He then made a full-body turn toward her, put an elbow up on the back of the chair, cocked his head and gave her a broad smile.

THEIR STORY HAS BEEN TOLD...

49

GOODBYE

Throughout the year after the Clearing Vision, Sam would often feel a presence.

Sometimes a touch on her shoulder or neck.
Sometimes the feeling that someone had sat next to her on the couch.
Sometimes someone was holding her hand.
Sometimes it felt like there was someone behind her as she would make dinner.

When it first started, she made excuses. It was her imagination. It was the ceiling fan, except it wasn't on. It was the dogs shifting, except they were asleep on their beds. It was the HVAC, except it wasn't running.

As the months went by, she stopped making excuses and began to absorb the calm and peace whenever it joined her.

On October 26, 2024, almost a year after it had arrived, and a few weeks after Sam had finished writing the first draft of this book, the presence left her.

It was 6:45 in the morning and she had just gotten up, played with dogs, etc., and then went into the kitchen. There was nothing visual aside from an odd glow to the room, but there was an overwhelming presence in front of her, and suddenly it spread out to envelop the entire room and seemed to fill her. She gasped in shock, and in that moment, the presence was gone.

In its wake was an emptiness that almost sent Sam to her knees, gutted with the same emotional intensity, the same crushing grief and sense of loss she had experienced with the Clearing Vision.

She knew in that instant, she would never physically feel the presence again.

As before, Gerry had left her—in October.

Only this time, he said goodbye.

50

LAST CALL

*I*t is said that truth is stranger than fiction.

This was our story, Gerry's and mine, and its evolution, from its beginnings as a collection of short stories to be left in the safe for the family after I passed, to its present novel format, was an adventure of its own.

Permission to Speak Freely was written as a novel because the times the two letters traversed and encompassed were of a time period two generations past, and so distant from today's reality. People were gone, places no longer existed, the fog of time clouded conversations long forgotten, and concepts were no longer relatable. The details of four decades past, having taken place before the age of computers and cell phones documenting one's every moment, had been lost to time.

In the interest of privacy for those who had been a part of our adventures, all personal names and details, the names of places, and the timing of events within this story were changed. Parts One and Two of this novel were fiction, where the details woven around events and the letters, were adapted to fit a storyline. Part Three, however, while still in story form, related this author's actual experiences.

The poetic license afforded to me by writing this story as a fictional memoir allowed me to tell our story from memory. But memory and perception are funny things. Two people can experience the same event and have very different perceptions, and thus, memories of what happened. I have no doubt as I wrote this story, Gerry repeatedly stood over my shoulder, muttering indignantly, "That is not what happened!" or "I did not say that!" And to that I say, "Look who's talking."

Case in point: Gerry exaggerated. That snake, the one from the cactus incident back in Arizona? It wasn't a huge diamondback. It was a medium-sized fella, and it wasn't in coil-strike position ready to take a bite of Gerry's rear. It was just lying there, minding its own business, and I did not pick it up and twirl it like a lasso! I just wanted to set the record straight on that.

Two innocent letters written in the spur of the moment became the foundation on which the telling of Gerry's and my story rested upon. I am proud, beyond proud to be honest, of our story, but it is our letters that have my deepest regard. Not so much for the actual words themselves, but for what they stood for and represent: commitment, trust, respect, and, of course, love. Our letters were filled with grammatical errors as sentence structure fell by the wayside in the flow of words written in the heat of the moment. Those mistakes, a part of the letters' essence, were not corrected aside from edits for clarity and repositioning excerpts within the story.

Twenty-three years ago, Gerry sat on an airplane and wrote me a letter, hoping it would remind me of what I had. He was hoping that through it, I would see possibilities, and it worked. It just took longer than Gerry had expected. It was through the writing of this book that it hit home just how phenomenal those times were, and just how special the cast of characters I had around me then were. Through the blessings of fate, I had spent twenty or more years with the most extraordinary people anyone could ever have the privilege of knowing.

My life hasn't always been easy, and many may say it hasn't been fair, but it has been good. I might even say, it has been miraculous.

    – *Sam Walker*

* * *

OVER THESE PAST MONTHS, I've been asked a lot of questions: What happened to so-and-so. How did you guys meet? What do I think about such and such? So if I may—my final thoughts on that amazing cast of characters, in descending order of appearance:

CAROL MATTHEWS

Carol Matthews has been an instrumental force in getting through this past year. We often debate the significance of the necklace's finding, with one of us maintaining that the necklace had to have been in the house all these years, somewhere, while the other likes a more surreal explanation. We still get together for dream analysis weekly, and like the times I had spent with my mother analyzing dreams, Carol and I often find ourselves laughing so hard, we can barely speak.

BETTY WALKER

My mother. My mom and I talked a lot during the writing of this book. Aside from Gerry, my mother was the best person I've ever known. Considered a best friend, a sister if you will, by virtually all who met her, she certainly was mine. I would have long talks with my mom, asking if she was okay with what I was writing of those last years. Much of the first draft of this book was written in longhand, with me sitting on a couch in front of a fireplace with a glass of wine. I would be writing and when finished, I would look over the pages.

The first time it happened, I laughed at what a coincidence it was —my handwriting had gotten to look so much like my mother's. The beginning paragraphs were in my handwriting, but by the time I had finished that night, the last paragraphs were in my mother's, not mine. And then, over the weeks, it happened again and again and again. The shift only occurred when I was writing for the book.

My mom also came to me in a dream. In this dream, she had read my manuscript and had given it back to me with notes. There were notations in the margins where she had written comments like "I would say this instead..." and she had initialed every comment so I would know it was from her, and that she approved. It took me a while to consider that, perhaps, I wasn't writing the book alone, and my mom was just fine with the words.

ROGER BELICAMPF

It would be an understatement to say if I hadn't met Roger, none of this would have happened. Roger was larger than life and he never met a day he couldn't enjoy, or an adventure he wouldn't go on. One did not apply to work for Roger Belicampf, for he did not have employees, he had comrades in arms. He was the adopted father to whom I told all my misfortunes, and from whom I learned there was always another side, another solution, another way to look at things.

Roger had a way of making his point. When Roger first met Gerry, he wasn't amused, let alone impressed, and he certainly didn't trust Gerry—not one iota. Gerry and Stan accompanied me one weekend to a seminar on flintknapping that Roger was giving. He had been listening to the two men mock and belittle stone tools when, of course, they had razor-sharp Army knives, so Roger issued them a challenge. Gerry and Stan against Kati Banyon and myself. Kati and I fashioned our own stone tools from rocks we had scavenged and Roger procured two road kill deer. The contest was to see which team, the boys with their metal knives or the girls with their stone tools, could butcher their deer the fastest. In a story that was worthy of a chapter all its own, us girls won, easily.

As Gerry and Stan stood there stunned, Roger had walked over to Gerry and told him with the sweetest of smiles, "I taught her everything she knows. You hurt that girl, I'll gut you like a fish, and I won't need some fancy knife." Roger retired in Colorado soon after I left for Ohio, but he always kept tabs on me, keeping me in the loop. We remained the best of friends until his death a few years back.

· · ·

TERRY RAINIER AND LUKE MICHAELS

By the time I met Terry and Luke, their military careers were behind them, and they were well into their second act. When Terry first rolled into the camp in Oaxaca all those years ago, I was stunned —thrilled, but stunned. Terry was not Rambo, not even close, but the man had an air about him that just oozed "everything will be all right." Even after all the chaos in Oaxaca had died down and there was no longer a cause for concern, Terry insisted on maintaining the night watch. I can still see him there, sitting upon the ridge over our camp in Oaxaca, a faint silhouette in the shadows of the moonlight, on watch. Terry was thrilled when I called him about this story.

When asked if he objected to me writing about him, in typical Terry fashion, he bellowed, "Hell no, but ya gotta make me tall, dark, and handsome. And suave, I wanna be like…James Bond." I could hear him over the phone cackling, "Yeah… the name is Rainier…Terrance Rainier." As we went to hang up, Terry had one last condition for me —his drink of choice was to be Bond's favorite, the Vesper martini, with a lemon slice. Terry passed away from old age during the writing of this book. I couldn't make his funeral, but I made arrangements for a copy of the Oaxaca chapter to be included in his coffin along with a martini—shaken, of course, not stirred.

Luke Michaels also lived out a long life, passing away from kidney failure a few years back. He and Terry remained the best of friends, often spending month-long road trips in the summer crisscrossing the country in search of adventure, many times stopping to visit me as they "just happened to be passing through" Ohio. The consummate storyteller, Luke could take the most mundane event and turn it into an evening of roaring laughter. He recovered from his bout of beer with tequila chasers that night in Oaxaca, although none of us ever allowed him to sing again.

KATI BANYON AND DOUG NIEVENS

My bickering duo. Kati Banyon, as I'm sure you have surmised, was a force of nature, and Doug was the perfect sidekick. They transformed otherwise staid and routine field seasons from a job into an experience. Kati threw caution to the wind, a lot, and it was Doug who always reined her back in. We had met while working joint gigs in Costa Rica. My introduction to her and Doug was when Doug sat down for a break in the jungle, in the path of army ants. Doug was new to the jungle back then and didn't realize, but Kati had seen. At the time, Doug insisted he knew what he was doing. He didn't need Kati telling him how to do things, so she had said nothing, and he was in no danger. I remember sitting there, not sure what to make of Kati as she roared with side-splitting laughter at the image of Doug dancing and disrobing, trying to get rid of the ants.

Doug got her back, though. A few days later, we were crossing a derelict vine rope bridge over a ravine, with caimans basking in the river below. Doug and I had crossed the bridge, and Kati was last. She was a stout woman who had some heft to her and, despite the fact that Doug, who weighed more than Kati, had already crossed with no issues, the rope bridge creaked with her weight, and for a moment, things seemed precarious.

Kati froze midway on the bridge, not willing to move, while Doug sat on the other side and teased her, pretending to be the caimans in the river below, "Oooh, look, snack time!" The withering look Kati shot at Doug was the beginning of the longest running Laurel and Hardy skit in history. Kati, a chain smoker, passed away from lung cancer in 2012. Doug, in his eighties now, is still with us physically, but is firmly held in the grips of dementia.

Brady Caldwell and Mark McIntyre

They were always in the background, but they were never second string. Brady and Mark were the framework upon which Gerry and I often leaned during our early years where we were still learning the logistics of our scheduling nightmare. One time, Gerry and I just gave up. We had been trying to work out when and where we could meet for a long weekend, but it just wasn't coming together. It was kind of a tipping point for us then. The juggling of our schedules seemed insurmountable at that time and we were beginning to think perhaps we weren't going to make it. But Brady and Mark had other ideas.

Gerry and Stan were on the west side of the country. I was on the eastern side. I was Brady's project, Gerry and Stan were Mark's. By train, by car, by bus, by air, by sheer dogged determination, Brady and Mark had made arrangements for us to be ferried to a common meeting, as if we all were part of the Pony Express. We all met in Oklahoma and it was there, at an Oklahoman truck stop, that Brady met the most gorgeous woman he had ever seen. They were married the following year.

Brady and Mark were my rocks after the deaths of Gerry and Stan —they took care of everything then and for years after. Both men retired from the Army when their tours were up. Brady and his wife Melinda moved back to Idaho where Brady went into the family business. On a family vacation to Seattle, Brady, while stepping out to get a pack of cigarettes, was caught in the cross fire of a drive-by shooting.

Mark returned to Las Vegas when his tour was up, where he met a dealer at the craps table who was better at craps than he. He did the only respectable thing a man could do—he married her. Mark and his wife Lydia happily lived out their days in Nevada, where Mark had gone into the IT business, but in 2013, Mark passed away from prostate cancer.

The Army

While the Army wasn't the focus of our story, it was a prominent backdrop upon which it unfolded. The Army had barged, uninvited, into my life one September day in 1981, and like a bad house guest, stayed for twenty years. Despite the Army having been a constant presence that I often had to dance around, I have a soft spot for the Army. Whenever they come on the news, or I see a soldier out and about, no matter how hard I try to stop it, a smile breaks out. My opinion of camo fatigues, however, still stands.

In reality, my time spent on bases was short—only a few hours a week at best, all told, if even that. I might have helped a soldier or two handle a "Dear John" letter, maybe showed someone how to diaper a bread loaf, or perhaps even embarrassed myself to no end by trying to relive my glory days running an obstacle course, but the honor of interacting with those young men, and being a brief, snippet moment in their lives, was all mine. I flitted in and out of those bases like a little bird hovering at a window, but sometimes I lit long enough to watch, and I learned a lot in those days about handling adversity, responsibilities and sacrifice. You might have picked up on a vibe that I have a soft spot for sergeants as well, and you would be right. They are an admirable lot.

Colonel Pernecki once told Gerry, "It's us brass that send our sons off to war, but it is the sergeants who bring them home." From what I observed from my short tenure on those bases, no truer words were spoken.

USHER SYNDROME

Usher's still continues to dominate my world. Found in .00005% of the world's population, it afflicts a total of 400,000 people worldwide. Originally described in the 1850s, there are now three types recognized today, with a multitude of subvariants. A fourth type was discovered and described as recently as 2022.While there are a number of studies involving genetics, biology, and technology treatment options, and some reports being published show promise, there is still no treatment available, or any on the horizon. The hope is that there may be something for the next generation of patients.

STANLEY IBBOTSON

Oh my Lord, what to say about that man. It took me a bit to warm up to him, but he became my dearest friend, my truest friend, and my most infuriating friend. Gerry and I used to laugh that after we got married, we would have to adopt him as a dependent since he was so incapable of functioning on his own. He was the warmest, cuddliest, most adorable puppy with the cutest antics—that you never could housebreak. But his zest for life just took your breath away.

I once made a crack to Lt. Colonel Lawson that I couldn't understand why the Army put up with Stan, that if I were his boss, I'd have fired him years ago. Lawson laughed that barrel laugh of his and told me that Stan was worth his weight in gold.

"You should see him when things go south," Lawson said to me. "Despite all his attention-seeking bravado, when it counts, Ibbotson is all business, stunningly competent and there are few better." Gerry and the others defended the incurable joker with similar words over the years, but to hear those same words from Lawson was comforting and it put a smile on my face. I would remember those words years later at Stan's memorial.

Stan was one of many in my life, who, if he hadn't been there, Gerry and I would never have had a story...and for that, he had my undying gratitude.

Stan and Gerry entered my life together on the same day and twenty years later, they both left it together, on the same day. In the early days after their deaths, I was angry that I had lost both of them, but as time passed, I was grateful that the same Fate that brought them both to me, saw fit to allow them to leave together.

Stan always knew just what to say and how to say it. Sometimes it was just a look or a gesture. Sometimes it would just be a simple hug, not saying anything at all. He always knew just when to show up with a pizza and beer, and chatter away about absolutely nothing. And oh that grin of his...it probably had them swooning up there.

SAM AND GERRY

Gerry and I will never grow old together. My boy from Boston will be forever middle-aged, always the handsome man with the devilish grin, and soft brown eyes, but he is always with me, now and in the future as I grow older.

The twenty years Gerry and I had together are my greatest pride and joy. They are also my greatest accomplishment. Writing this book was incredibly hard, and I will admit, I bawled through much of it. There were times I'm amazed that the keyboard didn't short out. The writing of this book also made me take a good long look at those years, and I marvel at it all. I marvel at how astonishingly lucky I had been. The people, the adventures, the friendships, the love.

I would have thought I knew everything about Gerry, but that guy continues to surprise me, even today. He left me a message in a dream not too long ago. The surprise wasn't that he had a message, but rather, what he said. You see, for a man who couldn't string three monosyllable words together, he's gotten downright poetic in his old age—he paraphrased a metaphor. In the dream I was sitting on a bench along a beautiful tree lined path in a park. The trees, magnificent and mature, arched overhead like a vaulted cathedral ceiling and their branches shaded the path in dappled light.

Gerry joined me, holding his hand out for me to take as I got up. As we turned to walk down the path, Gerry leaned in and whispered to me,

We have walked this together for so long,
the path is worn from our footsteps
– Gerry Martinez, January 2025

ACKNOWLEDGMENTS

No life's journey is taken alone and this book was no different. In the beginning, I wrote this book as a collection of stories to be put in a safe, but this book had other ideas. In its short lifetime, this novel has taken me on a remarkable journey where I have met a group of amazing people and reconnected with some old friends.

Throughout the writing of this book, I was blessed with a wonderful array of family and friends to lean on. In particular, my "Board of Directors" of Karen, Kathy, and Carole. Their support was astounding and I relied on these ladies heavily for they held my hand as this book took me on its journey. I am beyond grateful for their guidance, insight, ideas and encouragement.

There was another group of women who also were irreplaceable companions on this book's journey. I had never written anything but scientific reports. To put it mildly, I didn't have a clue as to what I was doing. As luck would have it, I stumbled across Amy Suto of Suto-science LLC and her talented colleagues.

Throughout this book's technical journey, Amy guided, goaded and coached me, providing a steady hand during the entire writing, editing and formatting process. Her instincts were spot on and her patience seemingly limitless! Being legally blind, computers are my lifeline to the world, but they are not always my friend. Documents and websites can be difficult to navigate. I have been especially grateful for Amy's willingness to accommodate and work within my limitations.

The associates that make up the rest of the team also contributed to a phenomenal job. Ashley Munson designed the book cover, including the drawing of the necklace. Line editors Sierra Campbell and Phoenix Grace endured and fixed my writing quirks, and Proof-reader Kathryn Underwood corrected my numerous grammar slipups. The expertise and professionalism of this team made this project not only easy, but a joy.

While I am immensely appreciative of those mentioned above, I am most grateful to Gerry for pushing me to make not only a leap of faith, but to take that first step.

ABOUT THE AUTHOR

A chance encounter while repairing human skeletons for the medical school as an undergrad led Samantha Walker down the road toward an unconventional career in forensics. In the 1980s, as a forensic osteologist, she participated in various field projects throughout the US, Mexico, and Central and South America. While in the field, she worked forensic and archaeological sites analyzing human remains, or as a member of a medical research team. In between her field seasons, she could be found in a lab doing research or on a campus teaching biology and science classes.

Diagnosed with Usher Syndrome, she retired from field work in 1991, but remained in forensics as a consultant. After retirement, her adventures continued as she traveled the world for as long as her Usher Syndrome permitted—lying in a tent on the Serengeti listening to lions roar and riding on dog sled teams with the Russian Yupik, among others.

Currently, Samantha Walker enjoys a more sedate lifestyle and resides in the American Midwest with her two dogs.

You can connect with Samantha at https://samanthawalker-permission.com/